THE DEPRAVED PRINCE

IMMORTALS COUNTRY

LEXIE AXELSON

The Depraved Prince Copyright © 2024 by Lexie Axelson

All rights reserved.

No part of this book may be reproduced in any form or by any electronic or mechanical means, including information storage and retrieval systems, without written permission from the author, except for the use of brief quotations in a book review.

This book is a work of fiction. Any names, characters, places, or incidents are products of the author's imagination and are fictitious or used in a fictitious manner. Any resemblance or similarity to actual people, places, events, or establishments is purely coincidental.

First Edition: September 2024

Paperback ISBN: 979-8-9906844-3-0

Copy Editing by K. Morton Editing Services

Cover Design by Austin Drake

CONTENT WARNINGS

This book is for mature adult readers (18+).

This is a tragic, captive, dark vampire love story. If any of these content warnings may be triggering, **please do not proceed**. It contains sexually explicit material and scenes that include blood play, primal play, breeding kink, stalking, dubcon, breath play, mentions of domestic violence, depression, graphic violence, death, Stockholm syndrome, manipulation, mental illness, and attempted suicide. This book does not have an HEA.

The Depraved Prince includes:
-Obsessed MMC
-Virgin Heroine
-Multiple POV
-Enemies To Lovers

For a complete list of content warnings, please visit the author's website.

Your mental health matters.

https://lexieaxelson.com/

For those who want to be taken by a vampire psychopath.

PLAYLIST

Enter Sandman by Metallica
Smells Like A Teen Spirit by Nirvana
Creep by Radiohead
November Rain by Guns N' Roses
Forever Young by Alphaville
People Are Strange by The Doors
Sleepwalk by Santo & Johnny
Enjoy The Silence by Depeche Mode
Wildflower by Billie Eilish
Put Your Head On My Shoulders by Paul Anka
Desire by Meg Myers
Summertime Sadness by Lana Del Rey
Born To Die by Lana Del Rey
Bat Country by Avenged Sevenfold
i like the way you kiss me (burnt) by Artemas

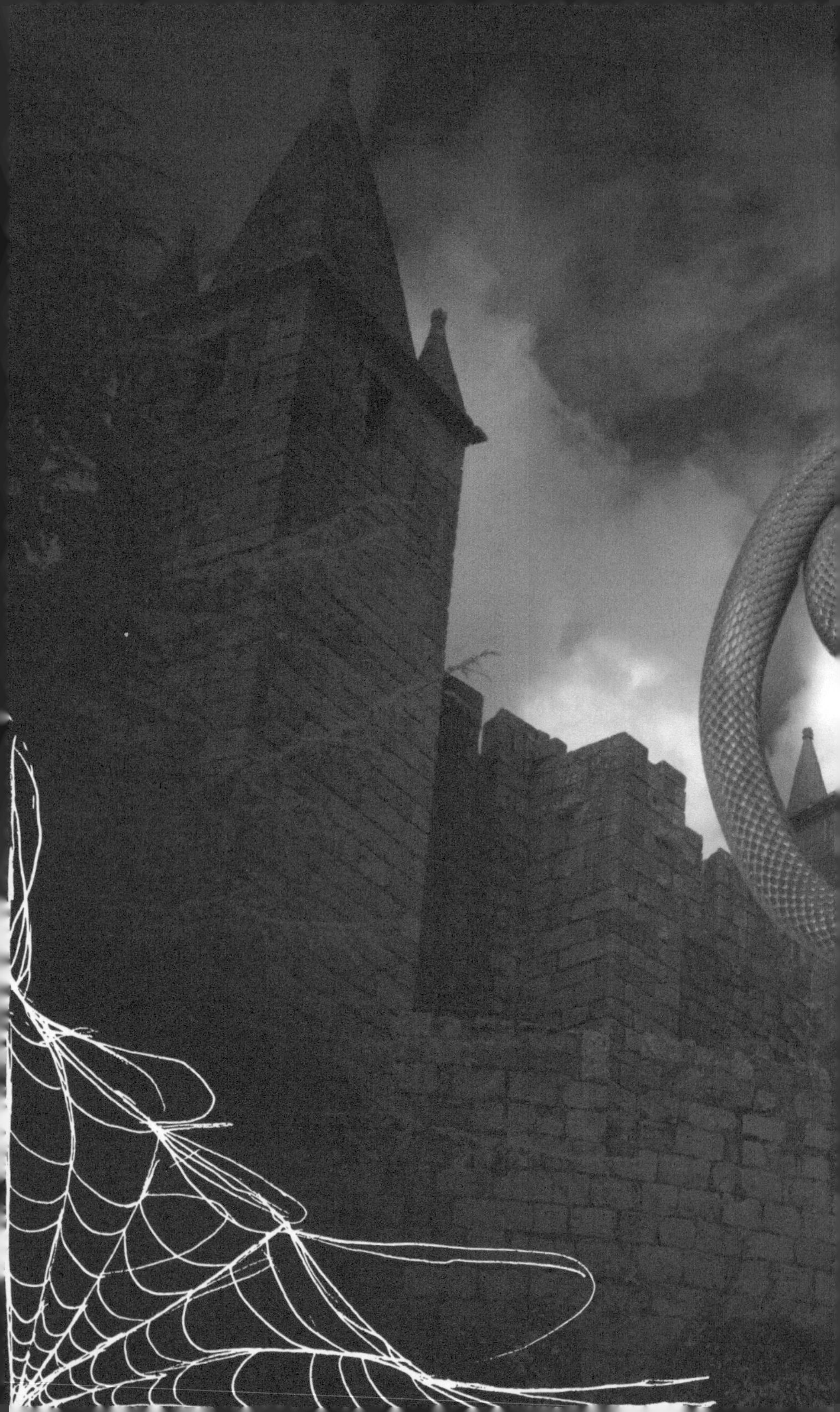

PROLOGUE

HAYDEN

"YOU MUST MARRY HER. I don't understand your interest in rebelling against tradition and your responsibilities to this family." My mother scolds me as I listen with my head hanging low. I love my mother, but I can't face the disappointment in her eyes. Truthfully, I'm tired of her looking at me like that.

"Hayden, have respect! At least pretend to care and look at your mother when she is speaking to you!" My father roars and is in my face at warp speed. I sit on the couch in the living room by the grand fireplace. Red and orange pools of color flicker behind them. My elbows are on my thighs, and I focus on the dark wooden floors, lost in thought. I lift my head to face my father's wrath. *He's fuming*. His eyes convert to a dark red from his original ice-blue eyes.

Fuck.

He's mad.

I inhale deeply, sensing the anger festering within me, too, but I cannot hold back my frustration of being cornered. I stand with a hiss, meeting my father. We are about the same height, but I'm slightly taller at 6'4.

"Mother. Father." I tilt my head at them. "With all due respect, I will not marry Eleanor. THIS. IS. CLICHÉ. For crying out loud! The firstborn son has to marry the daughter of another king to strengthen alliances?" I question them like I'm doubting their sanity. They don't move. They're frozen like statues, unwavering in their decision. They won't back down or change their mind, but I must try to get myself out of this ridiculous request. If they won't back down, neither will I. I've always been stubborn that way.

"We aren't living in the 1600s, and I'm not going to do this," I continue as my eyes change from ocean blue to dark red.

This is common for creatures like us. Our eyes shift to our immortal ones when emotions get too high and all-consuming.

Marriage has never interested me. When you can live forever, why attach yourself by law to stay with the same person for eternity?

This is not in my nature.

My mother sighs, frustrated, and bobs her head from side to side. Her hand massages her temples, contemplating her thoughts. I know what she's thinking. She's been asking herself the same question since I was born. Where had she gone wrong loving and raising a son who grew to be so stubborn, irresponsible, and rebellious—raising a son who doesn't want to take over the role of being the new Northern King?

My father wants to retire from his royal duties. My mother wants to go back to her roots in Europe. Three hundred years have passed, and he felt it was time for me to take over. I'm enjoying the responsibility of having *no* responsibilities. In this vampire world, there are other immortal royal families worldwide.

Four royal vampire families reside in the United States of America, divided by location. We ruled the northern parts of the U.S.

THE DEPRAVED PRINCE

The Southern King has caused my entire bloodline pain and misery. To dissolve it, he offered up his daughter. My father agreed and wants me to marry Eleanor Davenport—an easy escape and proposal so he can leave his duties as King.

Eleanor is a southern vampire princess. Marrying her would strengthen our troubling relationship with the family of Davenports. The Davenports ruled the Southern region—States like Texas, Oklahoma, Louisiana, Arkansas, etc. But Eleanor's father is a madman. I will never accept him as my father-in-law. He has expressed interest in becoming the only Vampire King in the United States, and he wants to start with taking over the North. The southern vampires are more substantial in numbers but not in strength or intelligence; I don't doubt we'd win if it ever came to a battle between the north and south.

Eleanor's father, King Davenport, tried to convince my father to join his plans to take over the country, but my father refused. Instead, he offered that his son marry his daughter and strengthen our families together as a peace offering.

I'll never want peace with King Davenport, not after what he did to my uncle. But my father has a good heart. Fortunately, I do not, and I take pride in being soulless. Life is just more fun that way.

My father believes in order, peace, and following the rules, no matter how outdated they are.

But me?

I believe that rules are made to be broken. I love life. I love being immortal. I love waking up after I've fucked and partied the night away. I. Love. Life.

"Kallum is the more suitable son to marry Eleanor and become king," I huff. Kallum, the second-born son. My little brother. Everyone calls him The Cherished Prince.

He's the exact opposite of me. Kallum is the calm one,

always following the rules, *the gentleman*. Always kind and polite. Most of the time, naïve, always believing everyone is good and has good intentions. Everyone in the North loves him, and he fulfills his duties to the people. I fulfill my duties when it comes to military or war aspects, and I thrive in that role.

"Hayden...Kallum could never be king." My mother says it like it's painful for her to admit.

"Why not?" I exclaim.

"Because he's not you! You are the one who is fierce. The strong one. You're the one who can make the hard decisions without blinking an eye. Kallum can be weak sometimes. He's too nice. He's too good—"

"And I'm what?" I cut my mother off. I press my brows together, looking at them with piercing frustration. My fangs are starting to grow out of anger. When I realize my instability comes through, I close my eyes and turn away to face the floor again, ashamed of my outburst. My fangs retract and unsharpen as I calm myself down. With each deep, shallow breath, I slowly return to normal.

Whatever normal is for us. It's our mask to blend in with humans.

My anger turns into sadness as the realization hits me like a train.

"I'm what? A villain?" My un-beating heart sinks. The facts hurt. My own parents think I'm a monster. They are the only two people destined to love me, programmed to love me by chemistry, and it's almost impossible for them.

I'm not a victim. I made it impossible for them. I take responsibility for that.

My behavior lately hasn't been the best. I've grown addicted to being reckless. I spend most nights drinking and partying with other vampire friends. I'm doing anything and everything I can to avoid conversations about my future like this.

My mother and father look at each other in defeat. They can't get through to me no matter what they say. I will never agree to marry into a family of mad people or take over for my father. There's a reason why I despise the Southern King, and he wants me to marry his daughter so he can gain points with our people. To repair his tarnished image after he turned on his own kind.

I'm unforgiving.

It was always the plan...*their plan*. Never once had they asked me what I wanted. They never thought to ask themselves that maybe it's time for things to change in an ever-evolving world.

Although, in reality, I still don't know what I want. Even though I'm over three hundred years old, I still don't have the answer if they ask me truthfully.

What do I want if I already have everything money can buy?

Then, they both turn to me with cold, deadpanned expressions.

My father looks through me as always and treats me like an heir and not his firstborn son before telling me with a distant tone.

"You are a villain when you need to be."

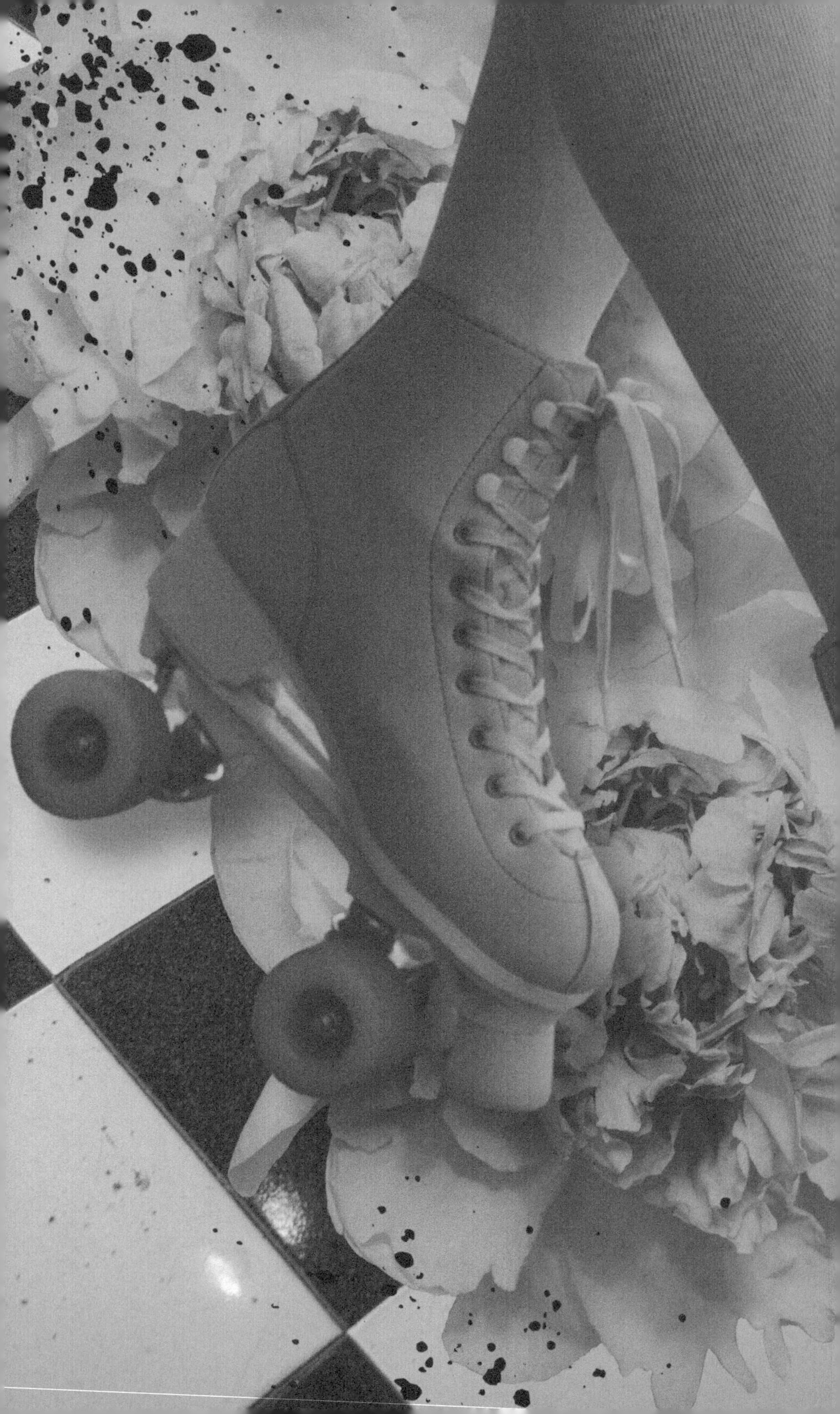

1
MILLIE

MARCH 23, *1993*

"Again, Theresa? Look at the fucking floor, cochina. There's a stain right there by the stove! How long has it been there? And this? Why don't you tell your worthless daughter to fold her clothes and put them away!" My mother's fiancé shouts at her, as she sits on the couch, shame written all over her tired face. Her cheeks and neck turn a bright red shade.

As always…I watch her take his unprovoked wrath. My own rising beneath me as I helplessly have to go through another one of their fights.

"I'm sorry, Santiago. A drop of the soup must have fallen," she tells him as she adjusts her posture on the couch. She had just finished dinner while he was out gambling their money away.

I sat there, anger simmering, waiting to blow but having to stay quiet so he wouldn't take it out on my mom further.

"*Eras una puerca! And so are your children!*" He calls her and my brother pigs. His tone hardens with disgust.

What had my mother done to deserve this treatment? What had we done? And most of all, what did my mother see in him?

I've had enough. Ever since he entered her life, she was ruined in all the wrong, dreadful, self-deprecating ways. My mother's spirit is tarnished and never coming back the longer their relationship continues.

He throws my clothes on the floor, making that the last straw for me.

"Don't fucking talk to my mother like that, you piece of shit!" I stand from the couch, screaming at the top of my lungs, as a lump in my throat forms. If my mother can't stand up for herself, I will. I'll be the armor that she doesn't have the strength or courage to wear. She's my mother. I'll always have this protective instinct; I can't help it, and right now, punching Santiago in his face after built-up frustration of hearing him beat her down with disgusting insults and unprovoked fights sounds like a fantastic idea.

I've had enough of watching this abusive relationship grow with no ending in sight. Every time he's around, my mood shifts, the air feels dense, and everything gets clouded in his demeanor.

At first, Santiago stood still, with flared nostrils and a protruding gut over his belt. His hands balled into fists and sweat-drenched the sides of his shirt.

I don't understand why he has to react like this over small things that can be fixed with gentle requests or inquiries.

To get back at me, he does something I will never forget or forgive.

My collection of snow globes from every school field trip, dating back from Pre-K to my junior year of high school, comes crashing down to the floor when he sweeps his heavy arm through the dining room shelf.

Glass shatters, and thousands of pieces spread across the white tile in a massive puddle of water.

My heart can't take it. With a trembling body, I watch my trophy memories fade before me.

"Why would you do that?!" I cry out as I do everything I can to stay standing. My legs want to give out from the blackened emotions boiling inside of me with no way out. I step forward to pick up the pieces, but my mother's broken voice cuts through the tension.

"Millie! Please stop." She demands through gritted teeth. Her eyes widen.

She's angry. Finally! She says something...but then her eyes narrow. And they're not directed at Santiago.

She's angry at me?

"But mom, look at what he's doing! Doing to YOU! Look at what he's saying—"

She cuts me off again.

"Millie, shut up!" She demands of me once more, and my blood runs cold. Tears fall down my cheeks as I watch Santiago walk into the kitchen with sick satisfaction. He has a curve on his thin lips and smug shoulders. He's turned my mother against my older brother and now me.

My older brother moved out a year ago because of their relationship, and I stayed, hoping things would get better.

"Mom!"

"Callate lo sico!"

The way my mom forced me down like I was the one who overstepped and crossed lines reminded me that I was no longer the center of her world. Have my brother and I ever been? It's a question I'll never get the answer to because I'm too afraid of the raw answer.

The center of her world remains clear.

It's a man named Santiago, and she's lost in her dark depression, plagued by his sickness, and there's no more trying to save herself. There's no more fight in her because she chose him.

She's lost.

And...so am I.

The reality strikes my chest like a stab in my spirit.

My mother chose him over her own blood.

All my life, no one has ever chosen me. People are genetically programmed to feel something: protection, loyalty, love, selflessness, or guidance.

I'm jealous of everyone who has these things from their parents. Every time I go to school, I see my friends have their parents cheer them on when mine are nowhere to be found. I never got to experience moments like my mother and father kissing me on the cheek when I was a pre-schooler and telling me to have a good day at school. Or to have a warm bed and house to go home to.

I grab my backpack and flee from her apartment until I end up on my estranged father's doorstep.

-Millie

I date the entry from when it happened. Five years ago. I'm twenty now, but the hole is still there. The damage is done. The past is permanent. The pain of losing a mother who's still alive is like a wound that constantly bleeds.

I close my journal. Reading and writing have been my own self-medicated form of therapy since I was a child. I needed help. I still do. I craved to be shown that love exists and that demons don't have to consume me. There is light within my troubled past and future, and I refuse to let everything I've been through taint me permanently.

I push away from my desk and roll on my chair for a second before I get ready for work. I slide the all-pink journal across my desk and stand, tying my long black waves of hair with a band.

My hand is cramped from writing. It's been healthy and freeing for me to pen down my thoughts finally. My parents don't believe in depression or anxiety. They've never entertained the idea of mental illness.

So...writing has been a way for me to escape my horrid reality. I place the diary back in my drawer and slip on my barista uniform while staring at my new collection of snow globes on the shelf. I stare at the Alaska one more specifically. I haven't been there but one day, I will.

"Alright, babes, we just gotta clean up, then we can lock up and enjoy our weekend." I cheerfully hype up my coworkers as we close down the local coffee shop. I give Leah and Hayes a smile to disguise how I'm truly feeling. I'm beyond exhausted. I've been working since eight in the morning, and it's now eight at night. My body aches, and I begin to sweat. Even though lately I haven't been feeling like myself, I've been self-taught to keep going and to maintain positivity throughout rough moments like this. Bad days don't always have to stay bad. They can end with a smile on my tortured face.

I've been working at the 'Nostalgia Coffee' shop for the past three years. It's a flexible job that fits in with my full-time college schedule. And when I heard I could wear roller skates in a 1950s-themed diner that also sells comfort food, I jumped at the opportunity.

After I finished cleaning a coffee spill that left sprinkles of stains on the pink salmon walls, I move on to clean the checkered floors. Photos of 1950s-1970s rock stars, country artists, and singers are framed amongst the walls.

Paul Anka plays on low volume, and the sound of the television in the top corner of the lounge room grabs my attention as Hayes quickly grabs the remote and points at it. He raises the volume and puts his hand over his mouth, covering a gasp. It's the local news channel with a breaking news alert. I stop in my tracks, balancing myself off the broom, and read the title of the breaking story.

In bold red letters:

ANIMAL ATTACK LEAVES 1 FARMER DEAD AND 2 IN CRITICAL CONDITION

"Another animal attack? Hayes, please walk us to our cars. This is getting a little scary. Those attacks are getting closer and closer to town," Leah says as she pleads with a terrified Hayes. His hazel eyes skim over the news reporter, observing the TV like it's going to come alive and bite him. Leah turns around with her back to the TV and continues to wipe down tables that have not been cleaned yet. She throws the towel over her shoulder, and her other hand holds the cleaning spray. Her blonde, wavy hair is pulled back in a ponytail, though strands have escaped her gelled back style, hovering over her brown freckles.

"Sshh! Let me listen." Hayes ignores her request and hushes her instead.

I roll my eyes at both of them. Hayes and Leah are the two co-workers who constantly bicker and gossip at work. Still, I wouldn't trade these two goofballs for the world.

"I mean, what kind of animal could this be? We live in Texas, for crying out loud. There are no bears. There are no alligators nearby," Leah continues. It's sort of true. We live in the southern region of Texas, south of San Antonio, away from all busy city life in a town called Santana.

"Leah, I'm trying to listen. Maybe if you let me listen to the news reporter, I can answer those questions!" Hayes hisses, hushing Leah once again. He holds the mop close to his chest for balance. His ponytail whips to his back as he shakes his head.

I've had enough of this. I'm tired, and I want to sleep. My threshold for negativity has met the maximum limits tonight. I stomp over to the television, get on my tiptoes, and turn it off.

"Millie. I was watching that," Hayes complains. I quickly grab the remote from his hand before he can turn the television back on.

"I know, but we're still on the clock." I turn to a worried Leah. "That attack happened far away from here, by the way, Leah. So, stop worrying, and let's finish cleaning so we can go home." I put my professionalism mask back on. I hate when I have to do that.

"Actually, Millie. That happened just a couple miles from here." Hayes corrects me. An uncomfortable, eerie pause lingers between all three of us as "Sleepwalk" by Santo & Johnny continues to play softly.

Our supervisor, Cole, pops his head out of the kitchen and swings his backpack over his shoulder. "Millie is right, you guys. Please focus on closing and not the TV. I have to leave right now, so I'm leaving her in charge." He points to me with a tired smile.

I lift an eyebrow, return the smile, and lean on my hip. Cole leaves through the back of the shop and locks it with his keys.

They both stare at the now turned-off television, digesting the news. I place the remote near the television and go back to cleaning. I don't understand why I'm feeling more tired than usual. It's only eight at night, yet it feels like one or three in the morning.

Leah sticks her tongue out at Hayes, and he returns the friendly gesture. Finally, after their little quarrel, they're over it.

Suddenly, our front door to the coffee shop opens, making the bells attached to it chime. I quirk a brow, immediately disappointed that I hadn't locked it yet. I felt like I didn't have to with the practically empty parking lot and *We're Closed* neon sign on the front window.

A tall blonde man with the brightest blue eyes emerges. He's dressed in a white shirt, black jeans and boots. He looks to be around his mid-30s. He comes walking in like he owns the place, confident yet *scary*. He turns straight to me, looking deeply into my eyes, and smirks. I tighten my grip on my broom.

"Sir, we're closed. You can come back tomorrow for coffee when we open. We open around eight a.m.," Hayes shouts politely over the register. The blonde man doesn't break. He continues to stare at me. It's cold and unreadable, making every second unbearably uncomfortable.

I don't like this.

I stiffen, and finally, he moves with a smirk.

What a creep.

I look away from the man and return to sweeping the floor in hopes that he'll understand that I don't welcome this type of attention. He needs to stop looking at me like that.

"I don't drink coffee," the man replies with a deep voice.

I peek with my peripheral vision to see him turn to Hayes in annoyance.

"I'm sorry, we don't really sell much else," Leah says as she walks over to the store's front door. She opens it and holds it open for the man, hoping he'll notice and leave. He turns to Leah and then to me. He flattens his lips.

There's a moment of intense silence before he speaks again.

"You know, you guys should really stop closing after sundown. I hear there has been a lot of..." he pauses, and a sinister smile replaces his once-thinned lips. "Animal attacks at night. You guys shouldn't be out...it's dangerous," he tells us cruelly. His ice-cold voice is laced with mystery.

We all stand in silence, watching him, perplexed by his cold demeanor.

Then, the man walks out the door without another word, and Leah quickly jumps at the opportunity to shut the door behind him. She reaches into her pocket for her set of keys and locks it. We all walk towards the window, plastering our faces against the glass to watch him. Instead of getting into a car, his tall figure keeps walking into the night until we can't see him anymore. Our coffee shop is located in a newly built area, so there aren't any other nearby stores.

That was weird.

"That guy was kind of creepy," I say as I sweep the floor.

"And hot," Leah mutters through a cheeky grin.

Hayes and I turn to Leah with the same confused look.

"Don't judge me." Leah rolls her eyes.

"*Judging,*" Hayes and I reply, synchronized with a laugh.

After we finished cleaning, Hayes walks us both to our cars. After he walked Leah to hers, he followed me to mine.

The humid Texas air blows through my hair, and I push the loose strands out of my eyes with my hand.

"Goodnight, Hayes. I'll see you next time we're on shift together."

"Yup. Goodnight, babes. I can't wait to tell the boyfriend about how I got to clean up vomit after the group of college students came in drunk."

"Yeah...that wasn't fun." I grit my teeth as I get into my car quickly, and Hayes closes the door, biting his tongue. I watch him enter his car, and then he zooms out of the parking lot.

I turn on the air conditioning, take out the tight ponytail from my head, and drive to my house, which is about a twelve-minute drive away from the coffee shop. The entire time I drive, the blonde man's interaction lingers. Leah was right about his looks. He's very handsome. He's got that mysterious, intriguing look about him. Yet, there was a dark aura he carried—it was almost tangible.

Even though it was a short and distinguished encounter, the way he was staring at me made me cringe and grip my steering wheel tighter.

Once I get home, I pull the door open, knowing my dad is still awake, sitting in the same spot on the couch as he always does, watching TV in the living room. I close the front door and lock it. He always leaves it open for me around this time. I hang up my purse and keys in the entryway and approach the kitchen, where my dinner plate awaits me in the fridge.

Grabbing it and placing it in the microwave, I heat it for about a minute before taking it to my room to eat. It's the same uneventful routine I've come to love. I walk by the living room and turn off the TV when I realize my dad has fallen asleep, waiting for me. I gently shake his shoulder to wake him up.

"Go to bed, Dad. I'm home."

He raises his head from the couch cushion, and his snores abruptly stop. With sleepy red eyes, he groggily nods his head.

"*Mija*, you're home. How was work?" He yawns while he gets up from the couch and walks to his room.

"Good, Dad. Get to sleep. I'll be in my room, turning in for the night. I'm tired."

He nods again and waves his hand over his shoulder as he sleepily drags his feet to his room.

Our all-black male German Shepherd, Cooper, is on my

feet as I move towards my room. He kisses my hands, probably telling me he missed me while I was at work. I give him gentle pets as he follows me.

I set my dinner plate at my desk once I'm in my room, and Cooper lays down next to my window.

Huh?

Now, that was not part of my usual routine with him. Usually, he sits on my bed, giving me the best puppy eyes he can muster at his five years of age, trying to get me to feed him from my plate.

I take off my shoes, turn on the TV in my room, watch my favorite comedy show, and eat the brisket with potato salad. My father is a fantastic cook with a passion for barbecue. I don't doubt that he has all the barbecue tools in the world. You walk outside on the backyard deck, and you would think he owns his own barbecue business with all of his top-of-the-line cooking machines.

I open my mouth to take a bite of my potato salad but I don't get to eat it. I jolt in my seat from Cooper's unexpected change in behavior. The food falls from my fork and back onto the plate when Cooper's growls roar.

I'm jumpy these days.

I turn to watch his ears shoot up, and he stands looking out my window between the curtains on high alert.

Cooper repeatedly barks. His snarls are indignant. The fur on his back rises like he's ready to intimidate or attack.

Is there a cat outside? Another dog?

"Cooper, stop it. You're going to wake up my dad." I scold him and try to calm him but he doesn't stop. I roll my eyes, get up from my chair, and get ready to open my curtains to investigate. It's probably a harmless squirrel.

As I get closer, I grow more weary. What's bothering Cooper so severely that he starts to scratch the windows?

I walk beside him as he continues to snarl, and I sweep my blue curtains to the side to check it out.

Oh my god.

My eyes widen, and my heart falls to my stomach when I realize *who* he's barking at. I drop my fork as blood rushes to my ears, silencing my ability to move or breathe.

It's the same blonde man from the coffee shop across the street looking at me with a wicked grin and abnormally bright blue eyes. His head tilts forward like he's taking pleasure in watching me. His smile isn't welcoming. It's taunting. I freeze as my mouth drops open. My voice is caught in my throat as I try to croak out for words, but nothing comes out. I'm unsure of what to do in a situation like this. He flashes his teeth, and I can see large canines, sharper than usual.

What the hell?

I blink fast and open my mouth to scream for my dad.

"D-Dad!" I blare as hard as I can after finally finding my voice. I rip my vision from the stranger, turn towards my bedroom door, and bellow out again.

"Dad, come quick!"

I hope he can hear me over Cooper's continuous barks. I turn back to the window, but I'm met with no one. I grip my curtains tighter and search vehemently for the man, up and down the street, every single tree…but nothing.

He vanished.

"I swear—" I mutter to myself.

Am I seeing things?

Where did he go?

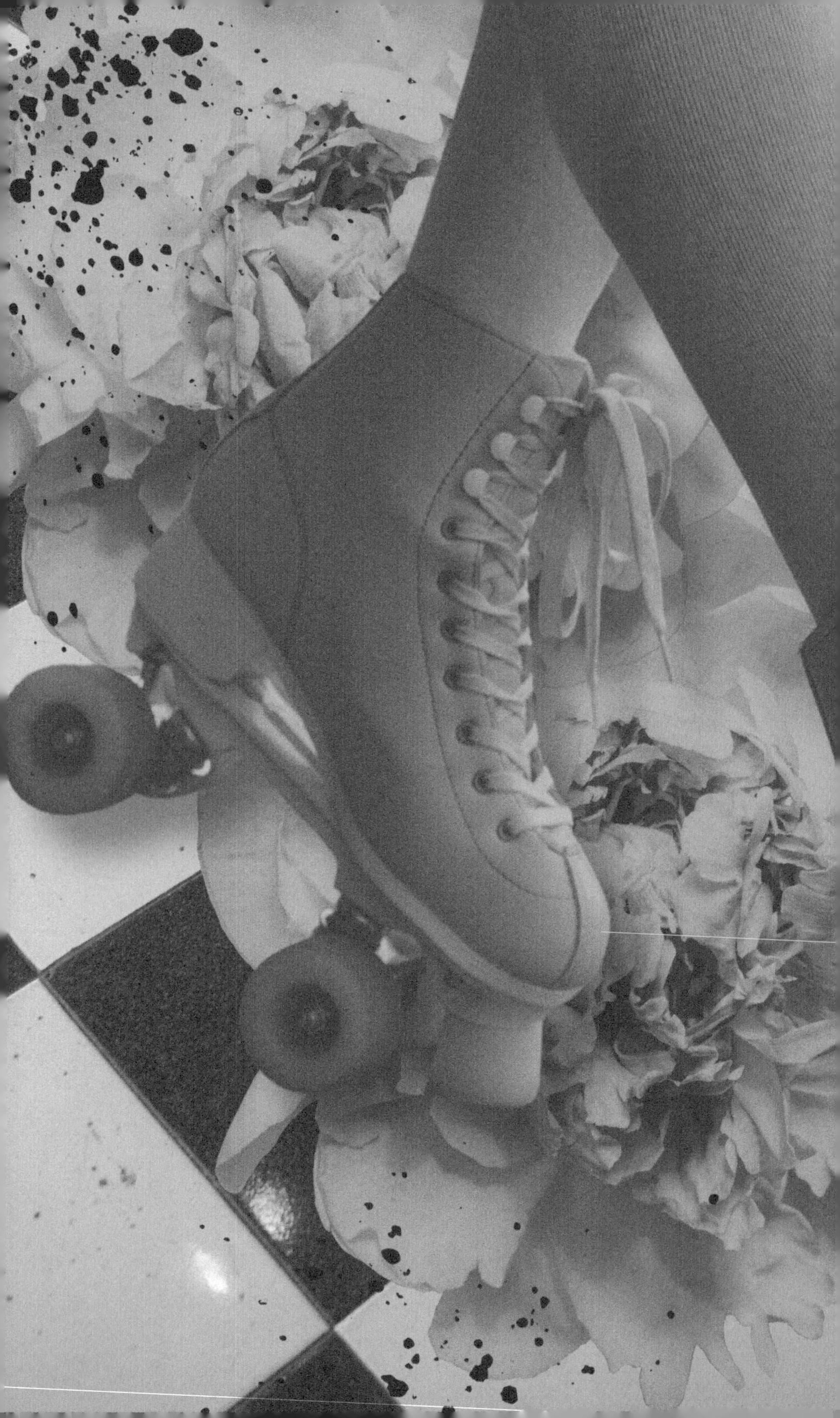

2

MILLIE

THE FULL MOON illuminates the sky as I open the curtains further with my trembling fingers. I check all of my neighbor's homes. All lights are off.

Could it have been my neighbor? Did I make a mistake? Or did this man follow me from work? Am I seeing things?

I shudder at that thought and tuck it far back into my head.

Cooper lets out a huff from his nose and walks away from the window. He's satisfied with himself and curls beside my bed on the floor. I stay at the window, making sure that the man is gone. I bite my lip, feeling my heart still erratically pulsing hard.

I contemplate what I should do next. Should I wake my dad and tell him? I shake my head. I don't want to worry him.

I stand there for a while, watching the front of my house to ensure he doesn't come back. I close the curtains and double-check that my windows are locked. Pulling up and down, it doesn't sway. So far, so good.

Cooper is very protective of me. If anyone entered our

house, he wouldn't hesitate to attack. He's become my new best friend.

Ever since I moved in with my dad late in high school, things have changed for the better. It was strange at first—it felt like I was moving in with a stranger instead of my father—but now I feel safe with him.

I check my computer for any missed IMs. I see that I have one from my supervisor, Cole. I guess he's not just my supervisor, but it's easier to pretend that he is sometimes so I don't have to confront my feelings and reflect on our complicated relationship.

> Wonderwall83: Have a good night. Sweet dreams, beautiful.

After I finish reading his message, I smile. I reply with a simple goodnight, change my status to 'away,' and shut my computer off.

Cole and I have been on a few dates. He wants to further our friendship, but I don't feel the same way. I see him more as a friend that I can laugh with and talk to about anything in the world, and we just get each other...but I don't want to take it any further. I like him, too, but I'm unsure about becoming something more. Cole understands how I feel and doesn't push it, but he wants me to know that he'll always be here for me.

I get out of my work clothes, put them in my hamper, and change into my pajamas. It feels so good to lay in bed after a long work shift finally. My feet are sore and throbbing. I reach for my right foot and start to massage it. I call Cooper onto my bed by patting my hand three times at the edge, and he joins me immediately. He snuggles at the corner, facing the window like he's still on high alert.

Two loud knocks thud against my door, and I yelp.

"What's going on? Did you call for me?"

Dad.

"Dad! You scared me. I-I did call you like ten minutes ago!" I exaggerate.

"*Todo bien, hija?* Can I come in?" He twists the knob but doesn't enter.

"Yes, come in."

He opens the door and pokes his head through. His dark hair is peppered with grey strands, and his dark brown wary eyes are pinned on me before they dart everywhere else in the room like he's checking if I snuck any boyfriends in behind his back.

"Everything is fine, Dad. I just...I guess I watch and read too many scary movies and thriller books. That's all. I'm good. I thought I saw something outside, but it's all good now." I scoff out a laugh and bring the blankets up to my chin as I try to find a comfortable spot.

He places his hands on his hips and leans forward like his lower back hurts. He walks to the curtains and watches the empty street for about thirty seconds before he turns to me.

I know my dad. His silence means he's trying to get something out. He's holding something in by the way he looks side to side, avoiding my gaze.

"Spit it out," I sing-song.

He chuckles with no humor attached to his tone.

"You know...I'll never stop apologizing for leaving you and your brother." He grips the edge of my bed and finally meets my eyes. I inherited the same brown eyes and dark hair from him.

"Dad..."

"I mean it. I was a teenager when I had Nash, and then you came along at a time when I was already drowning. Drowning in my own demons. My financial problems and instability. Your mother and I were best friends who were never supposed to get married. But that doesn't mean I regret having you guys. I hope you can understand and differentiate those two things."

I give him a soft smile as he leans on my bedframe.

"I do, dad. I know you're sorry. I can feel it in the way you always make sure I get home safe or when you try to invite me on those fishing trips to Lake Rockington. Even in the way you look at me, I can feel the guilt that haunts you. I'm just grateful I still have you and that *you're trying. Trying means everything* to Nash and me. We acknowledge you're making an effort to right your wrongs and doing things to better our relationship between my brother and me. It won't erase the trauma we endured, but...it's a step I will never take for granted."

He swallows my words. I have no idea how I was able to say those things without breaking, but I'm glad I did. The pain and memories of growing up, having fights with my mother, or when I wished my parents would come together and give each other a second chance...all hit me briefly. It stabs me in the chest as we hold each other with our silence.

He feels the weight of his actions and the consequences of not being a parent to us when we needed him badly.

"I won't let you punish yourself forever, Dad. We have a fresh start, so let's not move backward, okay?" I tell him, trying to lighten the mood.

He gives me a nod, with relief glimmering in his tired eyes. He walks away from me and closes the door. I stay staring at the door a little longer before a wave of exhaustion hits every nerve in my body. I get comfortable in bed, forgetting about the strange man on the street, and think about my parents as teenagers, laughing and holding each other. Something I always dreamed of witnessing as a child but never got. Now, as an adult, it doesn't give me the same feeling. It's weird to think of them that way together. I fall asleep in the hope that one day, I'll find a relationship that teaches me all the things my parents could not. With someone or alone, I'm determined to find something unconditional.

"I SWEAR I SAW THAT SAME BLONDE GUY AT OUR SHOP LAST night outside my window. It was weird and scary." I take a sip of my water bottle and watch Leah's reaction. I told her what had happened when I went home.

We sit across from each other, eating lunch in the break room. It's small but fits about five people, with a mid-sized table and a light green room decorated with 1980s horror movie posters on the walls.

Leah's eyes widen. "Dude, are you serious? Did you call the police?" She asks, looking down at her salad. She pokes at the avocado and chicken before eating it.

"What were they going to do? He ended up leaving so quickly anyway; in a blink of an eye, he disappeared. I think my dog scared him off." I grab a piece of leftover barbecue my dad made me. He turned the brisket into a sandwich.

"Damn. You didn't even give him my number? What kind of wing woman are you?" Leah giggles.

I roll my eyes.

"So you have a thing for creepy stalker guys?" I tease.

"No!" she bites out, but then she ponders and looks away, ashamed. "I mean, in the book world or movie world, *maybe*. Maybe I kind of like the idea of someone being obsessed with me...what about you?"

I stop chewing and actually think about it.

Huh.

I open my mouth, but Cole cuts in and opens the door to the breakroom loudly.

"If he comes back to the shop, we will refuse service," Cole says as he walks into the break room and sits down next to me. He kisses me on the cheek as he settles in, making me smile.

Cole is everything I could ever want in a boyfriend, but we're just friends. He's handsome, sweet, caring, protective, and intelligent. He's currently in medical school studying to be a surgeon when he's not bossing us around as our supervisor. He plans to work only for a few more months before starting his residency.

"You can't do that. He hasn't done anything." I knock his shoulder with mine playfully.

He's being overprotective.

"I'm sure he won't come back. I'll call the police if he does," Cole says as he takes a bite of his chicken wrap. Leah stands up and leaves the room, forcing me to be alone with him. She knows Cole wants to be more than friends, and she's rooting for him.

I take the last bite of my sandwich, then turn to my left and catch Cole watching me like he always does. The way he's looking at me is the same way he did that one day on Thanksgiving.

A Thanksgiving neither of us will forget.

I clear my throat, breaking our intense exchange because the memories are hitting both of us hard. I stand up, throw my trash away, and clock back in.

My shift goes by so fast, and I feel so tired again. I feel sick but not ill at the same time. I've been feeling more tired every day, and I don't know why. I made a mental note to make a doctor's wellness appointment. Maybe I just have low iron.

Cole told everyone to leave early because he wants me to get a headstart on learning how to close on my own. When

Cole quits, he's recommending me as the next supervisor. It's a great workplace, and I'm used to it...at least until I graduate.

I lock the doors to the coffee shop, and as soon as I turn around, I bump into Cole's chest. He's standing right behind me. I let out a startled sigh. I playfully pat his shoulders away, making the distance between us more significant.

"You scared me."

"Sorry. I didn't mean to do that. I don't like seeing you scared," he admits. A warm flutter hits my chest. I look up at him as I try to catch my breath and cool down my heated nerves. But then he's giving me that same look. He palms the wall behind me and leans in. At 6'2, he has a height advantage over me.

Is he going to try something?

I give Cole a comforting smile as I walk toward my car, dipping under his cornered embrace. It's a full moon tonight, and I hear all the night critters making noises around us. Famous Texas insects sing all night but quiet down when we get too close to them. Humidity coats our skin as we continue to walk, and the smell of rain nearby wraps me up.

"Hey, Millie. I was wondering if you wanted to grab a drink right now. At the local bar?"

"Oh..." My heart sinks, knowing I have to reject him. Why can't I feel the same way? Or am I scared of falling for him? Am I afraid of someone treating me well? Cole is good...he's always just *good* to me.

"Cole, I'm actually really tired. I have a date with my bed tonight with a man called sleep," I joke, but he doesn't laugh.

Crap.

It's not a lie. God, I hate this. He means a lot to me.

Cole swallows harder than usual and forces a tart curve of his pink lips. I try to change the subject.

"What about this weekend? We can invite Leah, too." I

look up at him, reassuring him. His smile widens, and he lowers himself to meet me. I tip-toe to give him a quick kiss on the cheek.

"Sure...whatever you would like." Cole returns the kiss on my cheek. He stares at me for a few more beats and withdraws himself, masking his emotions with deadpanned dark brown eyes. He turns around, walks across the parking lot, and takes out his car keys. I watch him get into his car and leave.

A part of me wants to give us a chance, but I know I don't feel the same way towards him.

How will I know if I don't try?

I'm scared of growing attached to someone.

I stick my key into the car handle but stop in my tracks as the noise around the trees erupts in front of my car.

Maybe a rabbit hopping around?

I quickly get into my car, pivoting on my feet. I close and lock the doors as soon as I'm entirely in. All the worst-case scenarios are going through my head.

A boar? A snake?

I twist my keys urgently, and the engine roars. As soon as I look into the rearview mirror to reverse out of the parking space, I see *his* ice-blue eyes staring right back at me. The creepy guy outside my window last night is inside my car in the backseat, grinning at me...with sharp teeth and glowing eyes that remind me of lasers. Before I can think or breathe, I scream at the top of my lungs.

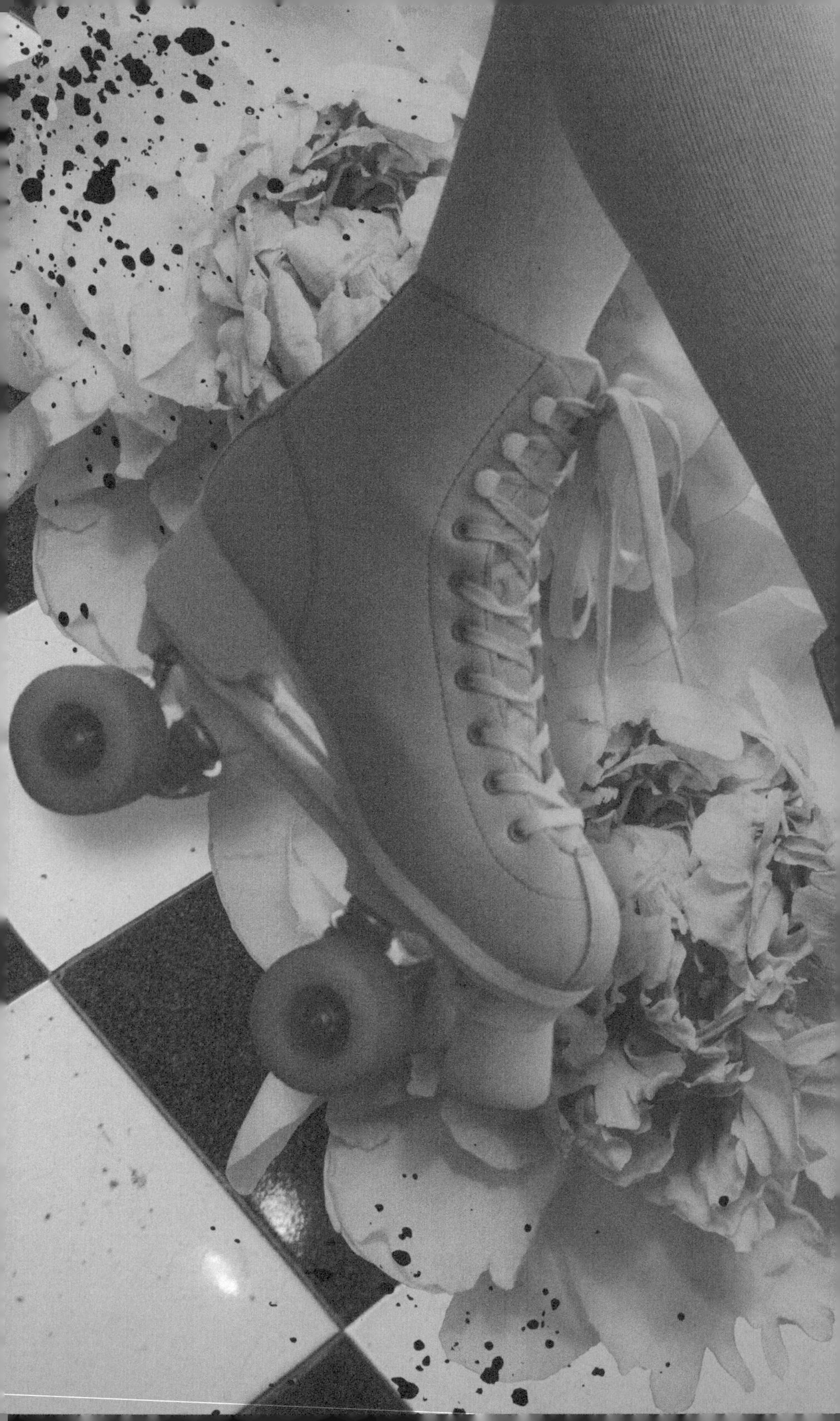

3

MILLIE

BEFORE I CAN SCREAM any longer or move an inch, at least attempt to escape my car, my screams are muffled by the stranger's freezing hands. His hand presses so hard against my squirming flesh that I bite my tongue on accident, and iron floods my mouth.

"Don't worry, darling. I won't hurt you...*yet*." His cold breath clouds my neck. His voice doesn't sound human; it's laced with profound horror.

My eyes are wide with fear, and hot tears start pouring out. My chest hurts, probably from my heart thundering so hard and tight. I try to sneak breaths through my nose, but my breaths are muffled by his large, freezing hand. I can barely breathe by the way he's pressing it against me. I stare back at the familiar dangerous man through the rearview mirror, with fright written all over my pale face. He inches closer to my neck, over the seat.

What do I do? How do I get out of this? Why does he have really sharp teeth coming out of his mouth?

I'm hoping Cole turns back around. My wishful thinking is

going hundreds of miles an hour. We're essentially in the middle of nowhere with new construction.

His lips trail my skin, and his nose dips into my neck as he smells me.

What the hell is going on?

With shaking muscles, I try to reach with my right hand for my phone. I need to call for help. I need the police!

It's in my purse that I dropped in the passenger seat. Hoping he's distracted by his strange decision to sniff me, I take advantage. I close my eyes and continue to cry softly against his hold, and I lift my hand quietly, my fingers reaching in the direction of my purse.

I barely make it over the center console when his hand quickly snatches my wrist and twists it until a loud pop bellows into the car. Excruciating pain drills into my senses, and I scream harder.

He broke it.

He broke my wrist.

"You humans are so weak, so delicate, so tempting." He roars with laughter like a monster, and before I can try to run away or call for help again, everything goes black.

"Are you sure she's a Valkyrie?"

"I'm sure of it. Her scent is strong. She has the blood."

"There's only one way to find out if she's a Valkyrie. I will take her to King Davenport myself. I'm the one that found her."

Voices.

That's how I know I'm conscious again.

I hear two men around me. One of their voices is familiar—the one that broke my wrist.

I guess I'm still alive. He must have knocked me unconscious somehow in my car.

Where am I?

I hesitate to move.

Fuck, have I really been kidnapped? The possibility alone makes me not want to wake up and face my new reality.

Do it. Just get it over with. You need to find out where you are.

Finally, I suck in a small breath and open my eyes slowly, careful not to make any sudden movements that will attract their attention.

Dark blue fabric.

I'm lying face down, on my stomach on a couch. My hand is in front of me, swollen with purple bruises. The evidence of a broken wrist is in front of me. And that's when I register the pain.

It hurts so damn bad.

I tilt my head to the side and blink fast. My eyes are dry and I'm doing everything I can to hold the anxious storm at bay inside me. I want to fall apart already.

I'm in a small space that looks like a bar room. There's a large pool table in the center, shelves with liquor and crystalized bottles on them, large TVs mounted on the walls, and shelves full of books that look ancient. What catches my eye the most is a massive map on the wall with a large, cryptic, gothic font.

Immortals Country

It looks like a map of the United States. I recognize each state, but it's divided into North, South, West, and East—each region with a name. A vast text that reads *King Davenport* is all over the Southern States.

I look up and see *King Drago* in the Northern States. I move my eyesight to the left to read the Western States, but I'm interrupted. Cold hands in my hair pull at the base so hard that I'm forced upward.

I yelp and squeal from the sensation.

"Stop! Please! Let me go home!" I plead. He pulls me off the couch and throws me over his shoulders. I thrash and hit him as hard as I can with my one arm, but I'm only hurting myself every time I hit the man. His body is hard like a rock.

The two men who were conversing earlier laugh at my weak attempts to escape. They're all wearing white sweaters with light blue jeans, and those same horrific, abnormally bright eyes look at me like I'm something to devour. One of them crosses his arms against his chest and gives me a creepy stare.

"We should drain the girl right here. Forget King Davenport!" He spits with glee.

What the?

"Drain me? What do you mean drain me? Let me go! Please, I promise I won't tell anyone about you guys. Please let me live. Don't hurt me, please!"

"Hmm, her scent is very tempting. I think you're right."

"Don't you fucking touch me, assholes!"

He ignores me like my voice doesn't matter. The other man gets closer to me and lifts my hair off my shoulder so he uncovers my face. He, too, has sharp canines coming out of his mouth. His eyes are ice blue, and he's tall with strawberry-blonde hair, combed perfectly back with gel.

He gets near me and invades my space, but then the door to the room blasts open with a loud thud. The man throws me off his shoulders violently. I hit the wall behind them, and it knocks the air out of my lungs, stunning me. I gasp for air and wince. I try to pick myself up with the palm of my hand, bending my stressed elbow, but fall back to the cold wooden floor. I'm too dazed by the blow.

"Drago." The blonde man startles out his name, rolling the r in rigid disbelief. "What the fuck are you doing here, Prince Drago? You know this room is only for the southern immortals." The two men align themselves until they're side by side, like a barrier in front of me, as if they're trying to hide me. They glare at the man who enters the room.

The man at the door stares at them with bright red, amused eyes, and then his lips form into a haunting smirk. I glance over as I cough repeatedly and groan. His teeth also have pointed canines across his bottom lip. He folds his sleeves and looks at his Rolex watch. He's in a black suit, and he isn't alone. He has other men with the same bright red eyes by his side.

"Tsk. Tsk. Tsk. I'm here on vacation before I have to fulfill my duties as the new King Drago. I'm here to visit my future father-in-law. Wanted to check out your guys' nightlife...and man," he hollows his cheeks and whistles quickly before continuing. "You guys really do know how to party. I love this nightclub!" he exclaims with sarcastic enthusiasm.

"Get the fuck out of here, Hayden. This room is only for us. No other vampire from any other region is allowed in this room. Go back out there and enjoy yourself. Finish your drinks and go home."

Hayden grins, shakes his head, and pouts his lips like a petulant child. He's enjoying getting under their skin. Then he notices me just as I sit up and hold my wrist, and a tear falls down my cheek.

"Who's the girl?" he asks the men mockingly. Hayden's men close the door behind him, and their eyes beam ruby red.

This is a fever dream, right?

"None of your business." The man who broke my bones snarls back.

"Oh, you see, that's where you are wrong. *It is my business.*" He sneers. Hayden is absolutely beautiful and out-of-this-world handsome. His smile and everything about this stranger is undeniably attractive. The longer I stare at him, the more I feel like I'm in a trance. I blink the gathered tears in my eyes as I try to think of how to get the hell out of this room.

"You Davenports have caused quite the stir and trouble lately. All these killings of innocent people have caused a massive amount of commotion. It's raising eyebrows amongst the council and other Kings. *Why?* You guys know the rules...so I will ask again, who is she?" He taunts them for an answer like he already knows the truth. He's toying with them.

"Just say the word, Hayden!" A man with bright red eyes shouts.

"Gerard, do we have to remind them of what they call me? Because I would love to," he snickers wickedly.

The two men with different sets of eyes look at each other before they face Hayden in silence. They both start to snarl, and I gasp, palming my mouth from the unfamiliar feral growls. The sounds they're making are definitely not human. I cover my ears and squeeze my eyes shut. I hug my knees closer to my chest to try to make myself smaller. Something terrible is about to go down, and I need to figure out how to escape.

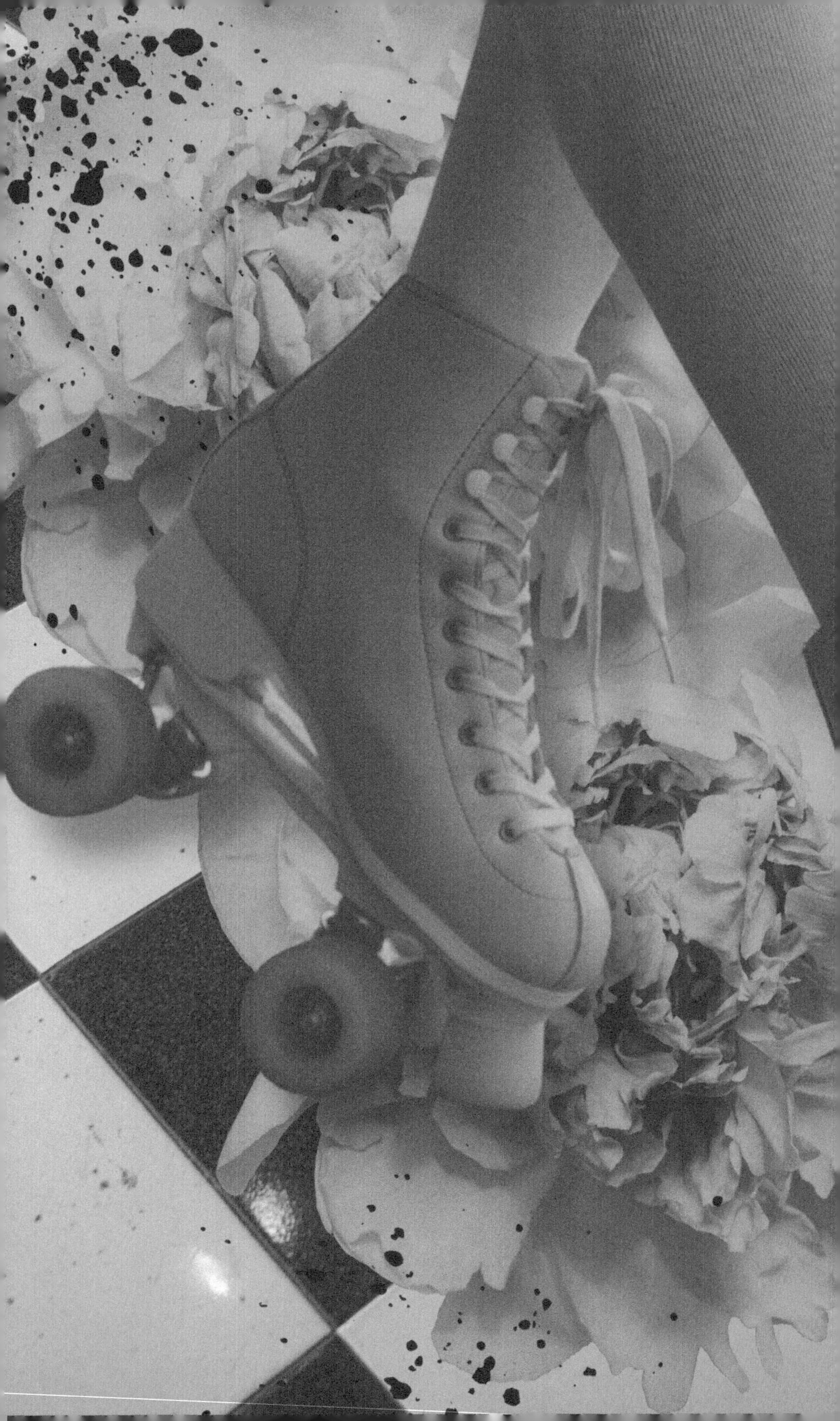

4

MILLIE

ANXIOUSLY, I peek an eye open and see the men who are holding me against my will in a position of attack. Suddenly, the man who took me lunges forward and aims an insanely fast punch at Hayden. Hayden dodges it, and I can no longer physically keep up with the ensuing fight. All I hear is snarling and bodies hitting the floor, echoing against the room's corners.

I'm still on the ground, trying my hardest not to scream. Hopefully, they forget about me, so I can try to run for it. Loud music blasts outside the other wall where the door was previously opened, and I think this is my perfect chance to try and escape. I keep my broken wrist close to my chest to protect it and decide this is my moment. Snarling, glass breaking, and the sounds of the room being destroyed by these fanged monsters are causing me to panic. My chest heaves dangerously fast, and sweat forms all over my body.

Then I hear blood splatter across the wall, and it looks like a bucket of dark red paint has been thrown against it…

I'm going to be sick.

Who are these people? Why is my troubled mind thinking

of Vampires? Well...it's the long teeth, vibrant, glowing eyes, strength, and speed. However, I try to put those thoughts aside. I need to concentrate on leaving. I quickly get to my feet and make a run towards the door. As soon as my hand touches the doorknob, my shoulder is squeezed, and it feels like I'm about to have a second broken bone.

I turn around to meet with the ice-blue-eyed man—the same one who took me from my parked car.

"You're not leaving!" he shouts as his nails dig into my chest, splitting my skin open. Before he can do more damage, he's cut off. Hayden throws him away from me. The blonde man flies in the air and lands across the other side of the wall, knocking over the bookshelves. As soon as I'm released from his grip, I open the door and bolt.

To my surprise, I really am in a nightclub. Loud music blasts and lights flash in bright colors—purple, pink, green, and blue. Those rays of light shine over a crowd of people dancing hypnotically. I run through the crowd of drunk people and spot someone I think would be sober. I run towards the bartender frantically, with convulsing gestures.

"Please help me! I've been taken against my will! I need you to call the police. Please. You have to get me out of here!" I plead as my voice shakes. I grip the bar top tight and swallow anxiously. I'm screaming at the poor guy, but it works because I have his attention. At first, he's annoyed and rolls his eyes like I'm someone talking nonsense, but then his gaze turns wicked. Another bartender appears and checks me out with him. I take one step back with knitted brows, confused by their demeanor.

Why aren't they helping me? Why aren't they concerned for me?

They nudge each other like I'm a joke to them. "Looks like someone's snack is trying to make a run for it." They both chuckle, and that's when I see those familiar sharp teeth. My heart sinks, and I shake my head vehemently.

This can't be happening!

I must be in a nightclub full of them.

I'm screwed.

I slowly back away from the bartenders, but their stares linger as if they're hungry. They whisper like they're conjuring a plan to take me for themselves.

I back up into what feels like a wall. I slowly pivot to a face I recognize. The red-eyed man, Hayden, *Prince Drago.*

For some odd reason, I feel safe with him. Something about my situation makes me feel like he's trying to help. Yet, I'm terrified of the unknown. I clench my broken wrist toward my chest again.

"She's with me." His deep voice towers over me, almost in a protective, possessive kind of way. He gives the bartenders a menacing warning with one depraved stare. The bartenders nod with no argument from them and scatter away as if they're afraid of Hayden.

He looks down at me and gives me half a smile like he's unsure of what to do. His red eyes are still bright, but his fangs return to normal-looking teeth.

"I don't know who you are, but please, sir, don't hurt me."

I don't realize I'm crying until Hayden looks at me with sympathy. He wipes away my tears with his thumb, his hand caressing my cheek carefully. He's cold, just like the other men. My eyes never leave his. With one hard blink, the once menacingly red shade transits into a beautiful bright blue. I can melt into this stranger's eyes if I stare any longer.

"If I'm going to get you out of here, we must go now." He leans down and whispers his determination into the shell of my ear. It sends chills throughout my body. The men that were with Hayden initially finally catch up to us. He grabs my hand,

and I follow him as he leads me through more drunken vampires. He gestures for me to walk in front of him so he can watch me as I walk.

Soon, we're out of the nightclub's doors, and Hayden rushes me into an all-black Mercedes SUV. I don't know why I don't choose to run away, and my instincts are telling me I'm safer with Hayden than with the men who hurt me.

I take one step forward on the sidewalk and hesitate. Should I trust him?

I stare at the door as thunder explodes around us in the sky. Rain is about to pour down hard. Then, I look to Hayden for reassurance.

"I don't know *what you are*...but please don't hurt me. Take me home." I'm begging him for mercy.

Hayden looks down at me like I've told him he's God's gift to mankind. It's like he's enjoying my pleas for remorse. He squeezes my shoulder gently.

"Get in the car, beautiful girl. We need to go now," he replies as he pushes me gently into the vehicle.

I nod and climb into it. I'm trusting this stranger with my life. Trembling, I try to click my seatbelt on. After three jittery attempts, I succeed. Hayden sits next to me. As soon as he closes the door, the driver presses on the gas hard and hauls out of there fast with screeching tires.

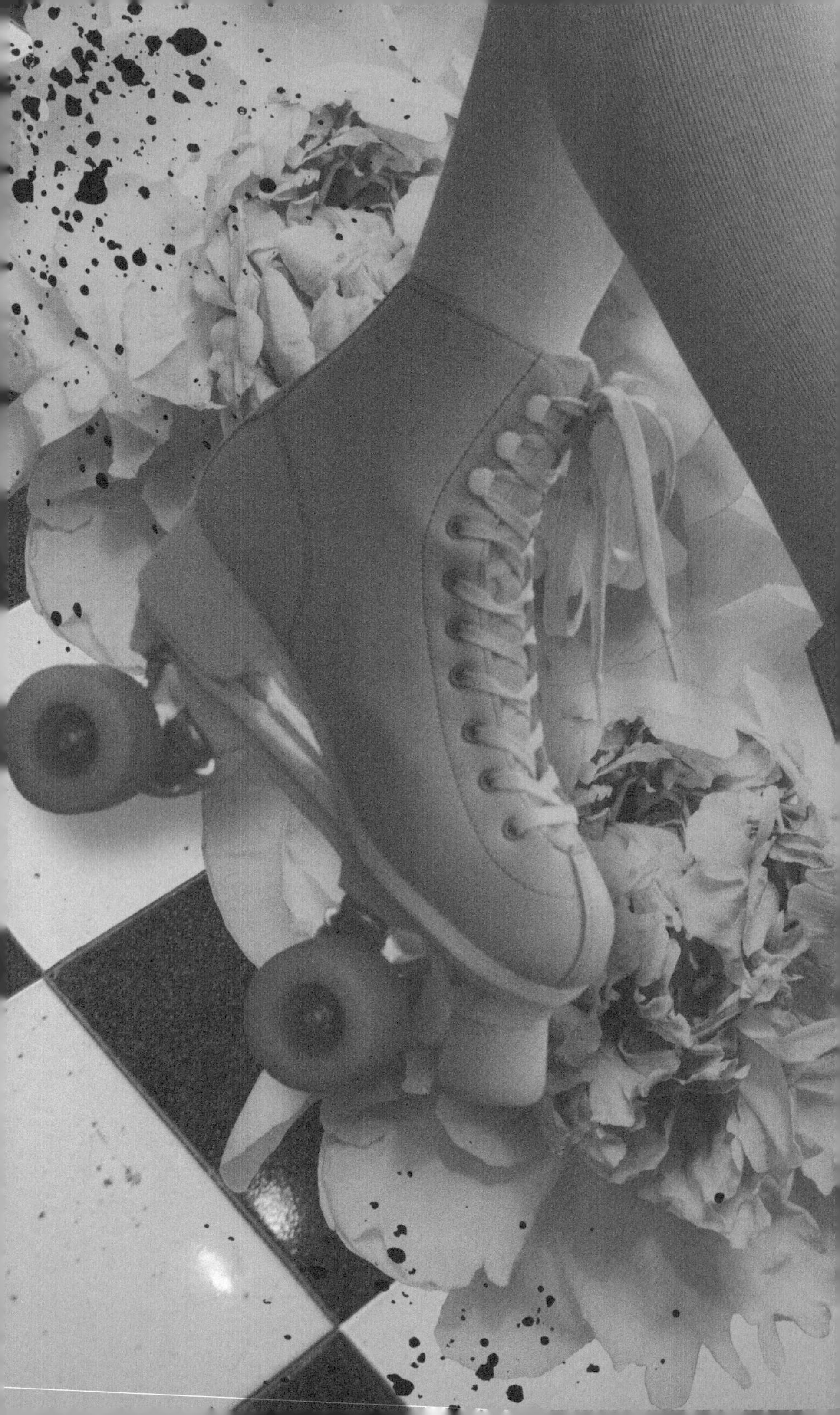

5

MILLIE

I HOLD my wrist like it's my new safety blanket. I'm trying to protect it from getting more damaged. It's throbbing, aching, burning, and there's nothing I can do to relieve the pain. The driver speeds, and every time we hit a bump, I whimper—pure agony.

I need a damn doctor.

I don't know what the fuck is going on. Where I am or who I'm with. I don't have my pepper spray on me—nothing to defend myself with. I'm kidnapped just to get kidnapped again by a man they call *Drago*. My heart thumps with adrenaline and fear. I can feel it in the base of my throat with each thud, and my chest tightens.

I'm on the verge of a panic attack. My dad is probably worried sick out of his mind. He always waits for me to get home to go to sleep.

Where is Hayden Drago taking me? Is he going to kill me? Thoughts begin to swirl about not seeing my family again. I don't want to die just yet. There's so much more I want to do. I never got to travel to Europe. *Alaska…*

I never thought I would be kidnapped. Hell, I never believed vampires existed. What I saw in that room when Hayden burst through those doors were things that wouldn't even appear in my worst nightmares. The way they snarled at each other's throats. The sound of blood splattered across the walls and floor when they were fighting. I can confirm that these horrors of trauma are engraved into me for the rest of my life.

There's no way I can sleep again, knowing these monsters exist in this world. The way their eyes turned from ordinary to vibrant colors when their vicious, sharp teeth would flash outside their mouths like rabid creatures. I tap my leg up and down and fidget with my fingers.

I'm shaking uncontrollably, my breathing shifts into deep, fast breaths, and tears flow down my cheeks. I look out the window, trying to hide my face from the strangers in the vehicle. I'm breaking down.

"Let me go home. I'm not supposed to be here. Please," I beg, watching the night sky through the tinted window.

Hayden chuckles. I turn towards him and glare. He throws his head back, still laughing. His mouth opens, entertained by my cries and pain. His teeth are displayed, and I can't help but notice how perfectly white and straight they are—his Adam's apple bobs with each husky laugh. The street lights shine against the giant ring on his middle finger. There's a snake wrapped around a bat engraved into it with words below, but I can't tell what they are.

What's so damn funny? How can my situation make him smile? As impatience and anger riddle my blood, my emotions get the best of me. I clench my one hand that isn't broken into a fist and narrow my brown eyes at his dashing face.

"You're sick. You're just like them, aren't you?" I seethe with venom, hoping he catches my off-putting tone. I'm going to die, but I might as well go out the way I want to. I'm still unafraid to speak my mind.

Hayden slowly stops laughing; he tilts his chin toward me, opens his eyes, and changes his face. Time stands still for a moment. His eyes are dark red again; the beautiful, mesmerizing sky blue is gone. Disdain in his iris, and it feels like he's burning a hole straight through me with just that look.

Before I can blink, his hand grabs my broken wrist tight enough to make me scream. What the hell? A few minutes ago, it felt like he was on my team, and now it's like I'm his victim. With my other hand, I claw at his skin, digging my nails to try to loosen his hand, but to no avail.

"Watch your words, Bambi. You're still alive because I'm allowing it," his deep voice growls. A sharp sob escapes me as I try to make him stop, but nothing works.

"Or I'll shut you up with my cock. By the time I'm done using you, your throat will be so bruised from my fucking…you won't be able to say the word *please* ever again," he dares as he smirks like he's already picturing his dick in my mouth. The image crosses my mind, and I don't know how to feel.

Finally, he lets go.

I have no words. I hold my broken wrist to my chest and let my hair fall over my face, using it as a way to mask my humiliation. *He really is a fucking monster.* I can still feel him staring at me as I concentrate on the seat before me. The only thing I can hear is the car engine and the air conditioning with blood that rushes to my ears. I want to tell him off once more, but I decide against it.

"And Bambi, you'll be begging me to shut you up again and again after you get a taste of me."

Finally, he wins. I give him a blank gaze as I lick my lips nervously. Hatred is an understatement with the way I breathe. All I see is his smug grin and red eyes. I hate that as I look at him with such rage, I can't help but notice how ridiculous and stupidly beautiful he is.

I hate myself for noticing. I stop sobbing and start to pray silently. I need to get out of this situation.

Street light after street light whips by like blurs of bokeh. My eyes fall heavy as I lose myself in my head. I'm exhausted from the pain, the running, and everything I've gone through these past few hours.

What time is it anyway? It has to be well into the night. My best guess is that it's around two or three in the morning.

We sit in silence for what feels like hours. A book occupies Hayden. Thoughts of my original kidnapper flood my mind.

What happened to the blonde man?

"Did-did you—" I'm stuttering. Fuck, why does he make the air so thick with uncertainty? Just looking at Hayden is so intense and intimidating that I can't handle it. I fear him.

"Did I what, Bambi? Spit it out," Hayden snaps calmly, still staring at his book. I flinch at his demeanor. He's unpredictable.

"Did you kill the men that took me?"

That catches Hayden's attention. He looks at me as if he's hesitating to answer that truthfully. Then he zeroes in on the book again, unbothered, and turns a page.

"Yes." Hayden clenches his jaw briskly.

Relief washes over me. They're gone. They can't get to me anymore.

My breathing finally reaches an average pace, and I let my head rest against the window as I try to flush out the dark thoughts of my unknown future.

If he wanted to kill me, I think he would have done it already. Sitting next to my newly made enemy, I wonder *what these people are*. What can grow sharp teeth like that? How can their eyes switch colors? Why do they want my blood?

Vampires? Animals? Aliens?

Soon, the physical and mental exhaustion catches up with me with each passing minute. I close my eyes and try not to think about my reality as I fall into the darkness that pulls me.

"Put Your Head On My Shoulder" by Paul Anka starts to play softly, and I swallow anxiously, following the curve of my lips. I love this song. Even when I'm enduring the most disastrous uncanny night of my life, the music still manages to distract me.

"Turn it up," Hayden orders the driver, and the volume rises seconds later. I focus on the lyrics and let myself succumb to my exhaustion.

COLD, VELVET SHEETS ARE UNDERNEATH ME, HUGGING MY body. I blink rapidly and take in my surroundings blankly.

I'm in my bedroom again. I'm in my bed, on top of my brown cozy blankets. I'm okay.

I try to remember how I got here, but does it really matter? Sleepiness still clouds my brain, causing fog. I can't help it, but a small smile forms as the safety of my room warms me.

Familiarity.

It all must have been a horrible, vivid dream. I'm on my stomach, looking at my lamp and snow globes on my shelf. Everything is lined up perfectly—nothing out of place. My white and pink roller skates are tucked underneath my desk like I usually place them when I get off work. My Garfield clock ticks and that's when I notice it's around five in the morning, and the sun hasn't greeted me yet. The only lighting in my room is the fairy lights above my headboard.

I groan into my brown pillow, and the dreadful memories of

last night come crashing into my brain like fire erupting in my heart and soul. I move my wrist, and sure enough, it slaps me back with a large amount of pain and radiates throughout my arm.

I hiss as I try to relax my muscles and joints. I close my eyes and grind my teeth. Nope. It wasn't a dream. The memories set in. They all sink me down a black hole, forcing me to remember that I was kidnapped *twice* in one night.

What happened?

The last thing I remember, I was in Hayden's vehicle. He kidnapped me from my original kidnappers.

The fighting, the snarling, all the dark blood.

If I wasn't awake before, I really am now. A familiar, deep voice interrupts my thoughts, making my heart sink so low I'm afraid it will never beat normal again.

"Bambi girl, sleep alright?"

Hayden Drago.

I quickly flip up from my stomach and sit up, ready to defend myself. I rush away from the direction of his voice, pushing my legs down onto the mattress to support my back. I scoot until I hit the headboard hard.

No, no, no, this can't be happening.

I bring my knees to my chest, holding them so rigidly it hurts.

"I'll scream," I threaten. My vision blurs as my heart pounds. I know my threat is useless.

Wait, where's my dog?

Cooper is nowhere in sight to protect me, but maybe if I scream, my dad and Cooper will hear me and rush in. Maybe even the neighbors will call the police to complain about the noise.

"I'd prefer you didn't if you want to live. *If you want your dad to live.*" Hayden casually warns me as he leans against my door, still dressed in his suit from hours ago, playing with his Rolex watch nonchalantly. He's so simple about everything while I'm deeply disturbed.

His dark brown hair is rustled in a mess—his blue eyes are hidden and focused on his watch. Being in my room makes me take in his height and frame. He's tall, just around what seems like 6'4, with a muscular frame, but he isn't overly muscular. He...

No, stop it, Millie. I won't think about these things. No matter how undeniably attractive he is, I'll fight against this magnetic pull to him.

"How do you know about my dad? Did you touch him? I swear to God if you touched h—"

"Don't get all riled up, Bambi. He took the dog out on a jog early this morning. He's alive...for now." His blue eyes pin to mine with tension around his jaw. He walks toward me, and I clench my blankets for useless protection.

Why is he still here? Why did he let me go home? Wait... how does he know where I live?

The closer he gets, the more my body stiffens. He grins wickedly as he stands over me. He leans on my headboard with one arm. I do everything I can not to look at him, as if he'll get the message that he's unwanted here and he'll disappear.

Suddenly, I feel his hand grab my throat tight. With his other one, he grips my jaw and turns my head, forcing me to look up at him. It's like he's upset I'm not giving him the attention he craves. Our eyes lock together, and after he blinks once, his crimson eyes make a devastating return. He smirks as he leans forward so we're face to face in dire proximity. His lips are close to touching mine, and his cold breath kisses my skin. A scent of whiskey, cigarettes, and mint surrounds me. I try to wiggle out of his grasp, but he tightens his grip like he's punishing me for trying to get out of his hold.

"Again, you're alive because I'm allowing it. Don't. Forget. That." His fingers and palm on my neck tighten.

The air in my lungs comes to a standstill. I can't breathe as my circulation gets caught off, and my head wants to explode. He's choking me. But I don't panic this time. My eyes squeeze shut from the pain, and I let him choke me. He wants a reaction; he wants me to fight and struggle, but I refuse to give him anything.

Finally, I see stars and black clouds threatening to pull me away. Just as I think I'm going to dive into darkness, he lets me go. And like a moth to a flame, I'm gasping for air. I choke and cough from the soreness. I hold onto my throat as if it'll help, even though I know damn well my neck is going to be severely bruised. While I struggle to breathe, Hayden turns his back to me and walks away with slow, indignant steps.

"And Bambi? Try to stay out of trouble. No one is going to be there to rescue you again."

Is that what he calls what he did to me?

Rescuing?!

I swallow and bite my tongue, trying so hard not to call him every name in the book. I think of some very colorful words to use, but then I remember his threat when we were in the car.

"*Watch your words...or I'll shut you up with my cock.*"

Slight heat throbs at my core as I remember how he makes threats feel like foreplay. What the hell is wrong with me? The exhilaration in my chest should not be present. It has to be a monster trick. I hate myself for this.

"If you tell anyone about what happened to you. You're dead. Not by me. No, no, no," he sing-songs. "But by those people that took you. For your safety, *for your father's safety*, you won't say anything. Will you, smart girl? If you do, they'll know where to find you." He sighs like he's annoyed. I watch him move, and even in the way he steps and the way his back sways, it does something to me.

Hayden opens my door and takes one step out. He's leaving me. He's actually going to let me live tonight. I bite my lip as I watch him grip my doorknob.

"It's Millie." I don't know why I felt the need to reveal my real name, but I did.

He turns his head over his shoulder, allowing me to see only half his face and strong jawline. His confusion is evident by how he knits his brows together and his eyes crease.

"My name is Millie, not Bambi," I whisper low as I correct him.

I hate it when he calls me Bambi. But it only elicits a smirk, and his eyes return to a mesmerizing frozen ice-blue color.

"In this world where I exist, you'll always be Bambi," he says darkly.

There's a short pause between us. I don't know what to do. Should I throw my beanie baby at him? It's the closest thing to my reach. Then he continues, "This is the last time you'll ever see me. Consider yourself lucky. You better start praying to God that you never do...you're going to need him in your corner."

For some reason, I unveil a glimpse of raw emotion when he tells me this. But it's just that—a *glimpse*. I'm unsure of what I'm seeing, but before I can overthink it, Hayden closes the door behind him.

I expect to hear his footsteps follow after, but there's nothing but an eerie silence with crickets singing outside my window. I hold my breath, concentrating on trying to hear a door close...*anything*. But it never comes.

I wait a few minutes before I fall apart.

He's gone. He's really gone this time. And finally, I can

breathe without feeling like I need to hold it in. I exhale heavily and start to sob uncontrollably.

I can't tell anyone about tonight. How am I going to live like this? How am I going to explain how I got a broken wrist? How am I ever going to be okay knowing that what I just went through wasn't a nightmare? It was fucking real.

All of me is terrified, horrified, thinking that men like the blonde man who took me would come back and search for me again. And another small part of me...*a very small molecular part* that I hate, is disappointed I won't see Hayden again.

Because I have questions, but right now, I'm more focused on surviving. I'm not sure I want to know the answers anyway.

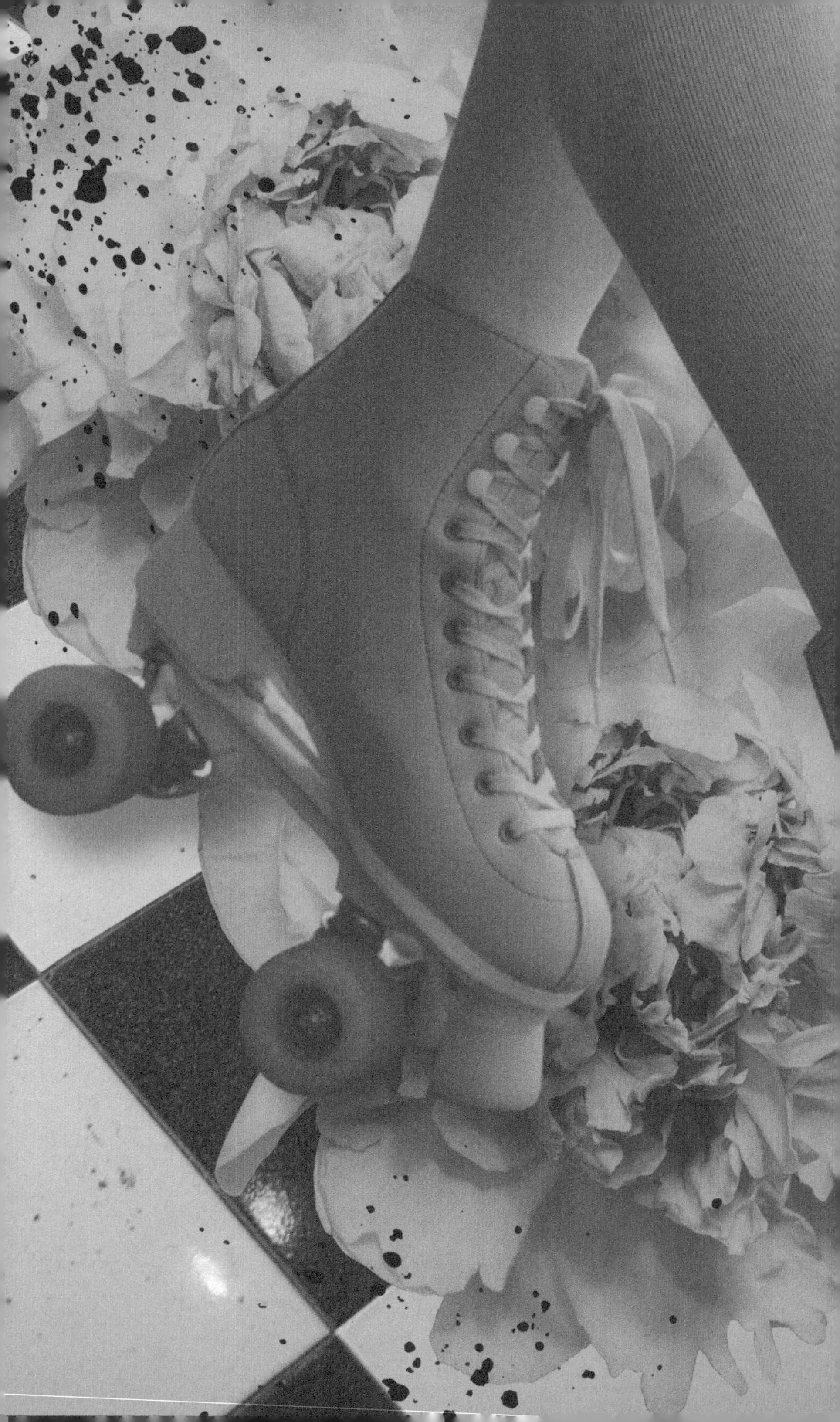

6

MILLIE
THREE MONTHS LATER

I CAN'T CONCENTRATE. I couldn't concentrate at work, at home, or even in the hospital when I got a cast on my broken wrist. The doctor said it was a clean break, but it should be able to heal after a few weeks. The doctor wanted to run blood work on me, but I refused. They wanted to do so much when I checked myself into the ER and did more unnecessary tests, but I declined.

I came up with the excuse I had fallen on my wrist and crushed it with my body weight when I went on a run in the middle of the night. I tripped over my own feet. It was totally unbelievable, but it got me through without any more questions asked.

My dad and friends asked me how I broke it, but how was I supposed to explain everything?

Should I start with, *I got kidnapped by this non-human guy who broke my wrist when I tried to call the police?* Or maybe *I got rescued by another villainous man who gave me bruises on my neck and threatened my life if I exposed their kind?*

Hayden Drago made it clear. I'm not allowed to tell the

truth. He warned me before he disappeared that if I told anyone what truly happened to me, people like the blonde man would come back for me.

I haven't seen him in three months, and yet it feels like it's only been a day. His scent and voice are stained into me like scars that don't fade. Those eyes are images I can't forget. Those lips, the way he moved, and the way he looked at me. Those raw emotions aren't easy to decipher.

All of what I endured replays in my head every single day like a broken record player.

I hate Hayden. I hate that smug look he wears so perfectly. The way he laughed at my pain and pleas for mercy. He enjoyed it. Thankfully, he hasn't reappeared. He only appears in my dreams, and I swear I can hear his voice while I sleep.

I haven't encountered another vampire or alien. Whatever they are. He kept his word. As did I. I haven't spoken about what truly happened to me, and it's eating me alive. I'm terrified. My anxiety is on another level. I can't sleep. I can't eat. I can't do anything I enjoy anymore because I'm living in fear that they'll come back for me. Every time someone comes into the shop or when I walk from class to class on campus, I lose myself in my head while I look vigorously for any features that resemble the creatures from that night.

Like right now. My strange gaze penetrates the man before me as he gives me his order of an iced latte with vanilla creamer. He holds out cash for me to take over the pink counter, and I'm just waiting for him to snarl or open his mouth wider so I can verify if he has abnormally sharp canines.

"I'll take that for you, sir," Cole interrupts me at my side. He lifts an eyebrow at me curiously. He takes the customer's payment, and I clear my throat. The man looks me up and down dubiously, probably wondering if I'm on drugs. I shake my head and look away from him.

"Sorry, I thought you were someone else." I force my best corporate-friendly smile and turn around, embarrassed. I grip the counter where we make coffee and suck in breath after breath, desperate for some relief. Cole takes over for me, giving me a gentle hand squeeze, and I return the gesture.

I really need to get my shit together.

It's my favorite time of the year. Fall.

Our manager loves to join in on the holiday fun, so we do what we always do every year when the weather changes and October is near.

We decorate the coffee shop for Halloween.

I don't know what it is about it, but the spooky aesthetic, leaves changing color, and spending nights watching horror movies soothes my soul. And yet, this time around, the excitement has been stolen from me. Now that I know that the creatures I fantasize about and adore are real, it *scares me*. They're not romantic or fun. They're dangerous and horrifying. They're out for blood and murder.

Are they the ones responsible for the local animal attacks?

"Millie. I'm worried about you." Leah sits down next to me on my lunch break. Why wouldn't she be? I'm constantly messing up customer's orders and dropping the bakery goods we sell. The last straw for me today was when I messed up one of our frequent customers' coffee orders by mixing up the flavors. She had a whole fit and started screaming at me for everyone to hear because I gave her hazelnut instead of vanilla. Cole intervened and told me to take my lunch break earlier.

He's always so sweet to me.

I have a small decaf iced coffee in my hand, but I haven't taken a sip. Instead, it's the swaying trees in the distance that encapsulates my attention outside the window of the shop. I dismissed Leah's comment unintentionally. I'm so lost in my head, and I can't snap out of it. I scan the area for anyone suspicious. I watch the customers and families with children walk in and out of the shop. Cars are parking and leaving, but everything seems normal—no one has eyes that change colors.

Leah's hand suddenly waves in front of my face. It breaks me out of my thoughts.

"Millie, what's going on? What are you looking for?" Leah's eyebrows pull inward as she tracks my vision.

I sigh, ashamed. I bite my lip and tap my fingers on my coffee cup, shaking my head nervously.

"Nothing. I...nothing," I murmur as I pick up my coffee and finally take my first swig.

"Millie, you haven't been the same since you broke your wrist. You're losing weight, your under eyes can use some concealer, and you're always so jumpy." Leah looks at me with her brown, worried eyes, studying me hard. She's waiting for a reaction.

Well, damn, that was...*honest*. I take her bluntness with a grain of salt.

"I'm just not feeling well." It isn't a total lie. It's true. I'm always tired. I'm getting headaches often, and sadness creeps over me like a shadow most days. After what I went through, I'm pretty sure this is all normal behavior.

"Well, how about we look into a therapist?" Leah asks as she takes my hand in hers and gently squeezes it.

Her touch feels warm on my hand, and I appreciate Leah so much for trying to help. I've been avoiding most of our hangouts because I'm too afraid I'll get comfortable enough to tell her what I've gone through. I'm isolating myself from everybody, and it's affecting me. Depression starts to claw its way into my soul. The same type of depression that makes you feel lonely and numb. The kind that makes you do things you may regret. Living in fear isn't how I want to live, but I have to deal with the cards I've been dealt.

"Look... I appreciate that you're concerned, but I'm fine, *really*." I lie. It hurts to lie. I always pride myself on honesty. I feel other sets of eyes burning into my left cheek.

People are staring.

I look over their shoulders to find Cole and Hayes talking to each other behind the register. They keep their voices low while their stressed gazes are pinned on me. Great, all my coworkers are judging me. They probably think I'm out of it.

Maybe I should quit. I've been thinking about it for the past few months. It's the end of summer, anyway, and school will start up again. I'm so close to earning my bachelor's degree in literature.

My fingers tighten around the glass as I fidget in my seat and stare at the coffee. The noise I've been blocking out is summoned like incoherent ghosts of whispers. I can feel the frustration building up and my heart reciprocates the harsh dwelling stress. It's all warm and hot in my chest.

I can't take this anymore.

I break.

I get up from the booth, remove my work barista uniform, and throw it on the table. I'm taking off early today. I don't care anymore.

I'm tired of all the glances this past summer. The worried looks from my coworkers wondering when I'm going to finally have a mental breakdown and fall apart in front of them. I refuse to give them, or anyone, that satisfaction.

"Millie, wait. Stop!" Leah pleads as she watches me walk away from her seat helplessly. She turns to our coworkers for assistance, but no one moves. Nothing and no one will stop me now. I've made up my mind. I storm towards the front door of the coffee shop, hearing Leah's footsteps behind me. It grows louder the closer I get to the exit.

Then I feel a hand pull me back.

"Let me go," I snap. I whip around to find *Cole*. Leah remains seated at the booth while I stare at handsome, sweet, sunny Cole. His tall frame towers over me as he holds my bicep tight but not harshly. The guilt from my sharp retort already settles in. He always wants to help, and he always wants to see me smile, yet I'm cold toward him. I can't help it these days, I'm wrecked.

"Millie, where are you going? Just talk. If not to Leah, then to me, maybe?" Cole begs softly. His dark eyes search through my brown ones. He's trying to get through to me. He knows that whenever we speak, our conversations flow so easily. He makes opening up about anything complex or controversial *effortless*.

My expression softens, and my facial muscles relax, but then the concerned whispers grow louder around us. I look around to see that we're attracting attention from customers. My eyes begin to blur, and there's that familiar sore rock at the base of my throat.

"I quit," I breathe only enough for Cole to hear.

Cole's eyes widen. "No...Millie. Don't say that, please," He begs as his grip loosens. I pull my arm back until I'm successfully out of his grasp.

I push open the door with force, and it swings open. I don't know what's gotten into me, but I need to be far away from everyone. Luckily, I've been cleared to drive just a few days ago.

I want to go home and never come out of my bedroom.

I stare up at the ceiling with my hands on my stomach. I'm thinking about Hayden's eyes again as the wings of my fan sway in circles. I'm obsessing over what happened to me. A small part of me wants to tell the world. Vampires, or whatever they are, *are real*. Monsters are real.

The way their clear, bright irises switched from blue to red. Then, the Blonde man who took me joins in on the infinite loop of dread in my mind. The way he broke my wrist so easily and fast. Grievous flashbacks of how they were all fighting, the sounds they were making, and blood everywhere. *The walls, the floor...*

Damn it. Why can't I stop thinking about all of this shit?

I cringe and shut my tired eyes tight.

How are these images still haunting me?

I concentrate and replay the events on a timeline of how it all began in my car; then it shifts to when the man woke me up with their discussion of "Valkyries." I almost forgot about it. One of the blonde men called me one.

What in the world did he mean by that? What is a *Valkyrie*?

I shift onto my side, and the self-isolation catches up with me. I won't cry. I need to learn how to move on from that night. I tuck my hands under my cheek as I try to keep my eyes closed. Maybe I'll fall asleep and dream of normal things tonight.

All I want is my mother. I want her to make me a warm bowl of chicken soup. I need her to listen to me talk about quitting my job and ask for her guidance. I want her to accompany me to a bookstore on Friday nights as we talk about the latest celebrity gossip.

But things are different.

My mother and father separated when I was under five years old. They had my older brother and me a few years into their marriage. I still remember when they shut their door, but the walls were still not thick enough to block out their shouts when they argued. Or when my dad left again and again. Even as a child, I understood and felt their resentment toward each other. It lingered, so potent it tainted my brother and me. We knew they didn't love each other anymore, even when they did everything they could to hide it.

I felt it so hard.

My mother became a woman who always put herself first, no matter what. She had custody of us, but my brother and I chose to leave her when she morphed into someone we didn't know anymore.

She met an abusive man named Santiago and decided that he was her one true love. She fell hard and decided that he was the only thing that mattered.

She wasn't always bad. She tried when she wanted to and had some good days. But once Santiago came into the picture, he kept bringing out her worst qualities. Santiago doesn't have kids.

He hated that he couldn't have kids, so he didn't want my mom to enjoy being a parent to her children.

Still, memories like when I had a throat infection stick with me like gum under my shoe. No matter how much I want to take it off or get rid of the evidence, the residue will linger in the soles of my heart. I was sick with fever and throat pain, and I begged her to take me to the doctor's office. I wasn't getting better on Tylenol.

Santiago was so angry because she had to spend money on me for the co-pay her insurance didn't cover. As we waited for the nurses to call me in the doctor's office lobby, Santiago fidgeted, upset.

"I can't wait until she goes away for college, so you don't

have to be taking her in whenever she gets a cough anymore," he snarled under his smelly breath.

My heart sank at his cruel words and my mother's tense silence. All I could do was stare at my feet. My worn-out green Converse tapped side to side as my anxiety crept in. Because if I tried to defend myself, I would get shut down, and she would get belittled if I tried.

Am I overreacting? Is it really just a cough? Self-doubt plagued me, and I felt bad for asking them to bring me here.

I turned my head in the other direction and focused on the television playing Rugrats. I silently hoped the doctor would help me the entire time I focused on the little TV in the corner. He had to tell them how sick I was, right?

Which he did after evaluating me. It felt good knowing the doctor justified my symptoms and suffering.

Well, Santiago got his wish. I was away at college now, out of their house. I'm away from him and her. I'm still in Texas, but now I live with my estranged father, and our relationship is going in a healthy direction. Nash left sooner than me, not being able to tolerate their toxic relationship and abuse.

Even though my relationship with my mother has always been troubled, I never want to give up on it.

I sit up and face the door to my room, where our phone is attached to the wall on the other side of it. I bite my lip as I swing my feet up and down pensively. Maybe I can trust her with this story. Maybe she can help me out of this mess, and if she can't, all I want is for her to be the ears to listen to me.

I leave my room, my pajama pants dragging against the cold tile with each step. I dial my mom's home phone number. I know it by memory. Four rings go by before she picks up, and a blip of hope twists in my heart. I haven't spoken to her in years. So when her familiar motherly voice says, "Hello," I stand up straight and twirl the white cord in my hand, in shock that she picked up.

"Mom." I grip the phone tighter.

"Millie, how are you? It's been years."

I rub my nose and dry my cheeks with my palms. My back hits the wall as I get more comfortable to have the most *uncomfortable* conversation with her.

"I'm not okay," I say flatly, holding back the monsoon of tears that want to fall again as Hayden and the blonde man with blue eyes flash into my head like a horror movie.

"Oh..." There's a slight pause in her impassive tone. It's like she's debating on hanging up.

But why?

"Mom...I—"

I want to tell her about my broken wrist and word vomit about what happened to me. She lives farther away from my dad, so maybe there's none of those creatures near.

I trust her still. I trust her to keep whatever I tell her to herself. I can't open up to my father and brother like this. I've never been able to. I can try again with my mother. I need her right now.

"Millie," she starts just as Santiago's cruel, unsettling voice booms in the background. My heart falls and shatters at his callous cadence.

"Get off the fucking phone! You have to make dinner!" He's still as ruthless and uncaring as the last time I saw him. Familiar fury builds up within me again at the fearless disrespect he gives her. I will never be the type of person to stand by and watch my mother get disrespected.

"Mom. Tell him you're on the phone with me. I need you right now." My voice breaks midway as I plead with her. She may not be able to do anything about my story. But all I want is her comforting maternal presence.

She doesn't say anything as he continues to hound her with cruel, malicious words.

"He knows, but he doesn't care," she whispers like she's trying to hide from him.

"Mom, please!"

"I can't. Try and talk to your father."

"Mom..." I croak out through the anxiety mounting in my vocal cords.

Is she really going to hang up?

"I'm sorry." I can barely hear her apology, but the remorse is evident in her tone and volume.

The phone clicks, and I'm left puzzled. I'm breathing heavily as I cry silently. A familiar pain of hopelessness resides in my heart like it's normal. Lately, these feelings of isolation and sadness have become my new routine. Every night, I fear one of the vampire men with bright blue irises will take me, but this time, they'll finish me off for good without a stranger with red eyes to save me.

Cooper senses my wary behavior and sneaks his snout underneath my hand like he's trying to distract me from my situation. He begs and pulls at my arm. I hang up the phone and ignore the dead tone that echoes in my ears. I give in and pet him as I let the reality sink in.

I'm on my own.

It's such a dreadful feeling to be unheard, unseen, *unwanted*.

Especially by your own family.

All I wanted was loving parents. My dad is more present, but we still have our issues. My brother Nash promised me I could live with him after he secured his job as a general surgeon, and that was coming up very soon. He's at the university in Austin, Texas.

I'm counting down the days.

I go back into my room with sore eyes, get back into the bed, and stare at the ceiling as if it's a form of entertainment.

I groan and blink my vexation away. I wish I never worked at the Nostalgia coffee shop. Maybe then, I wouldn't have been targeted or kidnapped or experienced the unimaginable trauma of monsters that walk our earth.

Finally, after I forget about my situation for a moment, I can feel myself finally giving in to rest. The night before, I hadn't slept at all. I only got three hours of sleep before my morning shift at work. My breathing evens out, and the pace turns into slow, deep ones. I close my eyes and give into my drained body that requires peace.

For an overall of what felt like five minutes, my eyes circle and burst open when the sounds of an intrusion break me out of my light sleep. It's coming from the upstairs guest bedroom. My breath hitches as I try to concentrate on the hiccups above me. Was it a dream?

But then my fears are verified once heavy footsteps thud above me a second later.

Dad?

I could have sworn my father told me he was at a barbecue tonight with friends. My heart rate picks up, my lips tremble, and I grind my jaw as I think about the worst.

Oh no.

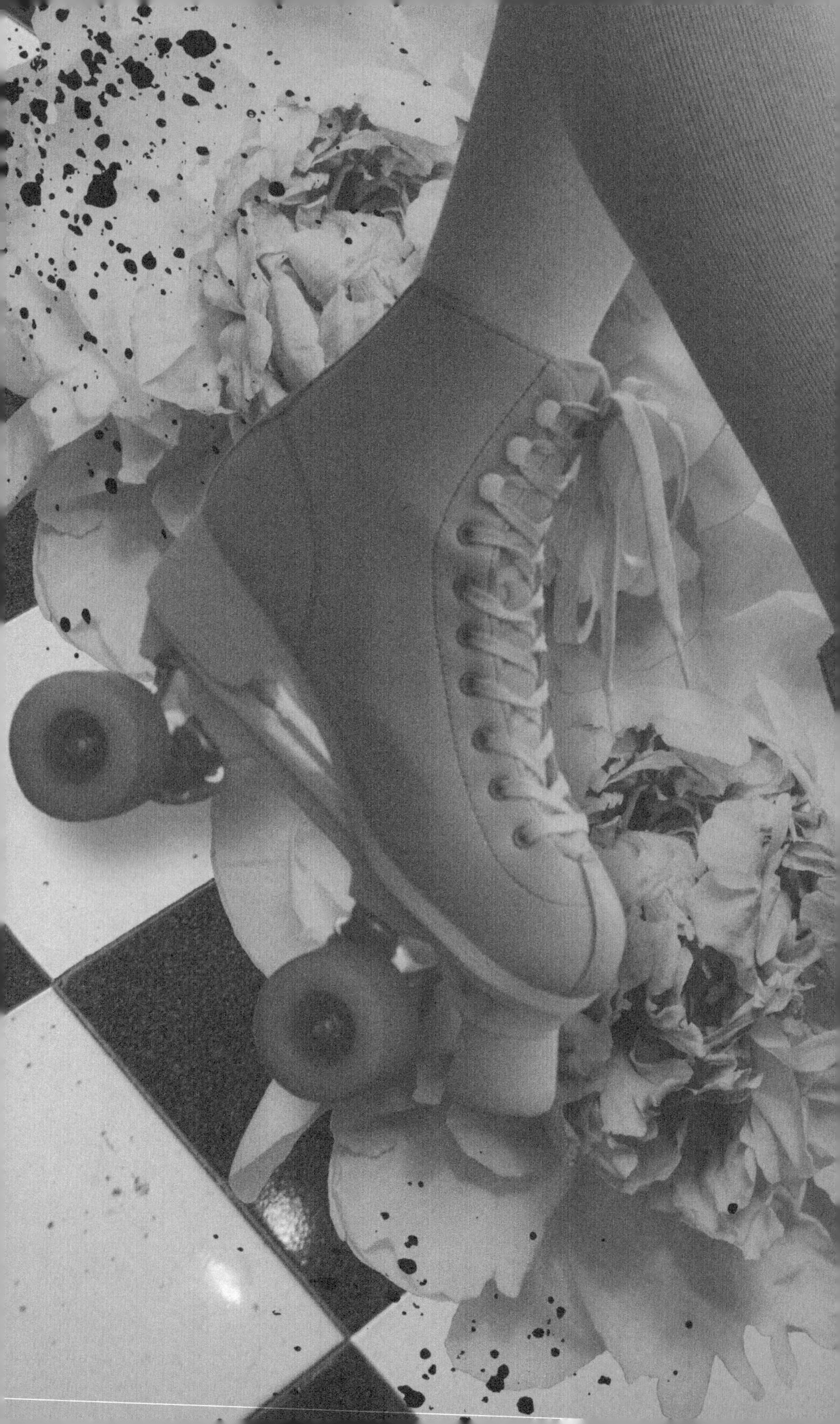

7

MILLIE

THE FOOTSTEPS DON'T STOP. Someone is in my house.

My entire body wants to coil into itself, and bile rises in my throat, burning it. I'm going to throw up...

What am I supposed to do? My wrist is barely healed!

If it's *them*. Oh, god. If it's them.... My mind scrambles for solutions.

I can't call the police because more of them will come after me. My heart pounds as fear reverberates with each beat. I palm my mouth hard to stop the whimpers from falling off my lips. Suddenly, the air runs thin, and the temperature feels suffocating.

I reach into the drawer, slowly but carefully, and grab a kitchen knife from my nightstand. I started sleeping with one ever since I was taken. I hold the handle tight until my skin burns. I rise out of bed and creep closer to my door, waiting for more footsteps, but nothing.

I turn the knob, ready to defend myself.

If I'm going to die, I'm going to die fighting.

The hallway is empty.

Every hair on my body rises like static. Why is an empty hallway scarier? My muscles tighten, and I hold my arms close to my body while the blade sticks out in front of me.

I look left and right, but...nothing. Nothing but the pulse throbbing in my ears. I close the door and retreat into my bedroom, putting a barrier between me and the unknown origin.

"Hello? Dad?" I call out, licking my plump lips.

I'm about to head back to my bed when I hear footsteps again.

Fuck it.

I swing it open, lunge forward, and swing the blade, ready to stab the intruder. My eyes narrow as I try to force my eyesight to rummage through the darkness.

It's Cooper.

His ears perk up when he sees me innocently, and his head tilts to the side in a cute, curious gesture.

Of course. It's just my dog.

It's just Cooper walking around. A high-pitched, short whimper falls from his mouth, studying me. I let out a deep breath and laugh softly. I swipe the small bead of sweat that forms on my forehead quickly.

I'm paranoid.

"I'm sorry, boy." I tuck the knife into my back pocket, walk deeper into the hallway, and rush to give him pets, scruffing his big ears and scratching him gently around his neck. He loves it when I do that. At first, he falls into my massage, letting his head nestle in my hand so I can get the angles he wants, but then his behavior shifts into something defensive.

He backs away from me, not letting me pet him further. The fur on his back stands up, his nose contouring, and he's flashing his teeth at me, growling ferociously like he wants to kill me.

What's gotten into him?

He's never behaved this way with me. I back away from him, taking three steps back as he continues to bark and arch his back. His tail points up like he's going to pounce, warning me to get away from him. His eyes lock onto me like I'm a target and not the person he's gotten to know over the past few years.

"Cooper, stop it. What's wrong?" I place my hands in front of me in a surrendering way.

His bark grows louder as I slowly step even further away from him. He then takes two steps closer to me, tempting me to flee.

"Cooper! It's me! Stop, please," I murmur softly.

He steps closer to me, barking like he's going to lunge at me any second. I keep walking backward until I reach my bedroom door on my right side.

But something stops me from walking further back, and Cooper's growls grow even louder. He looks rabid now that I've bumped into something hard.

What the...?

I slowly start turning, silently praying it's anything but a vampire. But my prayers don't make it to God in time because I'm staring into glowing, bright red eyes.

Hayden.

Hyperventilating and paralyzed with fear, my nightmares come alive. With tears leaking down my face, the mysterious man smiles with devious intentions, and Cooper closes the distance more.

Cooper has been trying to warn me this entire time.

I reach for the knife in my back pocket slowly as my chest heaves up and down wildly.

"I can smell your Valkyrie blood from hundreds of miles away. What makes you think you're safe, Bambi? Don't you know how mouthwatering you are?" He roars with husky laughter, but it's slow and conniving.

I let my bravery take over. I grab the knife from my back pocket, lift it into the air, and defend myself. I stab him in the chest, right by where his heart should be. It takes all of my strength for the blade to pierce through, but I barely succeed.

A sharp cry escapes my mouth as I let go of the knife, expecting Hayden to stumble back or shout from the pain, but instead, he looks down, unfazed, and smirks.

The devil in front of me *smirks,* like he's having the time of his life.

I walk into my room backward as I watch Hayden pull out the knife from his chest. He studies my weapon like he's impressed by it. He moves forward with one giant step and offers my knife back to me, holding it by the blade so I can grab it back by the handle.

What a gentleman. I roll my eyes.

He flashes me a hauntingly beautiful smile.

"That was hot. Do it again, but do it harder," he dares with a sinful, devilish smirk. A darker color soaks his suit—*he's bleeding.*

"You're insane," I breathe out as my knees lock to prevent me from falling over from all my trembling.

"I prefer the term Sadomasochist. But insane's easier to say, I guess." He shrugs nonchalantly.

"What are you doing here? I thought you were never going to see me again?" I take the knife back into my hand fast and hold it in front of me.

Hayden frowns in a snarky way, like I insulted him. He palms his chest and coos. "Aww, Bambi, you're not happy to see me? That hurts."

Cooper hasn't stopped barking. Instead, it looks like he's

ready to bite Hayden's leg off with the way he closes the distance, and his saliva flies everywhere with each bark.

"What a cute puppy! Call him off now. I would hate for your dad to lose his morning jogging buddy." His eyes turn into slits. The way his tone goes from joyous to villainous gives me a whiplash.

"You wouldn't dare..."

He crosses his arm against his chest and smiles.

"Want to try me? Want to see if I follow through with my threats, baby girl?" he taunts cruelly.

How does he know that Cooper and my dad go jogging every morning? Scrunching my nose hopelessly, I turn to Cooper.

"Hey, boy, it's okay, it's okay," I reassure him even though it's a lie. I don't think anything about this is okay right now. Cooper doesn't listen or stop. He looks at me confused but doesn't sway. I walk over to him, passing Hayden, and he watches us both with an unknown expression.

"It's okay, boy." I kneel down to meet Cooper's forehead and plant a kiss, putting on an act.

"Hurry up, Millie. Unfortunately for you, I'm only here to talk."

I roll my eyes again, and walk away from Cooper to my bed, crossing my arms defensively as Hayden follows me. He closes the door and locks it, forcing Cooper to whine helplessly on the other side.

What is he doing here?

"Unfortunately for me?" I mimic him.

Hayden sighs, rubbing his jaw, frustrated. He walks towards my window like this is his room. Or like he's been here hundreds of times already.

He lifts the curtains out of the way with his fingers,

glancing outside for a few seconds, and then he turns to me with his red, glowing, vibrant eyes.

"The pulsation in between your thighs and fast heart rate betrays you, Bambi. So, yes. Unfortunately for you, I'm only here to talk."

He knows my body can't deny the shameful attraction I have for him. Damn him. He sure isn't human if he knows how my body talks to him.

I clear my throat, take a deep breath, and force myself to relax. This is embarrassing.

"Then what is it? What do you need to say? You're the one that needs to hurry up and get out of here!" I point to the door.

"Why so hostile?" He quirks a brow. "You're cute when you yell."

I furrow my eyebrows at him. If my eyes could turn colors, they'd be scarlet and throw fire at him.

"You're kidding me, right? Do you really think I'd be happy to see you? I've been thinking about all the different ways to kill you if you ever showed back up here!"

Hayden sways his head back and forth, pondering, fighting the urge to smile.

"God, that turns me on. So you have been thinking about me, beautiful girl?"

I just told him I've been thinking about ways to murder him, and he sees it as me flirting. I tilt my head, confused, and mouth a curse word. I shake my head at a mischievous Hayden.

He's crazy.

"Okay, okay, you've got a point." His tone surrenders as he walks in a circle. He places his hands behind his back. "But my visitation is better than the alternative."

My eyebrows raise.

"What's the alternative?" I ask sternly.

"The Davenports," he responds, staring into my soul. Like I'm his prey. He clenches his jaw off and on, then licks his lips.

My heart sinks, and the flashbacks of the ice-cold blue eyes and blonde-haired men that took me come back like a train bulldozing the shell I've trained hard to have like steel.

"That's why I'm here, Bambi. The Southern King knows about you. He wants your blood. Your sweet, dangerous blood. He wants to suck you dry until you're nothing but skin and bones."

"Like I'm a human juice box?" He ignores me. I don't know why, but I believe him.

"When you say king? Like...vampire royalty sort of thing?"

He nods quietly.

"But I haven't said a word! I've stayed out of sight. I even quit my job today because I've been living in fear because of what I went through! Why does he want me?!"

"Because you're a Valkyrie," he states simply.

"Again, what does that even mean?"

"It means that you're no longer safe," he quips back sharply like he's over answering my questions. "It means that you've been marked for the reaper. It means you and your father are dead...if you don't come with me."

I flinch, but it changes to a glare of confusion.

"For your protection, of course." He shrugs.

I scoff.

"My protection, huh? Sounds like a lie. Do you expect me to believe anything that comes from your mouth? After you kidnapped and choked me?!" I cross my arms over my chest.

"I saved your fucking life," he tells me coldly as he turns to me disgruntled. "And you like being choked, baby girl. I know you do. No need to be ashamed of what gets you going. I liked it when I wrapped my hand around your dainty little neck. I liked it when I felt your pulse against my cold skin. I like many different things, and I'm not ashamed to admit that I'll bark like a dog and get on my knees like a good boy for a woman who catches my interest." He says it like it's a game to push me over the edge. My eyes widen at his candor and remarks. I purse my lips together.

"We're getting off-topic, Hayden. I'm safer in my own room than with you. Please. Spare me your concern, and get the hell away from me before I call the police—"

Hayden's mood changes, and his irises flash bright red again. He stalks over to me, stomping. With every step, he makes loud thuds of thunder, moving with a harsh purpose.

"What did I tell you about saying please?" he snarls. "I hate that fucking word."

I swallow. I sink down further as he towers over me. The way he's seething, full of wrath, makes me cower. I fall on my bed, my back on the mattress, and he climbs over me.

"Stop it. I won't go with you," I mutter.

He hovers over me, and his red eyes light up. He glides his nose from my cheekbones to my jaw, smelling me.

He's sick.

Then he opens his mouth and flashes me his fangs.

Is he going to kill me?

He pushes my body deeper into the mattress with his chest, his lips brushing against my artery. He growls, clearing his throat, while his teeth graze my flesh.

"You either come with me willingly or the hard way. If you don't and you stay here, your father will die when the Davenports realize there's someone else in their way when they pay you your final visit." He pulls back. "If you come with me, he lives. They'll find out you're no longer here, so they won't kill your dad in case he tries to protect you."

"*Why don't you kill me?* Put me out of my fucking misery. I don't want to live a life where I have to choose between which immortals take my throat! Just kill me already!"

I raise my hand to slap him, hoping that this will get him off of me. Because *damn him*, he smells so good. Whatever cologne he's wearing...it isn't fair. Or maybe it's just his natural scent. Either way, I need him off me.

He stops my hand before it gets close to his cheek, and thank God it's the wrist that hasn't been broken. His fingers press into my skin harshly.

He smirks villainously, handsomely. He kisses my forehead, and I glare daggers at him the entire time. When his lips touch my forehead, I squeeze my eyes tightly closed, wanting so badly to push his mass of muscles off me, but I don't want to risk another broken bone.

Finally, after the short kiss from satan, he retracts himself and then whispers into my ear, "Trust me... I will." He tells me with a satisfying tone.

Shivers run up and down my spine, and goosebumps erupt everywhere.

I'm going to die. Hayden is going to kill me.

Tears leak down my face.

"Aww, Bambi...we haven't even started yet, and you're crying?" He coos sinisterly, and then he kisses the tears that run down my cheeks.

"My name is Millie," I croak out raspy.

He scoffs, licking his lips.

Finally, he gets off me and re-adjusts his suit. He walks over to my window again. What is he looking for? It's like he's searching for threats in my neighborhood.

I sit up, and hold onto my pillow for comfort, as I watch him. I think he's really going to kidnap me. I don't think I'll have a choice if it means to protect my father. I have to go with him, right?

"Look, I'm not a total monster." He bows, smiling...but this time, he attempts to charm me. And fuck him because it comes so naturally to him.

"Your father will be safe. Your brother will be safe. And it'll buy you more time. I'll grant you a quick death while the Davenports..." He rolls side to side with his hands like he's lost in thought. "Not so much."

I arch my brows infuriated.

"How the hell do you know about my brother?"

He cuts me off.

"Oh, you mean, doctor to be Nash?" He lifts a brow.

My mouth falls open.

"I know everything about you, Bambi. Millie Flores. Hispanic. Mexican descent. She was born and raised in Texas. She loves to watch horror movies. She has mommy and daddy issues. But mostly mommy issues when she chose her new boyfriend over her children."

Asshole.

"Fuck you!"

He laughs, deep and seductive.

"Fuck me?"

He stalks back towards me and kicks my legs apart from me with his knee. He settles in between my thighs and puts his hand over my pajamas, right where my pussy is.

I inhale sharply, and the pulsations begin against his touch. My brain wants to make room for sensual curiosity. He scoffs before he slips his fingers into my bottoms and places his fingers over my skin. He stops right above my pubic bone, just a centimeter from my clit.

"If you want me to fuck you, Bambi, you have to beg. But get creative with your words because you already know how I feel about the word, please."

"Never," I rasp.

"Look at your cheeks, the color they make when I touch you."

"It's because I'm angry," I lie. I try to mask my flustered tone.

He chuckles profoundly and then slides his finger down my wet slit and smirks when he realizes how I'm dripping.

Screw him.

He pulls his finger out and holds it in front of our faces.

"Angry, huh? Your body has a wild way of showing that emotion." Then he licks his finger. He sucks my wetness with a deeply satisfied hum.

"Fuck...you taste so good. If this is the way you drip, I can't imagine how your blood will taste."

I've had enough of this.

I slap him across the face right before I grab my lamp and smash it across his head. My lamp shatters in pieces when it impacts, leaving many cuts all over his gorgeous, vengeful face.

I start crawling away when I realize my attempt to knock him out has failed, and my plan to escape is slowly withering away.

I crawl away until my back hits my headboard, and I hug my knees to my chest while I watch Hayden close his eyes, shaking his head like he's about to do something terrible. He faces all the broken pieces of the lamp on the floor, blood dripping down his sharp cheekbones and chiseled jaw. He grins, but he's beyond enraged by the way his eyes gleam a deeper shade of crimson and his pupils expand.

"While I love a good fight, I'm running short on time." In a blink of an eye, he's in front of my face, his hand over my mouth, muffling my screams. The vein in his neck bulges as he restrains me.

"Sweet dreams, little Bambi."

Everything goes black.

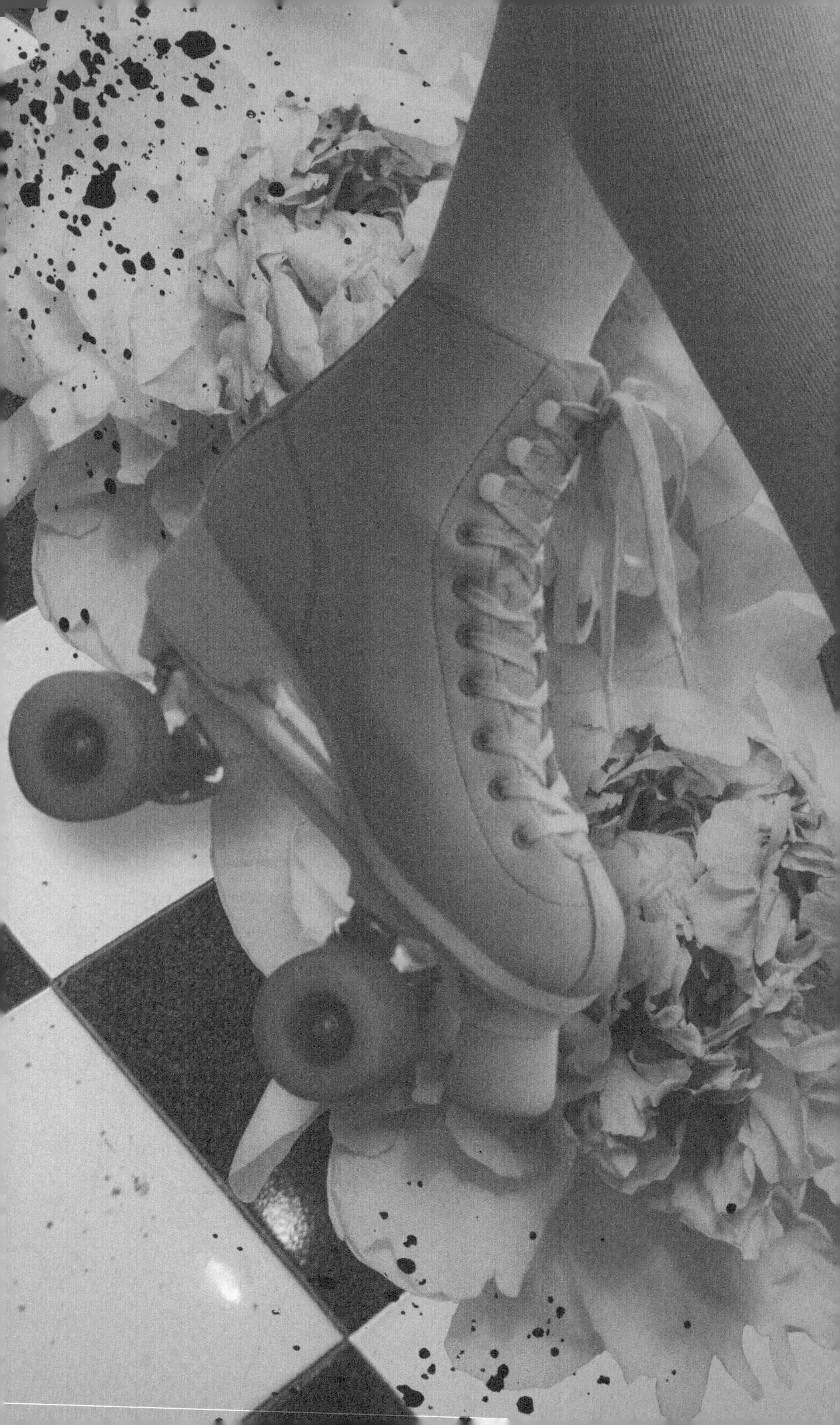

8

MILLIE

DARKNESS. Cold air. There's a soft foundation underneath my body. The contrary to the eerie feeling that surrounds me like a blanket of darkness. I feel like I'm in my bed. But it's different. I don't feel my beanie babies by me. I don't feel Cooper snuggling by my feet like he always does when I fall asleep.

All I can hear is my slow, quivering breaths changing into a quick, erratic rhythm. I'm scaring myself because Hayden's red eyes and sharp teeth sinking into my skin are all I can think about. It's a short movie playing in my mind, but it's fuzzy and blurry.

Am I dead? Did he finally take my pain away and kill me? Put me out of my misery?

The memories of me breaking the vase on his head come back like a storm, pummeling every ounce of bravery, shattering it in a way I'm not sure I'll ever recover. The fear he infiltrates sears into me like a permanent tattoo, poisoning my strength to fight him...and fight for myself.

How do you win against a monster you thought only existed in movies and fictional novels?

I want my life back. I want to live a life of being blinded to the mythical creatures that walk this Earth. I miss it. Maybe we're all naive. Maybe we're all forcing out the possibilities of eerie horror just so we can get by daily...*only seeing what we want to see.*

I don't know how long it's been, but I already miss my dad, I miss my dog, I miss the normal life of a college student trying to figure out if she made the right choice of courses she's majoring in.

I decide to break out of my weak moment and look around at my surroundings. Maybe he didn't kidnap me? Maybe this is all a bad fucking dream. Maybe I've watched too many horror movies, and it's getting to me. I can feel my pulse thunder in the base of my throat, and then the obvious hits me.

My heart is still beating. I'm alive.

So, I'm not dead yet, after all.

Nice.

"Is my little Bambi awake?" He tells me in a condescending tone, and shivers explode, crawling under my skin like spiders up and down my spine.

A sharp, high-pitched whimper spills through my chapped lips at his deep voice. He's here. He has me. *He captured me.*

Tears flow down my cheeks, but it's not the only thing that's damp. I realize my body is coated and drenched in sweat. My clothes hug my body, and I'm hot again.

My throat is dry, and my tongue yearns for water. Why am I so thirsty?

"What did you do to me?" I rub my forehead, forcefully blinking as I swipe a bead of sweat. "Did you drug me? Knock me out by hitting me?" I groan while sparing him a glance.

"Drug you? Ehh, I guess you can say something like that."

He shrugs nonchalantly. He looks at his watch like he wants to be anywhere but next to me. His bright blue eyes glow in the dark as they narrow in my direction. They look like Wolve's eyes. So detailed, sharpened with texture. Out of this world, *beautiful*.

"Did you meet your quota of beauty sleep, baby?" He teases.

Apparently, vampires don't sleep. Every time we meet, it's late into the night.

"Clearly, you don't get any beauty sleep, and it shows." I insult his prominent, handsome features. It's not my best work, but I think he'll get the point.

"Ouch. And we prefer the term immortals. Because we never die."

"But you bleed," I counter, spitting my words like they're a sharpened knife ready to pierce and wound him. I sit up and read the room. The air grows colder with hatred.

He huffs. A short snicker of a menacing laugh follows suit. He gets into my face, hands on his knees by the bed.

"We bleed," he agrees simply as he repeats my own words back to me with a sinful smirk across his undamaged face. Where'd all the cuts go?

"I'm going to kill you," I threaten. "I'll find a way. I'll kill you and get out of here."

"Sweet little Bambi, you can't kill the dead, silly," He tsks condescendingly, clicking his tongue three times and waving his index finger across my face. I narrow my brows.

"However, if you find a way to do it yourself, you'd be doing me a favor," he tells me. His devilish, sexy smirk fades away, and a cold, dead expression replaces it. His eyes betray him, giving me an insight. A flicker of pain spreads across his blue eyes. He leans in and kisses my cheek. The touch is slow and yet swift, but with no attachment behind it. It's like he knows his touch fuels the simmer in my veins. He wants me to bow down to him. I cringe but his touch causes an electricity of hatred and...*another emotion* I'm ashamed of feeling. I don't want to decipher it.

He gets into my face.

Another thought dawns on me as I chew on my bottom lip nervously. A light bulb turns on, and I reposition myself on the bed.

"You've never visited me during the daytime," I call out a possible weakness.

He stiffens, and his blue eyes dilate.

"Who is Cole?" He asks me, changing the subject.

My heart sinks. Oh God. I forgot he's been keeping tabs on my entire family and friends. Do the Davenports also know everything about my family?

"Why?" I murmur with a heavy breath.

"Nash has been calling your father's house nonstop. A woman named Leah keeps IMing you. And a man named Cole keeps leaving you these interesting voicemails on your house phone." He smirks. It's as if my capture entertains him, and the worry my disappearance has inflicted on my loved ones fills him with joyous satisfaction. He takes out a tape recorder, clicks a button, and I hear Coles's voice, making my blood heat.

"Millie, call me! Please. We're all worried about you. Come back to work! I just need to hear your voice. Please tell me you're safe and okay. I'll stop calling once I know you're okay. Please."

Cole's voice begs and pleads over coffee machines and chatter. He must have been at work when he left me these voicemails.

"He is so sweet, really. Why don't you give the poor guy a chance? He's taken you out on dates, right? He seems like a gentleman. Playing hard to get is your forte, isn't it?" He tucks a strand of my hair behind my ear. "I love it when you fight me. I love when the blood thunders in your heart when you look at me. I love it when you try to push me away, and your cheeks fluster when I grab you. Lie to me all you want, but I know your body well. I may know it even better than Cole ever has."

How does he know about Cole's and I's relationship? He's been stalking me...

"You've been watching me all this time since that night at the club, haven't you? You're the stalker that's been breaking into my house?" I accuse him.

All those nights, I woke up with a dreadful feeling. There was a shadow in my room watching me, but nothing ever ended up being there except for the gloomy possibility of me going crazy.

Hayden seizes his billion-dollar smile, and it transforms into something unreadable. "Yes...I despise Valkyrie's so fucking much. I've been studying you like a parasite."

He crushes the tape until it's in pieces, making my body freeze. He grabs a strand of my hair and sniffs it, closing his eyes as he inhales, fangs slowly appearing over his bottom lip as the strands fall over. I pull away, my heart thundering as I stare at the sharp points.

"Get those things away from me," I order him as my chin points high, putting on a fake façade of courage.

I've watched enough vampire movies to know how they use those things.

He frowns and licks his lips in disappointment, shrugging his shoulders. He's still in an all-black suit as he stands. He loves wearing his suits.

Oh God, is he going to attack me?

He doesn't pounce. Instead, his tall frame slips into the shadows with each step.

"No notifications from your mother," he says.

I'm not surprised. She probably thinks I purposefully ran away from home, and I'm sure she's not losing a minute of sleep over my disappearance.

Wait. How long has it been since I was out?

"How long have I been gone?" My voice shudders as my mind travels to the worst.

He grins. "Three days." He walks further away from me, towards the other side of the wall, slipping into the shadows. Shades of red light come from a large stained-glass window, barely illuminating the room and giving it a soft glow.

I swallow, tightening my fists. It's only been three days, and the ones who truly know me know this isn't like me to ghost everyone.

"Let me go back home," I whisper, shutting my eyes tight. My hands claw at the cold bedsheets underneath me. "Hayden...let me go." I sob softly, begging the devil before me for sympathy.

I'm going to die. If those other vampires don't kill me, I surely will die here...alone. I hate being alone.

"Go where? Home?" He teases wickedly. "This is your home now until you die." He looks at me like I'm his favorite meal. I scrunch my nose in defiance.

"I'll see you next moon, little Bambi," he tells me as he disappears, closing the door in a blink of an eye.

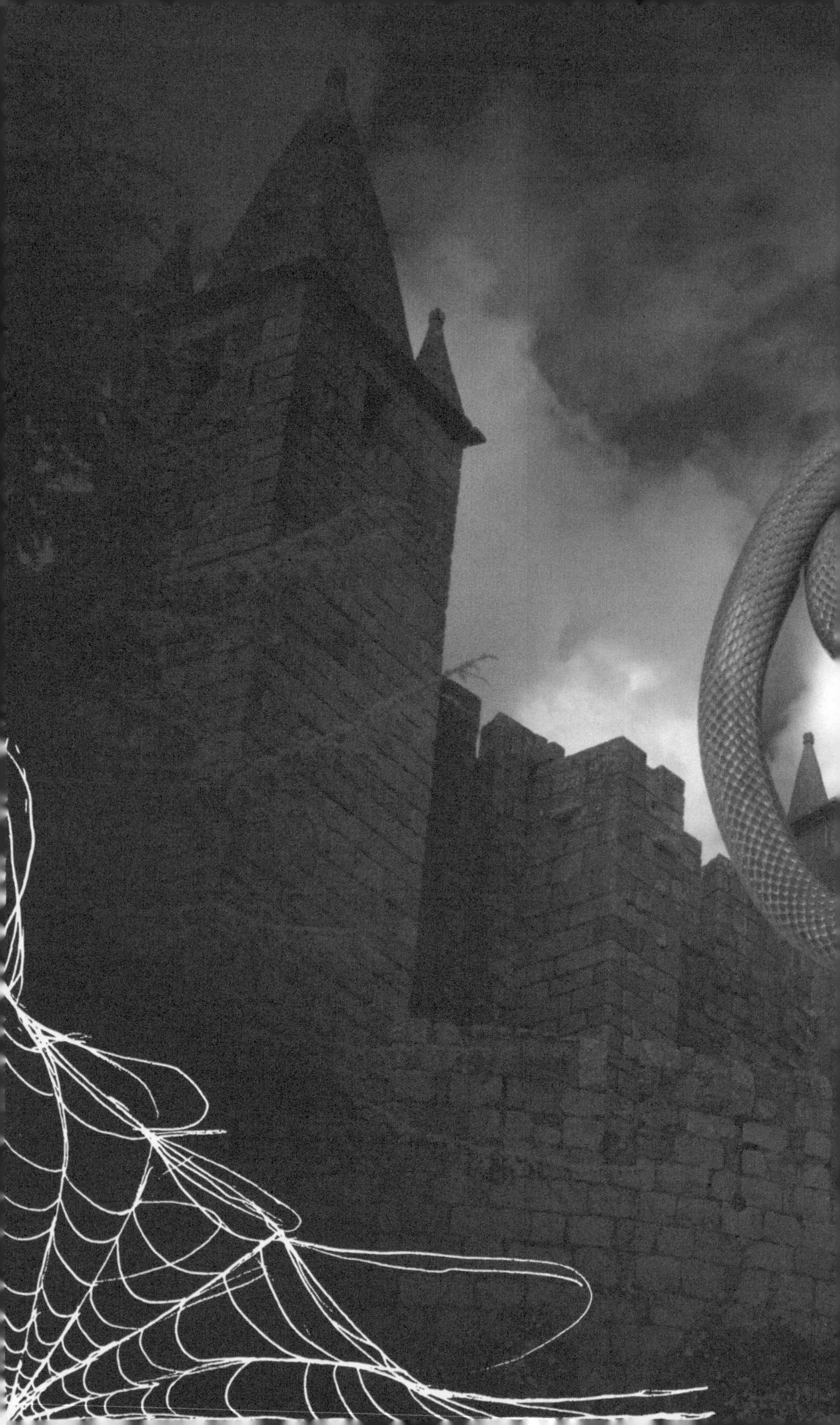

9

HAYDEN

Dear Diary,

I've never told anyone this, but...Santiago hit my mom when I was a freshman in high school. I didn't see it. I was too busy with homework, studying hard for my next exam in the living room. Nash stood up so fast from his bedroom, facing theirs across the hall. He charged towards them. Each step of his was loud and indignant, his balled fists at his side like he was ready to beat Santiago into a pulp. I stopped writing, holding my pencil in trembling hands, afraid of what would come next. Santiago locked the bedroom door on him before Nash could confront him. Nash banged on their door, cursing and threatening to kill him if he ever hit my mother again. Needless to say, Santiago didn't open the door, and my mother made excuses for his actions the next day, pardoning him and giving

Santiago another chance he didn't deserve. That was the last time Nash stayed at my mother's place and left for my father's. He moved there, and I stayed.

Because how could I leave my mother with Santiago?

She's going to need someone, I thought—a shoulder to cry on when he hurts her again mentally. But...even I had my breaking point. I left when he broke all my snow globes. I started my collection again, but it's not the same. But mostly, I left when my mother decided that her relationship was more important. She told me that again and again with her absent parenting. She chose him. She chose to leave me and my brother behind. Forcing us to be around this suctioning of evil. Stealing our light and innocence. To watch their toxicity toward one another like it was normal. My mom had plenty of chances to choose us. Santiago encouraged her to leave him over and over again. He's told her flat out that he didn't love her and is just waiting for the day she leaves.

She told me once that she regrets having children.

I guess some people may find it weird that I'm still writing about these things, but I worry about my mother. I worry about her every day and every night, hoping and wishing that one day, she'll see her worth. That one day, she'll change and be the parent my brother, and I need her to be.

She's beautiful, independently financially supporting herself, and most of all, strong.

Anyway, what triggered these memories was her birthday. She's turning forty-five. I called her to say happy birthday, but she didn't answer. She was on a plane going somewhere to celebrate with Santiago. Instead of singing Happy Birthday with her and eating cake, I worked until closing time.

-Millie

I CLOSE MILLIE'S DIARY. I've been reading it since I took her.

After Millie smashed the lamp over me, I became enraged to the point where I didn't have control and blacked out. My memories of that night are of a dark fog. All I know is that her father entered the house shortly after.

I walk into my father's council room, where he holds intimate meetings. It's his vampire man cave filled with blood in glasses that have rare jewels decorated on the glass bottles. He's pouring himself a glass of O-negative blood. We usually do this once a week to give into the cravings, to hold the temptations at bay. To prevent us from going into town and slaughtering innocents for their blood.

Our human servants bring them in for us.

"Hayden."

"Father," I fleer.

I sit down at the table, throwing my hands behind my head, and slip my feet onto the table, one leg over the other, waiting for him to spill.

"She's a Valkyrie. I can smell her. Once you entered the state, I could smell her. If the Davenports cross into our region and enter the state, they'll know she's here. They'll know we're keeping her, and the first war in centuries will fucking start."

"I know." She smells sweet. It's a cliche way of describing

her blood, but it's the truth. A Valkyrie's scent is so desirable and thick that it causes any immortal's fangs to extract just with a slight whiff and our eyes to go feral for it—like a shark in the ocean when it smells blood. A scent that is floral, fruity, serene, and lustrous, begging to be inhaled so much so that we become enchanted.

She's dangerous.

Valkyries are rare, after all.

"You were right, by the way. There were three Davenports outside her home when I arrived. They ran when they saw me coming."

"Of course, I was right. This isn't my first rodeo. I've been around for centuries to know that the Davenports wouldn't give up on finding her. *It was only when they would find her again.*" My father sighs.

"They're cunts," I spit.

"Hayden," he scolds. He lifts an impatient brow.

"What? I'm not apologizing for saying it. You're thinking it, too. Everyone thinks the southern king is a dick."

"Hayden." My father's right-hand man warns me with a low growl. "Disrespect of another king will not be tolerated in this cathedral," Holland challenges me. His ancient, bony hands curl against the desk until his knuckles turn white. Holland has been around just as long as my father has. He's never liked me. He's always favored my little brother Kallum over me. That I can agree with. Kallum follows the rules.

My system of rules results in grey areas. I don't believe in right or wrong. I don't thrive in a black-and-white mentality. I believe there's more to that, and that may be why my father and mother prefer that I take over than the latter...my brother. I love grey areas. I love problems. And I love when I get to choose the way I handle it.

"Forgive me, father." My tone heightens like I'm apologizing, but I'm not. "But I don't care." I snarl low. "I'm the only one that shows candor, and I won't change for you," I tilt my head towards Holland, "or for anyone." I lick my lips, leaning over the table. Flashing my white teeth with a big smile that can only be interpreted as *I don't give a flying fuck.*

"Enough, you two! Hayden!" My father roars and turns to me. I slowly let my back fall down until it hits the back of the leather chair softly. "There's only one way to be sure Millie is a Valkyrie."

I lift an eyebrow. I know what he's implying. He wants to feed on her.

I scoff out a bitter laugh. "Already wanting a bite out of Ms. Flores, father? Mom would find a way to kill you before you sink your fangs into her." I bite out a laugh, looking at my watch. I'm late for a party and with my midnight fling. Getting drunk and having an emotionless quick fuck, after a long night of traveling sounds like a good time to me, and I don't want it to go to waste.

"Not me..." He raises a glass to his lips, staring me down with those demanding eyes.

He wants me to bite her?

He's waiting for me to challenge him. Rebel against his order. Anticipating a clash of an argument, but an odd, unfamiliar emotion slithers into my chest.

I'm actually considering it. She's mouth-watering, after all. Her blood is so rare that wars have been fought over humans like her.

"You want me to bite her? You want me to commit a crime? Are you saying what I think you're saying, Father?" He's caught my attention. I lift my legs off the table and rest my elbows on my thighs, pressing him to tell me I'm wrong, but instead, he nods. He places the empty glass on the wooden table.

"No," I reply simply, almost robotically. I intertwine my hands together, clenching my jaw.

Once we bite a human from its warm, raw flesh, our emotions go rampant. Anger. Wrath. Lust. When they all mix together, it's dangerous and can result in their death. It's why we get it from blood banks most of the time. Over the years, we've studied and practiced getting it under control. It's what makes our soldiers, our warriors, our vampires so lethal.

Control. Strength. Reservation.

And if she's a Valkyrie, her blood will make me even more powerful. They say it's like being shot with adrenaline. Our basic immortal abilities like our strength, our speed, our thinking process is to the next power. And it's hard to stop from draining them, which results in killing them, and alas, our powers that await to be unlocked will reveal once the Valkyrie's heart stops beating.

"It's time you start taking over the tasks, son. You will take care of the North, our Cathedral, the military, and immortals will be under you whether you like it or not. I retire very soon. You are my son. You are a Drago!" He raises his voice with stipulation, each word louder than the one before. His eyes narrow down at me with blinding rage as he continues his outpour of frustration. "You were born a king. It's time you start acting like a fucking king!" He spits with venomous rage and uses his powers to spring over to the door in the blink of an eye.

I hold my ground, silently seething out of respect. I would never dare challenge him when he's in a state like this. His fangs protrude over his thin lips, and his eyes are transformed into a deep ruby red, glowing out of madness.

An awkward, thick silence fills the cold, dark, musty room.

I break it.

"Wow, Dad, you see? You ordering me around really brings out the color in your eyes. Maybe you should stay the king," I remark sarcastically. In a flash, I'm standing at the other end of the table, pouring myself my own glass of O-Negative blood. The delicious metallic fluid rolls down my throat and my fangs automatically point out. It's a reflex.

"Hayden," he scolds. He takes in a deep breath, his tone softening before he continues. "Take this seriously. If it's the one thing I have left to ask of you, take this role seriously. I cannot afford to lose you." His tone switches, unraveling a softer side, like he's hurt. Losing me means leaving my little, harmless brother to be in charge.

Kallum in charge would be a disaster in my father's eyes. In every single northern vampire's eyes. He's easily manipulated and easily taken advantage of, and we all know it. He would try to take a different approach when it comes to ruling.

My father pauses, sucking in a heavy breath like it's hard for him to continue.

It still baffles me to this day that even though we do not have a beating heart, our bodies act like we do. We act human when we're far from that.

"So, this is why you wanted me to kidnap her? Threaten her entire family's life? And here I thought you were a good man that followed the rules. I thought you had a soft spot for these fragile humans and wanted me to protect her. Not kill her." I shake my head. I'm all about breaking the rules. But even I know that taking a human's life means I go to the inferno for my execution.

It's specifically made to look like an arena. In the dead center, it's uncovered for the Immortals to be executed, specified for on-display executions. The sun is one of the ways to end us. That's why every cathedral in the four regions carries Stained Glass inside. If the sun is filtered with Stained Glass, it can shine on us without us dying or burning.

"After hundreds of years. I'm still learning something new

about my father. A side of him that I can relate to." I smile, flashing my own fangs. I bow my head, dipping my glass like I'm raising a toast of celebration. I take a sip, and my taste buds erupt. I clench my jaw over and over again.

"Ah." I sigh and lick my lips. My taste buds are going wild. "That's damn fucking good."

If I'm correct, he wants Millie because the southern king does.

Power.

King Davenport wants to inflict fear into every other immortal because once our powers are unveiled, no one would dare challenge a vampire if their powers are of use.

"A war is brewing. The southern king is upset you killed one of his sons. He doesn't want you to marry Eleanor any longer."

Thank fuck. Relief floods me. I'm not meant to be anyone's husband.

"A meeting has been called with all four Immortal Kings. I think I've been pushed into a corner here, Hayden." He grips the doorknob tight. Our family crest ring turns around his finger slightly. A black snake wrapped around a bat.

I stand up excitedly. A seed has been planted in my dark mind. *War.* I want to see it thrive with thrill. I've been wanting to see the Davenports go up in flames or his head detached from his body since the day he killed my uncle. My uncle fell in love with a Valkyrie. It's forbidden to marry them.

"I will attend. As the new soon-to-be king, I want to be there." I place both palms on the redwood table. "If he wants to start a war, I'm as sure as hell going to end it and make him regret the day he ever challenged a Drago. No one threatens a Drago and gets away with it. No one blackmails or taunts us, and I'll make sure to make that known once you step down and I take over." I spit with rage. I turn to Holland, then back to my father. "I'll send a message to everyone when King Davenport's head is in my hands and his eyes are on the throne I sit on."

"Spoken like a true king," My father says proudly. He smiles at me, and for the first time in a long time, his eyes glimmer with prideful glee.

"Not my style, a little over the edge, but uh—" my father admits as he trails off. He shakes his head once worriedly. He fears his own son. They repeatedly remind me that I'm a monster. "I think it's best you take her for your own. Bite her. Get it over with. Kill her. Initiate your powers and take over the four kingdoms. No one would dare challenge us. I'm sure the Davenports will track her, here, soon."

Holland's red eyes widen, and he glances at me, then my father, forcing his long hair to whip. "Are you sure you want Hayden biting her? Kallum is more suitable, predictable, he's—"

"Controllable." I interrupt his unnecessary rambling. Holland stiffens, slowly ripping his dark eyes from my father before pinning them on me like he's trying to control his seething.

He just won't quit, will he?

He won't give up on fighting for Kallum's ascension. A month ago, I would have been encouraging this. Agreeing to his outbursts and for my brother to wear the crown. But now? The chance to liberate my powers? The first immortal to do so in centuries? Well, that's just too much fun for me to give up now.

Holland stops talking like I've cut his tongue off with my blunt comment. He raises a white eyebrow, his lips turning into slits.

"He's controllable. You want to be able to control him, and you know you won't get that with me," I quip with a tightened tone. Holland will be my right-hand man when I take over. But I refuse to have someone by my side that continues to challenge my authority.

"That's not it at all, Hayden. You haven't been interested in being king for the past hundred years. Kallum has studied for this his entire life. He knows the laws. He knows how to rule with more peaceful procedures to keep us out of conflict with the other kings." His shaky, aged voice increases the tension in the air. My father walks towards him. Holland turned later in life. Probably right before he bit the dust.

"Holland, my dear friend." My father towers behind him. "You've been by my side since we were young, but my wife and I have made the decision. Hayden will ascend the throne. It is his birthright. Please stop challenging this." He places his hand on his shoulder, and Holland narrows his eyes at my father's gesture.

Then he turns to me, and with a smile, he says, "Davenports are after her. He wants power, and he won't stop until he's taken Ms. Millie for himself. You will be king. We're moving up your ascension. You don't have to get married right now." My eyebrows raise in relief. Good. I've never believed in monogamy.

"But you will wed. With an updated condition." I swallow, my body going rigid with anticipation. I watch my father flash to the door like he's about to leave, and Holland follows behind. The cold air whips by, making my dark hair sway.

"You can choose your wife now that the Southern King has gone rogue. The day you marry is the day you become king."

My heart sinks.

Fuck.

"What?" I murmur, my shoulders sinking.

Me? Choose a wife?

What the fuck.

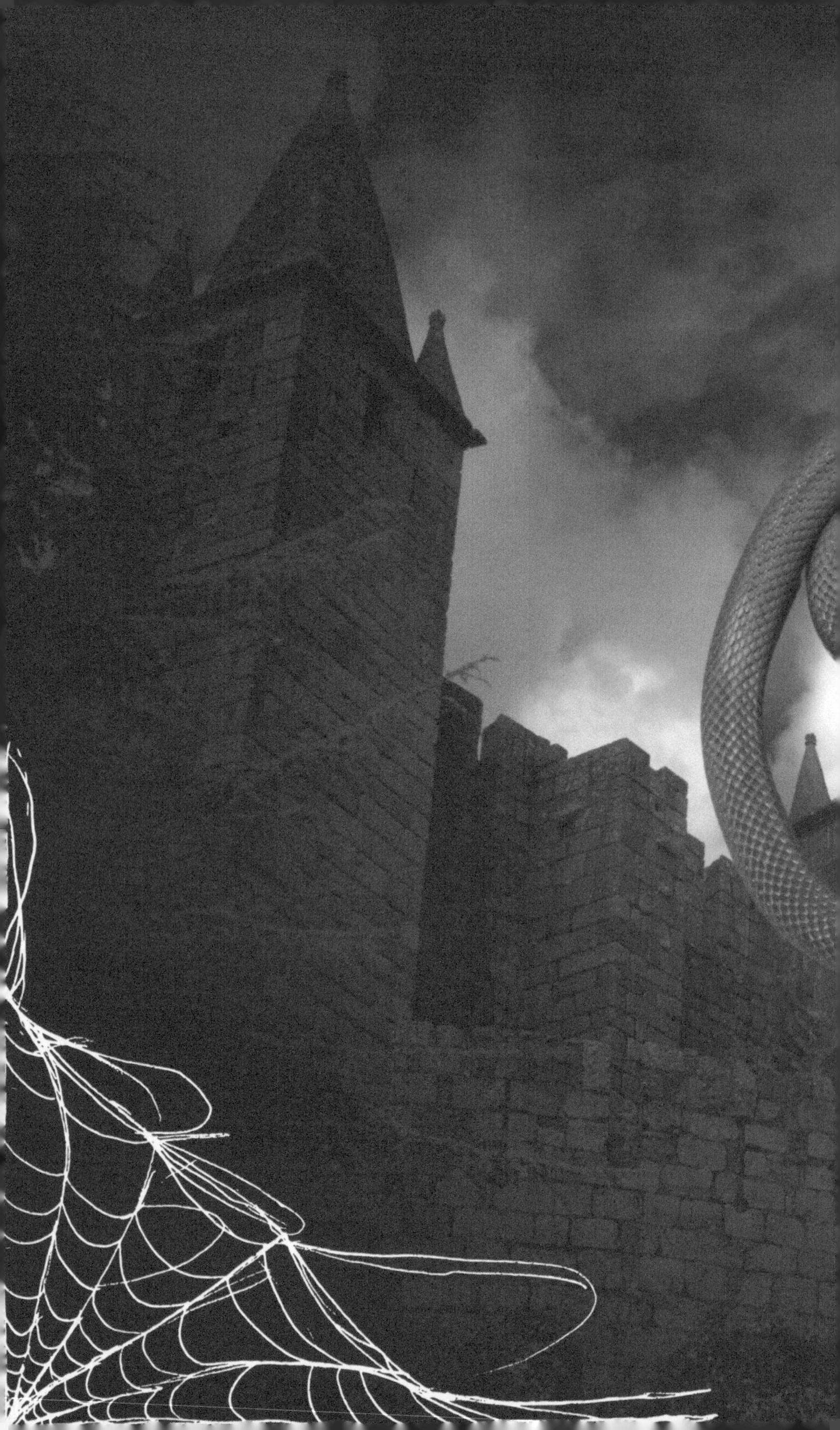

10

HAYDEN

MILLIE IS STAYING in one of our finest rooms in the cathedral. Stained glass covers one entire wall. The room is dark, gothic, and vintage. It hasn't been decorated since the early 1900s.

I had it arranged that way for a reason. My room is close but not too close. Kallum's room is down the hall.

My dad has tasked me with ensuring she is a Valkyrie, and I should just make it quick. But I want to make it painful. It brings me joy to hurt people. I only wear genuine smiles when I inflict and spread the pain I hold inside me to others like an unforgiving plague. It's so much fun!

I want to fucking kill her. I want to drain her until her veins are thinned with nothing to pump, and her blood is in my throat. I want to hold her black hair in my hands, pulling from the base as I sink my teeth into her neck, filling it with warm ecstasy. After all, her kind is what got my uncle killed.

I shake my head out of those thoughts. That wouldn't be smart of me. Like any other delicious rare meal, I must take my time with every bite and taste. I want to take what I want, savor every drop on my tongue, savor every swallow, digesting and marinating her blood in my mouth for weeks on end until it's time to make her heart stop.

"She's been banging on her door, screaming for us to let her out. Kicking on it while crying." Kallum stands by his door at the end of the hall, his glasses on the tip of his nose, with a book in his hand. I sense his unease.

I smirk. "Go to bed, little brother." I turn away from him and stare at the thick wooden door.

There are carved demons staring back at me, little gargoyles with horns on the sides, and our family crest and emblem in the center. All doors are designed that way.

I fix my suit at the collar. "Leave the family business to us," I say nonchalantly.

I can hear her take deep, even breaths from the other side of the door.

She's sleeping. There's a part of me that likes to watch her do that, but I force it back into the pits of my mind.

"A Valkyrie is staying one door down from me. How can an immortal like me sleep, knowing the most rare blood on the planet pumps by me? Calling my name. I've been having to retract my fangs all night long, and—"

I snap.

"They better fucking stay hidden!" I roar, fury and wrath slipping into my throat and the air, shocking both of us. He cowers from my ruthless demand. My little brother knows what happens when I get mad. *Everyone knows.*

I don't know where that came from or why I just came off as territorial. I don't care about Millie, but she's my property until I kill her. I turn away, furrowing my brows, gritting my teeth repeatedly. I force my fangs and blood-red eyes to vanish with deep, slow rises of my chest.

I clear my throat and watch my hand that's pointed at him fall back to my side.

"I'm sorry." I apologize weakly. "Father wants us to protect her from the Davenports. You know what happens when we taste human blood from the source, and I'm sure by all the books you collect and read, you'll know that once we bite a Valkyrie, it's hard to stop and—"

"We end up almost always killing them and unleashing our powers, which results in breaking the law. I know."

I nod, clenching my jaw, patting my pants for my cigarettes. I need to burn one. I'll check on my little Bambi and then head for a cigarette on my balcony in my room.

"I'm going to get some rest somewhere else until she's gone. Goodnight, brother. Or should I say, King Hayden Drago?" Kallum closes his book. "I heard Dad from here. You're ascending early. Good luck with finding a woman who'll willingly want to marry your grumpy self." He tells me blandly, fixing the glasses on the bridge of his nose.

I roll my eyes. "Yeah, and my first order as king will be to get you, your lonely virgin self, laid."

He scoffs out a laugh. "I'm waiting for the one. I want to be a little traditional in that way, brother. Not everyone wants to have meaningless fucks." He makes a dig at my sex life and flashes away. By the sound of his steps, he heads towards the guest room on the other side of the Cathedral, the farthest space from Millie's room.

Good.

Finally, I open the French doors slowly, expecting her to jump up and fight. I love it when she fights. My cock hardens at the thought; it's too fucking fun to see my little Bambi, hot and heated, ready to draw my blood.

To my disappointment, she really is dead asleep in a deep

slumber. Dried tears are down her cheeks, and her long black hair is knotted, probably from pulling it out of anxiousness.

I tilt my head to the side in awe as I stand over her. She's sprawled out on the floor, limp and exhausted like a pretzel.

That can't be comfortable.

Her chest slowly rises and falls. She's young but not naive. She's intelligent with a soul that's been hurt, and that's gone through way too much at twenty years of age. I've been watching her for the past few months, and my god, she is...*beautiful*. I can't deny that. Fuck, is she the most angelic, divine, captivating woman I have ever seen in my entire pathetic life, leaving stardust wherever she goes.

It isn't fair.

When I first met her, she had a broken and bruised wrist, tears overflowing so much so that they were dripping down her soft, blushed cheeks. Her soft lips quivered. Fear in her big brown eyes was evident with each rapid blink as she held her wrist to her chest. I could have fallen to my knees right then and there in the Davenport's vampire club.

Something hit me, an emotion that had me questioning whether I do have a soul after all. So, I pushed it away out of fear. Every time I look at her, I push it back into the darkest depths, hoping it'll fade, but her presence is a daily reminder that I may have a soul that hasn't gone to hell. It's still here, and I can feel it whenever I'm around her.

The sun will rise. I squint at the moon rays through the red stained glass. I track the rays and picture the sun instead. They hit my hand where I wear my ring. When the sun rises later, it'll beam on our skin, but it won't burn like it should because it's filtered through the Cathedral's stained glass.

I sigh, and the gloomy reminder that I need to rest hits me. It's almost time for me to head into my chamber and sleep.

"M-mom..." An angelic, innocent whisper leaves her sleeping lips.

I raise a brow and shift my gaze to Millie. She's talking in her sleep. I may or may not know all about what her parent's separation did to her.

There is a small curve on my lips, and I smile. Not because it brings me joy to see her still have dreams from her mother, but because she's still so hopeful at twenty years old. She hopes her mother and father one day find happiness. I know everything about her parents. I've visited her almost every night since I rescued her from the Davenports.

"My parents stayed together, Bambi, and look how I turned out? It's not all that it's cracked up to be," I whisper, ever so soft and low, hoping it doesn't wake her. She doesn't move or stir as I brush hair strands off her face.

I scoop her into my arms, careful and tactical, bringing her head close to my chest, her legs dangling off my biceps. She's featherlight. Being immortal gives us that advantage. Our strength is out of this world.

I lay her down, and she still doesn't stir. She's on her side, and I'll make sure to tell our cooks to prepare her a breakfast meal. I know all of her favorite meals. She must be starving...I know I am.

Fuck, I want a taste. I want her blood. I also may want the arousal too. It's inevitable once I bite her.

And I will bite her. But I'll spare her another night. She needs rest, and so do I. Because I love the fight, I crave the fight. I need her to fight me once she regains her strength because what I have planned for us is anything but holy.

I close the bedroom, lock it, and head to my chamber to rest. The meeting with my father ran longer than I thought it would. Our King's guard let me know my midnight fling has been calling nonstop, and she doesn't take cancellations mildly. Oh fucking well. I have a new plaything to chew on.

I'm inside my room in no time, standing in front of the mirror. I have no reflection so I don't know why I keep a mirror, but it makes me feel less like a monster. Maybe if I keep pretending, I'll feel less and less like one. Act like a duck, quack like a duck, and I'll eventually become a duck, right?

I undress all the way down until I'm in my boxers, then head for the balcony to light my cigarette. I push open the French doors, and stare at the full moon as I take a hit.

And for some fucking odd reason, I can't get a pair of beautiful honey-brown eyes out of my mind. Suddenly, the air shifts, and my senses come alive, signaling an uninvited guest.

My lips twist into a coy smile as I flick the cigarette bud until ashes fall.

"Eleanor Davenport. What did I do to deserve the displeasure?" I ask, unbothered, without acknowledging the southern princess.

"Was it worth it?" Eleanor Davenport stands next to me, beautiful and elegant as ever, in a beige dress that goes all the way down to her ankles and hugs every curve of her body in perfect ways.

Still...she doesn't hold a candle to Millie's beauty, even with vampire enhancements. Millie is majestic for a human, and her waves of beauty are undeniable.

"Was what worth it, princess?" I tease with a bitter tone. I blow smoke into the air in the opposite direction of the Southern King's daughter. I knew she was going to pay me a visit after I killed her brother to save Millie. They still don't know the Valkyrie is in our hands, just a few rooms down.

I've known Eleanor all my life. We've had our 'fun' and occasionally still do whenever we want or when fate brings us together. We've gotten along pretty well over the past two hundred years.

She wants a life of commitment from me, but I've never been able to give it to her. I've been honest, and she has a number of men lining up to meet the standards I can't. So, when she heard an arranged marriage was in the cards for both of us, she was excited.

The night I ran into Millie Flores, I was going to get on one knee and propose to Eleanor, as my father had wished not to break tradition.

Instead, I brutally murdered Davenport vampires by detaching their heads from their bodies, ending their lives, and beginning the start of chaos...a war.

"There's no way I can marry you now, knowing you spilled Davenport blood in the South. How dare you!" She hisses. She grips the railing tight like she's ready to unleash built-up resentment.

I raise an eyebrow at her, confused by her anger. I tilt my head to the side, just as a strong breeze blows through her strawberry-blonde hair.

Doesn't she know that her father broke the law? That he had his men kidnap an innocent girl? Break her bones and was going to suck her dry? The animal attacks that the humans have been reporting on the news are due to her father. Her region is casually slaughtering innocents looking for Valkyries, so her father can unlock his powers.

"You killed our kind for this human girl. When did Hayden Drago begin to have a soft spot for mortals?"

I roll my eyes, smirking, taking the last hit of my cigarette before I unleash my truth.

"I don't have a soft spot for humans. Ask your daddy to tell you the truth, Eleanor. I won't break your precious heart any more than I already have."

"What are you talking about?"

I cross my arms over my chest, a yawn following suit.

"Ask. Your. Father." I push forward into my bedroom, and she follows.

"I can smell her. You have her, don't you?"

I freeze momentarily. They can't find out we have her, or the Davenports will surround us like prey.

I keep walking until I fall onto my bed nonchalantly. Doing whatever I can not to give away my little Bambi. I cross my hands behind my back, and Eleanor watches my abs contract as I take slow breaths.

"What you smell is my new toy for the week. I have to quench my thirst some days. Even you know that, Eleanor."

She has her own victims and drinks from the source when the cravings get too loud.

"Are you fucking your meal too?" She flashes to my bed, standing before me.

"Jesus, Eleanor. Why so angry? Are you jealous?" I sit up, amused.

"Of course not."

"For someone who traveled far from Daddy's castle to question me makes me think otherwise. All the way from Texas to Montana. You flatter me, Eleanor." I palm my chest with an innocent, forced grin.

She bites her lip, and her eyes turn bright blue, as all southern vampires do when their emotions are high. Her eyes change from human-like green to ice-blue eyes.

"I wanted to marry you, Hayden! Now, I'm not sure we will be able to!"

"Eleanor! We both know you deserve more than me. An eternal life with me might seem like heaven to you, but it will only be hell," I snap, but I stay relaxed. Fighting the urge to change appearance. "I'm not capable of love, Eleanor. You know this." I stand before her in a second. Holding both her hands, granting her compassion I never give. "You deserve someone who will worship the air you breathe. Another man deserves the smile you bless anyone that's lucky enough to see it. Or when you enter the room, the man that adores you will fucking fall on his knees and kiss the floor that you walk on because you made time come to a stop for him." The more I ramble, the more I expose myself.

I've never felt like that with anyone before, but here I am, spilling a truth I didn't know resided in me. The minute I saw Millie...that's how I felt. The more I stalked her in the weeks that followed, it became more evident and clear to me that there was something different about her. I've been telling myself it has to be some sick game that Valkyrie's unknowingly inflict upon us...*it has to be that.*

It can't be that a human with pretty black hair dangerously pulls me in like a magnetic force. It can't be a girl who always smells so serene, like strawberries, that makes me feel like a weak man.

It can't be.

I blink like I'm trying to escape a trance. I realize I'm no longer looking at Eleanor, but at Millie's diary I stole from her room. The night she smashed a lamp against my face.

"Looks like you've found someone who makes you feel all those things. I'm sorry it wasn't me."

I tear my gaze from my desk and face a broken-hearted Eleanor.

A black tear falls down her cheek, and she quickly wipes it away, smearing it until it disappears. We cry black tears, unlike humans. She walks to the balcony, accepting the end of our argument after I let go of her hands. My throat rolls, and I blink away the intrusive thoughts.

"Eleanor, don't be absurd, darling. Like everyone says about me..." I clench my jaw over and over again, and my nostrils flare. "I don't have a heart. A true monster fit to be king."

My own parents have this to say about me. It's valid and justified after everything I put them through since I was born.

She laughs as another black tear falls down her cheek.

"That is what they say, Hayden..." she pauses. "Hayden Drago, the Depraved Prince." She forces a smile, and for a moment, I feel bad. Eleanor isn't a bad person. Despite who her father is. She's innocent in all of his actions. I just know it. I meant every word I said. She deserves a man who will love her all consumingly.

"Goodnight, Eleanor. Safe travels," I say as I watch her lift her dress. I hold the doors, ready to close and lock them.

She turns from me and jumps off the balcony. Her dress whirls in the wind and disappears in the shadows of the night. I close the doors and lock them with my skeleton key.

My room doesn't have stained glass—I don't take risks. It's windowless and dark, with a few candles lit in each corner.

I get into bed and stare at my finger as I get under the cover, the one that touched Millie's velvet pussy. Her arousal wetness coated it the other night. I'm unsure what comes over me every time I interact with her. I just let it flow.

I've fucked humans and still do from time to time, but it never goes past that. We are allowed to feed from them. Our fangs inject a type of venom that causes memory loss, so they don't remember the feeding afterward. However, on Valkyries, the venom doesn't work. So if I bite my little Bambi, she'll remember everything. Just like I want her to.

I put my finger into my mouth, sucking on it once more, hoping it still tastes like her, and close my eyes as I remember our encounter on her bed.

No woman has tasted like her. It was an appetizer—a little teaser of what her blood will do to me.

She's teasing me. The way she welcomes my touch even though her tongue tells lies. She's manipulating me into thinking she doesn't want me. But I'm ready to make her my full-course fucking meal until she succumbs to her fate.

The look on King Davenport's face when he finds out I have her is something I won't have the pleasure of seeing, but it'll still be satisfying. Avenging my uncle's death would make my immortal life just that much more fun.

Deep down, I know it's not the only satisfying thing a dead man like me can endure. Everyone I've ever known has experienced matching their soul to another, but I think it's pointless and overrated. But why does she intrigue me? I'll keep denying it until the end of time. I have to concentrate on the task at hand. Which is making sure her kind stays rare by eliminating her from this world.

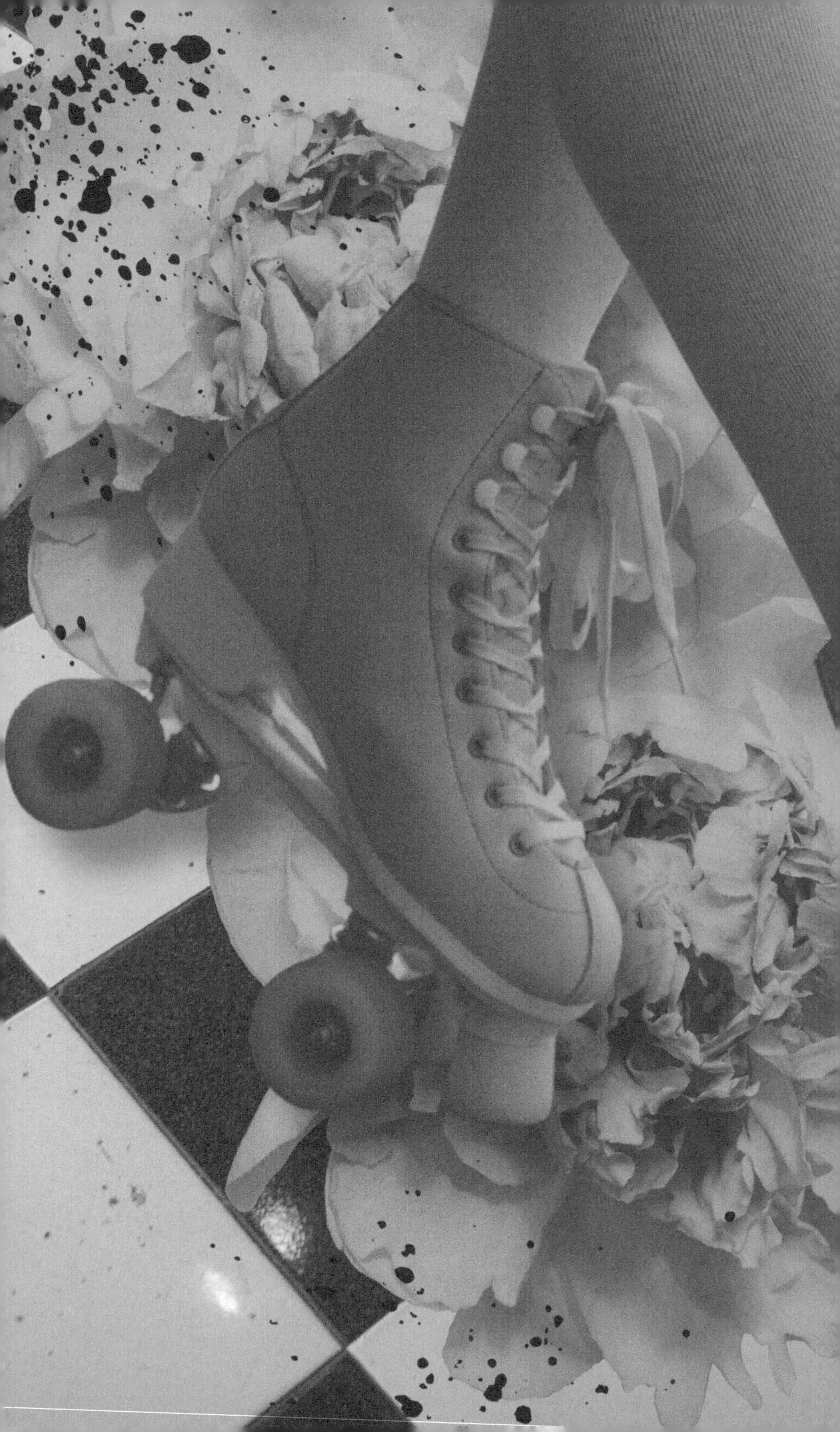

11

MILLIE

I WAKE UP WITH A RAGING, thumping headache. My stomach rumbles as red rays appear all over the room. I palm my stomach as my insides roll loudly and finally to silence. I groan, as I sit up. There are eye crusts in the corners of my lashes as I swipe slowly across them with the palms of my hands. I fell asleep crying until my throat practically bled from my screaming. No one is coming to help or save me. I don't have anything to defend myself with. I don't know where I am.

I have to save myself.

Despite my horrid situation, this is the best bed I've ever slept in. I peel the heavy, soft, luxurious black blankets off me and jog to the stained glass windows to see if I can see anything familiar. Or maybe I can break it.

With each heavy step, my feet meet cold wooden floors. Once the red light illuminates my body, I realize I'm in silky pajamas, contrary to my past clothing. I pinch the ultrasoft material, pull them from my thighs, and cringe.

I'm not in the clothes I wore when he broke into my house. Did he undress me?

Someone did.

Asshole.

I make it to the stained glass windows in ten distressing seconds. I place my hands on either side of the thick, red-stained glass, and the temperature strikes back. It's freezing to the touch. Ice-cold pricks at my fingertips, but I don't pull away. I continue my investigation, trying to gather as much information as possible to plan my escape.

How am I going to outrun vampires?

I won't be able to, but I can conjure up a plan to try and outsmart them. They must have ages of intelligence on me, but I need to find a way to survive. Hayden made it very clear.

He's going to kill me.

'Grant me mercy with a quick death.'

I squint and realize we're in high elevation. A river runs across from a valley. We're on top of a mountain, and a giant waterfall looks to run as big as a few miles. I watch the waterfall, mesmerized and taken aback by the beauty of the terrain and natural Earth.

I tilt forward and see tall trees with shades of orange, green, and yellow leaves everywhere. In South Texas, I've never seen the color of leaves change or that fresh wind everyone talks about when fall hits. I blink a few times, tearing my gaze away.

I look at the sky, and it's clear. No clouds. Just a blinding, bright sun in an abyss of blue.

He's never visited me during the day. I've only ever encountered Hayden during the night. There has to be a reason why, and the only thing I can think of is the sun. He might not be able to walk into the sun without getting hurt or dying.

If I'm going to have a chance at escaping, I have to use the sun to my advantage. I need to flee from them. I don't care where I am. Any place is better than being at the hornet's nest, where vampires live and sleep.

A knock at the door disrupts my thoughts, and I flinch. My soul practically leaves my body, and I jump up frantically as my heart sinks and my stomach flies to my throat. I tear my hand away from the glass windows and look around the room for something to defend myself with.

I grab a small gold Victorian lamp on a vanity across the room.

"Breakfast for Ms. Flores." The door opens, and a man pokes his head into the room.

He carries the tray to the bed, and I'm frozen. He looks like a butler. He wears white gloves, and his eyes beam bright when he steals a glance my way. He flashes out of the room in a blink of an eye.

He's a vampire. The butler is a vampire.

I run towards the door and turn my hands into fists, banging on the door with all the strength I've got. I get close to the door, the tip of my nose meeting the door first.

"Let me out! Please! Let me go, mister! Please! Let me go home! I'm here against my will!" I scream over and over again, repeating last night's events before I went to sleep on the floor. My voice squeaks out with each shriek, and the rasp follows.

"Help!" I mutter hoarsely. My screams transform into harsh sobs. My forehead rests against the door, shaking, as my hands fall to my sides in defeat.

No, I will not cry anymore. I'll get out of this.

I must get out of here.

I wonder if anyone is looking for me. Is there a search party? Is my dad okay? Is Cooper okay? I wonder if my brother flew back home to find me.

I wonder if my mother is worried.

Probably not.

Mom...

I miss her so much. Even though she's still alive, it feels like she's not with me with the way she's so absent from my life. All I want is her and my father's love. I'm twenty years old, and I still yearn for a relationship with them.

Does that make me pathetic?

I won't give up on her, no matter my age. She loves me. I know she does.

For some odd reason, Hayden left my silver cross necklace alone. It's the only piece left on me from that same night he took me. It still hangs loosely against my collarbones. I play with it as an attempt to self-soothe the anxiety that crashes into me every time I get desperate.

After about forty-five minutes of begging, screaming, and pleading, I give in to the natural need to eat.

I run towards the plate of breakfast: two strawberry pancakes and eggs with hashbrowns. I pick up the tray and sit down on a dining table on the other side of the room. This entire room is as big as my father's house.

Even the plates are luxurious.

I scarf down the meal in minutes as I continue to admire the incredibly detailed and well-designed room—a Gothic paradise.

"Hayden must be a millionaire," I whisper to myself as I take my last bite.

"Billionaire, actually."

Hayden's deep, hypnotizing voice corrects me and makes me storm upward. My knee hits the dining table as I stand. I hiss momentarily from the pain as I turn around to see him by the door in a leather jacket and dark jeans, leaning against the door. Handsome and dashing as ever.

He's quiet. I'm slowly dreading his next words. We stand in silence as I look around for any weapon. Finally, he looks at me after running his hand through his long, dark, wavy hair.

"Can you let a vampire sleep, little Bambi? If my cock is

buried deep inside you, will you keep that pretty mouth shut for me?" He asks with a dire smirk that will forever be engraved into my mind. He appears in front of me again, his lips by my ear as my heart thunders in my throat. Blood rushes to both my ears and cheeks. "Because that's the only time I want to hear you scream."

"Are you going to fucking rape me?" I seethe.

"Oh, Bambi, I've never and will never do that. You want to know why?"

I don't answer. His thumb brushes against my lips, and I turn my head, not giving him the satisfaction of seeing me scared.

"Because..." He begins just as he kisses my cheek, sending my heart to skip a beat. I push him with both my palms, pouring everything I've got to get him away from touching me, but it's useless; in fact, I think I made my situation worse. He's stronger than I've ever imagined. Instead of letting me go, he grips me by the back of my head, pulling my hair so painfully tight. I whimper as he gets a handful of it. Shivers dance down my entire body. Goosebumps form everywhere as he drags his nose across my cheek down to my neck as I continue to fight him.

Oh, no.

Is he going to bite me?

He pauses for a short, tense moment. "I make women's pussy weep for my cock. By the time I'm done with you, you'll beg for it, like I promised. Fight me. I love it when you do. I love the fight in you. It's admirable how you try to persevere in the unimaginable. Even when odds are stacked up against you."

I stop struggling, holding back the storm of hatred behind my eyes. I stare straight into his beautiful, crazed, dilated eyes, refusing to back down.

"Just fucking kill me already, Hayden. I refuse to be a slave here."

He laughs, letting go of my hair, and takes a step back from me. His hand brushes over his mouth and chin as he laughs.

"You're not a slave, baby. We're granting you mercy. The Davenports would have sucked you dry by now, probably have their fun with you before you succumb to your death, while you scream and they laugh. Consider this your safe haven."

"A safe haven with the devil," I spit out.

"I'm no devil, little Bambi." He enters my face, his mouth skimming through my hair, taking in a deep whiff of my scent. I shudder with our proximity. Something peril awaits with the way his tone deepens and his lips graze my neck. "I'm something far more horrifying than Satan. Even the devil runs and hides from me."

He walks to the door, getting ready to leave.

"Now, I'm going back to sleep in my chambers. I have to get some rest for my travels after all the mess I've done to keep you alive. I'm leaving for a while and don't know when I'll be back. Try not to miss me too much," he says with sarcasm painting his tone, before walkings away without another word.

Fuck him.

He's going to leave me here while vampires of all kinds are trying to hunt me down? No communication with the outside world? No way to know if my parents are okay? I want my old life back.

I start to break out in an angry sweat. I see red, and I'm blinded with rage mixed with panic at the thought of being here in this room for weeks, months...fucking years, maybe?!

I grab the butter knife that came with the tray of breakfast and throw it at him as his back is turned.

He catches the knife mid-air, a couple of inches away from the back of his neck.

How?

He faces the door again and keeps walking like I haven't just tried to kill him again. He drops the utensil, and it hits the floor with a loud, sharp noise; the metal chimes. He opens the door and takes a step out.

"I will not play your guys' games. I will find a way out of here. I will move to fucking Alaska if I have to!"

Alaska is almost always sunny. The sun has to be their weakness.

"Millie." He growls like an enraged animal. He turns to me. His eyes are bright red, and fangs make their appearance known again over his lips. He's turned into his creature-like self again like he's pissed off that I've threatened to escape him. "There's not a place, not a city, not a planet, not a fucking realm you could run to, and I wouldn't find you. You don't belong to anyone. You don't even belong to yourself anymore. You. Belong To. Me," he snarls and I back away from him further.

"Get used to being in Drago's Cathedral, little Bambi. I own you. Every single scream, tear, smile, until I kill you."

He shuts the door as I fall apart alone.

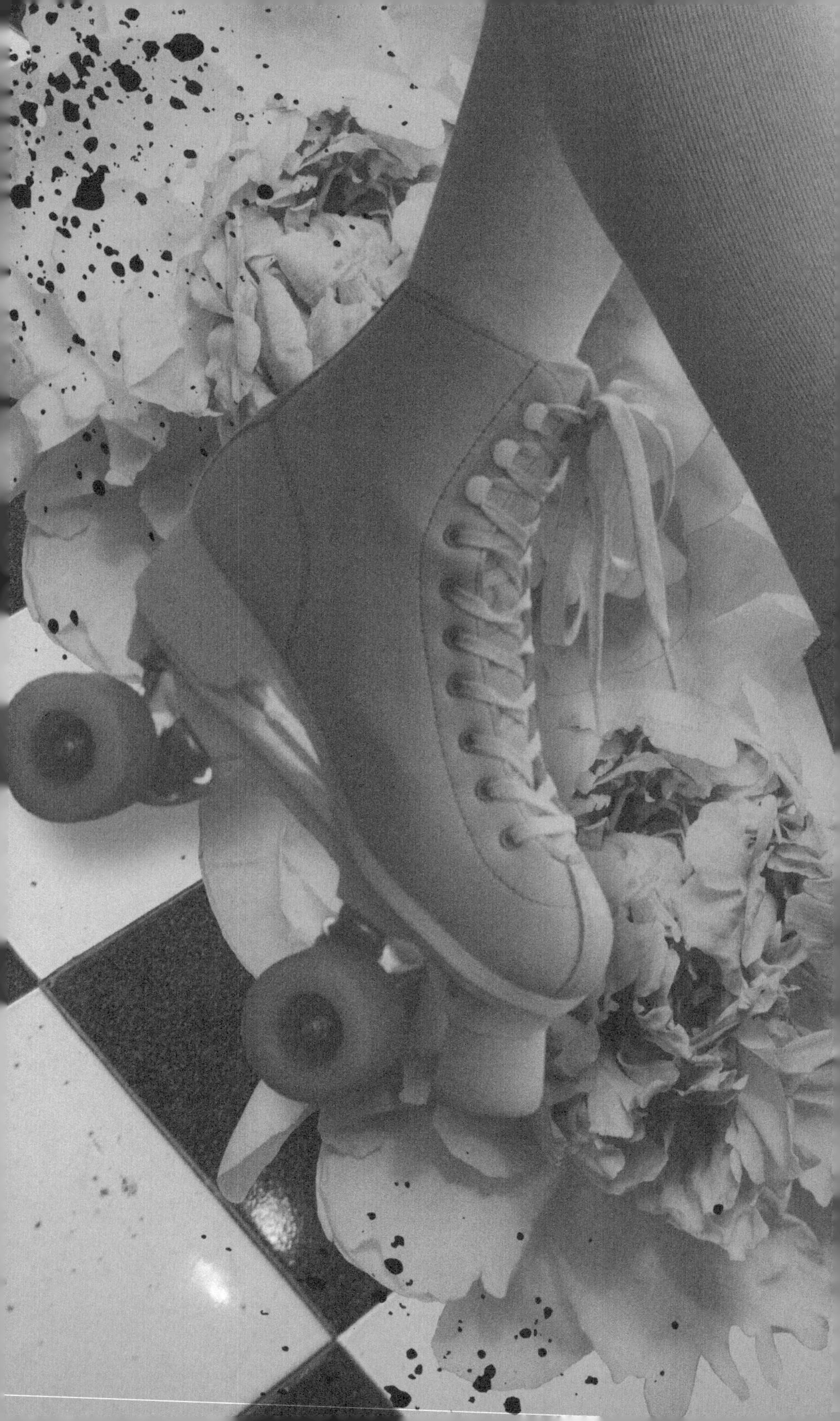

12

MILLIE

I DON'T KNOW how many days have passed, but it's the same thing over and over again.

I eventually crashed out hard after another day of being trapped in this room. I tried everything to escape. From screaming at the top of my lungs, throwing furniture at the apparent bulletproof majestic stained glass, but nothing. Not even a crack. It only resulted in hurting myself. There's a huge bruise on my ribs when the chair decided to fight back when it pounced off the glass.

There's a television in the corner of the room. I turned it on and watched reruns of one of my favorite comedy shows until I fell asleep.

That is until now.

I feel cold fingers trail my breast.

"Hayden?" I mutter, coldly mixed with grog and unease. I shift in my sleep, ready to put up another fight.

"Kallum, actually."

My eyes blow open at the unfamiliar, smooth voice. I jolt forward like I've been electrocuted. From the once comfortable side position, I end up falling to the floor with a loud crash, and my hips immediately shift movements. There's excruciating tenderness pressing my bruised ribs.

"Who the fuck are you?" I grab the same butter knife I threw at Hayden's back and hold it in front of me like a barrier.

I glance at the clock, and it's well into the night at three in the morning.

"Who did that to you? It looks fairly fresh." He points to the long scar across my breast.

I stare back at someone who looks like Hayden but has different features. I glare daggers at a sandy, dark-blonde vampire. He has glasses on, red ruby eyes, and fangs over his lips.

He's also incredibly handsome, but everything about him is softer. His voice, his body, and even his eyes seem anything but normal.

The complete opposite of Hayden.

"I'm sorry. I guess it was rude of me not to introduce myself properly." He lies back on the headboard, focusing on the TV in front of him.

"I'm Kallum Drago. Hayden's little brother. I'm sorry for waking you, but I just had to see the Valkyrie for myself, in the flesh and blood."

I'm quiet, backing away from him. Each step I take is pressed with distrust. I furrow my brows at the same word everyone calls me.

A Valkyrie.

"Stop calling me that. I am a person. I have a life. I am somebody's daughter. I have a boyfriend!" I lie, thinking about Cole.

"Boyfriend? Does Hayden know?" he huffs clearly entertained, followed by humorless laughter. "Anywho, it doesn't matter. Not anymore, Ms. Flores. You belong to the Depraved Prince, now."

"*The what?* Who?"

"Hayden." He says it so easily. "To everyone here in Immortals Country, he's known as the Depraved Prince." He places his hands behind his head like it's normal to have an evil brother.

The Depraved Prince?

"Why do they call him that?" My curiosity gets the best of me. He smiles, but it's anything but good. It's a sinful smile that holds secrets.

"Hayden has to serve his duties from time to time. Executing lawbreakers, or assassins, for example. He dismembers the guilty. Taking it upon himself to make statements. He killed an immortal by ripping his throat out for trying to get a hold of one of his human toys. He doesn't share or play well with others. That's why Father wants him to take the throne. It is his birthright, after all. I don't think I've ever seen my brother truly smile over anything gentle. He only smiles when he gets to hurt people."

I gulp.

"You're...interesting, to say the least. Every human girl who interacts with Hayden kisses his feet. But you...*you fight him.*"

"Why are you here, Kallum?"

I cut the small talk.

"I feel bad," he says nonchalantly. "No one should ever be alone for days with no social interaction. It's unhealthy. I can sense the stir-crazy happening in that pretty little head of yours."

He softens his tone.

"Or maybe I'm going a little crazy because everyone I meet has promised me death, and I've been kidnapped!"

"Yeah...that'll do it, I suppose," he retorts with humor present in his flickering smile.

Then it hits me, and I lower the butter knife to my side.

Kallum may be my way out. I can trick him into letting me leave. He's different than Hayden. He has remorse, while Hayden only bleeds horror.

I clear my throat, placing the butter knife on the nightstand.

I walk closer to him, and Kallum watches my every move like he's entranced.

"I should go now," Kallum says as I slip on the bed beside him.

I grab his forearm desperately. His skin is hard and like touching ice. Either way, I tighten my grip, hoping he can feel how desperate I am for his company and sympathy.

"No, please stay just until I fall back asleep. That's the least you can do for me? Hayden already told me my days are numbered. I would like just a flicker of compassion from *someone*." Not a total lie. Tears accumulate in my narrowed eyes as Kallum stares at me. He contemplates my request, his red eyes changing from bright red to brown as he fights with himself.

"Hayden just might kill me for this. I shouldn't be here, never mind *talk* to you."

"I won't tell him," I promise.

"You won't have to. He'll already know."

Kallum sits back into the bed and holds a book in his hands.

"Try to get some rest, now. I'm going to finish the last chapters of this book. So get to sleep, Ms. Flores."

We lay silently for a few awkward moments as I watch a horror movie play across the screen. This might be crazy. This isn't like me to do this, but if I'm going to have a chance at escaping. I have to do it now.

"Is my family okay?" I've got to ease into my plan.

He ignores me and continues to read.

"Are they looking for me?"

Again, ignored.

I try a different approach.

"It was a Southern Vampire that did it. That's what you call them, right?"

Kallum quirks a brow. "Did what?"

I've got his attention now.

"The scar on my chest. The one that you were touching."

"Ahh. That makes sense. The same one who broke your wrist?" He pushes, and a flash of compassion floods him. He turns a page and eyes my chest.

I nod.

"Hayden ripped him apart for it. He did it brutally, too. That's why there's a meeting right now," Kallum explains like he's proud.

"Is that where he is?" I pry.

He nods.

I turn over so I'm facing him.

"I think you're lying to me, Kallum."

My accusation rocks him harder than I thought.

"What do you mean? I don't lie. I never lie," he concedes like I've insulted him. His tone and body transit into stone like he's appalled.

Biting my lip, I mask my unease with a seductive expression.

I loosen the oversized silk shirt so that it falls over my shoulder, exposing more skin. I always sleep without a bra, so my nipples are hard and poking through the fabric. Kallum's eyes dilate, and he freezes.

"You crawled into my bed at three in the morning." I let my

shirt fall down more until it exposes my scar. Seconds later, a portion of my nipple is exposed.

"You touched my scar, and I felt how hard you were when you did. I felt the shape and neediness on my hip when I woke up."

His throat rolls as he grinds his teeth. He takes off his glasses and sets them beside him on the bed.

"Do you want to taste me?" I'm poking a vampire. Tempting and taunting him. I need to do this in order to survive. I'm using my rare blood to my advantage. I must.

"I consent to it. I won't fight you. Grant me a quick death, please. I'm sure whatever Hayden has planned for me isn't good."

He shakes his head.

"I don't want to taste you," he tells me in an unemotional tone that hardens. His body reveals the real truth, unlike his words. His teeth sharpen across his lip, and his eyes change once again.

He's not lying, but he's withholding part of his truth.

"But you want to have sex with me?" I ask with an unrecognized tone of mine, widening my eyes innocently.

God, don't judge me.

There's an eerie silence between us, and my heart thunders against my chest. I pray and hope he'll take the bait. Am I convincing him enough despite my tired eyes and muscles tensing up?

I decide to give it my all and go full send to hell with this newly adopted persona of mine.

My full breast escapes the rich fabric, cold air meeting my raw skin. I have full round breasts that plop out, and Kallum stares blindly from the consequences, and I stare back with pure, naive wide eyes. It's like he's on fire with how he starts to shake.

He drops his book, places it on the nightstand, and raises his hand too slowly. His big, veiny hand encases my breast, and I moan.

He's buying it. My gaze lowers to his very hard erection that's strained underneath his sweatpants, begging to release. *Begging to feel me.*

He trails his cold finger in between my breasts, giving me the green light just as his judgment falters, and I take full advantage. I might have just committed a suicide mission, but I'm still going to follow through.

I gouge him in the eye with the same butterknife I placed on the nightstand. It pierces through his organ, and he lets me go. I jump up just as he snarls an inhumane-like sound. A cold sweat breaks out against my forehead. It's a creaturelike wail that's so deep and agonizingly loud that my ears sting from the volume. A demonic-like roar of painful fury fills the entire room. It howls and echoes amongst the stained glass and vintage-like walls. I leave Kallum to attend to his injury, clutching at his eye as obsidian black runs down his face. He trembles and shakes from the pain as he collapses into himself, banging his back against the headboard. Immediate guilt simmers in every vein, but I will not apologize to my captors.

I take off from the bed and head toward the door without an apology. I want to, but I shouldn't. I need to focus on getting out of here.

I sprint like my life depends on it. My feet hit the floor, and I get to the enormous wooden door I've been staring at for days in seconds. My breaths are shallow and fast, my lungs burning with anticipation. My freedom awaits—my family...*my old life.*

I swing open the door and take in the unexplored territory.

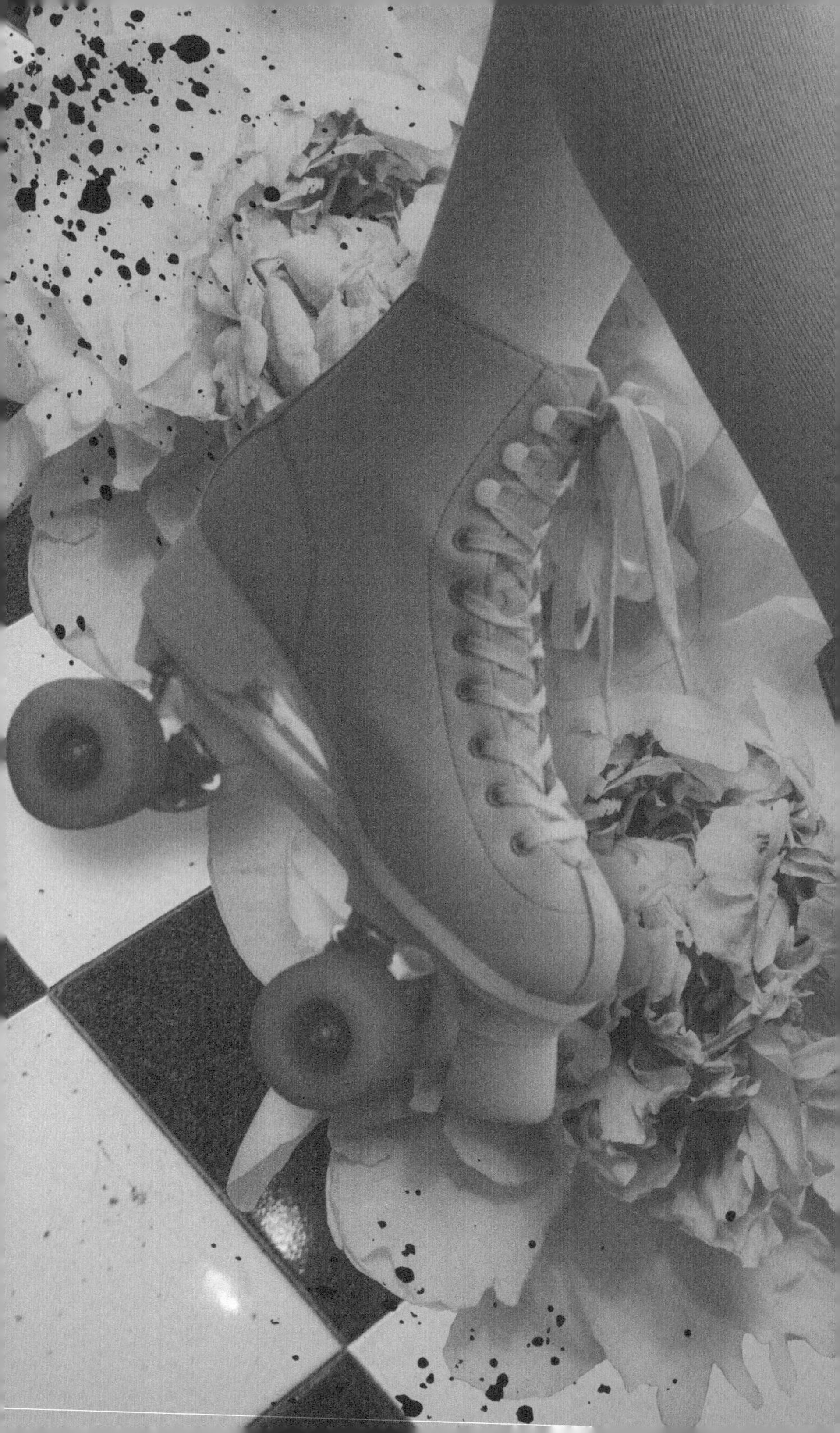

13

MILLIE

I DON'T KNOW where I'm going, but I run down the halls, trying to hold my breath as tears run down my face. I keep going, turning into hall after hall, taking guesses and hoping that God is on my side today. My bare feet hit the black floors as I try to stop myself from tripping over my own erratic pace.

I go down some stairs that seem to lead closer to an exit. I see massive stained-glass red doors. A small smile of hope slants my face when I see the sun is still out, shining through the Victorian windows.

It's almost nighttime. Just an hour or so, and the moon will rise.

I still hear Kallum's snarls in the distance. He's going to kill me if he gets a hold of me again. More snarls come from behind me, but they differ from Hayden's little brother. And they're close. Kallum's screams of agony must have alerted everyone, and now they're after me.

I don't look back. I'm either too scared or too focused on what's before me to waste one more second in this cathedral. I make it down the stairs just as more footsteps thud right behind me.

Oh no!

From what I can tell, it's just one pair of feet.

Dammit, Kallum must have caught up. Of course, he did. He's a vampire with speed. It's a part of their abilities.

Curse their abilities. It isn't fucking fair.

It'll slow me down if I check behind me. One wrong move, and I'll be snapped in half. I've seen what they're capable of doing. I'm like five feet away from the door. My entire body jolts with each stomp like I'm in a race—a race for my life.

I'm right here. One more step, and I'm at the exit. All my dreams of escaping are finally a reality. I'm so focused on getting out that I forget to blink.

It's real. I'm going to get out. The sun will give me an advantage to run. I have to try.

I lunge forward, grasp the black metal lever with the same design as Hayden's ring, and pull on it.

A ray of sunlight shines through the cathedral like a ray of hope, a lighthouse in the middle of the ocean, like a lifejacket. I smile with relief. Seeing the sun again after being in darkness the past few days feels so good. Something so simple never felt so grand.

I step out onto the pavement outside just as my hair gets pulled back, and I scream from an unexpected maneuver. I'm forced back into the Cathedral surrounded by red stained glass.

A large familiar hand slams the door shut, and my back gets pushed up against the doors.

"Ahh!" I bellow.

Red rays from the stained glass shine on him, but it's not doing any damage to the vampire before me.

How? It's the sunlight...

Shit. Maybe I got it all wrong...if they can be in the sun,

then nature's hopeful alliance is useless now. I need to think of another plan, but first, I need to survive the man I loathe.

Hayden.

My shamefully handsome captor is dressed in an all-black suit, looking at me like he's won a prize. I hate him.

A wicked curve of his lips turns, his sharp teeth shine, and I can see my pale reflection against them. He's in full-blown vampire mode.

"Where the fuck do you think you're going, Millie?" He questions me like I'm his property. Like he owns me. *His prisoner.*

He has me caged in with his big arms, and I'm frozen...but that doesn't last too long as my fight-or-flight senses kick in, and adrenaline is still vividly present with the way my chest is heaving.

"Home!" I slap him across the face hard.

He snickers like he loves it. He pins his hardened gaze back onto me slowly. His fixation doesn't waver. He tilts his head closer to mine, and a long lock of hair drops across his forehead.

I wince as he presses his hand around my throat, curling his hand all around. He squeezes my neck hard, taking my breath away. My eyes widen with my impending doom, and I quickly thrash against him. I'm slapping, hitting, doing anything and everything to get out of his chokehold.

"*This is your home now, Millie*...until you die." He growls, a monstrous sound painting the way he speaks. "You think you'll make it to Texas like this?" He takes hold of my top, letting it fall off my shoulder like it did for Kallum, exposing my scar. He licks his sharpened teeth as his red eyes flash with anger. "You're miles away from Texas—a week of traveling at most if you somehow get a car. You're in Montana. Far away from the South. You won't make it one mile before another immortal takes you for their own." He scowls at me like I'm a petulant child, but there's a change in his tone. It's almost like a warning rooted in worry.

There's no way he cares about me like that. He can't possibly be protective of me in that way. There's no way a heartless monster like him would feel an emotion like worry.

"I'd rather take my chances out there than spend another night with creatures like you," I sputter through his grip. Black surrounds the edges of my vision, and I know I'm going to pass out if he keeps holding me like this. I claw at him, scratching off his skin, knowing in the end, it'll heal back in a few seconds.

"You're hurting me, Hayden. Please. Let me go. I think—" I choke up as his grip tightens even further, shadows looming more and more, surrounding me like I'm going to fall back into a black cloud of quicksand. "I c-can't b-breathe!" Pressure fills my skull, and my feet leave the ground.

He smirks villainously. Hayden closes whatever distance there once was between us, and his icy breath is on my neck.

"That's the point." Cruel and sinister paints his tone. "But you like it. There's a pulse in between your thighs, baby girl."

Darkness paints each syllable, eliciting shivers to run up and down my body, hairs at the back of my neck rising from the unknown. I can barely hear anything anymore. My hearing is muffled as I lose circulation to my brain. My heart is beating so fast that it's the only thing that's crystal clear in my ears. My feet touch the ground again as he lowers me.

"Please!" My begging voice is low as tears fall down my cheeks onto his hands.

I want to go back to my room now if that's the only option I have left. I don't want to die just yet.

"There's that word again. *Please*," he coos wickedly, a vein protruding from his neck.

Cigarettes, alcohol, and masculinity waft into my nose. His

scent is so easy to get lost in. I wonder if it's part of a vampire thing or just a Hayden thing.

He loosens his grip, and I choke. I'm coughing hard, and my lungs get back to work. I'm desperate for air, and he stands there smiling beautifully and darkly.

I raise my hand to slap him again, but he catches it quickly. He kisses my knuckles, his eyes dilating large with each peck, while I flare my nostrils.

His fingers dip inside my underwear, causing goosebumps and my soft flesh to flush as he trails down until he's right where he wants to be. I clench my thighs together, trying to stop him even though I'm dripping. He pushes my legs apart as I fight. He invades my space, and a dark part of me grows excited.

It's the adrenaline. It's the adrenaline. I repeat in my head, forcing myself to believe it.

What the hell is wrong with me?

He pinches my throbbing clit, sending an electrocution to ripple through me. I flinch from the messed up salacity.

"You're. Mine." He dips two fingers inside me, both sliding in with ease into my welcoming pussy.

I hate him! I mentally scold my body like we're different people because it feels that way right now. It's wrong to feel two ways about him.

"I almost killed my own brother for climbing into your bed. Do you understand that?" He continues to thrust his fingers in and out of me as I listen to his cruel words.

"If you want to fuck your way out of here, you're begging the wrong Drago, little Bambi." He loosens his grip on my neck further, freeing me. I suck in a deep breath of air like I was drowning. Stars twinkle and glisten through my blurred, watery vision.

Then, something foreign happens.

Sharpness. Pain. An unforgiving stabbing sensation trickles into my neck. Dull and hard. My eyes widen with the dark realization.

He bit me.

He's biting me!

Hayden sinks his teeth into my neck, causing me to enter a fight-or-flight response.

"No! Stop!" I shout, but only a loud growl vibrates against my skin.

I'm going to die. Or worse. I'm going to become one of them. I need to get him off me. He's going to turn me into a vampire!

I'd rather die than live the life of a monster. I won't become something I fear.

I scream at the top of my lungs, doing everything I can to push him off me. My blood-curdling screams of desperation echo off the walls as I continue to fight him off my neck.

Hayden grips the back of my hair harder with lustrous need as he continues to drink from me. He pulls my body closer and closer until I can feel his massive concrete cock against my hips. He's hard, and by the outline that presses against me, he's fucking huge.

As seconds go by, I can feel another sensation burn through me.

Lust, madness, and *need* ignite like wildfire between my thighs. It roots from where he's biting me. Like I'm being injected with a potion at the same he takes from me. My nipples harden, and Hayden grips my naked breast with the palm of his hand that was once around my throat. He squeezes it, and my hard nipple grazes the rough callouses of his palm.

He sucks and sucks at the base of my neck, his bite slowly moves in deeper, and I'm scared he's going to bite my entire throat out.

He circles my clit with his thumb over and over again. Heat swirls inside my core, and what's worse is that I'm aching for more.

Damn him.

He continues to work my body through deep grunts and thrusts of his fingers. My own release is tipping over the edge. My mouth falls open, and I moan, staring up at the red-stained glass and painted murals on the ceiling.

"So needy, so fucking needy, and just for me, my little Bambi?"

I close my eyes, frustrated with the way my body deceives me.

"No," I mutter through another shameful moan.

"No? But you drip for me." He's condescending with pure satisfaction.

He pushes the finger he had in my pussy into my mouth, making me taste the evidence loud and clear. I narrow my eyes at him while he smiles with blood all over his chin and lips. *My blood.*

"My little Bambi is a liar. This pretty mouth of yours betrays you, but your body tells the inevitable, inexorable truth." He tightens his fistful of my hair more like he's sending me a message. "Before you die, I'll use you the way I please. I'll know every single way to make you scream with my name on your lips, and it'll hurt, but don't worry. You'll love it. You love the pain like I do?"

I tense up as he goes back to work on my insides. One finger slides back into my opening and one at the back of my rim. He's finger fucking both holes while using his palm to rub on my clit.

Thrusting in and out, driving me into an ocean of orgasmic immoral pleasure.

No one has ever touched my ass like that before. Cole,

well...that Thanksgiving day was amazing, but the demon in front of me snaps me out of those memories.

The build to my undoing climax grows stronger, and my will to fight him grows weaker. He's winning, and I'm not mad about it. He's hypnotizing me with euphoria. The way he talks, the way he looks at me like he sees my naked tormented soul. How he smells and feels, it's like I enter *his world*, and my own dissolves.

"Come all over my hand. I want to see if you can take it before the fun really begins," He demands as he plants a kiss on my bleeding flesh. "We're just getting started, Millie."

I tense up just as I push him away. I find my strength after my body escapes the state of shock.

"Never." I push against his chest until short, loud whimpers cry from my quivering, cold lips. They slip into the air repeatedly until finally, he lets me go.

He inhales sharply as he stares at my half-naked chest, and I attend to my open neck wound, hoping it'll stop the pain miraculously.

His bite burns.

I stare at the crimson wound, black and red twirling together and seeping down my skin onto my collarbones.

Not letting me continue to look at what he's done, Hayden grabs my face. His fingers dig into the hollows of my cheeks, forcing my mouth to open.

I'm in shock again. I never do well looking at blood. I grow nauseous in disbelief. I can't move or breathe while my face turns green. I'm so fucking scared and, at the same, the most turned-on I've ever felt.

What did he do to me?

Fear and lust hit me like a train, bulldozing my morals and common sense.

He licks my neck as his grip on my face strengthens. His

tongue warms me up like a bonfire, crackling every single vulnerable part of me. It's not warm like fireflies. It's hot, like the devil's lair in flames. Enigma and euphoric intertwine together and fuel my growing addiction to have his body on mine.

His thumb brushes my bottom lip back and forth sensually. I don't know why, but I let him. I stopped fighting for a small blip in time.

I think I'm falling into a hole I can't seem to claw myself out of.

"No one has ever tasted as divine as you." I suck in a breath as tears fall down once more. "I'm afraid I'm the one that's fucked. I'm the one that's ruined," his deep voice whispers as he kisses my neck, getting ready to go back for more. His red eyes glow like I've never seen before. Beneath all of those monstrous features, he's still the most handsome man I've ever seen.

"Am I going to become like you now? A vampire? A monster?" I whimper, my spirit dreading the answer.

"It's not as simple as that, Millie. Unfortunately, you're still human, and you're still my prisoner." He grins.

Oh, thank the Lord. I feel the weight fall off my shoulders, knowing I'm still mortal and I've avoided a life-altering transition.

From my peripheral, a group of his vampire staff gathers, watching us at a distance like they're ready to jump in for a slice of me.

I watch my crimson dark blood drip from his beautiful soft lips down to his shadowed beard that coats his sharp jaw. The feeling of my own blood outside of my body snaps me out of the trance Hayden placed me in. My senses kick in once again, and I'm fighting. My chest rises and falls with a new idea. It's cliché, but I'm hoping it'll work. He's a man, after all.

Throwing my shin forward, it connects with his balls.

Hayden immediately doubles over, an exhale of unforeseen chaos hits him, and he fully surrenders to his injury. He palms the floor as he grunts ferociously, an inhumane-like sound that's louder and more deep than Kallum's earlier unleashes.

I don't get a chance to soak in his well-deserved pain and my revenge. I open the heavy doors just as more vampires swarm the area, but for the first time, I'm able to outrun them into the light. Blood still falls down my neck as I jump into the Earth's sunset.

Hayden reacts quickly, escaping the raw sunlight from outside. He moves out of the way and disappears back into the shadows of his Cathedral, and I run further away as if my life depends on it.

I was right about two things.

One, if you kick a vampire in the balls, he will stop sucking your blood. Two, *the sun is a weakness for them.* The comics and movies were right.

The bottom of my feet touch gravel and rocks, making me stumble as I run, but the pain is not enough to stop me. At this point, nothing will. I have a chance as long as the sun stays above the ground.

"Millie!" Hayden shouts at me in a monstrous, inhumane growl. He sounds like a beast from hell. I dare to give him one more look over my shoulder as I run towards a bridge. I don't owe him anything after kidnapping and touching me...*even though I loved every second of his hand wrapped around my neck and his fingers thrusting inside me.* And drawing my blood.

Nothing.

"Millie!" he shouts again, demanding I return to him. Desperation laces his tone as his voice transforms into a creature-like roar. I don't know why I do it, but I give in to his clamor commands. Each shout louder than the one before. There's vexation mixed with sorrow in his tone.

I glance over my shoulder again before I turn a corner, which will make me lose sight of the enormous stained glass cathedral. I'm still running with burning lungs and blood dripping when I see that he's standing there with his shoulders slumped and pained, narrowed red eyes. He's hiding behind a line of shade, like a starting or finish line on a race track, not daring to step over it. He keeps himself behind the shadows of the Cathedral. A black tear falls down his cheek, making me question my sanity. I blink increasingly as the warm, dry summer air kisses my skin, making my hair blow in the wind.

I'm convinced I'm seeing things because there's no way in hell I just made a heartless monster cry. I turn back around and focus on getting away. Freedom to walk outside never felt like paradise before.

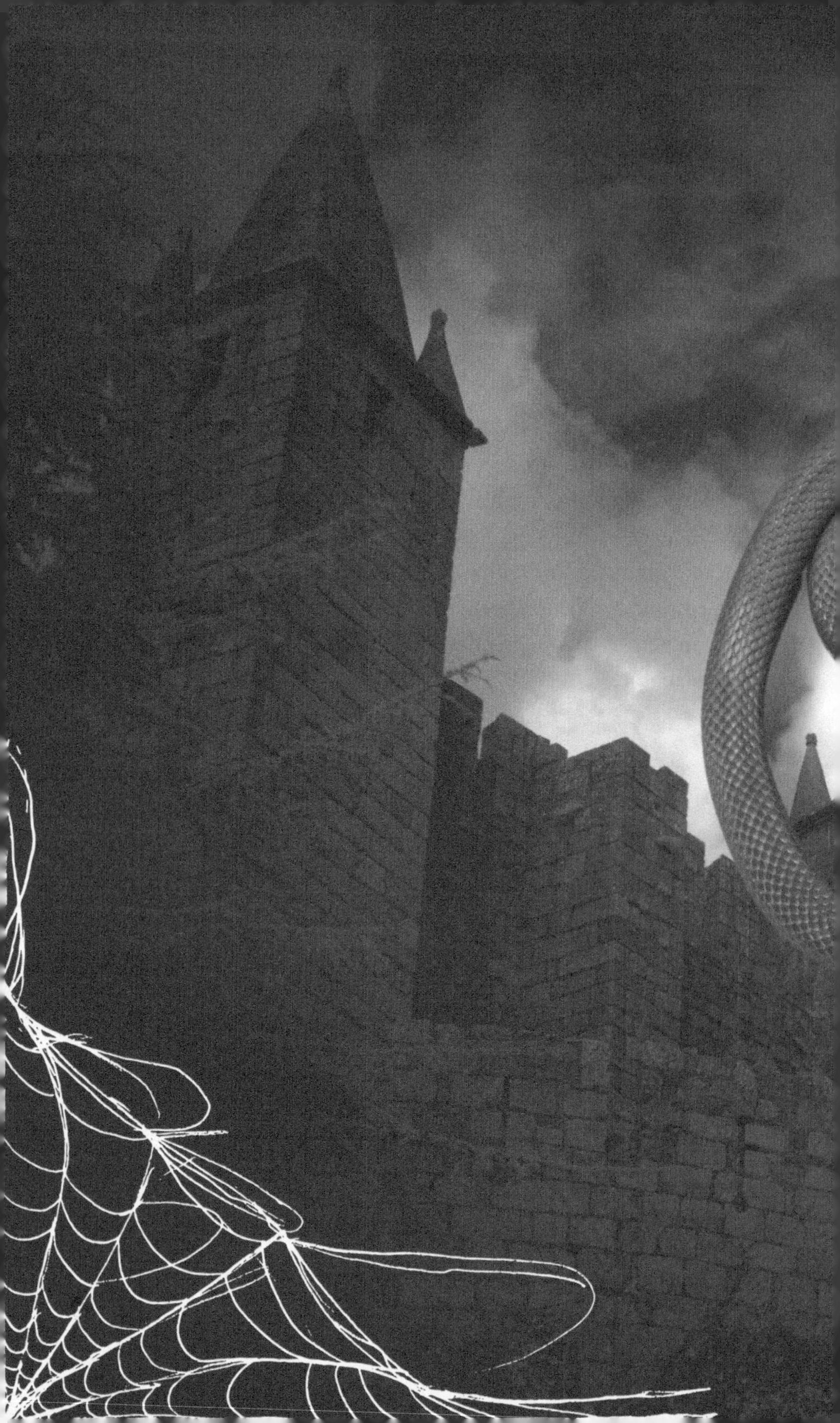

14

HAYDEN

"SHE'LL BE dead as soon as the sun goes down. She's bleeding all over herself. I shouldn't have bit her. Fuck!" I push a chair over after snapping it in half.

I miscalculated. I made a mistake. It's an oversight because she's distracting. Her beauty and blood will always have me at my weakest.

I was always going to bite her, but I chose the wrong time and place, and it cost me my little Bambi. My future powers.

She's...gone.

No.

"We'll find her big brother. The sun goes down in an hour or so." Kallum walks behind me as I grow tired. I should be resting. His eye has fully healed like Millie never stabbed him in the first place. I've got to give her more credit. She's capable of playing us so well. I let my fucking guard down, something I've never done with anyone. Not a friend, a family member, another vampire, my one-night stands. No one holds a candle to the wall I've built up since I was born...*except Millie.*

Again...it must be a Valkyrie trick.

Our King's guard steps behind me as I uncurl the cuffs on my suit. He's tense, and his nerves get the best of him.

Good.

The sleepiness I once felt drifted away once I heard Kallum cry out for help. I took a private plane with my father to attend the meeting. Our plane had just landed, and then I entered chaos. I'm tired. Beat. And longing for sleep. But that'll have to wait. I can only go so long without sleep, but I'll sacrifice anything to get my Valkyrie back.

Immortals need sleep, or they grow extremely weak. Our energy depletes completely, and we can't risk being weak in the presence of our enemies.

"I'm sorry, sir. I was—" I don't let the guard finish.

I turn around, and with both hands, I rip his head off. His headless body falls to the floor, and I throw it in the massive fireplace that sits in our living room. The flames turn to bright green as he burns. Usually, our bodies turn to ash when our heads get detached from our bodies but I don't feel like getting our floors dirty from an incompetent immortal.

"Hayden. That's the fifth fucking guard you've killed!" Holland roars behind me. He rubs his brows as he holds onto his crane with a limp.

I'm seething. It's his fault. It's Kallum's fault. Everyone's fault that she's gone. I'm wholly blinded with anxiety at the thought of anyone trying to get a hold of my little Bambi. She's a fucking goner. I know it. Her scent leaks into the air like a meal ready to be devoured.

"Then hire competent guards that can do their fucking job right. I lost her because he wasn't doing his job, and baby brother over here wanted to get laid, and Millie escaped! Which reminds me." I flash to Kallum's face. My teeth are pointed, and I'm ready to murder my only brother. "Breathe

the same air Millie does again, and I'll make the immortality ability a myth." I point to the deceased vampire on the floor.

My threat sinks into Kallum, and he swallows hard like he's ready to hide. His glasses fall to the tip of his nose, and he disappears into his chambers.

"Son, what is going on? Why is Mr. Pool dead?" Mother says sleepily as she studies our King's guard. Her trembles shake her nightgown, and she palms her mouth to disguise the gasp she wants to let out.

Then she looks at me like she always does.

Fear. Sadness. And most of all, disappointment. She's shocked that her son killed another immortal like it's a natural thing to do. She walks from me as the rage continues to thrive. I'm blacking out. I won't remember any of this in just a few minutes. I pace around, wanting to tear down the entire Cathedral. Growling like a feral hungry beast, I pace around, wanting to inflict more pain and hurt. The only thing that can satisfy my hunger is my little Bambi.

Mother shakes her head as she retreats to the fireplace, just as our cleaning staff comes into the room and removes Mr. Pool from the floor.

"Your son lost the Valkyrie. She's out there." Holland walks toward my Mother with disillusion. Every time I fuck up or make mistakes, it fuels his hatred for me further. I am proud of that, actually. But right now, at the brink of my interest in taking over the region, it backfires.

Holland continues to roar with an authoritative tone, "Now some commoner will get a hold of her blood and kill her. Who knows what kind of powers they will unlock? Never mind how hard it will be actually to kill them! You would be condemned to hell at the inferno if you were any other northern immortal. You—"

I've had enough.

"For a commoner yourself, you talk like you carry the Drago blood. You will remember your place in the Cathedral. I don't care that you're my father's best friend. I'll remind you to kneel and take orders." I spit. "I will be the King one day, and I will find my wife. And guess what?" I tower over him just as he shakes from his hatred. His green eyes flash to red. "You will sit in the first row at the wedding. Talk to me like that again, and my first order as King will be to cut off your tongue." Holland gulps as I threaten him. "And I'll cut it off over and over again for a month."

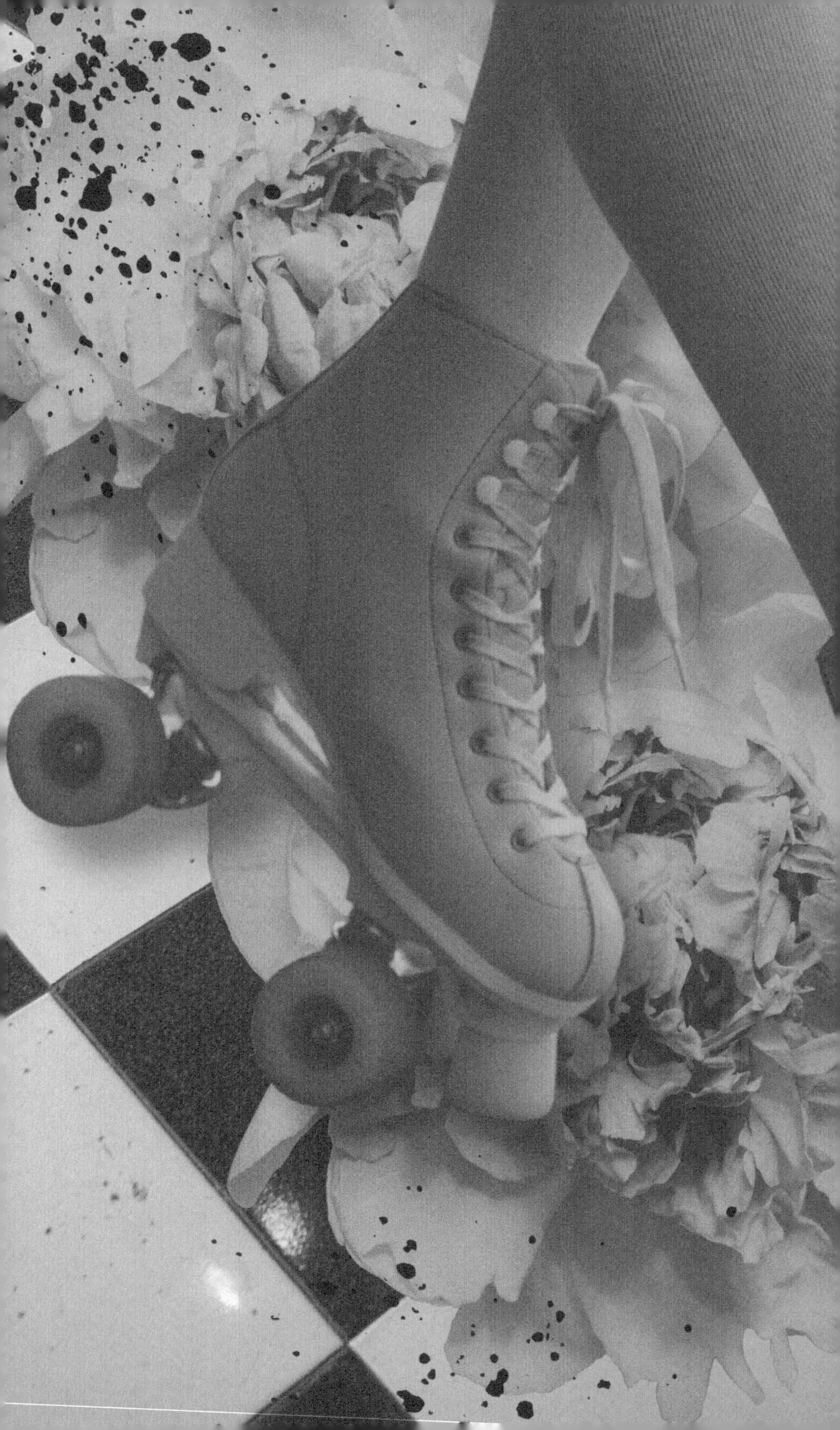

15

MILLIE

THE SUN IS DOWN, and the sky is black. After running over ponds, streams, and forests, surrounded by nature's elements, the sound of music called to me. It's muffled, but alas, I concentrated enough to pinpoint it. I kept following the sound like a light at the end of an obsidian tunnel until I found the treasure. I step over a hill, pushing through two thick brushes. My hair gets tangled in the leaves, but I keep moving forward until I see the opportunity of a haven ahead.

The wound in my neck clotted, and I stopped bleeding all over myself a while ago. Still, I've managed to cut myself through stickers, rocks, and trees. I'm hurting all over, but the thought of seeing my family again, my friends, Cole…even my mother again gives me the motivation to keep going.

My mouth falls open.

A concert full of people.

A concert. Full of people. I repeat in my head as my stomach turns into knots and my heart does backflips.

People. *Humans.* Non-vampire creatures!

Yes!

They're all dressed in costumes. Is it Halloween?

I walk down the hill, doing my best to stop myself from leaping over everything. If I take off running from the desperation, I'll just tumble down and hurt myself further.

I'm only a few feet away from what looks like a concert festival. A rock band playing 80s rock music gets louder. I smile when I spot young adults dancing and rocking their heads as the guitarist plays his solo. Everyone is lost in the song and laughter. A big sign on the stage says, "Bozeman Halloween Rock and Costume Festival."

*Something I should be doing...*not running for my life after being held captive by vampires. I'm still convinced I'm hallucinating everything, and this is all a horrific nightmare. Hopefully, the longer I'm away from Hayden, it'll feel like that—a bad dream.

Suddenly, I trip on a rock and tumble down the hill. I roll down, my body hitting every single rock and branch. I close my mouth, protecting it from dirt flying in as I crash. Finally, after a few moments that feel like forever, I stop moving, and gravity wins. I stumble into a crowd of men. Still lying on the ground, I face the night sky as they investigate me.

They circle every corner of my body. They all push their brows together and frown while they study me while holding beer bottles. They're clearly confused. I mean, it's completely valid. I'm covered in dirt, dried blood, and in my very thin pajamas with no shoes.

I feel like I can't breathe. I'm gasping for air, trying to focus on the moon above them. The stars aren't normal. They twinkle like they're moving, flapping their wings like small birds.

This can't be good. Unless birds are golden and they sparkle, I think I've given myself a concussion.

"Miss. Are you okay?" A man with a long red beard asks me.

I try to speak, but my voice doesn't work. My breath is caught in my throat. Finally, after a long moment of numbness and my vision spins in circles, my ribs scream at me. They got the most damage from the fall.

One of them reaches for my hand, and I take it without hesitation.

I'm able to stand, and I'm face-to-face with strangers. Energy kicks into overdrive, and I find my voice.

"I-I've been kidnapped! He's after me! They're after me! Can someone please take me back home or to the nearest airport? I don't have any money on me…I—"

"What do you mean someone is after you, lady?! Who? Who is after you?" A man with a husky build grabs a hold of my shoulders. His breath is heavily stained with liquor.

I want to shout: a monster. A vampire. A creature of the night. I want to warn them that monsters are real, after all, and out for our blood. But the way they're already looking at me, I refrain, hold my tongue, and give them the shorter version instead.

"A man and his family! Please help me. You have to help me." I manage to rasp out, my throat threatening to close up on me. I'm on the verge of tears again, hoping they'll take the little pieces of nonsense I'm throwing at them and believe me.

"Of course, we'll help you. Here, come sit down for a second. It looks like you could use a jacket and a nice water bottle." The bearded man guides me with his hand. I nod and agree faster than I mean to, but I'll take help where I can get it right now.

The loud music is still blaring, making it hard to hear anything.

He pulls me more into the crowd, and I hold onto the stranger's hand with no shame. No one seems to notice a girl covered in blood and dirt on her pajamas. Everyone keeps dancing in their witchy, zombie, and skeleton costumes, singing like they're in their own simulation of entertainment. A bubble that not even my frantic state could pop and deter them from partying.

Everyone is drunk and happy. Something I didn't even realize I missed. A life before I knew vampires existed. The things I would do to go back to that. What I would do to have never met *Hayden Drago*.

The crowd is heavy and littered with alcohol, dancing adults, and the smell of cigarettes and funnel cakes.

Finally, the bearded man sits me down near a taco truck on an empty bench. Seconds later, he and his friend surround me. He extends his hand. A water bottle is in his grasp, and I reach for it.

Why isn't the man moving with urgency? I need to get out of here. I need to find a plane or a vehicle, at the minimum!

"I just want to see a pretty smile on your face. It looks like you've been through hell."

A small curve of my lips pulls, and he breathes out, satisfied. He lets me take the water bottle from his hand, and I gulp it down so fast that water trickles down at the sides of my mouth as I rehydrate.

I finish the water bottle in less than a minute, and all the while, their eyes are on me, watching me like I'm some wild animal who got caught.

"Is that your blood?" the other man asks as he scratches his cheek.

I nod silently.

"Listen, I've got a truck in the parking lot. We can take you home if that's what you want. Where is home for you?"

"Texas."

"I love Texas. My favorite football team is the Dallas Cowboys."

"Mine too," I reply.

"I'm Cal, by the way." He gives me his hand to shake. The gesture scares me at first, but I give in, trusting him.

"Millie."

It feels weird to have a normal, friendly conversation again, unlike the usual fighting for my life the past few days.

Suddenly, a loud explosion of gasps erupts from one part of the crowd behind Cal and his friends. They all turn towards the commotion, and the heavy 80s music continues.

And like the Red Sea being parted by Moses...there stands the Devil's Advocate.

Hayden.

He's not alone. His eyes are beaming red like lasers, and he's dressed in all black and has more northern vampires at his sides. He's not even trying to hide that he's not human, which makes me believe that I'm not at any other concert.

The music still goes on. There must be thousands of people here, and most of them act oblivious to what's unfolding. The ones near Hayden begin to run the opposite way of him. Screaming and speeding their way out like blurs of rain.

Hayden and I lock eyes together. He stands with a vengeance, conviction written into his balled fists, a fuming creature ready to finish what he started earlier.

"He found me," I mutter sadly. I grab the man's wrist, standing from the bench, and hold onto his arm.

"We have to go. That's him! That's the man who took me!" I beg the man to turn and leave with me, refusing to let these men's lives be collateral damage.

"Millie, after all we've been through, we're still not on a first-name basis, my beautiful girl?" Hayden calls me over the music, and people watch him like he's a God. The way they look at him, it's evident they fear him.

I shudder at his penetrating voice. He plays with his watch on his wrist, ascending closer to me. The men gather in front of me like a wall.

"It seems my plaything got out of her cage. Please, hand her over to me." He motions his fingers towards him, but the men don't sway.

They block my vision from Hayden instead.

I'm about to say fuck it, and just run while I can. They're not listening to me anyway.

I spin around and take in my surroundings. Hundreds of cars and travel buses are parked in the distance, picking up and dropping off concert attendees.

I start to run, but someone pulls my arm back, and the husky man's fingers dig into my skin.

"What? What are you doing? We have to go! He'll kill us!" I stare at his curled grasp, but then a bright blue glow on the skin of my wrist catches me from the corner of my eye. My blood runs cold.

With a shaky, slow turn, I raise my head to see that the men who were supposed to be my saviors are actually Southern vampires. He pulls me in front of him, and the others swarm me. They force me forward, holding my limbs and the hollows of my cheeks, making me face Hayden.

"You think you can steal from King Davenport, Prince Drago, and there will be no consequences?" Cal taunts Hayden.

They pull my head to the side, and Cal hovers over my neck, baring his fangs like I'm nothing to him. I shout at them, but it only backfires. It fuels their tactics to restrain me more. People continue to dance to 80s music while these men stare each other down.

THE DEPRAVED PRINCE

"I would think twice about what you are doing with her. She belongs to me. *You are in my region. My kingdom.* There will be fatal consequences for putting your hands on her like that." Hayden narrows his bright red eyes.

"You started this war, Hayden." Cal chuckles, knowing his presence provokes Hayden's wrath more.

"If that's what you want to believe, then so be it. But I'll tell you this. I always finish what I start, and I never lose," Hayden replies.

Concertgoers begin to walk away from the two groups of men. They sense the battle that's about to ensue. We all do.

"The Depraved Prince." Cal shakes his head. "What are you doing out here anyway? Word has it that you haven't shown your face in a long time. Ever since King Davenport executed your uncle." Cal spits his words like insults. He licks my neck, causing Hayden to clench his jaw tight. His brows pull inward, and he snarls like a creature, almost like a warning to stop.

His uncle was murdered?

"We're going to take this Valkyrie to the rightful King. But it won't stop there, Hayden. We're going to rape and torture her just to spite you before we kill her. But don't worry, I will mail her head to you." Cal's grip on me worsens. Fuck it hurts so bad. Not even Hayden has grabbed me like this.

I whimper at the threat. Cal's friend, who is also a vampire, pulls my shorts down, and they pool around my ankles, stripping me of my freedom and clothes. I muster the strength, bite down on the man's hand, and elbow the other in his balls.

I'm free for one second, but that one second gives me a chance of survival—a blip of hope. I pick up my shorts just before I begin my escape.

"Run!" Hayden instructs me just before an explosion of chaos ensues, and I can no longer see what's in front of me. I

155

take off running through the crowd, desperate to escape everyone. I'm running from every single one of them, *including Hayden.*

It dawns on me. I can't trust any person here. This must be a concert exclusive to vampires.

I bump into body after body, weaving through the crowd frantically. Some swing around to confront me, but I don't stop moving. On any other day, I would apologize. Pushing and pulling through the crowd, I turn around to see if a pair of bright blue or red eyes is following me.

My head whips left, right, behind, and finally, a pair of familiar crimson-red eyes is right by me. About fifty feet from me, he looks at me with ferociously determined eyes, like I'm his prey. His deer. His little Bambi.

Suddenly, a southern vampire launches forward, blocking his tight vision of me. He raises his hand at Hayden, but before he can attack him, Hayden grabs his throat and tears it out. Red sprays everywhere.

I close my eyes again, praying and hoping it's a nightmare. He's killing each vampire that tries him, one by one, with ease. I tear my gaze away from the deadly battle he and his group of guards are engaged in.

"You know I love a good chase, Bambi. Especially when it's you running from me."

Hayden's voice echoes into my head like a fever dream. How is he doing this? What the hell is going on? How's he talking to me? Why does he sound so far, and yet it feels like he's inside me? Inside my head. Inside my fucking soul. I cover my ears as I continue my journey through the crowd.

"But you know what I love more?"

I don't answer. I feel like if I respond, I'm feeding this nightmare I'm so desperate to deny because I'm still trying to convince myself that monsters aren't real.

"Sending damned souls to Death himself. Granting mortality to immortality. The lives I get to take who try to look at what's mine, never mind steal. How does it feel knowing you will never escape me, little Bambi? Even when you close those pretty brown eyes to sleep, I'll chase you."

I continue to run as he continues to wreak havoc on vampires that get in his way to capture me—killing them one by one as I get closer to the travel buses.

"How does it feel to know I will never let you go? To know that I've engraved my obsession into you like cattle? The teeth marks on your neck were me branding you, little Bambi. It'll scar like a tattoo you'll never be able to get rid of."

Tears fall down my cheeks, blurring my vision.

He's in my head.

His enchanting voice taunts me. He's amused by the fact that he's in my skin. He's in me, and there's no way to get him out.

"How does it feel?"

His ominous tone paints his words as he repeats his question. His crazed voice echoes and bounces off the walls of my mind. It's soft, daring, and profound, making my cold blood spiral into fire. A riotous skip in the rhythm of my heart consumes me, and it beats all the way down to my core.

As soon as I emerged from the crowd, my feet hit the pavement—a straight road to the exit of the concert arena. I wipe the tears away, and my lungs constrict with that false hope again—a beacon of light in the darkness that has been thrust upon me unwillingly.

Suddenly, I get pushed up against a tree with hands around my biceps, pinning my back into the rusty bark.

I meet intense, bright blue eyes.

Cal.

"I wanted to take my time with you and bring you to the

rightful, soon to be only, King in the country. But fuck, you're too good not to take for myself." Cal pushes my hair to the side, digging his knee in between my inner thighs, and he snakes his hand into my underwear. "I'll make it quick," he declares with a snarl.

I call the only one who can possibly help me at this moment. I'll probably regret giving in to the man who has taken me against his will, but I have this weird, sick sense that he might grant me mercy, unlike these men.

"No!" I shriek, my voice trembling with disheartenment. My hands and eyes dart anywhere and everywhere but his cruel, uncomfortable infatuation halo. "Hayden!"

Cal backhands me when I spill his name, causing my face and hair to whiplash. I'm seeing stars while the ground spins simultaneously. Cal's fangs grow abnormally long and his mouth opens wider than humanly possible. I brace myself for the final chapter of my short life, closing my eyes and waiting for the final impact.

But it never comes.

Cal is off me, but I can't see anything because I black out from the havoc I refuse to acknowledge.

I fall to the floor and cradle myself in a fetal position by a tree that's right behind us. I tune everything out just as I cover my ears and stare at the ground. All I see are snowglobes while the sounds of snarling, blood splattering on the ground, and bodies hitting the floor linger above my head. I open my eyes when a pair of bright blue eyeballs with veins attached gets flung near my feet. They roll with a layer of blood and dirt.

Oh, I'm definitely going to be sick now.

I palm my quivering lips to stop the high-pitched shriek that wants to pour out of me. My brows narrow down at the organs, blinking away my horror. I close my eyes again.

I escape into my mind, creating my own snow globe. I travel

back to the day of my high school graduation. I don't know why this memory consumes me, but it does.

It had been a year or so since I'd been living with my father, but I would swing by to check on my mother every now and then. Unexpectedly, it was another dreadful start to her morning with Santiago.

I visited her for breakfast so we could celebrate my accomplishments and talk about the future I wanted.

"Mom, don't cry. Everything is going to be okay." I wiped away a tear that fell from my mother's cheeks. She got into another argument with Santiago, leaving her crying in the kitchen as she always did after a heavy, pointless argument.

She's quiet. She either can't hear me because she's too lost in her own mind, or she's choosing not to say anything.

"You know...one day, I hope you'll get your own happily ever after. Because, this mom..." My hands create an imaginary circle in between us. She pauses; the sponge in her hand stops moving in a circle as the soap drips down into the sink. Her red eyes and wet, long lashes meet mine. "This is not it for you. Just because you're older doesn't mean it's too late for you. You can still have your happily ever after...I know it."

She pauses, her once dull hazel eyes light up with hope.

"Maybe. Maybe some people are lucky enough to experience such a beautiful thing like that, or maybe some people are destined to have a life of suffering. Which one will you be?" She asked me. I watched her and asked myself the same thing over and over again.

I never understood that question...and I never had the answer.

My snowglobe moment shatters, depleting into a twisted reality. All of a sudden, I'm being pulled into another direction. I'm forced to stand straight up on my sore, cut-up feet. I accept my fate after I assume it's yet another vampire trying to sink their teeth into me and take my life. I see bodies everywhere. Music still plays as people crowd us in.

Then I finally register that it's Hayden who has me. He's covered in blood from head to toe—red streaks against his hauntingly vampire face.

He holds me with his big hands, squeezing firmly but urgently like he's begging for any reaction, but I'm still.

Death. So much blood. Teeth.

The terrifying snarls.

The way Hayden can go from charming with a devilish smile to a completely different creature and personality—the two clash against each other like different oceans from various directions.

I'm paralyzed with shock, and it settles inside me like poison in my brain because I know this is the beginning of something new, and I can't do anything to stop it.

I will never be the same again after seeing all of this. The trauma settles into my psyche.

Something washes over me. Everything gets tuned out, and all I can manage to decipher amongst the chaos I'm trying to wrap my head around is Hayden's soothing yet rushed, urgent voice.

"Are you okay, Millie?"

"Millie, you're okay, talk to me."

"Did they bite you?"

"You're safe. You're alive."

Maybe it's because I've never had someone care so much about me like this. No one has ever wanted to chase me. Nobody ever cared if I woke up the next day. I'm usually the one who does the chasing with friendships and my own mother and father, always begging to be loved in return. It's a fucked up way, but with each heavy deep breath, my eyes flicker between his red eyes and sharp fangs, and I react.

I react and send myself to hell, clashing my lips against his, and begin the ruin of my soul and spirit.

I kiss him, forcing the demons and doubts away and choosing to get lost in the only person that has made me feel cared about in a really long damn time...maybe ever.

Hayden stiffens, but he doesn't miss a beat. His brows furrow like he's in pain. I feel his fangs against my teeth as I kiss him, but they slowly fade away as we continue to brush our lips together like they were made for each other. I peek a glance and see that his eyes are still as deep, ruby red as ever. That hasn't changed one bit. He shuts his eyes and grabs both of my cheeks, pulling me closer if possible. He kisses me back harder and harder, pressing his massive body against mine, holding me like I'm his demise *and* his salvation.

His tongue quickly begs for entrance, and I grant it without hesitation. He travels deep into my mouth, exploring the depths of it, devouring me like he's trying to speak to me in a different language—a language of lust, sex, and danger.

I'm scared of Hayden.

I think I always will be as long as my heart beats. But at the same time, I fear him...he's the only one who could ever make me feel the safest in this world. A world I thought I knew but have no damn clue no longer.

Safe and fear can't go along with each other, can they?

He picks me up, forcing me to straddle him. My ankles lock together, and our height difference makes me look like a doll in his arms. He takes me toward the same all-black SUV I was in the first night we met. He's probably going to take us back to his Cathedral in the mountains. Miles away from the concert. Everyone continues to dance and party as if this is another Saturday.

My feet hurt from hiking, my lungs are sore from panting, and my body trembles like there's no cure.

His tongue dances with mine, and a feral groan escapes him. It's deep and mouthwatering, and it makes the pulsation in between my thighs accelerate further.

I want him.

I can't deny that, but I refuse to tell him that.

I don't think I have to. He knows when my body betrays my words. The way he makes me flush in my cheeks and my pussy. He just...knows. I assume it's a vampire thing.

I stop kissing him and instead bury myself in his neck, breathing in his cologne mixed with his natural scent like it's my new oxygen to survive. He cradles the back of my head closer to him, holding me like he's reassuring me that I'm okay.

"I got you. I fucking have you again, and I'm going to keep you," He whispers in my ear like it's an eternal promise he can't break.

Suddenly, he stops in the middle of the crowd when we're so close to his vehicle. I'm confused and exhausted, so I don't question him. I've witnessed this man kill for me over and over again.

"Does anyone else want to try and take what's mine?" Hayden dares the crowd, happily roaring with an ominous smile. His white, sharp fangs glisten across the concert lights. I breathe softly into his neck as I glance at the fearful crowd that stares at us like Hayden is an unpredictable, mad king.

By the very public fight, I think his own people now know I'm a Valkyrie.

He turns around while he holds me, coming face to face with strangers...other vampires; his hold around my legs tightens territorially.

We're returned with nothing but silence. I glance up at him, daring myself to watch my captor taunt his kind. Flames reflect in his red irises, and red-orange waves of fire dance back and forth from the stage where the rock band stands. He stands tall, holding his ground with me still in his arms.

"It's a beautiful night tonight, isn't it?" He questions the crowd again, and everyone takes a step back like they're waiting to meet their last day on Earth, the way their shoulders slant and their eyes peel from Hayden's to the ground, begging for redemption.

His nose scrunches with wrath, and he steps towards the crowd like he's ready to light the entire place on fire from the adrenaline that probably still simmers inside him.

I grab a hold of his suit, squeezing it tight in my hand.

Is he going to continue his wrath? Is he going to continue to embrace his depravity and unleash it on everyone and kill innocents? He's doing what he's best at...killing people. He suffers from a certain darkness that I recognize. Because I feel it inside me sometimes, I can only describe it as a vast emptiness that makes you hurt yourself.

"Don't," I plead with him.

He stiffens at my ghastly request like I blindsided him by my small outburst. I don't know why I'm asking him to grant anyone mercy...but I did, and there's no taking it back. He looks at my bloody hand, and his jaw ticks on and off.

He turns back to the crowd, and his enchanting face relaxes. His blue eyes return, and he glances at his bloodied, stony-faced guards.

"Hang their heads on spikes. Whatever is left of them...that is. I want to send a message," He commands them and walks away from everyone.

"Yes, Prince Drago." They all bow their dark-haired heads once, and the crowd disperses, leaving blurs of wind in their wake.

Blackness corners my vision, dragging me in, and my deprived mind wants to give in.

Hayden feels like my lifeline. It's because he is my lifeline now. Every single vampire that knows I'm a Valkyrie wants to take me for themselves.

He killed many vampires that got in his way while he chased me. He killed them to stop them *from killing me*. He did everything he could to stop me from escaping him.

As he walks toward a vehicle and away from dismembered bodies, I face my destiny.

There is no escaping an immortal vampire.

There is no evading his permanent chokehold.

There is no more life without this intoxicating man.

Hayden Drago, The Depraved Prince.

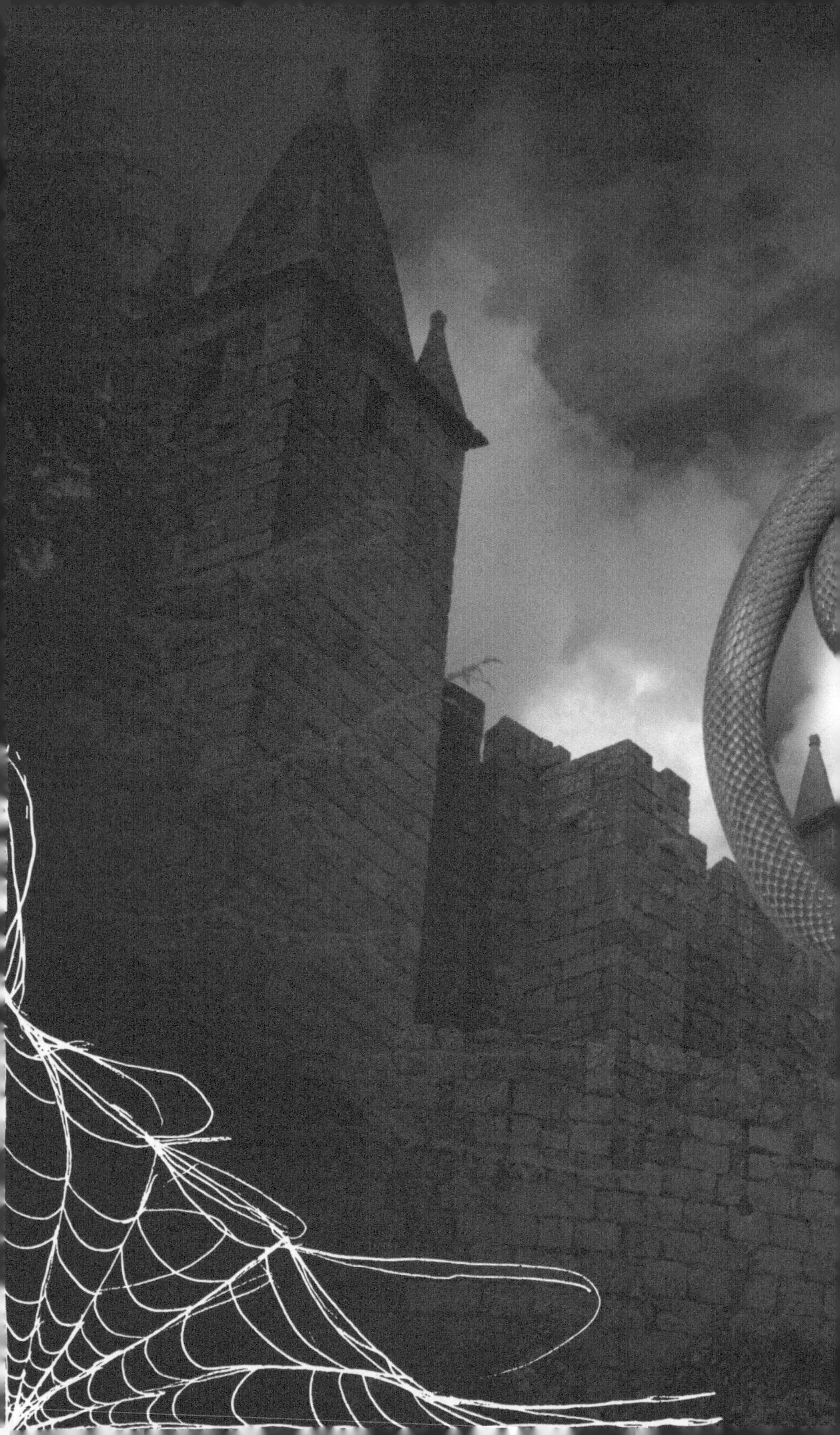

16

HAYDEN

I COULD HAVE RACED home with her in my arms. I thought about running the five miles she travelled, but I didn't want to wake her. Returning to the Cathedral would only take me minutes. But the look on the Valkyries face, when she slept, would be the ruin of me.

What the fuck am I doing?

Why did I grant everyone at the festival mercy?

I wanted to keep killing. I wanted to dismember my enemies myself while I wear the happiest smile of revenge on my face. But instead...I'm here with *her*.

I watched the moonlight shine on her glowing face as we drove home. The journey took around forty minutes due to the number of turns up and down the mountain. My father built the cathedral when he moved from Europe to the United States, painting it to look like a church with an elegant structure and engineering.

She passed out from exhaustion, finally reaching some sort of solace to rest on my chest as Kingsguard Charles drove us home. I couldn't tear my eyes off her the entire journey home. I'm afraid she'd wake up and try and leave me again.

She's sadly mistaken if she thinks I'll ever let her go. She's mine again—all mine.

My plans for us were to use and prolong her taste, mark her all over until she bled for me and me only.

But now?

The way I just slaughtered and dismembered southern vampires would give her nightmares for the rest of her remaining life, most likely replacing the ones she already has about her mother, father, and a dreadful man named Santiago.

We're back in the Cathedral, in her bedroom. What I really want to do is throw her in for a bath, but I don't. Instead, I've removed all her torn clothes and replaced them with clean pajamas. She sleeps deeply and doesn't wake as I tuck her into bed.

I'm covered in blood. In Davenport's sent assassins blood. It's likely they've been tracking her since I went to that meeting. I don't think it was some strange coincidence that they were at the concert when my little Bambi was going to be there. They conjured up a plan and followed her, waiting for the perfect moment to take her from me. I know it wasn't a coincidence because this is something I would have done. It's genius to watch someone you hate implode on the heartbreak you inflicted. To watch them die without even laying a finger on them by taking their purpose to live away from them while they watch, defenselessly. They wanted to watch me fold...break, penetrate the steel of armor I've been in since King Davenport murdered my uncle.

His only crime?

Trying to marry a Valkyrie. He wanted to marry a woman from Texas, and in the Immortal Law, it's forbidden. We have to leave them alone if we find one. However, King Davenport found out about his crime, and their secret attempted elopement. And sent him to the inferno, where he was executed like entertainment.

I looked up to him like a father figure, building a stronger bond with him than my own father. Ever since then, I've been out for revenge. I've been wanting to take something from him, like he took from me.

And what sweet revenge it will be to steal his Valkyrie and obliterate his plan to rule all the kingdoms. My plan for revenge is sweet, and I've been waiting for an opportunity to hurt him like he hurt me. Millie is my first-class ticket to do that.

I stare at Millie, and watching her breathe peacefully makes me enchanted. She has a few minor cuts, but the deepest wound of all is my bite on her neck. I smile as I stare at it. Every drop of dried blood has been washed off her body.

I almost killed her when I bit her. I wanted to so badly, but I wanted to take my time with her. I cringe at my own demons wanting to possess me. Shaking my head, I let an unfamiliar emotion coil into my chest at the thought of her not being here anymore.

I'm not fond of it.

I'm attached to her, no doubt. I convince myself that once I suck her dry, I'll move on with time. I've got all the time in the world, after all. There's no way I'd miss her.

I kiss the top of her head with a tightened jaw. It's such a simple gesture, yet its significance is more profound than ever. It's deeper than the depths of the Earth, and the emotions that simmer in my cold bones are longer than time itself. Every time I tell myself I'm not capable of tying myself to someone, every time I try to deny these sickening emotions that my uncle felt for his human, *it's more painful.*

Look where it got my uncle. Perished. Sent to hell. Leaving me alone with parents who care more about the crown than the interests of my brother and me. Instead of following in his footsteps, I should be more focused on avenging his death. But when Millie stirs in her sleep, she murmurs something pulling at the soul I thought I didn't have anymore.

"Don't...leave." A soft breath leaves her lips as her brown eyes stay hidden. A slow flash of her lashes flutter, and she grabs my hand. It's the first time she's yearned for me with her words. I'm paralyzed like a man seeing a shooting star for the first time. This is a moment, the beginning of a path I'm unsure of, with an ending I cannot see.

"Stay with me tonight," she whispers. "I'm scared. I only feel safe when you're here."

I don't know how to respond.

When she does things like this, it's distracting. Chipping away my plan bit by bit, and I'm letting her. I should just kill her and get it over with like Holland has been encouraging me to do. But just to spite him, I wanted to drag it out.

She grabs my hand and squeezes it gently in her warm palm.

My dick twitches with dark desire and pulses when she pushes her back to my chest, asking me to hold her.

So, I do.

"Prince Drago. Your father needs you, he—" Kingsguard Charles reminds me of my duties outside her door, and I despise it. Not now, not when I just almost lost her.

"I'll be there as soon as I can," I quip back, sharper than my fangs.

Don't piss me off.

A slight pause lingers in the frigid night, and then Kingsguard Charles shuffles on his feet, clears his throat, and leaves us.

I shift in the bed and hold her. I immediately get lost in strawberries, the staple scent of her hair. Or maybe it's just her.

Her black strands stare back at me while the rays of crimson red shine on her angelic glowing face. She looks serene. It's the first time I've seen her like this since I saved her in that vampire bar club. She's relaxed...at ease, and peaceful. The way she breathes is different, and it sends a message.

The first time I killed for her I was acting on emotions instead of thinking. I went to work, not thinking twice about protecting her or saving her.

I did it because it was the law. That's why, nothing else.

And yet, here we are—my hand over her waist, comforting a broken woman, with my chin on her shoulder, hearing her heartbeat like it's my favorite song on repeat.

I've never been a rule follower. My actions resulted in the end of my arranged marriage to Eleanor, whom I've known for years.

The back of her is pressed up against me, and every single muscle of mine goes stiff.

She's warm. I'm cold.

She's a fighter, and I'm a breaker.

She's soft, and I'm unmalleable.

This is more than just an opposite's attract idealization. Our attraction must be based on more than just chemistry. It's a spark that grows stronger with each moment that she breathes.

I've never stayed the night with a woman in the hundreds of years I've walked this earth...never mind holding one while she sleeps.

It's new, and it's uncomfortable. But it's also warm...like smelling a fall candle when the leaves turn orange. Or like standing in the cold sand, watching black waves in a winter ocean under the moonlight. Like inhaling the first salty, airy breeze that hits you, reminding you that even in the darkness, there is optimism.

My hand snakes further until it's tucked into her side, as

the temptation to do more rattles inside my hand like thunder after lightning bolts have struck during a rain storm.

I'm fighting the temptation to sink my teeth and cock in her heavenly depths.

I decide to move. I sigh as my hand travels to her chest and stops at the scar Prince Davenport gave her. I grind my teeth and soothe it with my fingertips, up and down softly, over her shoulders. An unforgiving urge to rip every single Southern vampire apart again rages on with no end in sight.

I want to kiss her. A genuine one that makes my cold, unbeating heart go up in flames. The gentle kind.

I kiss her naked shoulder, wishing I could stay in this moment, just like this, longer than one night, because the reality is that a war has begun—a war over my little Valkyrie. And every single immortal's world had been revolutionized when the battle of the Princes took place in Texas the night I found her in their club. Our eternal damnation on this Earth just got shaken, and a dance I'm ready to lead will explode.

But it won't be a war of swords, guns, bites, or mutilation. It'll be a game of chess. Dangerous discreet moves, and whoever can play the other better will win.

Thousands of footsteps thud amongst the cathedral walls, retreating to the shadows as the sun begins its path above the soil, and I know I'll have to withdraw myself from her.

The moon will not allow me to sleep. I wish I could have such a simple yet very intimate moment with her, like *sleep*. It's more intimate than sex.

But I can't sleep until the sun rises.

My abilities will not allow me to. When the sun nears, it frightens our kind away, and my energy drains. I seek the darkness to refuel. It's an inevitable trait.

Her lips twitch slightly as she hums sweetly.

I want to bite those, too, as I kiss her.

God, her lips.

She's too captivating. It's like I'm under her spell. All I want to do is fuck her in her sleep. I brush her hair over her ear, bidding my last farewell until I see her again in the next moon.

I look at the changed-out bedsheets from where Kallum bled all over her bed, and the reminder of her fleeing me comes back to haunt me.

I'm still angry. So fucking mad that she thought leaving was an actual option for her. For putting herself at risk. I almost lost her...and for that, she will be punished, but I want her to be awake for that. I want her to feel every single inch as I make her scream and sing me a pretty little word like my name.

She will bleed for me. She will always bleed for only me.

I hover over her neck, my lips softly brushing against her branding, a tilt of my lips as I make an ominous promise.

"I'm angry, Millie. I'm so fucking angry..." I grumble. "I want to wake you up with my cock," I breathe softly against her skin, pausing. Purposefully whispering my promise to her so she doesn't wake. "And don't worry...*it'll hurt* just how you like it to. You will be punished, Millie. I'm going to fuck you so hard your pussy will break and weep. So that every time you think about escaping me again, you'll be reminded of who you belong to. You'll think twice, *Bambi*."

I kiss her teeth-marked scars, and salivation brews in my mouth. There's a reason why it scarred. But I refuse to believe it. Again, it must be a Valkyrie trick.

My fangs fall away, and I blink away the painful urge to bite her. Furrowing my brows in agony, I lick the front of my teeth.

Her warm flesh always does something to me. When I touch her, it sends a bolt of electrocution, filling my hollow heart with lively fire. Our hearts don't beat. They can't beat. We're fucking dead.

They. Don't. Beat.

Then why does it feel like it wants to? And it wants to... *for her.*

I give her one last glance. I look at her cute silhouette underneath the red stained glass. Each step I take creates an agonizing distance. She is still mine to keep, my prisoner.

Why do I crave her acceptance? Why do I crave it more than my lust for power and revenge? Why do I crave for her to spill more than just her blood for me?

After tonight, after she willingly held onto me, after I showed her a blip of the lengths I'll go to destroy everyone, *she kissed me.*

I want more than that. *I need it.* I need her to be consumed by me, just like I am with her until I kill her.

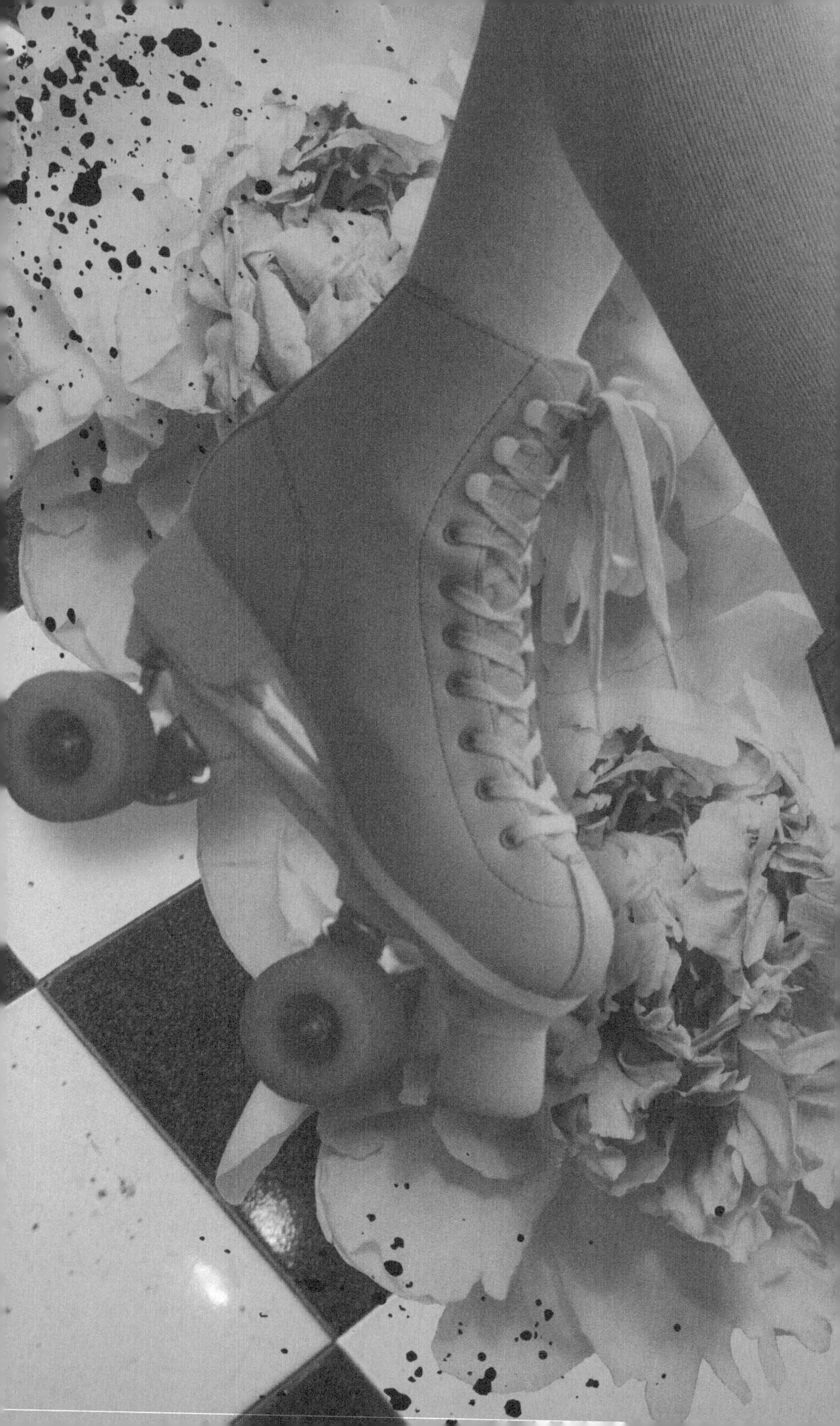

17

MILLIE

STEEL. Cold. Foreign.

It's...metal.

My first peaceful, heavy slumber in months is interrupted by a tightening of ice-cold metal around my wrists. I stir around, doing my best to escape the blurs of my sleep. I blink slowly, opening my eyes to see flashes of red from the stained-glass windows. It's still night.

I move my wrists, but they're conjoined together.

"What the hell?" I murmur through heavy breaths.

"You wanted to play a game of hide and seek, baby. Well, now we get to play my version of a game." Hayden's calm tone sends shivers down my spine. His cold, rough, long fingers trail down my naked stomach. His touch is ice, but what it does to me is the opposite.

He dips his fingers in, grabs the lining of my shorts, and pulls it down, leaving me in my underwear. He hums like he's satisfied with what he sees. He slaps my pussy, and my hips immediately jerk upwards. My clit heats up, throbbing, pulsating, and I want to scream at it to stop.

I peek down, and he's...shirtless. He has a body sculpted by God himself. He's covered and ripped in muscles. His abs tighten as he moves to my ankles. He spreads them apart with the same type of shackles. Faster than humanly possible, he rips my panties to shreds and throws them to the floor like it was paper. My legs are wide open, vulnerable, and exposed. "We're going to play now...and it's called Millie begs me to fuck her while covered in my enemies blood."

I whimper at his sick pleasure. My breathing escalates, tipping my head back against the pillow, exposing my neck. I frantically search for a way out...but nothing will get me out of these restraints.

"I love it when you cry for me," he purrs.

"I'm not crying, Hayden. I won't ever cry for you again, that's a promise I intend to keep," I seethe back at him through narrowed eyes.

Even through the darkness, I can see him clearly. He smirks sinfully and is wickedly amused by my unbreakable vow.

He doubts me...I can feel it. *He wants to push me.*

A dimple curves around his jaw, and a scorching spark hits me in the chest when he looks at me like that. It makes me feral with anger...and submissiveness.

"Don't you have a girlfriend? Someone else to occupy your needs?!" I pull on my restraints and clench on air.

Why do I like this?

"Millie. I'm not boyfriend material."

"Really? I would've never guessed!" I blare sarcastically.

He closes his eyes softly and bows his head until his chin almost hits his collarbone with a deep, lustrous chuckle of laughter. His abs tense as his balled fists relax at his side. He tilts his head to look at me, and a dark brow arches. His dashing ocean eyes are no more. Red, ruby, fiery eyes replace his blue irises instead. His sharp teeth protrude over his lips slightly, and a rush of fear ripples back like waves from an ocean I'm drowning in. Memories of his teeth inside me come back with no remorse, and I sink further down into the bed.

"Are you sure you won't cry for me, little Bambi? Because your pretty little pussy would disagree with you. It's dripping tears for me right now." I swallow and keep my brave face mask on as he lowers himself over me. Each one of his hands is on both sides of my hips as he dips forward and buries his face in between my legs. I try to push him out, but my tied ankles don't allow me to fight.

I'm all bunched up with nerves, my heart pounding in my chest, and my nipples harden with anticipation.

"I have to punish you. Let me hear my name fall from those pretty little lips. I need it more than I crave your blood," he growls slowly as his eyes gleam with sensuality.

He doesn't keep me waiting in the dark. His tongue meets my pussy with a soft, swift flick inside my slit. I arch my back, fighting his touch even when the darkest part of me relishes in his capture. His tongue drives inside my slit and ends at my clit. I grit my teeth as I stare at the waves of his dark brown hair at the top of his head, desperate to pull on them. To stop him...or to hold on for dear life because dammit.

Damn him because a moan escapes my throat, and I wince at the shock of pleasure it drills into me.

"I like it when you cry," he breathes against me. "But I like it when you bleed for me even more." He comes up, hovering over me. A dark wave of hair falls over his forehead as he positions himself with his full pink lips above mine. He crashes his lips against my swollen ones, but instead of kissing me, a shot of pain pours through me. He doesn't need to put much pressure or bite down hard on my fragile flesh to cut it open, and only when I taste the metallic iron at the tip of my tongue does he begin to kiss me. His teeth are sharper than a blade. The slightest touch and I'm lacerated.

He moves his lips against mine, savoring the taste of my blood as he intrudes my mouth with his tongue.

I don't move at first; I go blank for a few seconds, wondering what the hell to do. I want to fight him, but I can't. I don't want to. I kiss him back and it feels so good to let myself get lost in the way he makes me feel. *Craved.* He grabs a fistful of my wavy hair, pulling it at the base, and I mewl in submission, desperate to satisfy the ache in between my thighs by clenching them together but failing miserably because of my restraints. He growls against my lips. "You thought I wasn't going to punish you for the little stunt you did? For putting yourself in danger? For trying to leave the only monster on this fucking planet that can protect you?" He snarls at me in between kisses.

"Hayden..." I start but don't finish. He steals his own name from my lips like it's the most precious thing he's ever heard and hushes me with more feral kisses. He closes his eyes like he's angry, his brows pinch together, and I join him with closed eyes.

"I'm sorry," I moan out against his mouth.

There I said it, please fuck me now. Give me something.

He licks the bottom of my neck up to my cheeks.

"Now, be a good fucking girl, and let me feel how sorry you are. I want to hear you scream it!"

I give in with no more hesitation. He kisses me harder once my tongue competes with his. We move together in sync, and he pulls my hair harder. I feel his hardened cock underneath his pants. He presses his bulge against my clit, and I want to wrap my legs around him, temptation within me.

My body is almost begging for it like he said I would.

Shit.

"You won't break me. You might kill me one day when you're done with me, but you won't break me."

He grins sadistically after he pulls away from my bleeding lips. Red covers his mouth, and he licks it away and hums. He moves with vampire speed and rips my shirt open with ease, exposing my breasts and hard nipples to the cold air. He looks down at my chest and admires my body, taking his time.

"Fuck you're beautiful, and these tits are mine to sink my teeth into."

He takes my nipple in his mouth and sucks.

My body starts to tremble from the sensations, and like deja vu...pain erupts.

He sinks his teeth into my breasts, just close to my nipple, and drinks my blood.

Whatever pleasure I'm feeling reverberates through me like a virus of sinful, sick pleasure. My toes curl with an orgasm building like a damn volcano, ready to explode, and he isn't even touching my clit. His dick isn't inside my aching pussy, and I want to come.

He growls with satisfaction. His hand slaps my ass, and the sound fills the room. He squeezes my ass with his hand, pulling my pussy closer to his rock-hard cock, as he tries to suck even more from me.

My eyes roll to the back of my head, the emptiness inside my pussy unbearable. It's almost fucking cruel the way his venom inflicts on me like a side effect.

"Fuck, Hayden..." I rasp out as I squeeze my eyes shut. My pussy is wet and begging for him.

I give in.

I give in, letting the dark nirvana overrun and possess my mind, body, and spirit. I grab his soft hair and pull his head closer, fueled by my hatred for him and myself. I yank it closer, wanting to chase the feeling even more.

He knew this was going to happen.

"What was that, baby? I couldn't hear you over your sweet moaning melodies."

He bites my other breast, just below my nipple. Twinges of pain slither every time he cuts me with his razors. But it feels so damn good.

"Hayden...p-please."

"Please, what, Bambi?" He holds me tighter, bruising me with his handprints all over my ass cheek. He's claiming me with greed.

"Use"—he bites into my breast,—"your"—another bite—"words."

Fuck me.

"I hate you!" I shout a lie, my chest heaving as my words tremble. My shackled hands grind against each other as my fingers lose themselves in his hair. He continues to drain blood from me, feeding from me, driving me to the point of insanity, with lustful bliss.

"Funny you say you hate me because your pussy loves me."

Then he disappears, throwing my legs over his shoulders, and puts an end to my misery.

"Say you need it." He flicks my clit, and I practically scream out with circled eyes.

"I need it!"

"Say you want it." He kisses my pussy, and he groans like a monster. The sounds vibrate against my clit, and I shudder.

"I want it!"

He licks my clit, sucks on it, and begins to devour me. Pure fucking ecstasy hits me, and I'm in a dark abyss of bliss.

He moves faster, sucking, biting, his tongue working me harder and faster than humanly possible. Cruel salacity overrides my spirit, mind, and soul. My body feels like it's being burnt alive from how lustful I crave him. How badly I'm loving it. *Fuck him.* His body alone makes me want to fall in love with him. The way he's touching me, lapping me, devouring me...it's hard to deny him.

I've never felt this way with Cole... It's incredible.

I hold on to his hair as blood drips all over my chest from where he bit me. I move my palms all around it, spreading my own blood across my breasts and nipples. I bite my bottom lip hard, attempting to stop the mewls of destruction from escaping my throat, but to no avail.

Then he sinks his teeth into the inside of my thighs, right next to my clit, and I scream, pulling on his hair as he claims my flesh with his fangs.

"Oh my God," I beg for his mercy. I want to scream for his cock like I need it, but I hold my tongue, refusing to let him win his game.

God, I want him to fuck me so bad. I'm ready. So needy and ready.

As soon as God's name leaves my mouth, Hayden roars with anger, and he nips my clit. "The name's Hayden Drago, but I can be your new religion, baby. All you have to do is follow my commandments."

He pierces me with his tongue, diving inside me, fucking me with it. Stroking in and out, and he feels too damn good to fight. I come undone with his continuous lethal strokes inside my pussy and over my clit. I watch his back muscles move as he lets me finish my last waves of pleasure and ride his tongue.

"You get off on being tied up, your pussy is screaming to be filled with my cock. Maybe I should tie you up by your neck next time," he mumbles against my pussy like he wants to drown. But then he pulls away, and kisses my overly sensitive clit gently like he's saying goodbye.

Hayden

She's bitten all over. Marked, satisfied, and well fucked with my tongue.

She pulls on the restraints as she digests the wounds I've left all over her. I stand there, crossing my arms, proud. She loved it. She loved every second of my little game. She won't say it, but the evidence is all over her tits. She spread her own blood over her body as I ate her pussy.

And my god, the honey that I swallowed is better than her blood.

My pants grow tight since my cock is still very much painfully hard and ready to fuck. My balls are full, and they're calling for her...but I won't take her.

I haven't had blue balls like this since a century ago.

I stare at her pretty pink pussy and beautiful brown nipples as I free her wrists and ankles.

"You're a monster," she says, holding her knees to her breasts, and every syllable floats with unsure flinches of pleasure.

Aww, she's flirting with me.

"You have no idea." I wink at her. "You want me to fuck you, but baby, if I do that, you may not live through it."

She glares as her pussy weeps for more.

She quivers, her bleeding lips close, and she holds herself tighter. It takes everything in me and more not to fuck her into another oblivion, but I won't use my tongue the next time she comes, and she'll fall into an obsession.

"These will heal," I point to her open wounds that are starting to clot by her tits and thighs, "but the bite mark on your neck will stay forever. A scar from your *monster*."

She turns away from me and stares at the brightening red window, ashamed that she liked it. She loved every second of it. The thought of anyone kissing her body like I just did makes me want to set the whole world on fire.

I'm possessive over her. I can't handle the thought of anyone even looking at her the way I do, never mind talking or touching her.

I open the door and walk out of her room. I turn the skeleton key, locking it just as the sun rises, and I go to my chambers, sulking, angry, and rethinking my plan.

If this is what she makes me feel, no amount of power can do what she does to me. It's ruthless how she makes me ache for her when I sleep.

Maybe...my plan for revenge isn't worth it.

Maybe...The Depraved Prince has a soul willing to share, after all.

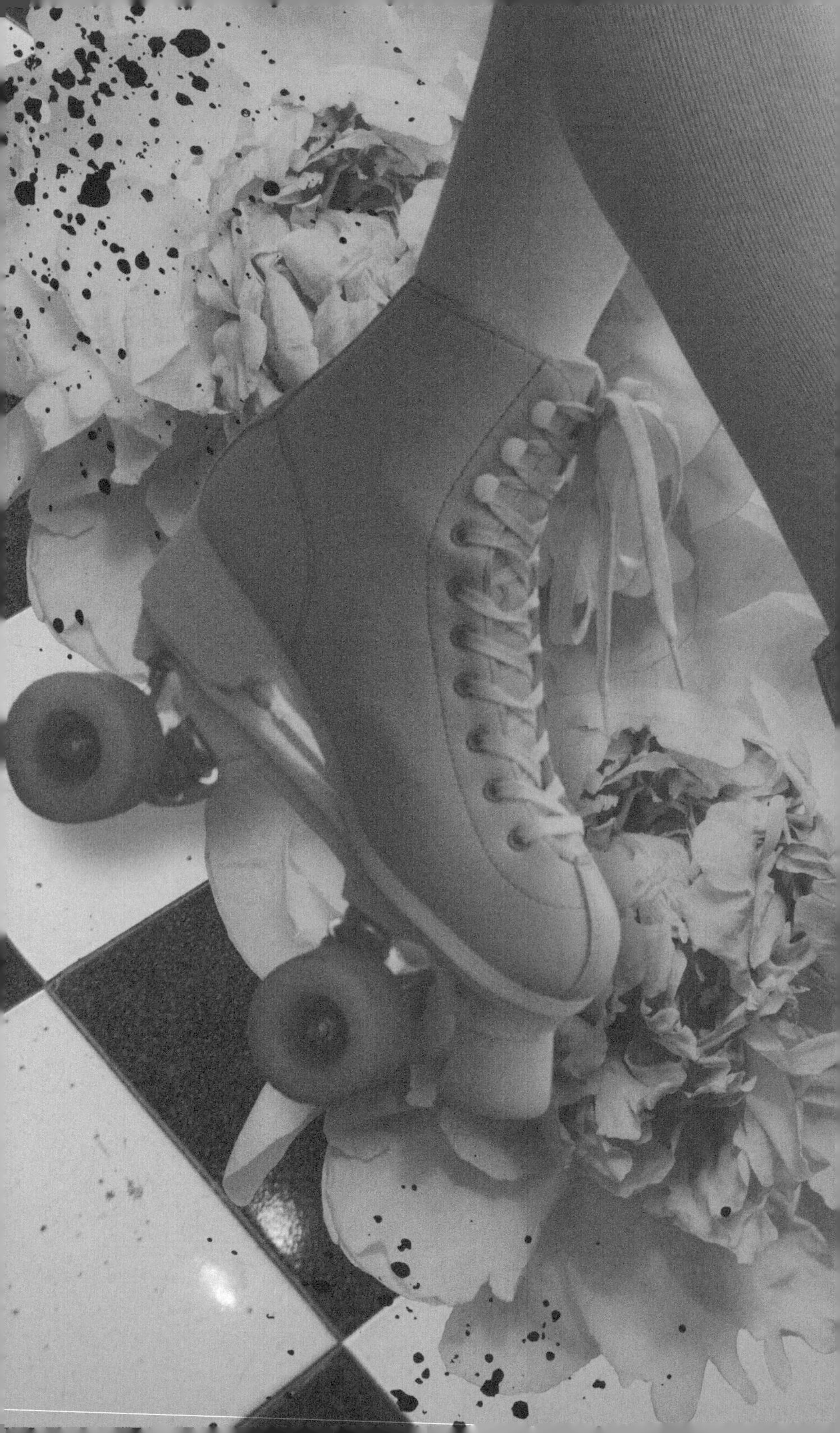

18
MILLIE

I PALM my neck and cringe.
Asshole!
I've been marked. I will forever have evidence of what he's done to me. Every time I look at myself in the mirror, Hayden will be there, tormenting me. A permanent reminder that I am his.

As soon as he closed the door, I wanted to scream in my pillow...because I just got tongue fucked by a vampire and loved every single second.

I won't let these confusing feelings hinder me from leaving him. I'll try again, and I will succeed. I must consider another approach and muster up a more calculated plan. There has to be a way to drain his abilities. There has to be a way to stun him for a hot minute, so it gives me another head start to run.

I heard everything he said while I slept. I knew he wasn't going to be able to resist his depraved urges to get what he wanted. I have a feeling that Hayden always gets what he wants, even if he has to take it.

When he threatened to keep me underneath his toxic shadows, it only sent me further into the dark hole he has me trapped in. A hole with walls that can't hide the reflection of what I feel. It's weird. I want to kill him. I want to escape him. But I want him inside me. He scares me, but the thrill of being chased by him...to be enjoyed by a man everyone fears does something to my soul, and I want to chase that feeling even more.

He fucked me with his tongue and then bit me all over while I was tied up, unable to fight him. The worst part is...I wanted it all, and I wanted more than his mouth.

I shift the blankets over me to examine the damage littered across my body. Bruises on my hips, bite marks that have already scabbed over; I jump out of bed and find a mirror that sits beside a dresser and the red stained glass.

I'm no longer in the blood-stained, dirty clothes. I'm desperate to rid myself of last night's evidence of a battle between two immortals with different eyes. I thought all vampire's eyes turn red when they shift into their authentic version. But I noticed that wasn't the case from their interaction in the club to the concert. It was a consistent detail. Every vampire that shares Hayden's trust has crimson eyes, deep and rich like blood. But the southern vampires had enriched cerulean blue, like a frozen ocean. Both were glowing and bright.

I wait for a few minutes before I head for the bath that's connected to my bedroom, naked and bloody.

When I open the door, I'm met with the familiar black walls, elegantly patterned. A brass-colored morphed mirror is nailed to the wall above the black sink.

A diamond chandelier made of red diamonds hangs in the center of the restroom, lit by candles that seem never to die out. The bathroom is also covered in red stained glass, which reflects vividly against the black bathtub.

This cathedral looked like a church on the outside, but what a Gothic daydream on the inside.

I touch the brass handle of the bathtub and turn it to get as warm as possible. I grip both sides of the tub as I lay my sore body in. I listen to the water run, staring at the water flowing and building, contemplating my next move.

WHEN I GET OUT OF THE BATH, I SEE SOMETHING ODD. Another delicious breakfast tray sits on a silver tray. The scent of organic maple syrup captures my attention. One of the guards must have brought it in while I was showering.

Pancakes, eggs, beans, and orange juice...and another tape. It sits on my nightstand with a player.

Did it slip from his pockets? Or is this some trick-or-sick game to torture me?

Still in my towel and drenched waves, I hold onto it as I sprint over. Water from my wet hair sprays the floor, but I don't care. Even when I almost slip and fall.

I'm hit with a rush of adrenaline at the thought of hearing my family again.

I put the tape in and hit play.

Nash: *"Look, sis, I don't know if you're going through some weird phase in your life, but this isn't fucking funny. You could at least give us a phone call and let us know you're okay, that you're alive, because you matter, Millie. Don't do anything stupid. You matter to us. We love you...you matter."*

Cole: *"Millie. I need to hear your voice. I've never in my life been so desperate to hear someone say hello before..."* he shuffles the phone against his shoulder before he continues. He inhales a breath, and it does that static thing against the speaker...he's nervous. "*I miss you. I miss seeing you here at the coffee shop. I miss seeing how you bite your lip when rush hours come in, and you're stressed. I miss the way I would walk into the coffee shop happy. Not because I enjoy being the supervisor but because I know you'll be there around me. I miss it. I miss you. Please... come back. How am I supposed to survive these shifts with Hayes and Leah? They're a pain in the ass. Come save me...*" He laughs, forcing a joke. But his laugh sounds different. There's a hint of a break, and it's painted with sorrow. "*Save me from another day of missing you. I hope you're okay. And I hope that when you do come back because I do not doubt that you will*" — he rushes out like a fact—"*I would love to give us a second chance again. When you return, I want to take you out on a date, and I'm not taking no for an answer. If I have to sit on your doorstep with your favorite flowers and chocolates, which I know are peonies, then that's what I'll do. I'll always care about you, Millie. I'll always want you.*"

I expect to hear more messages, but it stops playing. I hold it with my palms as the water drips down my naked chest, contemplating all that I've been through.

Even if I found a phone to let them know that I was still alive, what would I say? How could I put any of this into words?

Hey Dad, sorry I disappeared. A stupid, hot billionaire vampire has kidnapped me?

Hey Cole, I would love to give us another shot, except I'm not sure my heart would truly ever forget about the vampire I willingly kissed, even though he's kidnapped me against my will.

Hey Leah, I would love to catch up with you and tell you everything, but I'm scared I'll be putting you at risk.

Hey mom, I—

What would I say?

At the end of the day, I don't think those details would matter. Because if I were in their shoes, I would just be happy to know my loved one is safe and alive.

Would they think I lost my marbles? Check.

Would I risk their lives by letting them into my own snow globe of chaos and then return to Texas without protection? Check.

I glance around the room. There's an eerie silence like there is every morning when I wake up alone, and I refuse to do this over and over again until Hayden takes from me and no longer has any use for my body.

I demand an explanation. Everyone keeps saying Valkyrie this and Valkyrie that. Why am I so important? Why does every vampire look like they want to bite me?

Maybe there's a way to give them what they want, and I can still be in one piece and be able to go back and live an everyday life. Maybe a normal life with human friends and a human boyfriend...maybe with Cole.

His recording sent me back down memory lane and reminded me of how sweet, warm, and kind he always was with me. Patient and never demanding. The exact opposite of a certain atrocious vampire that has kidnapped and eaten me out like I was his last meal.

Footsteps walk down the hall with loud clinks stealing me from my reminiscence. A shadow flickers underneath the doors, signaling someone is walking by. I get up from the bed and place the recorder on the nightstand. I don't know what I'm doing, but I refuse to spend another day in the room alone with re-runs of baking and comedy shows.

Don't get me wrong, I love those things, but I'm going stir-crazy after the repetitive routine over the past few days.

I run to the closet and grab the first thing I lay my tired eyes on. It's a wooden closet full of laced black and red dresses, skirts, and tops. Red and black, no other options of color.

I slip on the first long black laced dress with a flower pattern on the long sleeves that meet my wrists and chest. It's gorgeous and hugs all my curves once I put it on.

I run to the door and bang on it with one tightened fist just as I turn the door knob with my other. I'm about to pound and scream, prepared for my throat to bleed with my ruthless begging like I did before.

But to my surprise, the door rolls forward slowly.

It's open.

I blink, taken aback by the massive oversight on Hayden's part unless it was one of the guards when they dropped off breakfast. Hayden wouldn't make a mistake like this.

Whoever it was, I'm thanking them. I take advantage and swing it open, ready to try and escape once more. Hayden should be resting. It's daytime; I assume every vampire is asleep except the guards.

I walk down the dark halls, holding the long dress just a few inches above my ankles to avoid tripping over it as I jog barefoot to the same exit as last time.

I walk stealthily down the same stairs and see the familiar big French doors.

This time, I know Hayden is asleep. I have this feeling...this weird connection to him, and I know he's far away from me, which makes me more secure to walk faster.

My salvation calls my name just as my heartbeat thunders in my ears and neck.

This time, the sound of a woman crying behind me halts me faster than I can process my movements. I stand there frozen on the black stairs and turn my head slowly to the woman's soft sobs.

She's dressed in all black, her hair just as black as her dress, and black streaks are down her face. I only get her profile because it looks like she's so concentrated on a male portrait from Victorian times that's mounted above the fireplace. A man with long dark black hair, blue eyes, and a mustache that sits above his pink lips stands next to a beautiful woman with cinnamon-red curly hair. She's tall, just like him, with freckles over her nose and glowing skin. She wears a bright yellow corset and a bright emerald heart-shaped jewel in the center of her neck. It's blinding...even in the painted portrait, the artist did an elaborate job of capturing little details of the encapsulating jewelry and features of the couple whose love is so visible that it's almost palpable.

A powerful tug of my bicep sends me off balance, and I almost fall the last two steps on the stairs. I turn to see a guard in a suit, with a long black beard and red eyes.

He hisses a creature-like sound through his pointed fangs.

"Queen Drago, it seems to me that Prince Hayden Drago's pet has gotten out of her cage again. I made sure to lock it after I dropped off her breakfast. This isn't my fault, I prom—" He trembles as I try to fight his overpowering hold.

The woman turns around, wiping her black tears away with the back of her hand. Her red eyes slowly change to brown, and she clears her throat to cut him off.

"Mr. Charles, it's okay. I believe you. I'm sure it was a mere oversight..." He still looks guarded, like he's trying to hide the fact he's pissing his pants because he might get fired and or killed.

"I'm not my husband, and I'm definitely not my son. You can go. I won't have you executed for a genuine mistake." She dismisses him with a gentle wave of her hand that has a massive rock on her ring finger. Her voice is serene, just like her smile. She looks like she has a gentle charisma about her, something warm in the way she talks with a British accent. She has a heart-shaped face. Her beauty is out of this world.

"Leave the girl," she commands gently.

Charles stops midway, loosening his grip, and I free myself from him.

I turn to the guard as his brown eyes jump back and forth between Queen Drago and me with a confused flattening of his pursed lips.

"Queen Drago. Are you sure? You need to rest. The sun is out. Let me escort Ms. Flores back to her room," he insists.

"Oh, Charles, it's the anniversary of my brother's death. I cannot sleep on this day, so I think this will give me a small chance to get to know the woman who changed my son's outlook on his ascension."

I furrow my brows, wanting to ask her questions, but I bite my tongue instead. I'm too scared to speak to these strangers, let alone breathe.

"She'll be fine with me," she reassures Charles as she lifts a perfect dark brow at me, "Right, Ms. Flores?"

I look to Charles and then back at the 'queen.'

"I-I," I stutter, unsure of what to do, but I think the best thing for me is not to disagree with Hayden's mother. I grab my elbows for some type of emotional support to speak, rubbing the laced fabric, and swallow nervously as I stand amongst vampire royalty. "Yes, you're right."

I look away from the vampires and fidget with my fingers instead, pinching at my laced black dress, hoping it'll calm my nerves.

"Good," she chirps happily, satisfied with my answer even though it wasn't as convincing. Because deep down, I do want to try and escape again. At the end of the day, I'm still human, a fragile, different kind of creature they can toy with and break so easily if they choose to.

The ends of her red lips tilt, and her white teeth make their presence known. Charles stays but keeps his distance behind me, watching like a hawk ready to whisk me away if the Queen gives him the word.

"I want to get to know you. My son tells me you like peonies." She drives her forearm between mine just as my heart skips a beat, and it palpitates so hard I almost choke on my saliva.

How does he know these big and little things about my life?

Her skin is cold but soft at the same time. She leads me down a large hallway on the first floor. We pass by more portraits from different eras the further we walk. Some have children in them, and various people I don't recognize. We pass by a portrait that says 1955 in small cursive handwriting in the right-hand corner.

There sits Kallum and Hayden.

Both handsome as ever, and yet still, Hayden's cruel, entrapping, handsome smirk glimmers back at me, and a cloud of bliss rings through my veins.

How does a picture of him manage to do that to me?

I clear my throat after Queen Drago catches my vision lingering on her sons.

"I do like peonies. They're my favorite flowers." I try to distract myself from getting caught.

I'm not sure how she's justifying this entire situation for herself. Her son kidnapped me! I want to shout out to her to do the right thing and let me go, but I'm sure once I do, Charles over here will whisk me away to my room for the rest of the day. I have to pretend that everything is fine.

"I want to show you my garden." She pulls against my arm harder. "Sorry, I just get so excited sometimes. I've never had a daughter or a little girl of my own to share my hobbies with, like gardening. My sons aren't interested in this."

I'm not her daughter, and I'm thrown off that she's so callous and dismissive towards my situation. I'm only here because they took me, and I'm being held against my will.

A minute or two passes, and I'm staring at acres of land through the red stained glass. The sun is out, and I still can't wrap my head around the fact that she isn't burning, in excruciating pain, or even getting lit on fire like in the movies when the red rays shine against her skin.

"Who was the man and woman in the portrait, Queen Drago?" I pry, my curiosity getting the best of me. The aura surrounding her makes me feel welcomed, and the words fall out so easily. I've always been good at reading people.

"Oh, please call me Cordelia," she corrects me delicately, palming my hand with her cold one.

"Sorry, Cordelia." We stare at her enormous garden behind the glass, acres of land with tall trees, other mountain terrain, and a giant lake in the far distance. It's beautiful up here.

"That was my brother, Amos, and his fiancé, whom he never got to marry." Her mood shifts, and her once warm voice turns cold with despair. She crosses her arms and looks into my eyes. Her light brown eyes turn glossy, and a black tear falls out. She wipes it away, and I refrain from comforting her. Whenever I see someone cry, I yearn to wrap them in an embrace so they'll know they're not alone. It's a reflex.

"He was executed at the Inferno for falling in love with a Valkyrie. It's a law. A law created out of fear that the living would be exposed to the underworld they live above. Everyone was afraid of Valkyrie's exposing our kind. That they would create a mass of destruction and start a massive problem for Immortals and humans, which would lead to the extinction of our kind."

"What's the Inferno?"

"A place where we hold our justice system. If you're found

guilty, you get executed by being burnt alive until your body turns to ash in front of council members and all Immortal Kings."

Damn, that's brutal.

"So kidnapping a human against her will isn't illegal?" My candor spills out before I can stop it. Cordelia stiffens momentarily but regains her posture.

"You are safer here. You have a chance to live longer if you stay here in this Cathedral. If any other immortal finds you, they'll kill you and take you for themselves, you—"

"Wife, will you come back to bed? Let Charles escort Ms. Flores back to her room." A man roars behind us like he's scolding her for sharing an insight into their lives. I jump involuntarily, and my stomach flips at his unexpected interruption. I palm my mouth to stop my shrieking. I'll always be on edge in this damn Gothic Cathedral.

"Arthur..." Cordelia pivots on her black heels and observes what looks like Hayden's father. He's tall, dark-haired, blue-eyed, and has a short beard covering his chiseled jaw. He wears all black. Black top with black sweats, and black socks.

"I was just showing Millie my garden. I want her to take care of it for me during the day when I can't." She smiles at him, and his face contorts into a frigid expression. His eyes beam black at us...and then he fixates on me. He leans his shoulder against the wall, unimpressed, and his hand bows forward, searching for Cordelia's.

I tense my legs up and change glances.

"Plant peonies for me. I want to spice it up from the usual red roses. Charles will help you get set up with that." She winks at me as she takes his hand, holds up her dress, and walks effortlessly and beautifully to her husband, who still stands furiously.

What have I done to him to receive this prejudiced, vicious

treatment? If looks could kill, I would be six feet under the ground with the way Arthur keeps his deathly stare on me...and on my neck.

He sees what his son has done to me. I know he does.

His gaze is sharp and venomous, glaring disappointment into the branding of his son's teeth on his captive's living flesh like he's connecting the dots to a puzzle he doesn't want to decipher. I can't hold his sharpened gaze, so I palm my neck and let Charles guide me back to my room, passing by a sympathetic Cordelia and a glacial Arthur.

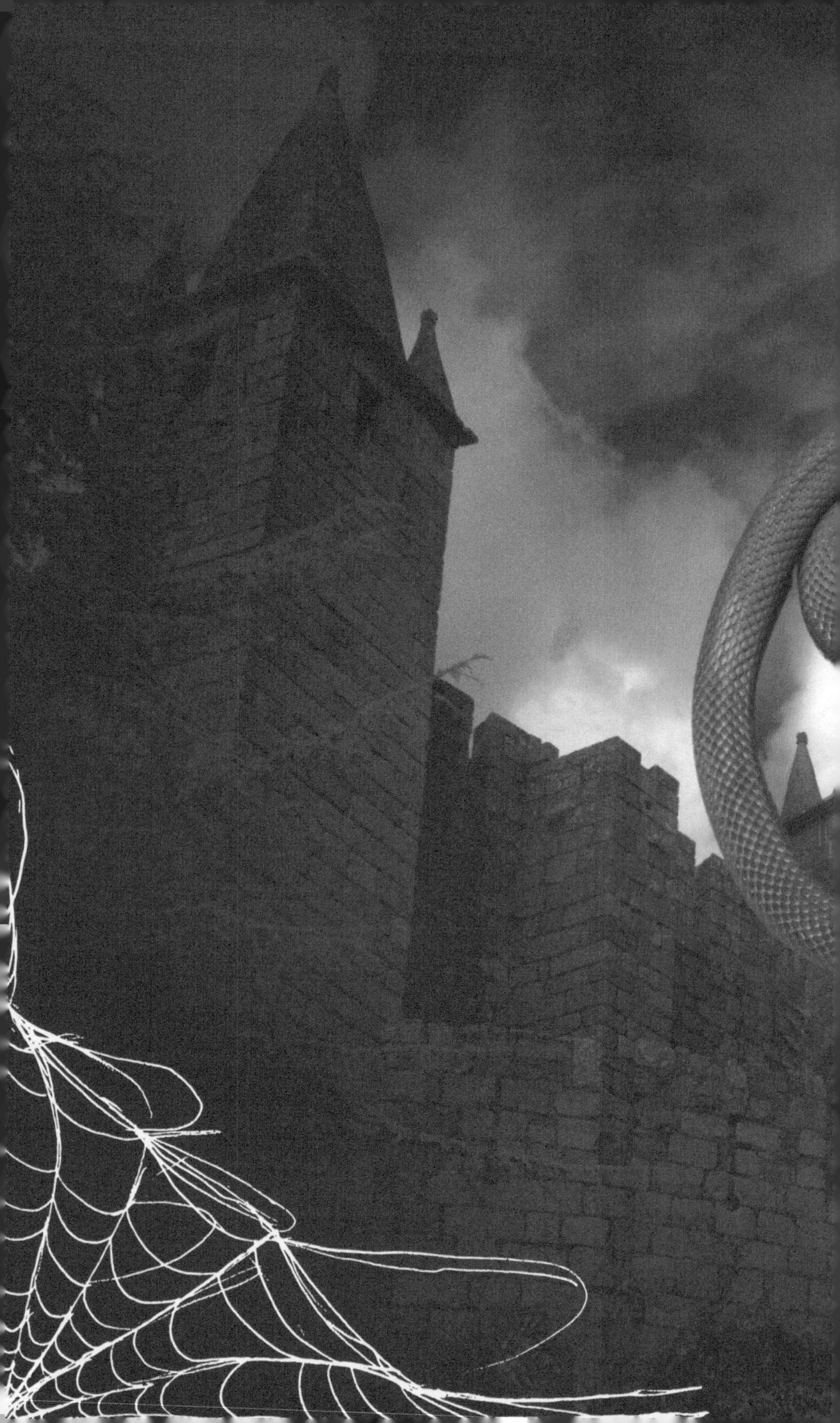

19

HAYDEN

Dear Diary,

Cole and I finally did something on Thanksgiving. It was like coming up for fresh air from drowning. Cole always sees me when others don't. But something was missing. I'm not saying he was terrible or didn't know what he was doing. Something in the way he kissed me, the way he moved against me, and the way he whispered sweet promises into my ear with gentle caresses.

I wanted more. And I wanted it to be hard. I wanted pain.

And when he wrapped his hand around my throat, I wanted him to squeeze it. I wanted him to take my breath away and force me to do strange things with him. I craved to be pushed past my limits *and my boundaries to shatter like they were never there in the first place.*

Is that wrong?

Instead, he let go of my neck and kissed my temple as he finished on my stomach.

After he finished kissing me down there, I was hesitant to go all the way with him. I'm still a virgin, technically...

Cole was careful, but I wanted the opposite. I didn't say anything or share my interests to explore more with him because I felt ashamed of my cravings like it was something taboo and immoral. How do I tell him I want those things?

There should be a connection with him, and I don't feel it. The fact that I'm questioning the durability of our relationship is what validates my doubts.

~Millie

I SHOULDN'T BE READING her diary, but I can't help it. I want to kill Santiago. But I want to kill Cole even more.

I guess I still can.

I closed her diary and drifted into a deep sleep, thinking of all the ways I was going to make them scream, cry, and hurt while I smiled.

I was exhausted, from council meetings to the little concert debacle, saving Millie from the Southern Vampires. I tossed and turned all night, and even when I was able to rest, the cravings wouldn't stop.

Her blood, her scent, her flesh. My cock was harder than a fucking rock and throbbed in pain when I closed the door to my room. As soon as I got done "punishing" her, I jacked off in an earnest manner until I spurted cum all over myself, and it still doesn't scratch the catastrophic itch that she inflicts upon me. Only she can do that. Being around Millie puts the pain at ease, and she makes me feel like I'm human, too, capable of masking reality. Because, at the end of the day, I'm a monster. It's like I can breathe, even though my lungs don't expand. Like I can feel a fire inside my cold, dead skin, even though my heart doesn't thump. She has been destructive of my old ways. Catapulting into my life at a very unexpected time...and I'm afraid I'm lost.

I can't think straight. My plan for revenge starts to crack. It began to fade when I met her, but then it really started to fuck with my head when I started reading about the most vulnerable moments in her life.

Holland came to my chambers to summon me at midnight. The reality is that my father still wants to step down. Our once peaceful alliances with the Davenports have wilted beyond repair. There will never be peace again after I killed his men to save Millie. Secondly, I have to choose a wife, and I know they're wondering why I haven't taken Millie to unlock my powers.

I walk into my father's headquarters with rejuvenated energy after a day of rest, and I can feel my little Bambi sleeping peacefully. I can hear the sound of her even-paced breaths. I wake up every night, voracious because I'm allured to the enchantment she places me in.

I push open the thick door and tighten my collar nonchalantly as I enter.

My father sits on his throne of jewels, a chair made up of the eyes of those who have crossed us. Our eyes, once plucked from our soulless bodies, turn into diamonds. The chair reflects red, green, magenta, and blue, bright twinkling like rare stones in the dark.

"Father." I stand before him, ready to be attacked with questions.

He narrows his eyes at me and intertwines his hands like he's ready to chew me out.

"The girl continues to live. I can smell and feel her. It's been causing quite a stir-up between the walls of this Cathedral, Hayden. The longer she lives, the longer the tension continues. King Davenport has already sent his men to surround Montana, hoping she might escape again." Holland stands tall beside my father like a prude wanting to rain on my parade of keeping Millie alive longer than they want. He wears a long black cloak and leans on his cane. He glares at me, unbothered to mask his true feelings toward me. Lately, it's been more truant.

"My God, Holland. Did you do something new to your face? It really brings out the miserabilist in your eyes." I point to my own and smirk. He mumbles something under his breath and shakes his head.

I love getting under his skin.

"Hayden," My father interjects with a cold tone. "Why is she still alive? Why haven't you done your part?"

"Father, let me play with my food," I argue.

"I want to step down, *and I want to do it today*, son. I'm tired...your mother wants me to retire so we can go back to London and visit her family, and that can only happen if you ascend with your wife. And your powers. I'm trying to convince the council to change the law about Valkyrie's. Maybe they'll bend the rules for me. I'm highly respected amongst the regions."

My cold smirk dissipates into a tightening of my lips. A somber pause loiters the dark red and black throne room as I search for the right words.

"Have you even chosen a wife since the proposition to

Eleanor has been shot to shit when you recovered the Valkyrie in Texas? When you murdered her brother and King Davenport's son? Everyone is breathing down my neck about sending you to the Inferno for that. But I told them that they were responsible for slaughtering humans, and of course, Davenport acted oblivious to it. He's playing pretend like he wasn't the one that tasked his son with killing innocents."

Another question daggers at me, like he's trying to get inside my head and figure me out. This isn't like me. I'm selfish and depraved; I'm a monster amongst our kind, and I'm sure the gossip has run rampant since the concert. The kiss we shared was on display, and I don't give one fuck what everyone saw.

I wanted them to see it.

"Her name is Millie," I say as I turn back to face my rigid father. He's bent over on his throne, eyeing me suspiciously.

I sink into my confused thoughts. I lean on one leg, rubbing a hand through my slight beard. I'm usually clean-shaven, but lately, that's changed. A lot has changed.

"Do you have...*feelings* for the Valkyrie?" he pries with a blanching grimace like he's stunned with disappointment that I could have any type of empathy for Millie. I can see why. It's what got my uncle killed. He leans forward, daring me to answer him truthfully.

I laugh. A dark and soft roar dwindles and echoes off the Victorian walls because the thought of me falling for someone is humorous and wild. It comes out so naturally and fast, but then my chuckle disintegrates slowly as I process his accusation because it strikes cords within me—cords that have me wondering the same thing—and it hits home.

I massage my lips with my fingers, and flashbacks of her nipples in my mouth and her lips on mine paralyze me momentarily. The memory of how she held my hand and begged me to stay the night with her fuels the impossible.

I'm falling for this girl. If it's not love, it's lust, and I don't mind lusting for this woman until she shows me what kind of version of love she needs me to accept and show her. It's what she deserves. After reading everything she's been through...I can relate. Although she's still full of hope, and I'm full of despair.

After watching her for months on end, stalking her, intruding on her safe space she calls a diary. She's never been shown unconditional love. Her family left Millie behind without a second glance.

Hell, I don't know what *love* is, but I would like to say that it's a privilege to have parents who want you and want the best for you. The guidance everyone requires when they're born isn't always given, and she never had someone to look after her in the right way.

I want to be that for her. I want to look after her. Even if I have to do it in the only ways I know how.

She bounced from parent to parent to grandparents; nothing was stable.

"If you're falling for this girl...you know how it'll end."

You don't need to remind me.

A relationship with a Valkyrie is forbidden. He doesn't need to remind me.

My father's icy grumble interrupts my brooding. I quirk a brow at him, and hope sinks into the pit of my stomach as nausea swirls into my mind at his dry empathy. No one wins in this situation, no one but time itself. I glance quickly at the portrait of my uncle Amos near the throne. My father catches my pinned vision and clears his throat before pinning his blue eyes on me.

"Do you want history to repeat itself by having the second-in-line son take over like I did for your uncle because he couldn't keep his private life private? Attempting to marry someone that's forbidden? Do you want Kallum to ascend instead of you because my patience has worn thin?"

I pensively place my hands on my hips and pace back and forth as I get lost in my apprehension. I'm never good at confrontation, and I like to avoid it at all costs.

Holland leans on his cane, grinning mischievously like he's won his small victory, challenging me to relinquish my right as King.

Not in this lifetime nor the next.

Through gritted teeth and all the courage I try to find within my broken soul, I muster, "I'll kill her tonight and find a wife by the end of the month."

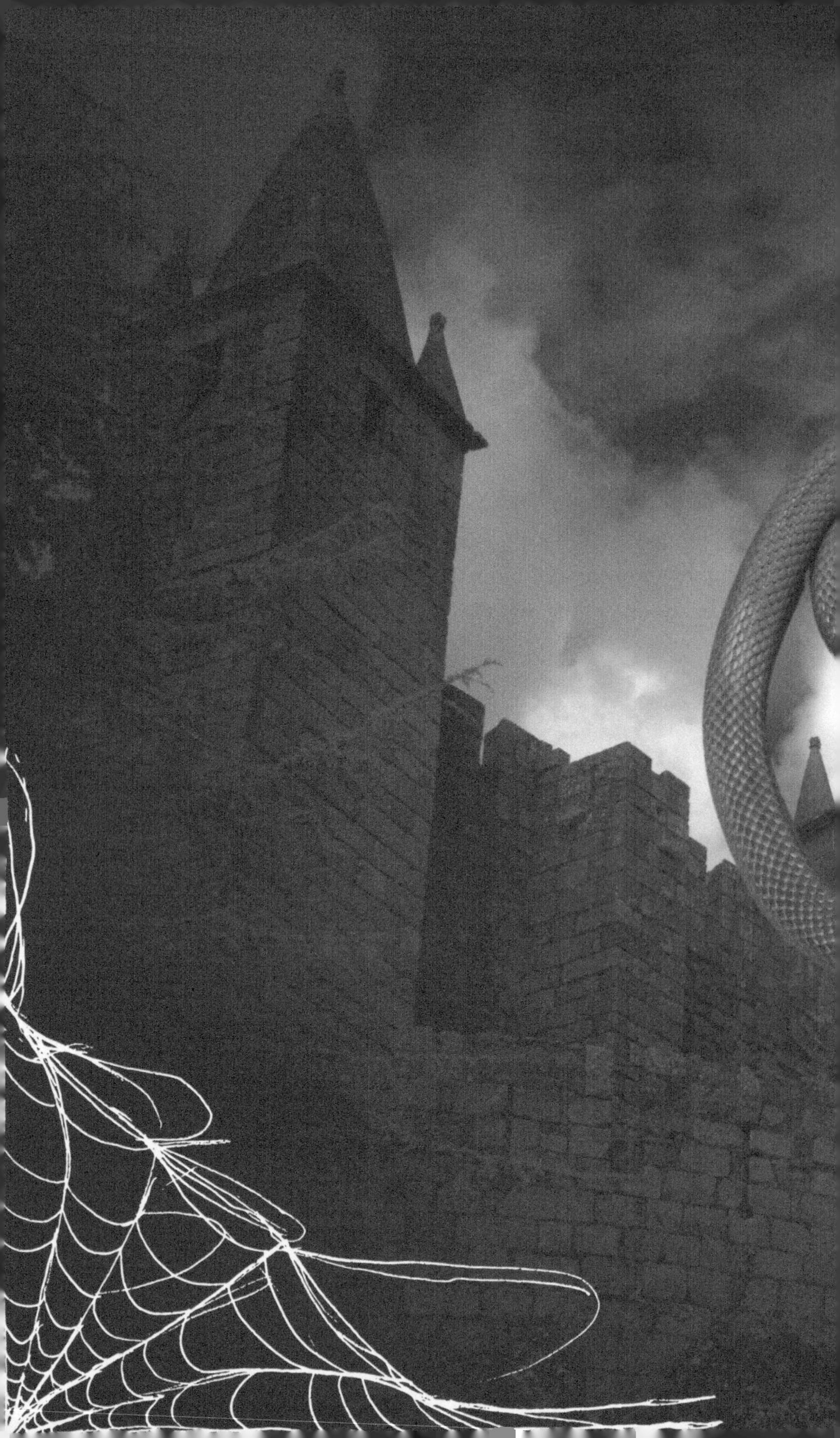

20

HAYDEN

Dear Diary,
  I dread the weekends.
  It's another lonely Friday night.
  No one is around. No one is around to talk to. No one is around to share a laugh with or the simplicity of their presence. My close friends don't know what I go home to. They don't know about the nights I endure. They don't know that I don't know how to think straight sometimes. No one knows that some days, I wake up and struggle to go on.
  Sometimes, I hate me too.
  No one knows...

IT'S UNFINISHED. The entry is unfinished because she always signs her name at the bottom. It's a bit all over the place. And there are wrinkled textured dots amongst the paper, most likely from tears. I close it.

Seconds later, I walk into the room where Millie is staying with a grievous plan I promised to do. She's been staying in the same room my uncle had his Valkyrie in before he was executed from this dark Earth at the inferno.

She's asleep, and even through the freezing Cathedral, she manages to warm up any room she's in. She emanates peace and vulnerability and tastes like what I suppose heaven is. A realm I'm eternally banned from entering...she's the closest fraction of heaven I'll ever get to experience, and my father wants me to dispose of it.

I lay down beside her, careful not to wake her, as my hips dip into the mattress and the scent of pure strawberries waft into my senses. I grab a lock of her hair, and my nose trails the soft, black, wavy strands. I could get lost in her forever. She is a mysterious maze I would gladly never find the end to, and I would happily live like that.

My cock is immediately erect, and my God, it takes everything in me not to tear off her clothes and have her suffocate my dick with her mouth, her cunt...or her ass. I'll take them all if she lets me.

"You're here," she breathes out, and I pause my movements. She's awakened, and my plan to sink my teeth into her and drain her blood until her heart stops is already having hiccups in the process.

I don't want to do this...but I must.

It's either me or another immortal that finds her. Even my brother might get a shot if I don't follow through with this.

"I'm here," I reassure her, masking the dread that wants to paint its way into the conversation.

"What time is it?" she questions me as she stays still, not bothering to open her eyes yet.

"Three in the morning," I tell her truthfully. She pauses and does something that has me questioning what's left of my sanity. She dips her hand over the blankets and finds mine, snaking her fingers through them and intertwining us together.

"Maybe I'm crazy, but I'm going to thank you for saving me at the festival." There is a short pause as my eyelashes rapidly flutter with amusement, and a vivid smirk crosses my face, and she knows it. "You're still an asshole for kidnapping me, though," she spits out and places both our hands over her hip, sliding them until they meet the soft mattress that she's sleeping on.

"You still said thank you somewhere in that statement. You just made a confession that you lust for me as I do for you...I'll take it," I tell her wickedly as I pull myself in closer to her body. I need it on mine. Once her back hits my chest, images of my father sitting on his throne—the throne I will one day own, flashback with malice.

I resent my father's order. I don't want to kill her anymore.

How can I after finding out what she tastes like? After she's placed some sort of trust in me?

Her blood is rare, and on top of it all, it tastes too damn good to let it die with her. When she touches or looks at me, it puts me into a fucking bubble, and I'm *her prisoner*. Granted, she looks at me like she *wants* to hate me, but the way her heart flutters irregularly like it's fighting its own battle to regain a constant normal rhythm again that flows to destroy the feelings that simmer in her veins when I speak to her, speaks mountainous volumes.

I know she won't say it or admit it to me, but she thrives on being forced and choked. She loves it and craves it. I've read most of her diary, and she wants to experience it. She wants me to lose control just to feel her...and I lost that control months ago in Texas when I first laid my eyes on her.

In return, she makes me feel like maybe I do have more to give than to take. I'm willing to fight wars to keep her tethered to me and only me for the rest of my pathetic existence. My selfish need to acquire my powers is starting to dwindle and be replaced by another selfish need—or rather, my obsession with her existence.

I pull down her black-laced nightgown until it reveals her naked skin, and she doesn't fight it.

The scars on her breast that King Davenport's son gave her stare back at me mockingly. A loathing reminder that I failed to protect her entirely; someone else scarring her makes me livid, and I see black.

"You say you're going to kill me, but here I am, breathing in a room that my entire house fits, wearing clothes I know I'll never be able to afford, in a Cathedral that looks like a castle high up in the mountains...in bed with you." Her voice stabs my ears with determination. "I crave you, Hayden when I know it might be fucked up to feel this way. You have me in a dark fog, and I'm unsure I want to escape it. I know nothing about you... and yet you know everything about me. How is that fair?"

Her skin is warmer than usual. Her heart rate is faster than normal, and I sense something isn't right about her health.

"Are you feeling okay? You're hot." My hand slicks across her warm temple. Is she sick?

"I'm fine!" she lies. "Don't change the subject. I want answers, Hayden. Plea—" She refrains from using that word, and I twitch when she does.

She turns around and lets my hand go. An aura of emptiness flares into me cruelly at her absence. She turns to face me with beaming brown eyes, glistening even underneath the darkness; her eyes have a chokehold on me.

Mulling over her gentle yet destructive words, I'm hesitant to respond.

Because I came into this room with the intent to put an end to her life and an end to this brewing war, but the way she wreaks havoc on me, already dripping honey in between her thighs, is a reminder I want her alive more than anything in this world. I don't want to betray her trust. Fuck. I don't want to see the look on her face when she finds out the truth.

"You fail to realize that all I've done for the past six months is risk my right to the throne, my eternal damnation, standing up for everything I believed in to keep you and your family alive. My ways of doing so may be depraved and frowned upon in your fragile human world, but it has to be done. Keeping you away from the Davenports, your family, and the life you once knew is necessary."

She narrows her eyes at me, and a tear falls down her cheek. I want to wipe it away, but I hold my ground. I need to get this out.

"Why did you try to commit suicide at sixteen years old?"

She stiffens.

"What? How do you know about that?!"

"Answer the question. You know what I'm talking about. Why did you try and take your own life?" I scowl at her. I care about her. Reading her journal has me invested and captivated.

She touches her arm—the one where there's a scar—just hidden behind the sleeve of her black nightgown.

I read the unfinished entry in her journal before entering her room. The scar on her arm...it all adds up. I always assume the worst. I hope she'll tell me I'm wrong, but she doesn't deny it.

"Don't make me talk about it. I hate going back there." Millie's shaking, her eyes fade to hopelessness, but I need to know what happened.

Who do I need to torture?

"Back where?"

"That dark headspace where I hate myself." she claws at her hair.

My brows knit together, and I ball my fists. "Why on Earth would you hate yourself?"

"Because!" she snaps, cutting me off.

The collected tears on her dark lashes fall down her reddened cheeks.

"If the two people who are supposed to love you unconditionally didn't want you, why would I want myself? If they didn't want to live for me, why would I want to live for myself?" She's shaking and grips the scar on her arm tighter until her knuckles turn white. "If they hated me, I would hate me too." She rubs it up and down.

She's having a panic attack. A lump forms in my throat as I jolt forward and scoop her into my arms as she bellows in my chest. She punches and fights me, but I just hold onto her tighter.

"Let me go!" she sniffles, trying to push me off, but I just encase her more. I need her to feel how much she's wanted.

"No." I kiss the top of her head.

"Hayden!" Another push.

"No." Another kiss.

Finally, she stops fighting me and grips my suit tighter. I let her cry and whimper while I soothe her back.

"They don't hate you, Millie." I kiss the top of her head. "They made mistakes they will never be able to take back. But don't let the trauma they inflicted on you drown you. You're still here, and you should be proud of yourself for that."

She holds onto me tighter and whimpers softly.

I want you, Millie. If they don't want you. I want you.

I'm tempted to say it, but the fact that she's almost asleep in my arms makes me hesitate.

I don't want to disturb her peace or say something that I'm still trying to figure out myself. I have an attachment toward her, and I don't know how far it goes, but I feel like I must take care of her.

I want to take care of her.

I don't want to become the next most powerful king there's been since King Killian, from centuries ago. He was the last vampire to have powers before he died at the Inferno.

I don't know when she contracted the fever, but maybe she got it from the concert. I gently lay her back on the pillow, and she lets me. She nestles into it, and I stand.

"Wait. Don't go," she pleads.

"I'm coming right back," I assure her with a gentle tone.

What the hell is going on with me?

I flash out the door to grab Tylenol from our storage for human necessities. After grabbing the pill bottle, I ask one of our chefs to cook chicken soup for her. Then, I head back into Millie's room. It all took me about three minutes.

I hand the pills to her. She pushes herself up against the bed with her hands, eyeing the pills suspiciously.

"What is that?" she asks as she takes them. I give her a cup of water.

"Tylenol. For your fever."

I watch her swallow the pills and climb back into bed with her. Kicking off my shoes, I take the glass of water away from her and place it on my nightstand.

I grab her body, forcing her to turn on her side so that she faces the red stained glass and her back is to my chest. She's shivering, clawing at the blankets to warm her up more. She's already at a 102 body temperature. I force the blankets off her, and she whines. She tries to grab them again, but I snatch her arm and scold her.

"Your temperature will get higher if you do that. We need to get your temperature down, not up."

"But I'm cold," she stammers with chattering teeth.

"That's your fever talking, Millie. Let me help." I take off my shirt, knowing full well my body is cold, and embrace her. She hisses and fights my hands off her at first, but I keep my embrace tight and like steel.

"Why are you doing this? Why are you being nice to me? Don't you want to kill me?" she asks me as she continues to shudder against my body.

I pause, contemplating her question as I grip her hips to keep her still. I don't know how to answer that.

She's warm. But it's not the fever. Millie is warm all the time.

"When I was still a human...*before I turned*, I got sick sometimes. My mother and father were always too busy running the kingdom and with other matters that didn't concern a child. It was my uncle that took care of me."

Just then, there's a knock on the door, and the Chef comes in with Millie's food and drink. I stand, take the tray from him, thank him, and he closes the door as he walks out. I turn to Millie, and she sits up with rosy cheeks and pale skin. She's still shivering, but not so much as before.

"He would always make me chicken soup. This is his recipe." I place it on a wooden bed tray so she can eat while sitting comfortably still tucked into the bedsheets. She hovers over the plate, smells the warm fumes, and I can feel her mouth watering.

An overwhelming urge to touch her...*gently* consumes me. The urge is frightening and unfamiliar. I grit my teeth and resent that temptation. I like her. I like her a lot.

I grab my shoes and shirt before I'm at the door. I watch her take a few bites while she sits on the bed, and for some reason, I can feel my uncle's ghost haunting me in this room. The cathedral holds history. I grip the door, and my mouth opens before I can stop it.

"Imagine being hurt so much that you lose faith in humanity. Imagine being betrayed so many fucking times that you can't feel anything anymore but numbness? Imagine being hurt so many goddamn times you lose trust in everything and everyone? To the point where you can't even trust yourself?"

She stops eating, and she freezes. She holds the spoon in her hands and doesn't move, but we stand there watching each other. We lock eyes. Compassion floods through her slow movements. I'm opening up to her. Giving her a small window into the life I've lived. I've never been able to open up about my life before with anyone, but with Millie...I guess I can't stop talking about shit I'm ashamed of.

Three Hundred Years Ago

I throw rocks at the lake behind the Cathedral. I know I'm not alone, and I don't want anyone to know that I'm hurting. I've been taught not to cry. It's weak to cry, father and mother say.

"My parents treat me like I'm different." I stare at my eighteen-year-old reflection.

"You are different, though in all the best ways, Hayden." My uncle comforts me once again since my parents are lost in their daily lives that don't involve my brother and me. They're always absent when I need them but always present when it's time for me to execute duties I dread.

"I'm different because I'm a monster."

"What'd you do?"

I throw a rock at where my face is, and the water breaks into waves. "I beat someone up."

"Why?"

"Because they were bullying me. He started a fight with me... so I ended it."

My uncle Amos sits next to me. He brings his knees upwards and places his crossed forearms against them as he watches me.

"And what did this boy tell you? What did he say that triggered you to unremorseful madness that you beat him almost to death?"

I shut my eyes tight as I recollect the boy's bloodied, bruised face. I liked seeing him bleed red. It gave the demons inside me joy.

"Everyone notices how my parents have never been there since I was a child. It's a small town. Everyone notices how quiet I am and self reserved. Everyone in school thinks I don't belong in this world. If only they knew the truth about how I came into this world."

"Hayden," he scolds. "What did he say?"

"He said that I'm pathetic because I search for a sense of family through my teachers because I go above and beyond with my studies. That I'm undeserving of loyal friendship and compassion and that I'm so worthless that my own parents and brother feel the same way, too. That nobody will see me like a man, but only a monster who says please too much when I ask for things. I'm just being polite, which got me into a fight."

"Ignore them, Hayden. But don't ever stop standing up for yourself. Defend yourself and your light. Don't let a cruel world beat you up until all you feel is anger. Be stronger than that."

I snap out of my thoughts and close the door before she can respond. I don't know if Millie was going to or not, but I'd prefer if she didn't have an answer.

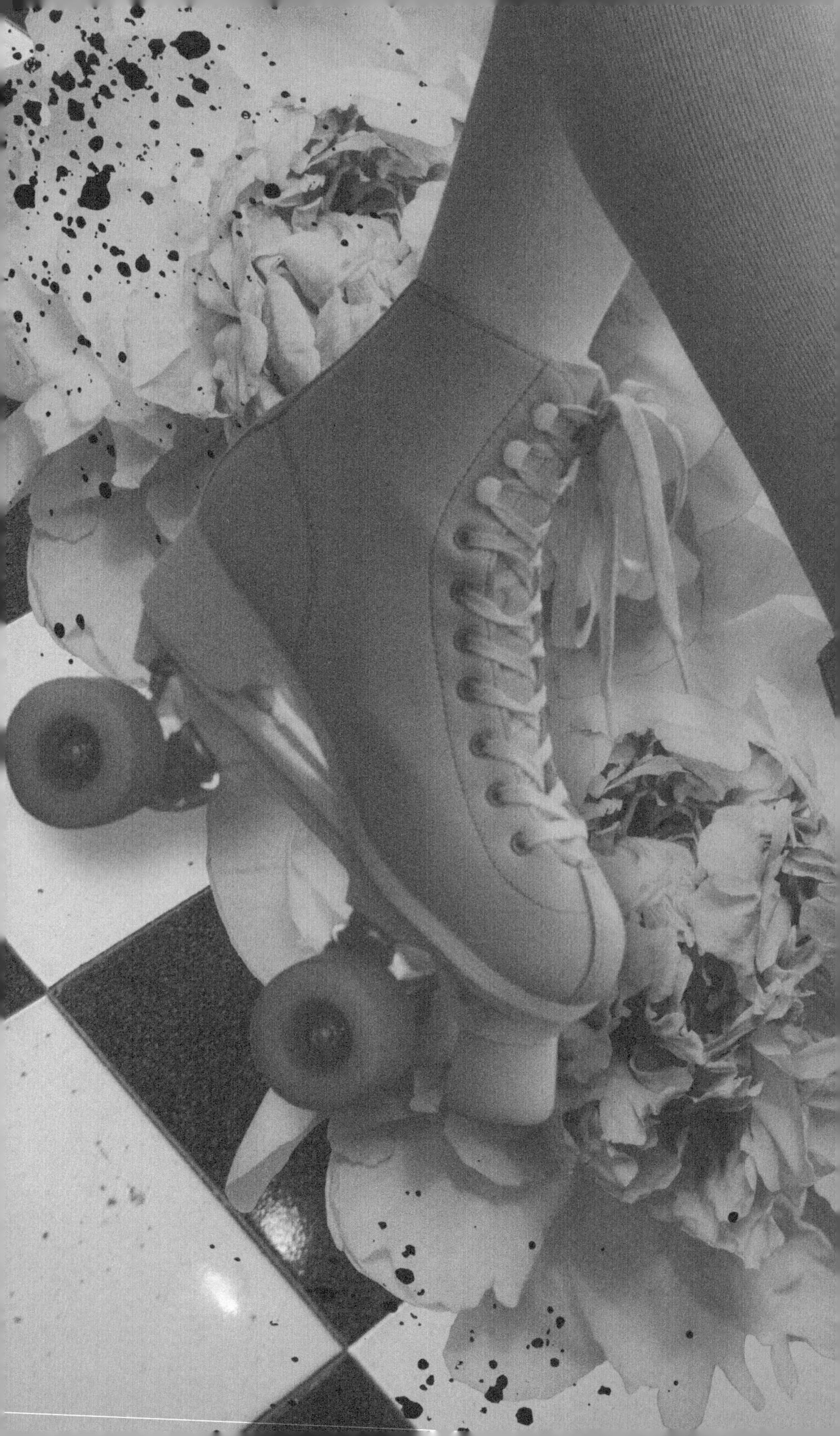

21

MILLIE

"THAT WAS VERY stupid of you, Millie. To run away when you're safer here than anywhere in the world. People know about you now. Bad people that want to kill you for your blood. I'm the only one in this world that can protect you!"

My fever disappeared after a week, and Hayden has been spending all his time with me, watching movies or even lying together in silence when he isn't busy with work or taking care of his bloodlust. His presence is enough for me to feel okay.

I hate being alone.

But tonight, we're having our routine back-and-forth moment where we argue about me wanting my freedom back. Hayden Drago is gone, and The Depraved Prince is back.

I've never been so confused in my life. There's a dark chemistry between us, and I'm unsure what to do about it. He hasn't touched me like the night of the festival when he 'punished' me even though I want him to.

He's beautiful in the way he talks, walks, and moves. He craves me and brings my darkest fantasies to life. It's like he knows what buttons to push, and I'm letting him.

I'm drawn to this game, and there's no more denying it.

"And you're telling me that you aren't bad? You want to kill me too! What makes you different from everyone else?" I drawl, pointing my finger at him. His shoulders fall in a guilty fashion.

Silence. He doesn't reply. How can he? He knows I'm right.

I decided to pour out all my inquiries, desperate for answers. Maybe there's still a way to go back home, and maybe we can both pretend this never happened. He killed southern vampires like it's a sport he's good at. Perhaps they took the message and will steer clear of me.

I walk up to him when he doesn't answer, only stopping when we're practically chest-to-chest.

"Why did the entire Cathedral look like a tornado went through it?" I bristle. He goes rigid, his face turns to stone, and he looks down, meeting my inquisitive gaze.

I woke up that night of the festival when he had me in his arms after he slammed the front door shut. The entire place was torn to shreds, and glass was everywhere. Furniture destroyed and ripped open. A headless body on the ground...

I couldn't move or speak, so I stayed still and tried to go back to sleep. Sleep has been my only place of solace here lately, but that's changed. Now I feel a haven when I'm only around Hayden after witnessing so many attempted assassinations on my life.

"What are you talking about?" he groans out, frustrated, furrowing his brows and waving his hand before me like I asked him something wild. Maybe he doesn't remember.

"The Cathedral was trashed that night of the Halloween festival," I point out, not backing down.

He sighs and shifts on his feet. He palms his hips after

running a hand through his dark hair. He looks away from me, ashamed.

"I...I don't know. Sometimes, when I'm enraged, I black out and can't remember. Kallum told me I destroyed everything and killed one of our guards when you left me." He gets closer to me. "And I would do it again."

Shivers run up and down my spine. I swallow the nerves that possess me when he tells me this with a dark, cruel tone.

"What is so special about me, Hayden? Why does everyone call me a Valkyrie?"

"Because Millie!" He roars, flashing his teeth, his eyes igniting into red flames. His true self emerges and explodes with fury. His beauty is still there...but it's also terrifying. He starts walking forward, forcing me to walk back until my legs hit the bed, and I scramble away from him. He's pissed.

I flinch at his rusty outburst and sit up until my back hits the wooden demon-carved headboard. He stands from the bed in a split second and paces in front of me by my vanity with a large window full of luxurious cosmetics that fit my tone. I haven't touched it to spite him.

"You're just going to have to trust me on this. Your blood is the rarest in the universe. If a vampire is lucky enough to find one, they kill them, and there hasn't been a Valkyrie in a really long fucking time. It's illegal in our world, but that still doesn't stop anyone. You hold a vampire's treasure beyond just blood that runs through your veins."

"Explain! Please. I deserve answers," I declare, trying to reach for his face to cup his sharpened jaw, but he pulls back before our flesh can connect.

He sighs. His entire body shakes with madness. He turns around, his suit straining against his stiffened muscles. His face darts to the door, and when I think he's going to flash out of here, he changes his mind.

"All vampires have powers, more that go beyond our natural abilities. It lives within us like a virus that stays dormant unless we suck the blood from a Valkyrie." His loud voice depletes into a soft murmur, and he palms my chest. I shiver as he presses his cold, calloused hand into me. "And if their heart stops beating while our fangs are inside them, the virus becomes active, and we find out what kind of powers hide within us."

"What type of powers?" I elevate my curiosity. There's a moment of vulnerability in Hayden. He's letting his armor down, and I need to take advantage of it.

He looks at me with pinched brows and a wall drawn up so high. Seconds pass by, and he tries to withdraw himself.

"Don't you dare pull away now. I want to know."

"Millie..." he murmurs with disdain.

"More p-powers?"

God, what other powers could they have?

"More than your speed and strength? You already have immortality. Please tell me, Hayden. What kind of powers and why me?"

He shrugs with unease. "It could be anything. From flying like a bat out of hell, healing, lasers for eyes, controlling the weather, becoming invisible, reading minds."

I tear my eyes from his tall stature.

"The rule is we cannot interfere in a Valkyrie's life. These laws were put in place centuries ago to save the human population so that the world will remain balanced. Humans outnumbering vampires. These rules were put in place because innocents were being slaughtered left and right—even children. Immortals became desperate when they learned King Killian had killed a Valkyrie and became the most powerful of all. Thousands of humans were being killed searching for Valkyrie blood, and all the kings of Immortal Country agreed to peace... to stop us from killing each other. For greed. For *power*."

He hovers over me in a blip, brushing my bangs from my face, looking at me with glints of desire in his ice-blue eyes.

"But the Southern King has declared war on everything and the law the minute he started slaughtering innocent humans searching for you. There's a war. And the only thing that will put an end to this is if someone kills you. Taking the initiative in activating their powers. Because once they do, they'll be the most powerful immortal that anyone has seen since...since..."

My brows raise at a sight I'm extremely unfamiliar with. Hayden is clearly tormented by inner turmoil and is not composed. There's a break in his concrete shield, with a hint of remorse.

"Since when?" I pry harder. I scoot closer to the bed until my feet dangle at the edge.

Instead of answering me, he reaches into his pockets and pulls out a cigarette. He sticks one in his mouth, lighting it with the hand that carries the ring with the bat and snake.

I want to scold him for smoking around me, but I don't want to kill this moment of raw vulnerability.

"My uncle Amos..." He takes a hit, and smoke lingers in the air, his voice painted with grief. "If we're hard to kill now, it's tripled once the powers are active. He didn't go out with a fight. His only crime? Falling for a Valkyrie," he scoffs, amused like he told a funny joke. His eyes reach mine, and I swear there's emotion attached to it. "I don't know why it's you, Millie. I don't know why you carry Valkyrie blood, but there's no use dwelling on something that I cannot change. You're a target, and you're a target with a rare, delicious prize that's caught the attention of all the Immortal Kings. Especially Davenport.

Don't you get it, little Bambi? The only reason why you're still alive is because of *me*."

He walks closer to me with a pained, beautiful smile, closing the distance until his cold, sultry breath hits my lips like a wind of mint. My own breathing comes to a dangerous halt, blood rushing to my face. Just the ministry of his presence does this to me. It catches me off guard every time, sending me into a mess.

"Now that I know you, I despise you're a Valkyrie. But you are."

He closes his eyes and leans in. His gaze is intense, full of a trillion emotions with a hint of pain. He cups my cheek, leaning in for a kiss, but I don't let him touch my lips. I pull back, and he groans.

"You scare me."

"I would be a little worried if I didn't."

"Please...maybe you're right, Hayden. Maybe you're right about everything. But let me go."

Let me go home. Please. You know that's what I want.

"No."

"Hayden."

He smiles. His red eyes flash, and my pulse quickens. His teeth slowly graze his bottom lip, and he hovers over my neck. He pulls me to him, and I'm bracing myself for him to bite me again. Our hips are pressed together, and I feel the hardened mass of his cock straining his pants.

"Don't we intrigue you, Millie?" he coos.

He pulls away. He cups my face in his hands, holding me firmly like he's eager for my answer. He walks me to the vanity until we're in front of it. My heart thumps like wildfire, and I love the thrill he gives me. He forces me to face the mirror while his hands are all over me.

I gasp when his reflection isn't behind me like it should be.

"We don't grow old. We don't get sick. We don't die. We live our lives fearlessly, traveling the world, partying all night, sleeping all day." I'm palming the vanity. He presses his body against me, and in a second, his massive, hard erect bulge is on my ass, and he thrusts into me. I whimper as the front of my thighs hit the wood rough, and he grips the back of my hair as I stare at myself. It looks like a ghost is moving me around, my hair getting pulled back by nothing.

"We fuck whenever and whoever we want without ever getting tired. Don't you want to be an immortal? Don't you want to live life to the fullest with no regrets? Don't you want to fall in love with life a little more?"

My neck is exposed, and he pulls my head to the side so that I feel his cold breath on my neck.

"Don't you want to live forever?"

That's an easy question with a simple answer.

"I would rather die than become a monster. You kill people, Hayden. You're selfish. Cruel. Depraved. You take, and you take. You're trying to take pieces away from me, but I will never let you devour me completely. Don't you think it's rather boring? The mask you put on to play pretend doesn't fool me, Prince Drago. You're bored." I push my ass back against his cock. It wants to come out and destroy me. I'm playing with fire, but maybe I want to get burned. "Hundreds of years you've walked this Earth, and you're still unhappy. And maybe...just maybe, I make you feel alive, and that's why you don't want to let me go." I grit out my truth as I rub against him, and he quivers beneath my touch. His nose trails my jawline, and then his head falls forward like he's in pain and wants to let me go but can't.

Am I scared to die? What I do know is I'm scared of leaving my loved ones. I'm scared of being alone in the afterlife. I'm scared of dying before I get to experience what being in love feels like. I'm scared of becoming like Hayden and his family.

He stops caressing my cheek with his knuckles. My words don't get through to him; instead, they fly over his head. He turns me around fast, picking me up and sitting my ass down hard on the vanity. My breasts bounce up and down while bottles of makeup fall off, and he has me by the throat, choking me.

"Tell me what it's like to fear death, baby," he breathes out cruelly with sinister promises. "I don't want to kill you, but the way you make me feel...you're a threat to the life I once knew and want to keep. A Valkyrie got my uncle killed. I hate your blood. *I hate you!* I refuse to let the past repeat itself with me. I won't get myself into more trouble keeping you alive than I already have..." Hayden is gone. The sweet, protective side of Hayden is replaced by the Depraved Prince.

His decision-making is giving me whiplash, but it doesn't compare to the way he stares into my eyes like he wants to erase me from this world. Hatred, pain, and lust intertwine together on his handsome features.

He chokes me harder with his large hand, as he smiles beautifully, and I take it. His other is gripped on my hip. Pure charm and masculinity wrapped into one monster. He sinks his fingers into my neck, the circulation slowly cutting off. Yet, he's precise not to damage my throat. He can't kill me, even when the demons tell him to...

I squint at him as I sneak in breaths through my nose. He smirks, the anticipation he seeks evident in his red eyes that glimmer with hardened lust and control.

I don't struggle or fight him because I know that's what he desires. He gets off on making me cry for him. Making me bleed and weep. A part of me craves to submit, but I want him to know that he's capable of showing me a side of him that he has locked away...probably forever. He's capable of forgiveness, compassion, love, faith, and peace.

I welcome his pain. I want to feel it.

"Give me your pain. Give me your hurt. I can take it," I dare him with nothing holding me back.

I grab a hold of his hips, pulling him more into me with my legs. He watches me in a stunned manner.

"Because I know what it's like to scream in a room full of people as they watch you drown. I know what it's like for people to think you're a bad person when they refuse to understand the origin story of how you became a villain. I know what it's like to hurt and never to trust again." He tightens his grip on my throat like he's begging me to stop talking. My words are gutting him profoundly. The vein in his neck bulges with frustration.

"I know what all those things are like. But do you know what it's like to hold someone or something without destroying it?" I choke out, stars dancing in the distance, and he loosens his grip around my throat. He tilts his body back like he wants to retreat. "Without hurting it?"

But I keep my hold on him with my legs, even though I know he can break away if he wants to. He wants to push me away, hurt me, and break me. I don't know why I want to show him that he's capable of more, as he's literally trying to kill me.

He doesn't deserve it. I don't know what his childhood was like but I'm still trying.

I stand, closing the distance between us. I tiptoe to meet his mouth and kiss his jaw. He closes his eyes and stiffens. I blink slowly, and he loosens his muscles around my neck. I kiss his chin over and over again, trailing soft touches with my lips up his jaw until I hover over his ear.

"Stop it! Fight me! Treat me like the monster that I am!" He punches the mirror behind me with a destructive strength. I shudder and shift on the vanity as the blow shatters all of the glass. Hundreds of glass pieces fall to the floor, but I'm not cowering away.

He's scaring me. He's a monster that wants me to feed into his mindset.

I won't do it.

I kiss his lips, and he groans like he hates the way I touch him, but the lust wraps up into frustration. He can't find the strength to let me go. To kill me like he's been promising to do. All of his emotions are turning into demons, making the darkness feel like quicksand, consuming the Hayden I've grown to know. I can feel the battles he endures with his morals.

He finally kisses me back, pressing his cold, full lips to mine like it's the last kiss he'll ever have, and lifts his hand like he's going to hurt me. I break the kiss and contort my face, preparing for his wrath.

He connects with the wood, which results in a significant dent.

"Why can't I be normal?! Why do I want to kill anyone that tries to take you from me?!" his roar crescendos loudly.

"Hayden. Stop. You're okay." I try to comfort him and wake him up from his spiral.

"Don't try and fix me. You cannot fix the dead!" he scolds me, but it's not me who he's trying to convince.

It's himself.

"Prince Drago. Let me help you. Maybe I can open your eyes to realize that revenge and blood aren't the only things that can drive a person. There's more to you, Hayden. I feel it when you kiss me."

He pushes my neck to the side, and I whimper from his forceful gesture.

His pupils expand, grabbing a fistful of my hair, and he snarls like he's ready to eat me alive. He resents me for trying to have a conversation with him. He mashes our bodies together, taking my breath away, and I can feel the tips of his teeth about to prick my throat out, but he doesn't get to follow through.

Two loud knocks on the door interrupt him.

"Prince Drago. They've breached the Cathedral. Davenport vampires are here to take the Valkyrie!"

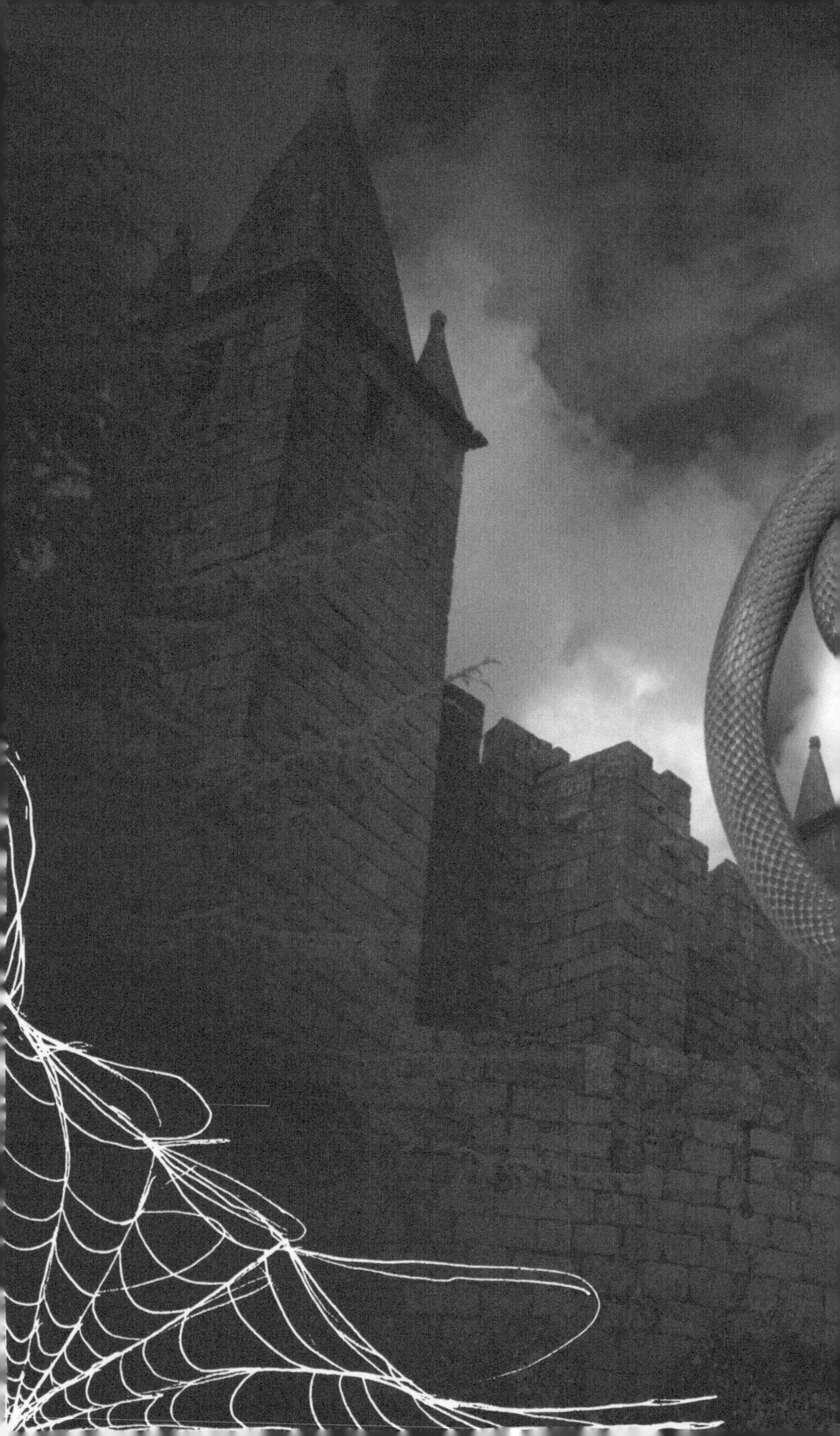

22

HAYDEN

I CURSE under my breath as I stare at my little Bambi. Her pulse in her neck tempts me to bite. I feel and hear the sound of her hot blood pumping, driving me insane as she usually does. Her honey that drips in between her thighs that has my cock hardened with impenetrable lust. The softness of her skin that I want to hold naked and treasure all night.

Her soul matches mine and fits my broken pieces perfectly.

And they're here to take her from me?

Not a fucking chance.

"Hayden...don't go. Don't leave me in this room. Take me home!" she begs once I retreat from her. She tugs at my arms with glassy eyes.

She still doesn't fucking get it.

"I am your home!"

I keep walking and reach the door in no time. I whip it open and come face to face with several Kingsguards.

"How did King Davenport get inside?!" I shout as I fight the darkness inside my head that wants to wreak havoc on others.

"We don't know, but they're in here!" Charles declares as he walks forward.

"Five of you stay guarded at Millie's door. Where's my father and brother?" I tear off my suit jacket. I throw it to the floor and start to fold my cuffs, clenching my jaw so hard, I'm not sure how my fangs haven't chipped.

"They're downstairs. Your mother is in her chambers, protected."

Good. Millie is protected, and so is my mother.

From a distance, I hear banging, snarling, and shouting. Another battle has begun and started without me. I rush to the living room, where I see my men and blue-eyed immortals fighting each other. Limbs are being torn, eyes are being gouged out, and my father and brother are nowhere to be found.

Are they in hiding?

Either way, our military is doing a good job fighting them off. I even see Holland joining in on the deranged, chaotic scuffle. He tears off someone's head by biting it off.

I smirk. I think I like him now—just a little.

"Hayden! You shouldn't be here. Get somewhere safe! You are the future king!" Holland shouts at me as he takes on another immortal.

Do I ever listen to him? Why does he think I would start now?

"And miss the fun?" I lick my teeth, and I fly towards a blue-eyed immortal that's right by Holland. "No way."

EVERYONE WHO TRESPASSED IS NOW BEING BURNT ALIVE IN our grand fireplace. We've stacked body after body, gouging their eyes to add to our throne and the crown. Hearing their screams while they burn gives me joy. I love it when I get to hurt people. Still, amongst the madness, King Davenport hasn't shown his face. But he's here.

We can all smell him.

"I've checked everywhere, Prince Drago. We can't find King Davenport." Charles informs me as his bright crimson eyes dart between me and Holland. He fears what I might do to him if we can't find him.

I purse my lips as exhaustion catches up to me. Where can he fucking be?

Suddenly, Millie's scream echoes throughout Drago's cathedral. My head spins toward the origin, my spirit crumbling at the sound I've never heard her conjure before. It's a strangled, horror plea for me. I don't hesitate when all I want to do is freeze from the sound she bellowed out. She's in danger. Her heart thumps, her blood is cold, and I know *she's in trouble*.

I run to the quarters she's staying in, which takes me about a minute or so. It's at the far end of our structure. I'm on high alert, convincing myself I'll make it to her room in time, trying to push out my worst fears. As soon as I turn into the hallway, I find all of my men dismembered on the floor, without their heads.

Did we underestimate King Davenport?

"Don't walk in here, Prince Drago. Or the girl is dead." King Davenport's rugged, threatening voice taunts me inside Millie's room. The door is broken down and shattered to pieces.

Wow, he's crazier than I thought if he thinks I won't try to end him. I don't give a fuck that he's more powerful than me.

I flash inside the room.

"Stay outside!" I order my men to stay put. I need to do this on my own. Charles and Holland grimace but hold their ground.

King Davenport is a few feet away from Millie. She holds a piece of glass from the vanity mirror I broke toward him to defend herself. He smiles cruelly at her; his aged fangs are tinted with yellow but still sharpened as ever. They're the longest fangs I've ever witnessed. He's older, more experienced, and has an unbreakable motivation to kill Millie. It's admirable that he doesn't give up and always goes for what he strives for. But not with my Millie. And I still hate him. I still crave revenge at every corner of my mindset, but not at the cost of Millie anymore.

"Wow, she's a beauty. Now I see why you took her for yourself." King Davenport starts to move toward my girl, and I lunge forward. He strikes me down fast like I'm nothing but a fly on the wall. My back collides and cracks with a dreadful collision.

I hear my spine shatter, and I go limp for a second.

Fuck.

That hurt.

Luckily, I'll heal in a few seconds, and my broken bones will repair like they were never damaged in the first place.

I never take my eyes off her as I stand again. My gaze is locked onto the girl from Texas like a moth to a flame.

"Don't hurt him!" Millie's strangled cry chips away at my blackened heart.

Davenport claps his hands and sneers. "Aww, you care for Hayden Drago? Don't you know about all the sick shit he's done? I don't think you do by the way you plead for his mercy." King Davenport nears Millie and I break fast. Pushing onto my feet, I manage to reach him this time. I pull on his cloak, and it rips.

But still, he's stronger.

Shit.

He tucks his veiny hand into my sides and launches me away; this time, he throws me into the stained glass, and it cracks—pieces of red fall onto the floor. I flinch when the pain from my broken ribs demands my attention. My face is cut all over as dark black blood drips into small puddles all around me. My lips, nose, and cheeks all burn, but it doesn't compare to the devastation I'll endure if he takes my Bambi away.

"She's marked." He emphasizes as he eyes her neck where my teeth marks are. "You love this girl, don't you?" he roars, bewildered.

I do. I fucking do.

I try to pick myself up from the ground, grunting and feeling a glacial wave of defeat over my shoulders. My unhealed injuries win against my decision to stand. I'm not ready to fight, but I don't care. I stumble as iron comes up my throat, and I spit blood onto the glass. Davenport chuckles and circles Millie like he's taking pure delight, watching me fail repeatedly to keep him away from her. I fall on my knees as hope leaks onto the floor. Every time I try to get him away from her, I'm beat back down.

If I'm going to die, I'm going to die trying. On my fucking own. I don't need my men for this.

"Now I get to make you suffer again by taking another person you care for away. But first, I think I'll rip your head off so you can join Amos in hell." Davenport stalks in my direction, each step thundering with ambition to ruin me. I swallow my nerves as I try to push myself up again. I'm not healing fast enough, and he's taking advantage—cruel bastard.

He forces me to look at him with his long nails stabbing my throat...but then Millie slits her wrist. The sound of her skin getting split open is like lightning hitting the ground so hard it thunders and vibrates the entire Cathedral. My whole existence shakes from the unexpected.

She's not doing what I think she's doing!

"No, Millie, don't fucking do this!" I snarl at her, but she looks at me like she'll do anything for me. Her honey eyes gleam with mercy, and blood immediately starts dripping down her arm. She watches it as her face pales. Her skin glows with a thick layer of sweat.

She's sacrificing herself. For me? I'm not fucking worth it, beautiful girl.

My fangs involuntarily protrude over my mouth, and I want a taste of her myself. But I've learned more self-control tactics from being around her so much this past year...while Davenport hasn't. Her blood pains me, and her enigma of sweet strawberry odor blinds King Davenport like a stun grenade before he can finish his intentions with me. He spins her way, his long silver hair whooshes through the tension, and his blue eyes glow even harsher and vibrant. He growls like a madman with nothing to lose and lunges for her.

Well, *Millie is my everything to lose.* She's it for me in every single fucking lifetime. He's fast, but I'm faster. This time, he's distracted, and I'm healed. I don't plan on losing. She's mine. She has always been mine.

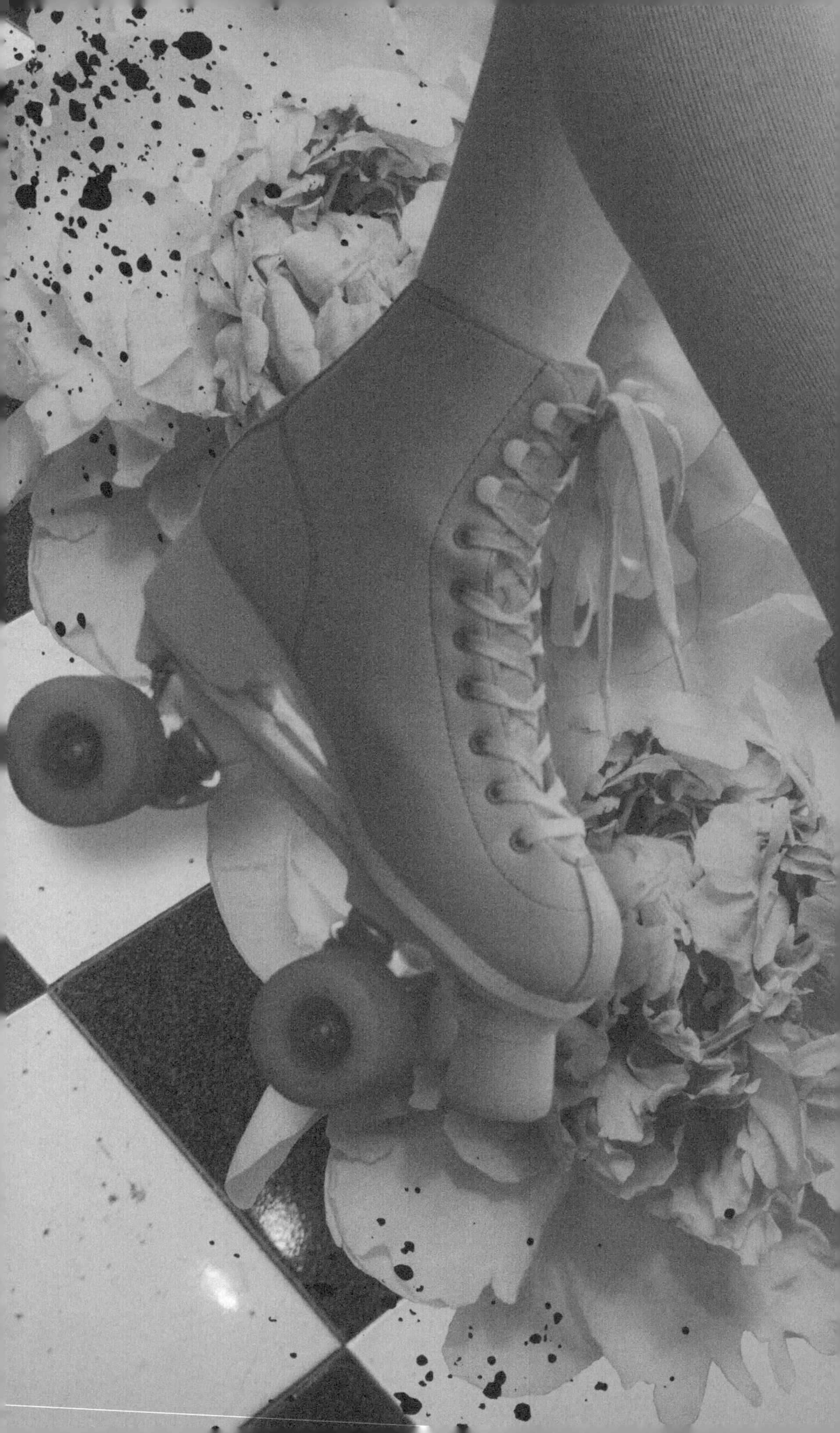

23

MILLIE

THERE ARE several reasons why I decided to cut myself like bait on a hook. It was to lure in the shark that's been after me. I've been treading their waters for far too long, and I'm ready for it to stop. I'm staring him down with pure, unwavering determination rooted in anger. Watching Hayden attempt to save me from King Davenport repeatedly but only resulting in failure...it's breaking my heart. So I'll do what I must. If I have to kill myself so that he can no longer spend his days in a constant state of mind of dreary over me, then so be it.

This Southern Vampire King is the reason why I can't be home with my family. With Cole. My friends. My school.

My father.

It felt like Hayden was in trouble...and as much as I'm angry with him—as much as I despise what he's done to me, I don't want him getting hurt, especially over me. It's an unfamiliar, weird emotion, but I don't want my captor hurt.

I focus on the blood falling down my arm, and it drops onto the floor. I'm breathing heavily as the pain from the cut still hasn't hit me yet. I tear my eyes from the vampires before me, realizing I may have cut myself too deep. The blood is overwhelming, so I shut down as I watch the one with bright blue, vibrant eyes launch himself forward like a bat, and I squeeze my eyes shut, preparing for my demise.

But it never comes. I wait and wait for it as my life flashes in my head—all the things I regret, all the good moments, and all the things I still want to accomplish.

I'm holding myself like I did at the concert when Hayden killed innocents and other vampires. Praying and wishing I was in my own snow globe again.

I close my eyes tight, and the pain in my arm no longer matters. What feels like hours lasts only minutes as I keep my eyes and ears closed.

"Baby...you're safe. Millie, look at me."

His dashing voice is muffled. I'm scared. I'm scared of the world we live in. I'm scared of hurting. I'm scared of *him*.

"Let me look at it," Hayden begs.

I shake my head.

"Is he gone? Is he dead? Is it all over?" I cry out softly.

"You're safe, baby. He's gone. You will always be safe with me...and *only me*." He says it like it's a promise.

"Let me take care of this for you." He gently holds my profusely bleeding arm like I'm going to shatter.

I can't look at him while he does it. I know what's coming.

His icy tongue grazes the blood. He's licking it away. After a few long strokes, a bandage coils over my wound. I bury my eyes in my other hand as he takes care of me. I try not to scream. I'm gritting my teeth so hard that soft whimpers follow.

"I'm so sorry. I'm so fucking sorry you're hurt, baby." He lifts me into his arms like I'm featherlight.

"My prince, we can take her to another room. It's already prepared—"

Hayden cuts off the Kingsguard. "No! She stays with me for the rest of her time."

Hayden's room is incredible. It's dark, with bookshelves everywhere—vintage decor from a century ago. Candles lit everywhere. The same candles that never seem to die.

"Hayden. I should go back into my room. I—"

"You belong with me," he clips out. He closes and locks the door behind us with a skeleton key.

I close my mouth as I watch him. Everything feels like it's going in slow motion. He's different with me. He's still aggressive as ever, but there's devotion in his tone. In his movement. In his eyes.

Action speaks louder than words when I'm with him.

"You're mine, Millie. Don't be afraid. You'll never have to be afraid of me. I won't ever hurt you."

He lifts off my blood-stained garments, leaving me naked and bare. I'm staring back at his muscled chest. Tan, perfectly contoured like the devil took his time creating this sinfully handsome bloodlust demon. He tilts my chin upwards to meet his cold, ice-blue eyes. His dashing face is still littered with deep bruises and cuts.

"What you did..." His smooth voice seeps into my ears, making my nerves coil with desire. His voice wreaks havoc on my body. It's soothing and deep, forcing my common sense nowhere to be found. He shakes his head disapprovingly. His dark brows pinch together like he's disappointed, but then there's a glimpse of happiness in those blue irises. I've never seen him like this before. He licks his lips and trails a slender finger up and down my neck where he marked me. The only thing I can hear is my fast breathing. The tension between us is so thick because I know what's coming.

"I need you...Millie. I want you. And I want you now. Surrender your soul to me. *Surrender every part of your body to me...*"

He doesn't have to explain in detail. I know what he means. I know he craves me *entirely*. I just thought...Cole would always be my first.

A tear falls from my eye, and he wipes it away with pained, narrow brows.

"Hayden...I've never—I—"

"I know."

"Please, Hayden. I just want to go home now. The war is over, isn't it?"

He nods, his jaw flexing like he's about to ruin me in ways that he craves.

He knows he has no reason now to keep me here. The war is over. The rebellious king of the south is dead. No one wants to break the law by killing me anymore because it'll result in them being imprisoned for eternity or burned in the inferno. Hayden exemplified the Southern Vampires at the concert festival by putting their heads on spikes. Now? He killed a King. I'm still new to this whole vampire world, but I think if anyone tries to challenge the Dragos or the law, they'll think twice.

"It's over. Let me go home. I won't tell anyone about your existence. I can forget about all of this. You can move on. I can move on," I plead with him, desperately in a high-pitched request. I do everything I can to keep my voice from shaking, but it's not enough to mask the pain in every syllable.

He smiles. And for a second there, I think he's going to

agree with me. But then his eyes flash to crimson, and the darkness in his soul comes alive.

"There is no moving on for me *or for you*. Don't you get it? You're the only light in my life. You think I'm going to let you go?" he growls low and sultry.

Another tear falls out of my eye.

"It's the right thing to do. Let me go home," I mutter.

"Why would you want to go back there? *What home?*" he spits out with amusement. "Why would you want to return to a place where you're always hurting? Where you're never seen? Where you aren't loved the way you should be?" He leans forward, kisses my cheek, and brushes his bloody knuckles against my face, leaving streaks of black.

His question blindsides me. I stiffen and ache all over. The truth gets slapped into my face.

I glance away from him and instead close my eyes as I whisper in a broken tone, "It's all I've ever known. *Pain and isolation are my home. I'm used to it.*"

Years and years of everything going wrong, watching my mother in an abusive relationship and always wondering where my father was, did something to me. It molded me into someone who's addicted to pain and fear because it's all I've ever known how to live with.

Maybe that's why I understand you, Hayden. Perhaps that's why I like you.

He smiles, but it's cold and more rigid than steel.

"You leave me, Millie...and I will burn my own damn kingdom to the ground. You deny me, and I will make everyone around you hurt for it. I will never stop. I have fallen in love with you. Don't run from me...don't run from *us*."

My heart drops and shatters.

"What do you mean?" I breathe out, my tongue trembling.

"You know exactly what I mean." His sinister threat sends every hair on my body to stand.

He's going to hurt everyone I love if I try to escape? If I try to leave him?

He's not giving me a choice to leave?

"I thought it was against the law in your world to marry a Valkyrie."

"I'm a prince. The Depraved Prince. No one dares to fuck with me. And I will be king soon."

I shift uncomfortably.

"Do you want something happening to your dad? To your mother...to Nash? Don't make me breathe that little co-worker of yours's name." He trembles with wrath and possessiveness. Even when he's in his vampire mode, he's still hypnotizingly beautiful. "I'll kill anyone who tries to take you from me. I don't care who they are. I think I've proved that to you since the night we met."

I freeze at his vicious words. When he mentions Cole, it's like venom taints the air, making it hard to breathe. It's like just the thought of Cole makes him want to lose his shit.

With watery eyes and a strangled whisper, I force my words to spill out. "You're insane."

He smirks devilishly at my insult.

"That's the point."

Is this what he's come to? The man who saved me from meeting my demise multiple times just to keep me chained to his world selfishly like a prisoner? Is staying here in this Cathedral to keep my parents, my brother, and my mother alive...*my only option?*

What do I say?

He's threatening to kill the ones I love if I don't choose him. I care for him. I do. But this is depravity and immoral.

"If you try to leave me again, I will drag you back here and make sure to hold you tighter than before," he promises me darkly and cruelly. Another shiver kisses every organ inside me like electrocution.

He caresses my palm with his hand, soft, heavenly, and warm. His touch is the complete opposite of his dark soul and malice promises.

"You could have anyone else, Hayden. *Anyone*. You need to be with another vampire to match your ways of living. I can't be what you need. I don't want to be a vampire. I don't want to live forever."

"*You want me though*, don't you?" He places his palm on my chest and smiles dashingly. "Your heart skips a beat every time I touch you. *I can hear it*. Your brown eyes shine brighter whenever you look at me. *I can see it*. You already confessed that I've altered your soul. *I can feel it*," he tells me in a rough, deep, lustrous murmur.

He's right. But this is all so wrong. It doesn't change anything. It doesn't change that he's a monster; his actions tell me he's far more sinister than the devil.

I can't speak anymore. I don't think he will listen to reasoning tonight...*or ever*. I can't deny that I'm attracted to him. But I still want a life of freedom. I want to go back to my life before I met him.

He removes his hand from my chest and carries me to his bed. He lays me down gently and hovers over me, careful not to crush me with his body weight. He settles in between my legs, and I'm tempted to push him away, but I refuse. I don't want to piss him off. And another part of me is addicted to the thrill he inflicts. My body yells the truth when my words deceive me.

"I promise you...you will have everything you could ever want or need. I have all the money and resources in the world to spoil you with. Do you want to go to the moon? It's done. You want me to buy hundreds of houses and the rarest of diamonds for you to wear? Consider it bought. Do you want me to be faithful to you until the end of time? I'll be hopelessly devoted to you, Millie Flores." His hair falls across his face, and I'm tempted to push it away. He's going to get what he wants like he always does.

"Say something," he pleads with wide, curious eyes, looking vehemently from my own, searching vigorously for a response. He cups my face, brushing his thumb in small circles on my cheek.

I'm still as my mind runs in about ten different directions.

It's the people pleaser in me.

I don't care that I'm hurting. I don't care that people beat me down until I can't feel anymore. I don't care if they just take and take from me. I just want them to be happy, even if they cause me pain. I refuse to let this dark world take the light from me. I don't want to become the monster they want me to be. I don't want to match their darkness.

I don't want to break. I won't let anyone break me.

I need to make sure everyone is okay...even if that means I drown.

"Do you want me to burn the world and everyone you love in it, Millie?"

I shake my head.

"Good girl," he breathes against my neck as he presses his mouth on the side of my neck. I feel the sharpness of his fangs. I'm already preparing for him to feed from me.

"Do you understand that there's nothing in this world that will stop me from having you? Not even yourself?" Dark adoration laces his hungry tone.

I nod.

"So then tell me, baby. What do you want?" He dares me as if I have a choice. "The war may be over, but that doesn't mean that's your sanctuary. *I am.*" He growls, and his teeth slice me open without him having to bite and suck. They barely grazed my neck when I felt the pain strike, and a warm trickle of red rolls down my neck. I groan and tense underneath him while he unleashes a beastly growl from his throat. He hums sadistically as he watches me bleed. "I've always been your sanctuary...*and you are mine.*"

He pulls back, his injuries and bruises already disappearing like they were never there in the first place.

I swallow as the demons in his blue eyes dance in devotion, consuming me.

"I do want you. I want you so much...but it makes me feel crazy. I can tell you what I don't want, and that's your money. I don't want it or care for it. And I also crave a life without vampires, Hayden. Let me go," I croak out through my tightening throat.

A minute ago, Hayden and I almost died. Now, he wants me to surrender more than he's already taken?

He stiffens, going rigid at my request, but then his fangs reappear like a threat, and it sends shivers down my spine. My heart thunders, and I want to melt yet run away. How can those two emotions and responses mesh together and co-exist?

"I can't do that. I can't lose you." He pulls back as he shifts into something horrifying. "Centuries on this planet, and no one, not one fucking soul, holds a candle to what you do to me!" He snarls as my denial suffocates him—a vein bulges in his neck, and my curiosity about his kind piques.

"You are rare, Millie. And I'm not talking about your blood. You carry something inside you that makes me forget about the dark demons that plague my numb, soulless mind when I'm around you...*please.*"

I gasp.

He said it. He really said the word, please.

"I'm begging you, baby. *Please*...don't run from us. Or I'll turn into something far worse." Another ultimatum to get me to bow down.

Worse? Can he do worse things?

I inhale sharply as if I got hit in the stomach. My heart skips a beat, and despite what has happened, I know what type of darkness he's talking about.

Demons that crawl into your mind without your permission. Demons that kill you on the inside and destroy you one day at a time. I know that darkness. It's the type of darkness I fight every single day.

I like him. I really, *really*, like him, yet I'm so angry with him.

The good that I try to keep within me prevails in this moment. I want to take his pain away. I want to make him feel seen. Maybe I'm the only one in his life who sees past his depravity and dives deep into the origin of his story. We all have a story, and I need his to change.

"Please," he begs again, his whole body intensifying as he awaits my answer. "Give yourself to me!"

Dammit Hayden.

I've already given you my heart the night we met. I just didn't know it yet.

"Yes... let's fight our dark demons together," I concede as heat implodes my veins, and I give into our game.

I look at him with wide eyes as a tear falls out and rolls down the side of my face until it's in my hair. I reposition myself underneath him. I open my legs and welcome his already hardened, thick, and massive cock that pokes through his clothes.

A victorious smile paints his handsome features. His sharp

canines glisten, and he unleashes that animalistic growl right before he sinks his teeth into me. I wiggle and cringe as he sucks at my neck. Pain with euphoric unreal pleasure erupts like the fourth of July throughout my body and mind.

It's like damn morphine every time he bites me. His bite is an addictive drug. He pulls my entire body off the bed with one arm, lifting me into him greedily, like he wants to tear my throat out and devour me completely.

"Do you realize the amount of strength I have to have not to rip you apart until all of your blood is inside me? You're fucking divine, Millie...and all mine."

My clit throbs, my pussy aches to be filled, and he presses his cock onto my pussy over our clothes. Dry humping each other as he sucks the blood out of me.

I yank his soft, thick hair strands, eliciting a vampiric growl. He gets off my neck and goes to my chest. He bites my breast, and I moan out. He returns to my neck, but this time, he goes to the other side.

His sharp teeth cut into me, and I pull on his hair, pressing his face more into my neck as if that'll stop the pain. I'm trembling and shaking, and my heart is hammering painfully because I want him inside me.

Suddenly, blackness clouds the corners of my eyes, but the morphine-like pleasure that makes me lust for him continues. It's as if every time he bites me, lust fills me like a curse, making me crave to get bitten, overpowering.

I start to see stars, and my hand falls from his hair as my muscles become mush.

"Hayden...I think...I think I'm going to pass out," I softly murmur as I grow cold and weak. He's never taken this much blood from me.

"Fuck, baby. I can't stop. Tell me to stop. Tell me to fucking stop," he growls weakly through his sucking.

I gather and muster all my strength and push at his chest with my palms. He's strong, rigid, and his cock is harder than concrete as he rubs himself on my pussy.

Everything feels so damn good, but I know if he doesn't stop draining me, I'll die.

"Stop! Hayden, stop!" I grit out my plea, and to my surprise, he listens just in time before my vision goes black.

He restrains himself. He grants me space but still hovers over my body as my blood drips from his mouth. He clenches his jaw repeatedly, with guilt evident in his eyes.

He's panting hard as his tongue grazes his lips, licking my blood off his mouth.

My senses come back, and I no longer feel lightheaded.

He reaches for the top of his shirt and begins to unbutton it. I watch his every move, enchanted, mesmerized by his beauty, and yet scared of what's to come next.

He's midway, and I'm staring at his muscled chest with heavy breaths. I cover my breasts with my forearms as the reality starts to sink in.

"Are you going to make love to me?" I whisper shyly.

He chuckles deep and mouthwatering.

"I'm going to fuck you, baby." He finishes undressing himself and goes straight for my clothes. His vampire powers kick in, and in a split second, my panties are ripped to shreds, and I'm completely exposed to him.

His eyes gleam with adoration as his gaze rifts up and down my breasts and naked pussy like I'm the most perfect dream he's come to know. He shifts in between my legs again, caging me into his body, and I feel *him* at my entrance.

My chest heaves at the unknown sensation.

"Once I fuck you, and I will fuck you...*you're mine*. If any man tries to touch you, I will hurt him. If anyone tries to kiss you, I will kill them. I won't even blink twice about killing for you. You're my property that no one gets to look at as long as you're with me. Do you understand?"

I nod.

"I need to hear you say yes. Or I'll stop. I'll stop this right now. I'll become a ghost, so you'll never see me again."

I contemplate. I'm actually thinking of saying no, but I'm trapped in the chains he has around my heart. I feel seen, heard, and *craved*.

"Yes."

I want him. I want him now. I want this.

He kisses my lips gently right before he positions the head of his dick at my entrance, teasing me. He slicks the tip of his dick up and down through my slit, circling my throbbing and needy clit with calculated motions. I sink my teeth into my bottom lip to prevent myself from moaning. I'm about to lose myself already, and he hasn't started. I tilt my head to the side and arch my back, still watching his intimidating, starving gaze.

"You make me feel alive. If this is what it's like, you'll never be free of me." He thrusts into me, and I scream from the unfamiliar intrusion I've never felt before. His girth stretches me in a way I know I won't recover quickly.

It. Fucking. *Hurts*.

My eyes widen, and I moan out a sharp scream.

"Oh, God, Hayden. Hayden! It hurts...*it hurts!*" I hold him tighter, but I don't want him to stop. *God, please don't ever stop.*

He kisses the tears running down my cheeks, making me forget the pain for a second.

He continues to move in and out slowly, breaking into me, dissolving my virginity, and I close my eyes tightly shut as I let my doubts go. I turn my head to the side as pain floods everywhere. He makes me feel too full. So damn full down there. I feel like I'm being torn and reborn at the same time.

"You're too big," I whimper.

"The pain will go away soon, Millie," he promises me as he continues to thrust slowly and passionately like he's savoring every second of being inside. He glances at his cock rocking into me and smirks that same sinful one that makes me melt. I dare to take a peek, and there's blood coating his veiny perfect cock. I feel like I'm on drugs. I feel like this is a dream. He's my bad dream I don't want to wake up from. Hayden is my monster, and tonight I accepted it.

Our harsh moans fit perfectly like a symphony that filters the silence in his room. I can't help the sounds that are coming out of my mouth. I watch my sinfully handsome vampire captor fuck me with perspiration leaking down his chest. He's losing himself inside me like I'm his haven. I don't ever want him to stop pumping, touching, and loving me like this.

I'm giving into this sick game of his and he's winning.

I claw at his shoulders, and he roars with satisfaction. He buries his face in my neck but restrains himself from biting. Instead, he licks at my neck, cleaning up whatever blood that lingers from earlier.

"Tell me you're mine," he commands.

Thrust.

"I'm yours."

"Tell me you crave me."

Thrust.

"I crave you." His cock starts to feel heavenly, and the pain is long gone. As I register his words, the headboard kicks into the wall with loud bangs.

"Tell me you love me."

I'm breathless as he picks up his strength and speed, pounding into me angrily and crazy.

"Ah!" I scream as pleasure rocks me violently. My eyes spring open from how drastically everything has changed. Before, it was slow and calculated. Now? His movements are messy and powerful. The muscles in his triceps tighten, and he tears open a pillow beside my head when I don't respond. The sound of fabric being torn open and holes drilled into the wall from the headboard ring into my ear.

"Tell me you love me!" He growls impatiently as he claws the headboard and crushes it in his grasp. The wood cracks and pieces of it fall onto the side of us.

"I love you! I love you, Hayden. I love you..." I moan out, and a sharp scream from my throat follows as pure bliss explodes; my entire body trembles and I'm in a dark paradise. Shutting my eyes, my climax possesses my body, nirvana inking my veins, and my pussy clenches down on his cock as I orgasm. Oh my God, he feels so damn good.

The thrill he inflicts upon my body is addicting, and I already want more. Hayden's eyes transform from blue into those crimson, vibrant, vampiric red eyes. They glow, and the obsidian in his eyes dilate.

"Fuck. Millie. Fuck!" Hayden powerfully thrusts into me faster as he grips my hips tight with his free hand, so hard bruises will form. "I'm greedy...so fucking greedy for you," he whispers into my neck as he comes undone, and his thrusts slow down, but they're deep and full of passion as he fills me with his cum.

"I'm sorry, Millie. You're mine now...and for that, *I am sorry.*" He sincerely apologizes as I ride the blissful surges.

It's like he knows *what he is*, and what he's doing to keep me isn't right. He knows he isn't being fair or reasonable. He knows I'm trapped but doesn't want to lose me. The lengths he will go to to have me with him are fucked up, and he's apologizing for it.

He cups my ass still, his fingers digging into my skin with no remorse as he still relishes being inside me. He doesn't want to pull out.

Our breaths are fast and deep, and I reach for his face, brushing my fingers through his hair. Hayden closes his eyes and tilts his head towards my fingers. He looks different. There's solace, a glimpse of a good man I know he is. I feel satisfied.

I groan, and I already feel the aftermath on my strained muscles.

"Are the demons gone?" I whisper with a shaky voice.

"Only when I'm inside you," he rasps and falls over closer. He kisses me, and I return the mutual passion. He cuts my lips open with his fangs, forcing the blood from my lips to join our dancing tongues. I like this side of Hayden. I love his gentle promises and caresses. The demons in his head and soul need to be silenced, even if it's at the expense of my freedom.

The demons are gone. My family is safe. The Southern Vampire King is dead.

Everything will be okay.

Everything will fall into place.

And I will find a way out of this.

He rests on his elbows and brushes his thumb against my cut lip. Red stains his thumb, and he licks it. He hums deeply and is animalistic. His cock grows harder while he's still inside me.

"As much as I want to fuck you all night, you need rest to recover. I took too much blood from you." He kisses my forehead, gets out of me, and pulls me onto his chest. I lie on top of him as he pulls the blankets over us.

He's cold and rigid, but I'm too exhausted to move. I'm tired, drained, and depleted. And yet, the man I fear is still the only person that makes me feel loved, safe, and at peace. He makes it easy to fall asleep. I blink uneasily as I remember how King Davenport almost took Hayden from me. I shudder against his cold muscles. My fingers lurch against the veins that run along the perfect V of his lower body.

"I'm not going anywhere tonight. Go to sleep, baby girl. I'll see you next moon." He knows what I'm feeling...*always*.

"I'll see you next moon," I repeat as I close my eyes for the night.

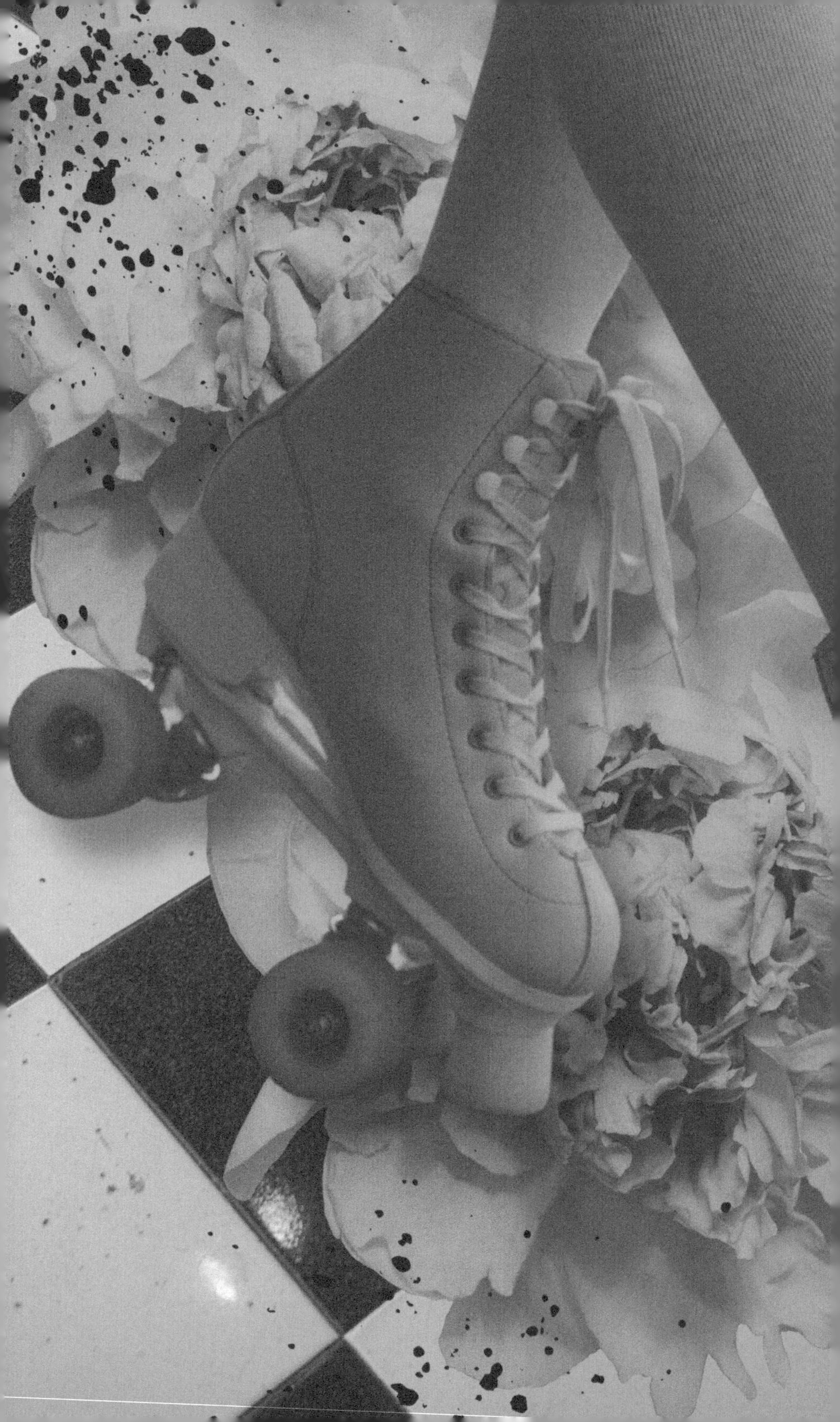

24

MILLIE

WHEN I WAKE UP, it takes a minute to gather my thoughts. I blink slowly as I take in Hayden's room. His arm is around my waist, securing me into him like he's afraid I'll disappear. There are no windows in here. The candles that never die out illuminate his room dimly.

I shift my legs, and soreness all over strikes back. Soreness in between my thighs, my hips, my wrists, and where I cut myself to distract the Southern King.

It's still wrapped up perfectly.

I pull off the bandage slowly. I hold it in my other hand and inspect it. I expect to see inflammation around the wound, but it already looks well into healing.

That's a good sign, I guess.

The memories of last night come back.

Hayden killed the Southern King.

His ultimatum if I try to escape again.

And then I surrendered myself to him...*entirely*.

He came inside me. I felt the evidence of it drip down my

thighs. The blood from him breaking into my virginity was left on his blankets, right underneath our hips.

I'm on birth control because I get painful periods. But in just a few days, I'll need another shot. Now that I'm actually sexually active...wait, will I even need it?

I want to wake him up. There are so many questions about how all of this works. How did he become a vampire? If biting a human isn't enough to turn them into a vampire, what is the process like? How does the vampire royalty thing work? When can I see my parents again? My brother? My mother? And...Cole?

I'm afraid of what he'll do to him or any guy that comes near me.

I peek a glance at Hayden and turn my head on the pillow. There's fluff and torn fabric everywhere on the bed. The headboard is crushed in that one spot where he gripped it violently when I didn't tell him I loved him right away. I could tell he was holding back his vampire strength when he fucked me last night. This man could crush all my bones with a simple flick but chose to fuck me as gently as possible as he could.

Since the war is over...am I able to walk around the cathedral freely now?

I can unlock his door. He thinks he won't try to escape since I promised him I wouldn't. It would be perfect to take advantage now that he's gone to sleep for the day.

I scoot away until my feet touch the floor, and his arm falls to the bed. I expect a creature-like growl to follow suit...or for him to pull me back into him. But nothing. A weight falls off my shoulders, and I wait a couple more seconds before I make my move to stand.

I watch him, and he's still. His chest rises and falls like a human would. He's on his back, his head tilted to the side, and all the bruises and cuts are gone from fighting vampires last night. It's like they weren't there in the first place.

He's out cold, sleeping like a rock. This is my chance. I assume it's still early in the day, so I have more time to put distance between him and me.

But then his ominous promise echoes into my mind, sending goosebumps trickling down every corner of my skin.

"You leave me, Millie...and I will burn my own damn kingdom to the ground. You deny me, and I will make everyone around you hurt for it. I will never stop. I have fallen in love with you. Don't run from me..."

"If you try to leave me again, I will drag you back here and make sure to hold you tighter than before."

The shivers are more robust, and I tuck that plan away.

I feel like a new person after sharing something I've never shared with anyone before. This was my first time being intimate...and my first time was with a vampire.

Just that thought alone has me questioning my sanity. Is this all real?

I rub my temples with my fingers as I search for clothes while naked. I blink hard as I go through Hayden's drawers and grab the first clothes I can find.

Black sweater and sweatpants that look way too big for me, but that'll do for now. I walk into a bathroom that looks very similar to mine and take a shower.

The entire time I clean myself up, I stare at his bitemarks and scrub them with a loofah, hoping and wishing they would disappear. Then I scrub the one that is a permanent scar on my neck until my skin is raw. But no matter how badly I wash, they're there. I think it's time to accept that I've become his own personal supply of morphine.

AFTER TAKING A SHOWER, I REALIZE IT'S ALREADY PAST noon. Being kept up late at night is starting to catch up to me. I'm getting closer and closer to staying up all night and sleeping all day like Hayden wants.

As soon as I open the door to Hayden's room with the skeleton key, two Kingsguards are waiting for me. They escort me down to a luxurious dining room. Red stained glass is everywhere. Showering red rays of the sun at a very long vintage wooden table that looks able to seat about twenty people. There sits a fresh breakfast plate with naturally squeezed and pulped orange juice.

Chilaquiles.

"Um, this is one of my favorite meals. I haven't had it in forever. How—"

"Hayden gave us a list of all your favorite meals." As if the Kingsguard can read my mind, he mumbles behind me with a deadpan look.

Of course, Hayden knows. He knows everything somehow. My stalker turned vampire captor.

I clear my throat as I stare at the meal before me. My mouth waters, and I go for the fried pinto beans first.

My grandmother made this for me growing up when I would spend every weekend with her because I couldn't stand being around Santiago.

After scarfing down my breakfast, I care for Hayden's mother's garden. I water the plants, and the anticipation of watching them bloom pulls at my heart. I don't know why, but it makes Hayden's mother happy to have me here...taking care of her plants.

I love peonies.

It's a few minutes before sundown. I smell the air, and if nature has a scent, this is it. Woods, dirt, the sound of the river flowing, and waterfalls are the white noise I dream about coming to life. Birds are singing, and I close my eyes, enjoying the outdoors. I purposefully take longer outside to enjoy nature. I've never been to this part of the country, and it hits me.

I need to travel more.

The sky is dark, full of shades of blue and purple mixed together. The air is fresh, warm, and perfect for a walk.

But that's a fantasy because as long as I'm here, I will always be a prisoner without freedom.

"Hurry up, Ms. Flores!" Charles barks from the door.

I grimace at his voice. Rolling my eyes, I mimic his commands like a petulant child with an immature mockery of silent words.

Charles is following me everywhere I go. As soon as I enter the Cathedral after watering the plants and caring for the garden, I see Queen Drago.

Hayden's mom.

"Isn't she such a delight?" She's dressed in gothic black garments. A long dress that goes down past her knees as she watches me. I walk in shyly.

"All watered. Should expect to bloom very soon." I smile, rubbing the leftover dirt from my hand on the sides of my clothes.

"Millie. It's been a while since..." She chokes up, and I swear I see blackness enter the whites of her eyes like she's about to cry.

"Since what?" I murmur softly.

"Since my son has smiled—a true pure smile he got from

not inflicting pain on others. It's been a while since something came into this Cathedral that made us *all* feel something good. You belong here, Millie."

I don't know what to say. It seems to me that they all want to keep me here...except Hayden's dad. Speak of the devil; he's down the hall. I peek over Cordelia's shoulder, and his eyes flash red. It seems to me he's trying everything he can not to murder me as the ends of his lips tremble from disgust.

This man hates me...

"Cordelia!" He shouts at her with a low growl that bounces off the black walls.

Her smile slowly fades. I stand there awkwardly, and she reaches for me. I tense up as her cold knuckles collide with my cheek.

Is she going to hurt me?

But then she slides her hand up and down, soothingly, like a mother would to her daughter—something my mother has never done. The gesture is unfamiliar but warm.

"You have something special about you. You're too kind...too—"

Come here, Millie.

Hayden's command echoes in my head like he's far away but so close. He talks to me the same way he did while chasing me through the crowd at the concert when he saved me from Cal.

I jump, my heart backflips, and my chest tightens at his deep voice. My body movements stop Cordelia from finishing her sentence. She watches me like she knows her son calls to me.

She smiles and walks away to her fuming husband.

Millie. I can feel you. Come to me, baby.

Dark butterflies swarm, and I react. After Cordelia leaves

with her husband, I begin my journey back to the vampire who holds me captive.

After about five minutes, I'm back in front of his bedroom. Charles opens the door to his room for me, and I walk in.

The first thing I see is the broken headboard. The wall has holes, and the bed sheets are torn. My brow lifts curiously. *Where is he?*

The moon shines through, and a gust of calm, cool wind hits me, making my black hair fly past my shoulder. I change my gaze to the night sky a few feet away.

Hayden.

He stands tall on the balcony with a cigarette in his hand. He's wearing a black sweater, dark pants, and black boots. His hair is combed back on the sides, and strands fall seamlessly on his forehead.

He's not in his signature suit.

He turns around and smiles as he flicks his cigarette. He motions me forward with his fingers.

I swallow nervously.

As soon as I step on the balcony, he grabs my hand and pulls me to his chest. He kisses me hard, pressing his lips to mine as he consumes me with his mouth. A flutter ignites in my chest, and my core pulsates. And then he pulls back. He cups my face in his large, cold hands.

"How do you feel?"

I sigh, with heat creeping into my cheeks as I remember him inside me. The memories of our bodies tangled forces my clit and chest to pulse. Fireworks explode inside my stomach as flashes of him, slicking in and out of me last night with sweat, anchor me into that familiar wave of euphoria.

"Sore," I murmur.

"That's normal. Have you eaten? Drank water?" His

concern for my health is evident. He almost destroyed me with his cock last night, and I loved every dark second.

"Yes, and yes."

His thumb brushes the scar on my neck, and he admires the branding he gave me with his teeth.

"Good girl." He leans in for a kiss. I tense up as he leans down, expecting him to cut my lips open again, but he's gentle. He stays there like he's cherishing my warm flesh on his cold one.

"I can't forgive myself for almost killing you last night." He grinds his teeth as he pulls away. He brushes my hair with his hand with a broken look. His blue eyes look lost in mine.

"It's okay. I'm here. I'm alive. Bruised...but alive," I joke with a forced smile, but he doesn't laugh at my dry humor.

"The thought of hurting you kills me." He tells me as he stares straight into my soul. His sweater hugs all of his tensed muscles so well.

"Hayden...I have a lot of questions on how all of this works. You came inside me."

He smirks like he's proud of himself. "And you're on birth control, are you not?"

I furrow my brows at his bluntness.

How does he know?

"How do you know that?" I step back, but he pulls me back into him again. His scent hits my nostrils, and I restrain myself from burying in his arms. Everything about him is so intoxicating.

"I've been watching you for months after I rescued you in the club."

"Can vampires get humans pregnant?" I palm my belly. The thought of carrying Hayden's child runs through my mind.

"Yes." He puts out his cigarette and leans on the balcony

railing. My eyes widen. I need to get my shot again or make the man wear condoms if we're going to continue to do this.

"Would it be such a bad thing if you carry my child? I do need an heir one day." He puts his calloused, cold palm on my hand as he gazes at my belly like he's imagining my nine months pregnant bump.

I stiffen and look down at our conjoined hands.

"And there's no way in hell I'm having a child with anyone else now that I've fallen in love with you, and you are mine," he says.

"Hayden..." I start but don't finish. I don't know what to say. He notices my hesitation and backs off.

"What other questions do you have, baby?" He turns around and crosses his big arms over his chest. He stares at his boots briefly before looking at me like he's mesmerized. Like a man obsessed.

"How do humans become vampires? If biting me is not enough, how does one become like you?

His face falls, and he's the most serious I've ever seen him.

"Do you want to be one? Because that can be arranged. Just say the word, and I'll turn you. We can be together for eternity. Have you changed your mind?" He takes a step toward me with hope written all over his body language. I swallow nervously and shake my head.

"I haven't changed my mind, Hayden."

He sighs and straightens his back in disappointment. His bones pop as he stretches.

"The powers are inevitable because of your blood. I don't care about that...all I care about is having you around for eternity."

"What happens to a Valkyrie when they change?"

"A Valkyrie has never become like us before. So I don't have an answer for you."

He turns around and looks at the full moon behind us.

I'm about to ask why, but he interrupts my question.

"In order to turn, you have to consent. It's kind of like the warning: never invite vampires into your home. Well, never invite a vampire to bite you. You have to invite me to turn you. More specifically, recite the words 'Volo unum esse cum morte' three times."

I quirk a brow when he speaks to me in a language I don't recognize.

"It's Latin, little Bambi. It means 'I want to be one with death.'"

I shiver.

"You have to say those words before I bite you or in the act. As soon as you finish, your heart will stop beating, and you will be immortal."

"Were you born a vampire?"

"No...my mother had me when she was still a human. I turned when I was around thirty."

"I thought you guys couldn't kill Valkyrie's? Our relationship is forbidden in your world. It is the law, is it not?" I point out, and he scoffs.

"Nothing, and no one, will forbid me from having you. I will be king and I wouldn't kill you. I would turn you...if you consent. I want to keep you with me." His tone tweaks with madness.

"Why are your eyes red and the southern vampire's blue?"

"Every vampire's eyes are the color of their maker. Northern vampires are red. Southern's are blue. East is green, and west is magenta. Whatever color your eyes are is the king you serve."

I place my hands on my hips and pace on the balcony. If he turns me, my eyes will be red like his. This is not a life I aspire to have. I want to stay human, but I can't confess it flatly. I need to convince him to let me go slowly over time.

"I want to finish college. I want to see my parents again." I concede when I stop in front of his chest.

He towers over and smiles like I asked him if unicorns exist.

"You will, I promise. First, I need to speak to my father about something important." He kisses my lips quickly but softly and starts to walk away.

"I'm going to watch TV if you don't mind?"

He opens the door to his room and turns over his shoulder.

"Of course. I'll be back because we have a celebration to announce tonight."

What in the world could we be celebrating? The death of King Davenport, maybe?

"And what is that?" I ask.

"You'll see."

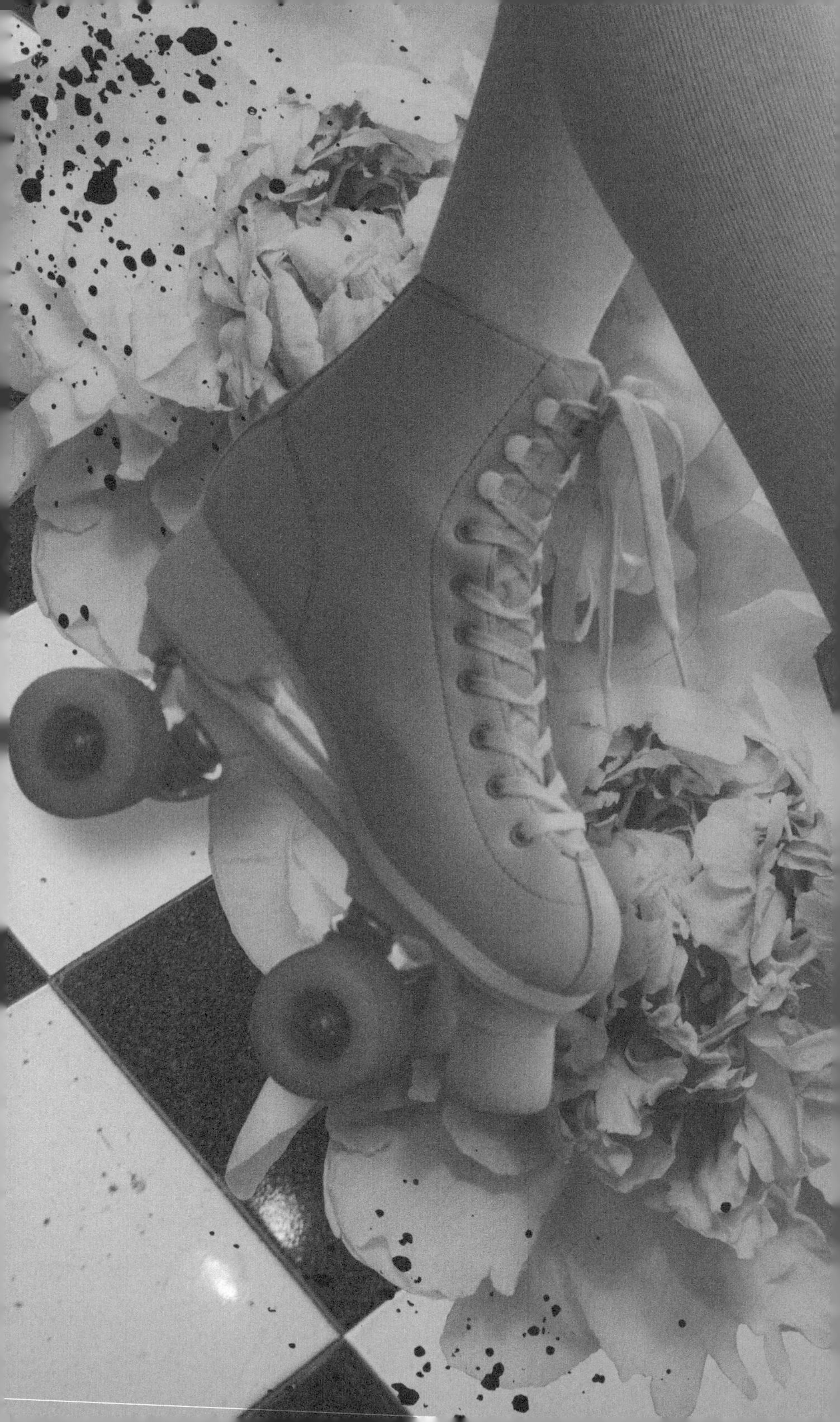

25

MILLIE

IT'S about an hour since he left. So I keep busy with a movie even though I'm starting to fall asleep. Nightmare On Elm Street is over, so I decide to look for another movie to watch while I wait for his return.

 I sit in the bed wearing a sultry black dress Hayden asked me to wear, my back to the new, unbroken headboard. I flip through the channels and realize Hayden has news networks on his.

 Sure enough...I'm staring at a photo of me with a substantial MISSING text on top of it. My brother is there but where's my father? He must be home. I can't imagine what my absence has done to him and everyone that cares about me. They're all pale, with sunken eyes and hollowed cheeks. And then I see my mother, holding onto my older brother, Nash.

 My mother! She's there, she cares about me, she's there, and there's no fucking Santiago in sight.

 They look distraught.

 Cole stands tall. His dark sandy hair looks longer than usual. He always keeps it short, but he looks different. Could it be my absence? Watching him takes me back to my days at the coffee shop. The days when he bossed me around, sprayed me with whipped cream when work was slow, and even our one intimate night during Thanksgiving.

"We all hope Millie is still alive." he stares at the camera like he wants to talk to me. "Millie, we love you. Please come back home. Whoever has her, release her to us. Do the humane thing," Cole begs, and my God, I miss that voice. *I miss him.*

I look at Cole, and my heart flips. My stomach turns to knots, and a tear slips out of my eye as I think about my old life. Leah stands behind him, holding onto my brother Nash.

"Millie."

Hayden's voice startles me like I was caught doing something terrible, and I turn off the TV before I can hear the rest. I pull my knees to my chest and let the remote fall to the side of my hip.

"Hayden...I—" I look at the dark television. "I was flipping through the channels when I saw the news."

He stares at the black screen as he stalks forward. He stops at the end of the bed and then back to me.

"I could feel you heat up when you saw him." Shit. He's referencing Cole. He had to be standing there watching me.

"Do you love him?" He asks me with a tone that sends shivers down my spine like he's ready to destroy the TV so I can never see Cole again.

I shake my head almost too quickly.

"I-I," I stutter. "He's my friend. I care about him, yes." As he clenches his jaw, I slip the words out of my tightening, dry throat. He brushes a hand through his wavy dark black hair as he digests my answer. He nods slightly longer than usual as his chest rises and falls like he's trying to contain his composure.

"You don't love him. You love me..." He walks toward me as

my entire body tightens. "Right?" His hand reaches for mine, and I look at him doe-eyed.

Do I love Cole? I do, in a sense. Being trapped here...held prisoner by a monster, has made me realize many things. It has made me wish I had tried to take things further with Cole despite my doubts.

"Right." I take his hand, and he pulls me up from the bed.

"I spoke to my father."

"About what?"

He smiles, and it takes me aback. It's a pure, genuine one without malice attached to it.

He gets down on one knee, pulls out a box, and presents a ginormous glistening ruby ring. His muscles pull taut as he gazes into my soul.

"Marry me."

My mouth falls open, and my shoulders slant. My thoughts are delayed by a landslide. Still, he looks as hopeful and handsome as ever on his one knee, watching my stunned gaze, with his rugged good looks and glowing blue sharpened eyes. I can't handle it when he looks at me like this. His majestic features are out of this world.

"Marry me. I have to ascend the throne immediately, and I want you to be by my side as I take reign."

I can't speak. His question is rocking my brain. Marriage? To a vampire?

"It's a little fast, I know. But...it feels right. Nothing has ever felt right to me before. You're the first person to make me feel like my disarrayed life makes sense. My purpose in life isn't to rule, little Bambi. *My purpose in life is to keep you*...and I want to prove that to you every day."

His eyes flash red. But they're not from fury, wrath, or lust. I swear it's from solace. I do that to him. He's said it time and time again.

"I love you...*all the time*. I knew you were mine even before we met. Your soul has always belonged to me. I just had to find you. Everything about you, Millie...*everything* makes me want to fall to my knees. I never want to blink, and I never want to leave you for the next moon because I don't want to miss one second where I can't show you how much I love you."

"Can I think about it?" I ask. I sink my front teeth into my bottom lip with trepidation.

His eyes squint, indicating enrage, or maybe he's genuinely hurt at my response. I'm afraid he might let his demons take over after my rejection, so I think quickly.

"It's just that...moments ago, you were promising to end my life, and now you're asking me to be your wife."

He softens his intense gaze.

It's not a lie.

He stands, closes the box, puts it into his pocket, and kisses me roughly.

"You're mine, baby. Even if you can't say it. Your heart, body, and soul do. And that's enough for me." He breathes against my lips, and my heart jolts. Electrical desire pumps through my veins every time he touches me. I can feel his body speak to me. It tells me the honest, raw truth. His actions reciprocate his words. Everything pulls together perfectly whenever he confesses his twisted love for me. He gets a hold of my hips and pushes his hard bulge on the front of my stomach.

"As much as I want to bend you over this bed, lift this pretty dress up, and fuck you in it, I have plans for us tonight."

His tongue grazes my bottom lip, begging for entry, and I welcome him.

"Why not?" I dare him and grind against his hard cock.

"Fuck. Don't do that. If I fuck you, we'll never leave this room..."

I groan as he thrusts back into my waist, forcing me to feel what I do to him. "You're going to make me cum in my pants like this..." he groans.

"What plans?" I complain as I kiss him back harder. The chemistry between us is palpable, and my body obeys without thinking twice about it. It's dark and disturbing, but I can't stop myself from being embraced by someone who haunts me like a shadow. I welcome his ghosts. I'm scared of him, yes, but I'm scared of how my soul comes alive and begs for him to hold me even more.

"I want you to meet my close friends, something I've never done with a woman. They want to meet the girl who's been keeping the Depraved Prince so busy and all to herself... wrapped around her wings."

He pulls my hair back, and I gasp at the quick maneuver. He hovers over my neck; his fangs brush my neck, but he doesn't sink into me.

He feels guilty for almost draining me the first time we had sex. He doesn't want to bite me again. At least not yet.

"Because you are my angel. And I am your demon."

HAYDEN IS DRUNK. HE SMILES AND LAUGHS WITH HIS friends while I sit on his lap. Everywhere I go tonight, he's right by my side, holding my hand or hip. His grasp doesn't falter. He's turned into my shadow knight. Ever since he almost bled me dry, it's like he's afraid to let the cravings take over, along with the lust. He made sure I ate at least one more time before he introduced me to his friends, along with hydration all day.

There are about five of his friends. They're all in leather

jackets and jeans and are also inebriated. One of them holds a cup of red, and I highly doubt it's fruit punch.

Hayden grasps a beer while I dangle my feet and move my head to the music that plays on a boom box. "Creep" by Radiohead. It's one of my favorite songs. I'm so lost in the music, and swaying my hips slightly to the beat, I hadn't noticed Hayden watching me... delighted and encaptured.

I stop dancing, and he blows out his cigarette. His sinful, dashing smirk and his blue eyes twinkle with desire.

"What?" I ask, slightly embarrassed.

"Nothing." He tells me with a pure tilt of his soft pink lips, and it causes a flock of butterflies to swarm crazily into my chest.

He flicks the cigarette and pulls me in by grabbing the back of my head. His lips are on mine, moving with harsh purpose. My entire body turns into fire, and I want to push him away because he's claiming my mouth in front of his friends.

The first thing I taste is the beer and cigarettes on his tongue. He's devouring me, and for a minute, I hesitate. I put my hand on his chest and push against it, but then he growls against my tongue.

"Don't be nervous. They need to know who you belong to. Kiss me back...*hard*." He squeezes my thigh with his huge hand, and I let out a small moan that floats into the fresh woodsy air, and I melt into his body like always. I obey and kiss him harder. I grip his hand on my thigh and squeeze as our tongues dance together. I close my eyes and tune out our surroundings. Hayden tilts his head to the side and does it repeatedly to get deeper. We continue to make out like we're about to tear each other's clothes off and get lost in something forbidden and dark.

"I need to talk to one of the guys about something, and then I'm sending them all home and calling it a night. I want to be in bed with you. I can't wait any longer." He whispers with a deep tone. Images of his teeth deep inside my flesh while his cock is deep in me, making me cry his name, flash through my head. I nod through his kiss, unable to hide the anticipation. I can feel myself getting wet, and my core pulsates with need. He's taken my breath away. I open my eyes to see that even though we're here in Montana, our souls intertwine perfectly together when he's with me, and we're in our own universe. He smiles as he repositions me on the couch. He gives me one last quick kiss on the forehead and stands.

A deadly kiss with my demon disguised as a charming, beautiful man will always be my favorite type of crime.

"I'll be right back, baby." Hayden kisses my lips, and dammit, I melt when he kisses me. He's been so gentle with me since I sacrificed myself for him...and since he fucked me.

I watch him leave, and just the way he walks with so much confidence makes me clench my thighs together. I clear my throat as one of the men stays behind. I wipe my lips and try to control my breathing and escape the hypnotization he always has me in when he touches me.

His friend looks familiar. I stare at him as he drinks his beer. He doesn't make our interaction comfortable, but it's nothing bad. When his eyes flash to red, I flop against the couch.

Why did Hayden think leaving me alone after everything we've been through was a good idea? After knowing the amount of people who've tried to kill me?

Maybe he trusts his friends.

I sink into it more until my back touches the leather. There are multiple reasons why vampires' eyes change...I just hope it's not the one I think.

He walks to me, and I ball my fists.

I don't trust anyone.

He holds his hand to me, and then his eyes change to

normal brown ones. He gives me a friendly smile, and dimples appear on his cheeks.

"Gerard."

I glance warily at his hand, then back to his face. I swallow and shake it.

"Millie." I let him go after two shakes and hold my knees to my chest.

"Why do you look familiar?"

He scoffs and takes a swig of his beer nonchalantly.

"I was with Hayden when we first found you at that nightclub in Texas and rescued you."

The memory flashes in my head, and it all connects.

He helped Hayden kill the men who took me from the coffee shop. I remember their snarls and blood and body parts everywhere. Sometimes, I can hear and see it in my nightmares when I fall asleep. Now, I'm in a relationship with said nightmare.

"Oh...that's right," I murmur. The memories settle in, reminding me that this is not normal. Being here in Montana, taken by a vampire, is not normal, and my heart starts to beat thunderously.

I need to get out of here.

Maybe Gerard can help me.

I need to stay calm if I'm going to try to make a run for it again. Hayden will sense my unease and flashback here in seconds.

"I'm glad to see that you're still alive. The law says we cannot kill you. So you don't have to be scared of me." He chuckles and looks at me like I'm going to join in on the joke and laugh. But instead, I look at him with a blank stare. I pin my vision to the back of him, side to side, looking for any sign of Hayden over his shoulders. They must have gone far.

He catches onto my body language, and I bite my lip. I'm trying to muster up the courage to ask him for help.

Keep calm.

Keep. Calm.

Or Hayden will notice the change in my emotion.

"What's on your mind?" He puts the beer down and walks forward, about to join me on the couch, but I stand up.

"Help me get out of here," I whisper, low with gritted teeth.

"What?" He takes a step back from me like I asked him something wild.

"If it's illegal to kill me in your world, it should be illegal to hold me here against my will, right?" I whisper, and if vampires can go pale, Gerard does and stiffens.

"He has you here against your will?" he asks me, shocked. Perhaps the kiss we just put on display for everyone to see has him questioning my intentions.

I nod fast and look over my shoulder.

All I see is a full moon and tall trees dancing in the wind.

"Oh, Millie. I can't. I'm loyal to Hayden."

"Please! I know there's good in you. Please help me get out of here?" I practically beg, and Gerard looks around us with fear evident in his pursed lips. No, I do not know if there's good in him, or maybe he's just as depraved as Hayden. Still, I need to take my chance.

"Keep it down, or he'll kill me for even considering this request of yours!" He sputters out so quickly that it's hard for me to understand him.

He looks around and then turns to me. He grabs my hand, and I immediately look around for my demon. If Hayden notices any other man has touched me, he'll lose his mind.

"I went to take a piss, and you ran. Okay?" Gerard offers a plan.

My heart flips with hope. Is he really going to help me?

"When he starts to look for you, I'll meet you at my car. It's a Toyota 4unner, parked just through those woods." He points behind him, and I see a bunch of cars parked together in the distance. They are barely visible, but they're there.

Hope is reborn, and tears spring in my eyes.

"Fucking go now, Millie!" He snarls, and I see a side of him that scares me. His fangs grow over his bottom lip, and his eyes pool red.

I nod and mouth my silent thank you. I take off running through the trees, not bothering to see if Hayden can feel me running away. I don't know the extent of his powers, but whatever is keeping him busy must be important.

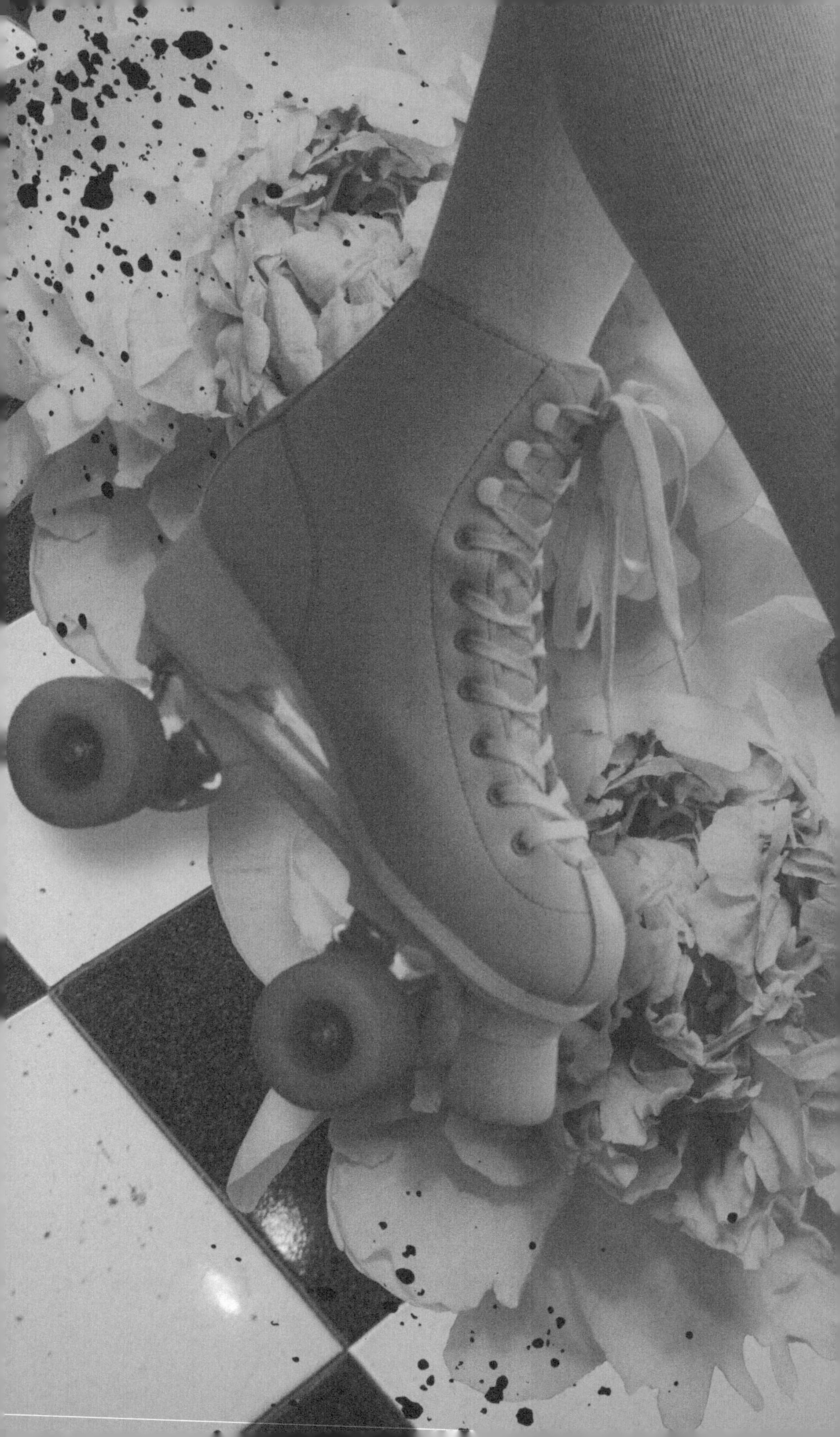

26

MILLIE

THE SOUND of branches breaking underneath my feet and leaves brushing against my body is not enough to overcome the sound of blood rushing in my neck, chest, and ears. At this point, I don't care if Hayden knows I'm trying to leave. I can't lose the fight in me. I can't let the complexity of our relationship blind me forever. My shoes are in my hand as I trip multiple times, but I manage to keep my balance.

"Smells Like A Teen Spirit" by Nirvana plays from the stereo I left behind, and I focus on it to stay somewhat calm as I run through the trees. As I get farther, the volume feels like it's being lowered.

After a few minutes, I make it to the car. My throat burns from breathing in the cold air, and my tongue dries. Even though the temperature is cool, sweat forms above my brow, and I swipe it with my hand. I palm the tinted window of the silver forerunner and try to open it, grasping the handle and trying to pull it, but it's locked.

I pull on the handle desperately over and over again, but to no avail. I'm shaking all over, and I think about ditching the car and Gerard, but then someone grabs me by the shoulder. I squeal and palm my mouth with my hand to muffle the scream.

It's Gerard.

"He's looking for you already. Let's go." He jabs me with his words.

He opens the door, and I glance at the empty seat. I don't know why I hesitate, but something in the back of my mind screams at me to ask the question.

With tears running down my cheeks and adrenaline pumping through my veins and into my fragile, petrified senses, I ask, "Where is he?"

"I told him you went back into the Cathedral. We have to go if you're going to have any shot at leaving this town without him thinking I had something to do with it. Get in my car now, Millie!"

He races to the other side and unlocks his vehicle, and I hesitate to open it. The guilt of leaving Hayden hits me like a train. His ominous ultimatum to submit to him echoes off the walls of my racing mind, and I do a double take from the passenger seat and the Cathedral.

"Get in! What are you waiting for? I'm going to give you five fucking seconds before I change my mind!" Gerard whisper-yells at me as he holds the passenger door open for me while he leans over the console. His eyes are beaming red, but his urgency isn't sufficient enough to snap me out of the chokehold my captive vampire has me in.

I turn back to the black-colored, incredibly detailed architecture, with bright red stained glass in every window...and it stares back at me like it's alive. I see figures moving through the halls of the Cathedral, and the reminder of what I saw on the News Network screams at me.

My family needs me. My father, who was desperately trying to right his wrongs with me, is waiting for me. My mother needs someone to remind her every day that she can get her happily ever after, and I will be that person despite the horror I've seen and been through. My brother and I can strengthen our sibling connection when I return.

I climb into the vehicle and close the door. Gerard puts the vehicle in reverse before I can even put on my seat belt. The tires rasp against the grass and branches, and he turns his car around so fast that I hit my head on the window violently; a pained moan leaks into the air from my throat, and I palm my head.

Ouch.

"Shit! I'm sorry. I have to get you out of here before he catches on." Gerard explains in a jumpy tone and a shaken voice. "Cars are usually slightly faster than us when we run."

After rubbing the spot where I hit my head, I realize that the burning sensation doesn't falter right away. There's a familiar wet sensation. I drop my hand to see blood on my palm, and I swallow. My hair clouds my vision, and I pull it behind my ear. Even through the darkness of his car, the moon gives me just slight illumination to see the extent of my injury. I have a cut on my forehead.

Gerard finally turns us around and puts the car into Drive. The uncomfortable space between us makes me wonder. I ran from one vampire to another, but he's a stranger. I know nothing about him, but I trust he can do the right thing...right?

"Why are you doing this? Why are you helping me?" I place my hand on the center console, with my palm facing the ceiling of the car, not wanting to get my blood on anything.

We're barely nearing the end of the trees when Gerard tilts his head to the side like he's amused and entertained. His eyes turn red, and he grips my bloody wrist tight. Deja vu of the first vampire that took me while I had just gotten off work comes back clearly. A sinister smile replaces his once-welcoming one. "Because it's the right thing to do."

He doesn't get to finish. A loud, animalistic snarl roars behind him, and the window to his side shatters, making the car swerve for a second before it slows down.

I scream and scream at the top of my lungs as I watch Gerard's head get detached from his body in a split second, and dark blood splatters everywhere in the car, but it misses me entirely. I can't watch more death surround me. I'm going to have a heart attack.

I leap out of the car and fall over to my knees, greeting the forest floor unforgivingly. My knees scrape rocks and branches as I try not to hurl my stomach acid. One of Hayden's friends is there, as if he expected me to climb out. He restrains and stands me up, turning me around and making me face a raging Hayden. I jump like a scared cat when I see what Hayden has done to his innocent close friend who tried to help me. I watch Hayden walk toward me; each step is slow and unforgiving. He towers over me with murderous eyes and vengeance written all over his handsome face. He looks at me like he wants to punish me, yell at me, and devour me at the same time.

The moon shines over us, and a large number of bats start to flap their wings vigorously and chirp as they fly over our heads under the moon and out of the trees. They fly over him as he continues to look at me like he's in pain. I did promise him that I would stay with him, and now...I'm caught. I went back on my promise.

The rest of Hayden's friends show up behind him with bright red eyes and fangs over their bottom lips. *These men* are truly loyal to him and out to drag me back here with him. They're all breathing heavily as they come toward Gerard's body and continue to dismember him like nothing. Each limb turns into ash. They laugh like they're going to enjoy watching

Hayden punish me. Their laughter dies down as they head towards the bonfire that's still going behind us.

I don't think I'll ever get used to watching Hayden murder people.

His friend lets me go, and I take it all in while the blood on my forehead still drips down my face and onto the side of my cheek.

The horror of it all sends sickness to crawl into my system, and I'm tempted to throw up. Bile rises in my throat as nausea takes over my dizzy head. Gerard is dead because I asked him to help me. The guilt starts to eat me alive already, even when his true intentions are still hazy.

I don't know why I thought running now would work, but I tried.

I turn around and take one step, but in a flash, I feel his strong arms cage me in and pull at my waist roughly. Hayden throws me over his shoulder with so much force it gives me a whiplash. I start to kick, scream, and cry with distress in every pull of my muscle.

"Please! Let me go, Hayden!" I pound on his hardened, muscled body, but it doesn't work.

He lifts my dress up as he trudges into the Cathedral and slaps my ass in a vindictive way. Immediate pain floods the area, and I wince. My skin throbs in response, and I try to pull my dress down, but he doesn't let me.

Slap.

He does it again and harder. I close my eyes as I continue to wiggle and pull at his wrists, but he's too strong, and I'm just a human. I can't kick him in his balls from here. He releases an animalistic growl with no words, vibrating against my hip.

"I'm sorry! I'm sorry, Hayden!" my firm apology goes through one ear and out the other. He doesn't care. I'm returned with silence. And that scares me even more. His silence says more words than anything, and I just know I'm in fucking trouble.

He's beyond pissed off.

I'm scared of what he'll do to me now. Will he chain me up in his room? Will he finally kill me now that he realizes I lied? As I continue to thrash in his torturous hold, I close my eyes and prepare for the worst.

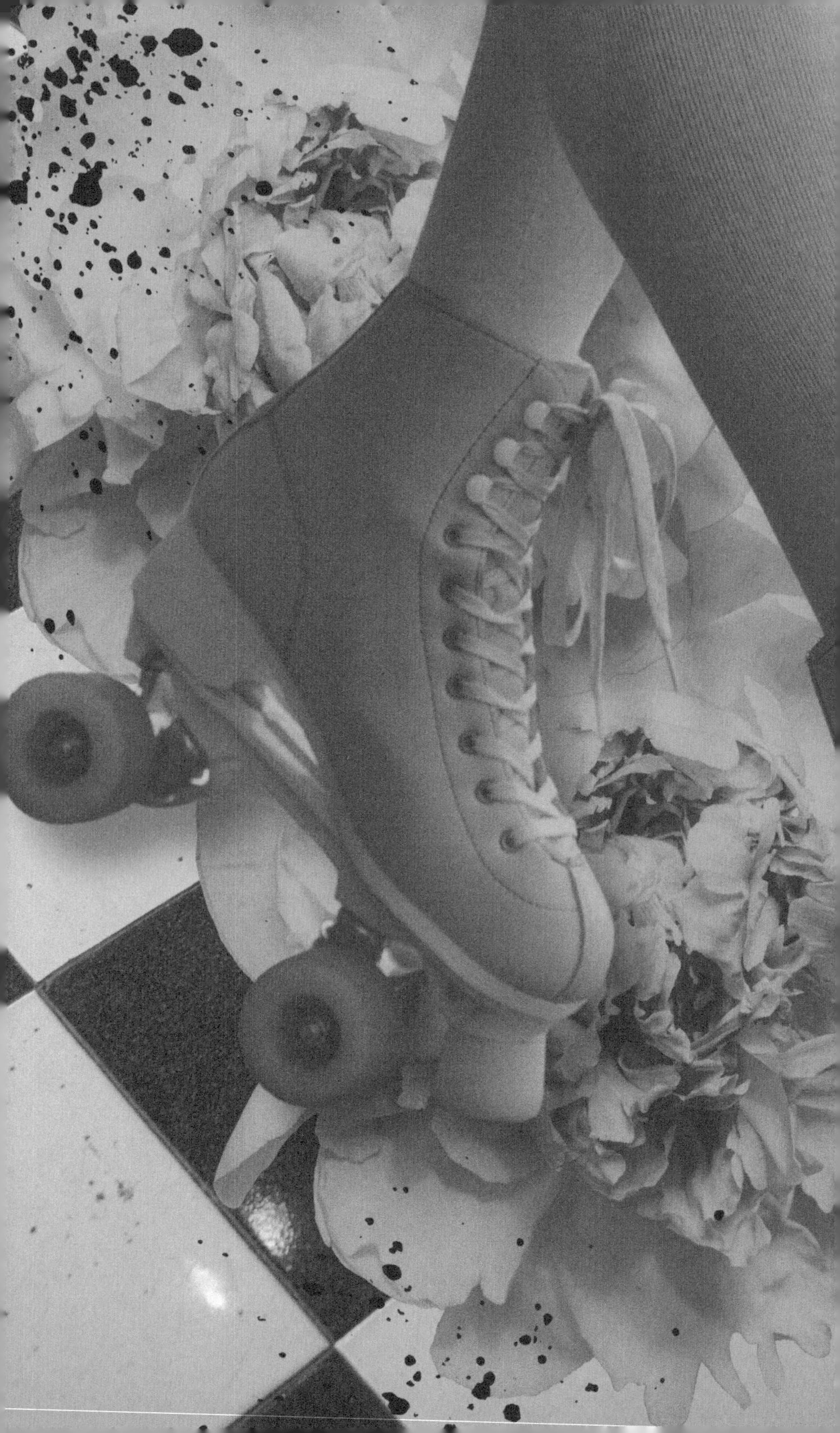

27

MILLIE

"YOU PROMISED you wouldn't try and leave me!" He shouts, kicking the door to his room closed with his foot. He grabs me like I'm featherlight and puts me on my feet. I stumble, and I'm about to fall onto the floor, but he catches me just in time before I can hurt myself. He protects me from the fall and makes me stand back up.

He locks his door and runs a hand through his hair anxiously. The veins in his neck bulge, wrath evident, and I'm biting my lip as I try to stay calm. He paces around me...circling me like a shark.

"Now I killed one of my close friends because he was going to take you for himself!" He kicks his desk with his boot, and it breaks in half. It's like he's having a manic episode. The darkness and depravity take over him so easily.

I hold myself and watch him.

"He was not going to hurt me! He was helping me get back home!" I shout at him as I suck in a breath and clench my jaw. I'm so stressed out that my teeth grind against each other, and I can't do anything to loosen them up.

He turns to me, and his jaw ticks off and on.

"Look at your head! He hurt you! You bled!" He shouts like his demons are back, and they are here to stay.

"That was the car. He was not going to hurt me!" I push at his chest, but he doesn't move an inch.

He turns to me and cups my face with both of his hands. His eyes are still blood red, and he smirks with flaring nostrils and narrowed brows.

"Aww, my poor naive little Bambi. You forget that he's an immortal, just like I am. I could feel his intentions with you through my dead bones, sweetheart. He was going to take you for himself, probably take your blood, and then turn you into his personal pet and fuck you. You don't know him like I do."

"Again, he was helping me go back home!"

"It doesn't matter anymore. He's gone. He touched you...he touched what's mine, tried to take you away, and paid the price. I can't believe you tried to go with him. He looked at you the way I fucking look at you! Who's next, Millie? I told you what would happen, right?" He gets in front of my face and caresses my cheek softly. I stand there with my hands at my side, feeling defeated.

I break down and sob silently as he watches me intensely. The same realization I had at the concert hits me again. I'm never going to escape him, am I?

"I'm going to remind you of what will happen every time you try to run from me. Should I start with your co-worker?"

I shake my head and lick my trembling bottom lip as he tilts my chin up, forcing me to meet his gaze. A tear falls down my cheek, and he clenches his jaw. He wipes it away with a quick swipe of his thumb.

"Cole?" He taunts me in a wicked way with a feral, rough smile.

I freeze at the mention of his name.

My silence makes him angrier. He looks at his watch, adjusting his cuff, and smirks sinfully. His fangs grow longer and make a dreadful appearance.

He wouldn't dare hurt Cole...

"I can take the Drago family private plane right now to pay him a visit. The way he was pleading for you to come back home gives me just the motivation I need to remove him from your life. Your blood should only heat up for me!"

My eyes bulge. He's not bluffing. He turns around and heads for the door. He's there in half a second. Air whooshes through my hair and over my shoulders from how fast he jumped.

"I'll take everyone you love away so that the only family you have left is me! You only have one choice. I'm only giving you one choice, don't you get it? I will kill everyone you care about. I'll kill all of your friends and family so that the only person you have left is me. I'm your family. Your parents abandoned you just like mine have. I've lived and experienced that type of absence and heartache. I'll kill them all off one by one until I'm the only person that you can trust and count on. You. Will. Fucking. Devote. Yourself. To. Me! Your father left you, remember?! Your mother has never considered you. Nash dipped and left you behind. *But I will never leave you behind.* They don't deserve your forgiveness. They all treated you like shit! I love you more than myself. I've watched you for months, and I know you, Millie Flores! I truly know you better than anyone in this world. I will love you the way you need to be loved, and I will *never* leave you alone."

Oh my god, he's insane.

Before he can grab the doorknob, I react and scream.

"No! Hayden, stop, please!" I bellow out. "Don't kill him! Don't kill anyone! They are all innocent in all of this. I'm yours! I'm sorry. I..."

How do I stop him? How do I make him believe I won't try and escape again?

"I love you!" I blurt out in a sharpened tone, quick and curt, hoping it's enough to make him believe me.

Hayden stiffens and stops. He straightens his back and turns his head. His dark black waves fall over his forehead, but he doesn't make another move. He's still looking at the floor like he's contemplating his entire life. He's unsure, and it shows.

"Your words aren't good enough anymore," he murmurs like he's the one that's broken. He opens the door and takes one step out.

I hesitate as he continues to leave. I know what I have to do. I have to succumb to my forced future.

"I'll marry you!" I seal my fate with those three words. I reach out for him with my dried, bloody hand. "Please. I'll marry you."

My candor seems to paralyze him. He stops walking, and it feels like forever that we both stand there with the heaviest of emotions howling over our souls. My promise strikes him hard. I can see Charles ready to go wherever he needs to be.

"Sir? Prince Drago?" The King's guard asks in an attempt to snap him out of his thoughts, but Hayden stands there with balled fists and a blank, furious stare.

He doesn't buy it, does he?

But then he slams the door shut, surprising me, before Charles's stressed gaze and locks it. I stand there, and he's standing over me faster than the speed of light. I look up at him, doing everything I can to stay on my two feet.

"You'll be my wife?" He asks in a soft whisper, slowly raising his head with a pointed chin as if waiting for me to take it back. He looks at me skeptically, his tone deepening, rough and rugged. His brows are furrowed like he's trying to read my mind.

"Yes...I'll be *anything* you need me to be. I'm sorry. I want you, Hayden. Maybe...maybe I ran because I'm scared of the way you make me feel. It's a feeling I've never experienced before. Like it's wrong to want someone like you—someone who loves me so dangerously and is willing to do whatever he needs to to keep me. Maybe I ran because I'm scared that..."

I don't have any more control over my words. It's spilling out of me like a demented sickness. *I'm giving in to him.* Letting my dark fantasies win the battle I've been fighting against.

I grab his hand, and dammit, warmth rolls down my cheeks from my sore eyes, and I let my heart talk and shut off my mind. I place his hand on my chest like he did when it was my first time with him. "That I'm consumed by you just like you are with me. You can feel it, can't you? I know you can." Before I can finish, he grips my waist and pushes it against his, and I feel his hard cock wanting to rip through his jeans.

I'm just pretending to be his good little prisoner. *Right? This is all fake...right?*

I question myself when I already know the damn answer. Before I let shame plague my emotions, Hayden interrupts them.

"Don't let me stop you. Finish your sentence and show me how much we've consumed each other." He growls like a beast that will burn down the world if he doesn't touch me. He whips behind me and grips the back of my dress. Before I can blink, talk, or turn around...let alone process my thoughts, he tears my dress open from the back with his hands. I'm in my bra and panties while looking at the luxurious dress I'll never be able to wear again.

He unhooks my bra while trailing his nose through my hair and down to my neck, smelling me.

He hums. "Strawberries."

He kicks my feet apart with his boot, and I look down to see what he's doing. He kneels and grips my ass with both of his hands and squeezes hard. I fall forward with my hands on the end of his bed. He pulls my panties all the way down until they pool around my ankles.

"Hayden..." I breathe. I wipe away my tears with my hands and let the dark, blissful lust I get from the way he touches me possess my body.

"Go on. I'll be on my knees for my queen while you finish your sentence."

He goes in between my thighs, and I know he can see that I'm already dripping for him. How can this happen? The chemistry between us is there. It's just...*there*, existing, and I can't deny the sensual havoc he inflicts upon me. The way my body immediately craves to be loved and wanted, whether it's toxic or not.

I need it.

Hayden sees me. He's uncovered my layers forcefully, one by one, only to discover there's a hole in my heart and spirit. I'm as empty as him, wanting him to fill it *for me* when I can't for myself.

I can feel his smile as he breathes deep and rough against my tender flesh. I suck in a breath and blink hard, trying to concentrate while battling my inner demons.

"Go. On." He demands, and I feel his tongue go through my slit and up to my aching clit.

Oh, fuck.

"I want you forever," I confess truthfully as I grip the sheets of his bed, clawing them as he continues to make detrimental magic movements that have my toes curling. "My heart skips beats for you." I look behind me to unveil the demon who haunts me like a shadowed protector on his knees like he's worshiping me.

The darkness that exudes from his beautiful face falls, and he smirks victoriously.

"I knew you felt the same for me. I knew it then, and I know it now. You bleed for me, you ache for me, *and you lie*, but your body tells me that you love me." He cups my ass cheek with his large rough hand and kisses it. His lips vanish after a split second to be replaced by his sharp canine fangs. He bites me there, and I groan as his teeth sink into my skin and flesh.

"Oh..." I whimper.

He doesn't suck but only watches my blood fall down the back of my thighs after he pulls back. He smacks my ass, watching it move, and he smiles like he's proud of the sight of marking me.

"I'm going to fuck this soon." He spreads my cheeks apart and licks my rim. My eyes bulge, feeling the tip of his tongue graze my sensitive back virgin hole. "Not right now, but soon." He promises me darkly and stands. I'm about to turn around, but he pushes the bottom of my back forward, forcing me into a bent-over position.

I gasp in the air as I watch him tear off his clothes over my shoulder, and I stare at his god-sculptured body like I'm entranced. The veins over his v-like torso and abs are contoured perfectly. And his hardened thick massive cock springs free, with pre cum already glistening...

"Promise me something? My family can be here for the wedding?" I try to make my own attempt at an ultimatum. I look dead straight into his eyes and beg him to give me back the one thing I feel like I need to fix—my relationship with my family.

"They don't need to go on with the emptiness in their hearts that you and I feel and carry every day. They need to know I'm alive. I am yours, Hayden. I promise. Spare them, and I am yours." I blink rapidly, biting my lip. It'll be complicated to reveal where I've been, but I'm sure Hayden can think of something.

"Anything for my little bride."

With that, he scoops me in his arms, and we're in the air. My back hits something, but it all happens too fast; I can't process it quickly enough. I look down to see that we're floating, and he has my back pinned into the middle of his wall. His bed, TV, and furniture look miniature from up here. His room is that wide with tall ceilings.

My breasts bounce from the collision, and he growls when he notices. He immediately reaches for one pebbled nipple and takes it into his mouth, sucking on it, and pinches my other breast with his hand.

"You mean your little prisoner?" I dig.

He chuckles low and deep and shakes his head. He's gone into his vampire mode, and his fangs grow bigger, sharper, and scarier. I'm panting as he lifts my legs, and I secure them around his waist.

"You think you're the prisoner? You have my unbeating heart in the chains of your soul. Don't you get it, baby? The key to freeing me doesn't exist anymore. You have me, Millie. You fucking have me."

He cups my face with his hands and looks down at my pussy. I grind my teeth and hold onto him, intertwining my hands together around the back of his neck. My wetness welcomes him as he pushes his cock inside me, but he isn't slow or soft; he's ruthless. He starts to fuck me hard and passionately against the wall, and my hair and breasts bounce with each thrust of his hips.

"Don't you feel that? How perfect your body welcomes me? I'm your home. We were made for each other, Millie. It took me centuries to find someone like you, and I would wait centuries more if it means I get you in the end."

I'm breathing hard as he rails me with no remorse. As he continues his deep thrusts that make me feel like I'm being split in half, he goes to my neck, and I scream because I know what's coming.

"Do I need to carve my name on these tits so everyone knows you belong to me?" He bites me, and my entire body goes electrocuted. His teeth sink into me, and I close my eyes, while my mouth gapes open. He starts to suck and suck as he pulls me into him like he's full of greed and no one else can have me.

"Oh my god...Hayden! It feels so..." I moan, and my back hitting the wall, our skin slapping, and his sucking fills my ears as he continues to work my body like I'm his haven and dark affliction.

"It feels so fucking good, so fucking heavenly? Doesn't it? Why would you ever want to escape how I make your body feel again? No one can fuck you like like I can, Millie. *No one.*"

He grants me space and starts to flick and circle my clit with his finger, and I enter a fucking dream I never want to wake up from. It feels so good. He feels so good. How does he make the darkness of his actions feel so right? His cock is so hypnotizing, hitting *the* spot inside me I never knew I had.

"You feel so good. I won't leave you again. I promise!" I moan out and suck in air into my narrowed lungs as we continue to fuck while we float against his wall.

The mirror that fell when he kicked his desk catches my attention. It's split in half but yet remains intact. My reflection stares back at me while Hayden watches my pussy get rammed by his thick cock.

Hayden doesn't have his reflection...but I do; I'm naked while blood runs down my neck and down my breasts onto my stomach. Rivers of red are painted across my brown-toned skin, and my thigh is indented with his hand prints from his grip to hold me up.

It looks like I'm getting fucked by a ghost.

But then I can feel my climax so close, and he knows it. He reaches over and sucks on my breast as he shouts and circles my clit, and fucks me harder.

"I want to hear you come. I love the sounds you make when you come for me. Do it, baby. Scream for me!" He growls against my breast before sinking his fangs into me, and I obey unwillingly.

"Hayden!" I moan out a high-pitched and torturous bellow. I come undone, and my orgasm rips through me like a storm of emotions. Ecstacy unleashes in our chemistry. His cock thickens at the sounds I'm making, and my muscles twitch. I throw my head back as he continues to move in and out of me ruthlessly. I'm seeing stars in his darkness that I'm swallowed in like an ocean that doesn't have an end.

"You're being such a good girl for me. Fuck!" He growls, and he quickens his pace. Deep and calculated thrusts, and he reaches his own peak of bliss and slows.

He's filling my pussy up with his cum, and he makes sure I get every drop. He pulls out and watches the cum drip down onto the floor, and he smirks devilishly. He grabs the rest before it can exit my body and plugs his fingers into me, pushing his cum back in.

"My babies belong inside you. You'll never be alone again, my beautiful fiance. I'm going to hold onto you tighter and fiercer now...just like I promised."

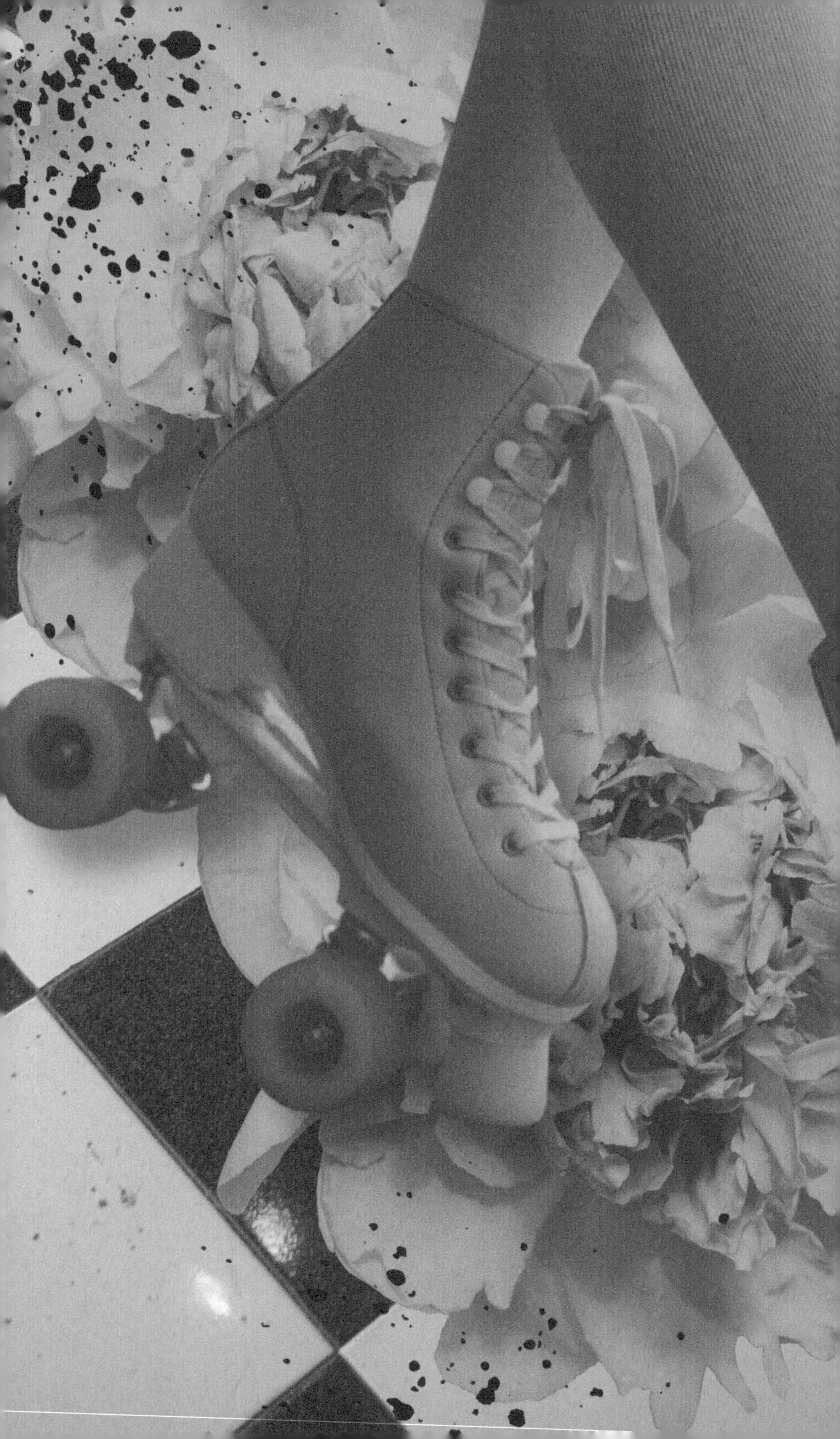

28
MILLIE

IT'S NEARING three in the morning, and I just want to sleep. Hayden wouldn't let me rest until *after* he made sure to take care of my wounds after biting me several times and having rough, angry sex with me. I'm exhausted. Just like the first time he made love to me. Everything is sore, and he hasn't let me sit alone and process everything. One minute, I tried to escape. The next, he killed his friend for trying to help me, and now... I'm engaged to a vampire. The guilt over Gerard is depleted when Hayden explains how horrific Gerard is known to be. He had a reputation himself. He was cruel to humans, and whoever he claimed as his blood supply for the week would endure pain and crimes. It turns out Hayden was already suspicious of him, so when he tried to help me, Hayden didn't hesitate to end him.

I inspect every detail of the giant ruby glimmering ring on my ring finger through the bubbles. It's an oval shape that takes up much of my finger and has natural diamonds on the rim.

I can see my drained reflection amongst it.

After he fucked me hard against the wall while floating, his eyes haven't left my body. It's like he's afraid I'll try and leave, but honestly, it's justified.

But I meant it. I meant it this time. I'm not leaving him. At the cost of my family, I can't do that to them. Plus...I don't think I want to escape him anymore.

I either marry him, or he'll kill my friends and family.

I've accepted him and everything that makes him depraved. He's my monster. And I'm going to sleep in the bed he's made for us.

We both brushed our teeth, and he made sure to grab me pajamas I could actually fit in for the night. When I hop into the warm water, I watch the water turn a lighter shade of red and swirl around me.

It's my blood.

This time, he only took minimal blood from me so that I didn't pass out or near my death. He controlled himself, and I'm sure that wasn't easy for him to do.

We're in his bathtub, and I sit in between his legs as he grabs a loofah and cleans off the countless bite marks on my body. The bite mark he left on my neck isn't clotting as fast, and it keeps dripping.

He squeezes the loofah angrily until his knuckles turn white, and soap falls onto my shoulder and down the middle of my breasts.

"Are you upset?" I ask softly, dreading the answer. I don't like it when he's mad. Because when he's angry, his depravity takes over him like a virus with no cure. It's hard to snap him out of it.

I yawn softly, trying not to fall asleep. He pulls my head back until I'm resting on the left side of his chest. He pulls my neck to the side so that it's exposed to him. I don't fight him. I can feel the pulse in my neck pump hard, and he's eyeing it closely.

"Yes. I'm mad, little Bambi. I'm mad at myself. I fucking bit you too hard here..." He leans forward and licks my neck. He drags his cold tongue like he's savoring every drop. The blood continues to fall, but he's trying to stop it. "I'm sorry, baby." He apologizes with remorse in every single word. I can feel the sincerity in it. He licks my neck once more until, finally, no more blood runs down my neck.

"Everyone fears you, don't they?" I don't know why I said it, but an impulse struck me hard, and the words fell out of my mouth before I could stop them.

He scoffs and palms both of my breasts. He squeezes them gently as he kisses my shoulder.

"I suppose. But you don't...do you?"

Shivers roll down my spine.

Yes. You scare me.

But I don't tell him that, even though I know he senses my unease and how the rhythm of my heartbeat quickened.

"You don't have to be afraid of me anymore. I won't ever fucking hurt, hit, or kill you." He grabs my chin, forcing me to look at him. His light blue eyes darken. "I'm not your parents. I won't leave you no matter how much you push me away. Do you not get it? I won't be okay if I don't have you. I love you so much that it fucking hurts. I'm a man who's been beaten down so much over centuries that I'm numb. I can't feel pain...but you? The thought of you not being with me? I'm in fucking agony. I'm obsessed. You're the only one that makes this life bearable. Like maybe I'm not eternally damned to hell after all...like maybe God does have a soft spot for me if he gave me you by crossing paths that one night in Texas."

He concedes his feelings for me once more, holding my chin in the palm of his hand, tight. His eyebrows pinch together like he needs me to believe him. Why wouldn't I? He's never lied to me since I met him. He's always followed through on his promises and threats.

I can see through him in this moment. It's slapping me in the face. Hayden has never been shown or taught how to be gentle, patient, or loved in a normal and healthy way. We're both searching for it, and I think we've found it in each other. He needs me just as much as I need him.

I reach over and pucker my lips to meet his. He doesn't let me move a centimeter more when he realizes I'm reaching in for a kiss. His lips are on mine, moving against me fiercely. He forces me to open my mouth with his tongue, and as soon as I do, his tongue dances with mine, and I melt in his arms. Once again, I'm giving in to him fully.

I'm surrendering to someone who loves me so deeply that it fades all of my bad memories away…all the scars I wear on my skin and in my soul. It's like it's just us two in a cruel world. When he holds me, everyone around me, every single person or thing that has ever hurt me, disappears.

How can he be so dark all the time yet so gentle with me when he wants to be? It's confusing me…but if this is my new life that's being forced upon me, I will accept it slowly over time.

His hand moves from my breasts as we continue to kiss, down my stomach and onto my pussy. He slaps my clit with his hand gently, and I squirm in his arms, making the light red waves of bath water move around us in the black tub. My heart begins to hammer, and my clit starts to throb, craving to be stimulated.

"Why me? You could have anyone, Hayden. You're beautiful, rich…" *and you fuck like a God.*

I break the kiss, and that's when I realize I'm straddling him in the bathtub with his hands on my hips and ass.

His dark hair is wet, and he watches me closely.

He stands quickly, and I stay there on my knees, watching him with his hardened cock as he strokes it. Water drips down his body and into the tub, while some gets on my face, and I blink it away.

"How many times do we have to have this conversation?" He asks as he reaches behind me and opens the drain. The water starts to dissipate and lower. I'm about to exit, but Hayden turns on the showerhead.

"Is it so wrong to become obsessed with someone that drives you to irredeemable madness? Is it so bad to have fallen in love with you because you didn't even think twice about sacrificing yourself for me when Davenport almost got the upper hand against me? You slit your veins open, leaving you vulnerable. You knew the consequences of those actions. You provoked the Mad King to keep me here. You did that to save me. And now...I want to save you."

How does he know so much about me? How does he know about my upbringing, my childhood, my mother, and my father? These small details? How does he know things I've never told anyone? Before I can put the missing puzzle piece together, Hayden hovers over me and pulls me up by my hands so that I'm standing.

"That's why I want you. I've never wanted to commit myself to anyone more than just a good fuck and blood supply. Never. Because it's not in my nature. I thought I wasn't capable of what I feel for you. *You are the one who broke me!*" He growls sensually and pushes me against the wall, making me face it. I palm the tiled black wall and bite my lip until it hurts. I turn around fast to watch him. My long black hair whips around, slaps the other side of my cheek, and sticks from how wet it still is. I wait for him to continue, heaving and rubbing my thighs together for relief.

God, I want to make him happy.

"Humans are made for fucking, and eating...*not for love*. That's what we're taught, you know? It's engraved into our dead brains when we turn. But you're teaching me that the laws we live by are a broken system. It's all a lie because you exist, and you were made for me!" He starts to finger my clit, kicking my feet apart, and nudges the crown of his cock in between my ass cheeks. His chest and abs are on my back as he rubs his cock against my rim like he wants to fuck it, but he holds back from entering.

I tilt my head back as he fingers my clit, and nirvana clouds my senses. I'm submitting to him just the way he wants me to. *Just the way I have to*...if I want to survive him.

The shower head continues to hit our hips as he kisses me. His fingers go lower, and he pumps three fingers inside me. I almost buckle over, and I moan his name over and over again.

"Hayden...Hayden...God, I want you inside me. Make me feel loved. Make me feel like I belong. Please."

"Oh, I will. You won't ever have to beg to be loved ever again." He removes his fingers from my pussy and instead puts one in my ass. He starts to stroke his finger in and out. My eyes widen as he stretches me, and he doesn't need to say where he wants to put his cock next.

"Good," I murmur. I close my eyes as the dark thoughts swirl, rooted in the curiosity of what it feels like to have his dick inside my ass. "Don't get me wrong, Hayden. I'm still very angry with you. I despise that you always take what you want from me. You make me crave you and fall in love with your demons. I will always want to fight this feeling with you because our beginning is..."

"Is what?" He snaps, pissed off, as he pushes his cock inside my rim. He shuts me up by filling me up with his thick shaft, and I gasp. I press my hand against the wall harder as my calves tighten.

I didn't realize how sensitive this would be! It hurts, but it feels...*good*.

I like the pain. He knows it.

"Traditional? Cliche? Like a romance-comedy movie?" Hayden taunts me for the answer, knowing damn well he's taking my ability to remember my own name away. He pushes his girth inside me more, and he pulls on my waist, forcing my ass to go up higher and making me stand on my toes.

"Our beginning was horrifying, and our journey still is terrifying," I spit out with lust and hatred wrapped into one. My voice breaks when he starts to quicken his pace. His balls slap against me as he moves.

He snickers as he starts to pump inside my ass. His skin slaps against mine with the shower water, and I whimper as I take it. My orgasm is already knocking on my door, waiting to obliterate me. I can't remember the pain of my past or my present while he's inside me.

"Good. Horror movies have always been my favorite." His darkened tone gives me goosebumps. "Touch yourself. Make yourself come all over your fingers while my cock is so deep inside your ass that you'll feel it in your soul for the rest of your life!"

So I do. I obey as always and reach for my dripping pussy and start to fuck myself with my fingers while he takes me from behind. He pulls on my hair like a leash and yanks my neck back as he continues to follow through on his promise...like he always does.

"Your eyes are rolling back, huh?" he grips the hollows of my cheeks, forcing my mouth to open. He smirks as he claims and stretches me. He hovers over my shoulder, spits in my mouth and shuts it tight. "Swallow it all like you will with my cum."

So I gladly do.

"I want it harder, Hayden," I admit through a moan.

"Harder? *Jesus*. I fucking love you," he growls. "I want your ass dripping with my cum."

I nod and bite my lip as he ruthlessly fucks me.

"Let me turn you. Join me. Please?! And we can live forever...*together*. We can fuck like this and never tire. We can travel and explore every single country together. Let me buy you the prettiest dresses and fill your jewelry box with the rarest diamonds in the world." He proposes another deal with him. He wants me to be immortal like him. He wants me to be his prisoner forever. "You'll always be protected and safe, baby. You wanted to fix me? Well, fix me! Drown me with your love. I'm begging for it. I'll always be good to you and make you feel loved like you deserve. You'll never be alone. *I know you hate being alone.*"

Again, how does he know that's one of my biggest fears? I furrow my brows as I try to figure it out, but then he bites my shoulder, and the pain knocks my thoughts away. He doesn't suck. He lets blood fall down and watches it like he's hungry but doesn't want to give in to the cravings. He's already taken enough blood for the night. He can sense it.

"Let,"

Thrust.

"Me."

Thrust.

"Turn you!"

He's fucking me so deep and feral right now. Water splashes every time his hips collide with mine. He's begging for it violently. He's using my body as a tool to get what he wants. *But this*...I can control it. My choice to be mortal is a decision I get to make. He cannot make me change or take that from me, and it's killing him on the inside. He desperately wants me to chant those Latin words three times to consent to become a creature of the night like him, but I refuse.

I shake my head fast and vehemently. "No, Hayden. I won't be like you!" I cry out as I come all over my fingers. My orgasm bursts through me like fire, from head to toe. My mouth gapes open as he continues to brutally fuck me. I want to fall over from how hard I came, but Hayden forces me to stand and continues to wreck my ass as I ride my torturous amazing high.

He's my drug, and I'm afraid I'm addicted to the way he floods my veins.

He growls that same animalistic roar, wraps his hand around my neck, and presses his fingers into my skin, slightly taking my ability to breathe right away. I don't need to turn around to see that he's in Drago Vampire mode again with crimson eyes, pupils blown, and fangs ready to slash into me.

He punches the tiled black wall in front of me, causing it to shatter. Pieces of the wall fall to the bathtub floor and run down toward the drain. He's impatient and urgently begging me, full of wrath. He doesn't like being told no.

"You're the only woman who has ever denied me. Say it! *Volo unum esse cum morte!*"

But I shake my head, denying the future he so badly craves. "Say it!"

No.

He continues to work my body. Before another minute can pass, he grunts and matches my orgasm. He comes undone as his own climax gets pumped into my ass. He lets go of my neck and grips my hips so tight as he pushes his cock as deep as it can go, and he's making me hurt for denying him. More bruises will be added to my collection, along with the rest. I love it when he marks me like that.

He keeps driving his slow thrusts until his balls are empty, and all of his semen is inside me instead. "I need you to be a good girl for me every day and a bad needy slut in my bed when my cock is inside you."

If I was exhausted before, I'm completely drained.

He pulls out fast and turns me around rapidly. He lifts my chin up with his finger and kisses me hard, rough, needy. His eyes are still dilated and angry. I kiss him back, matching his speed, and we eat each other's sins, matching our broken pieces like we always do when our bodies collide.

"You will consent. You will do as I say. *You are mine, Millie.* You will say those three words, or must I take someone away for you to realize that you will not escape me by dying from old age or sickness by staying human," he drawls again psychopathically. "Cole? Nash? Leah? I'm your family. I'm your home. I'm your haven." His husky voice taunts me again, daring me to tell him no so he can try and break me into agreeing.

"Stop it! I already agreed to marry you. Leave them alone!" Horror creeps into my tone as I shout and push at his chest with my fists. I'm tempted to punch his jaw, but his sinister smile makes me hesitate. He grabs my wrist before it connects with his face. I try to pull back, but he doesn't let up.

"Do I have to fuck your resentment away until you stop fighting me?" he asks cruelly. His eyes darken as he smiles ominously like he's enjoying looking at me succumbing to him. He licks the bottom of his front teeth across his fangs, and I scrunch my face to stop my whimpers from escaping. His red eyes charge like he's obsessed with everything that makes me me.

He forces his soft lips on mine, pressing into me like he needs me to understand that I'm not going anywhere, reminding me of my place in this life together. He pulls back, and his eyes are emotionless, dark, and depraved. He smirks and tucks my hair behind my ear, gentle as always, but his next words have me riddled with fear again.

"I may love you with all that I am. But don't forget WHO I am. You will commit to becoming immortal, and I'll give you some time to accept that when I say forever, I fucking mean *forever*. Now, let's get you to sleep, baby girl."

He leans forward, kissing me slowly but harshly.

"I'll see you next moon," he tells me after he pulls away.

I swallow as I try to ignore the pulsation and lust and try to snap out of my dark thoughts. The same demons he fights.

He carries me to our bed after drying and clothing me with fresh undergarments. I slide under the blankets just as he lays down next to me. Before I fall asleep, my heart thunders, and then it quiets as he kisses my neck where his mark is. We watch one of his favorite classic movies as he holds my breasts and continues to kiss my neck every other minute. His big hands roam everywhere until I eventually feel some sort of peace as we watch the movie together.

"I'll see you next moon," I whisper my final goodnight, and I can hear his deep hum of satisfaction behind me. His cock is erect, but he doesn't act on it.

I fall asleep.

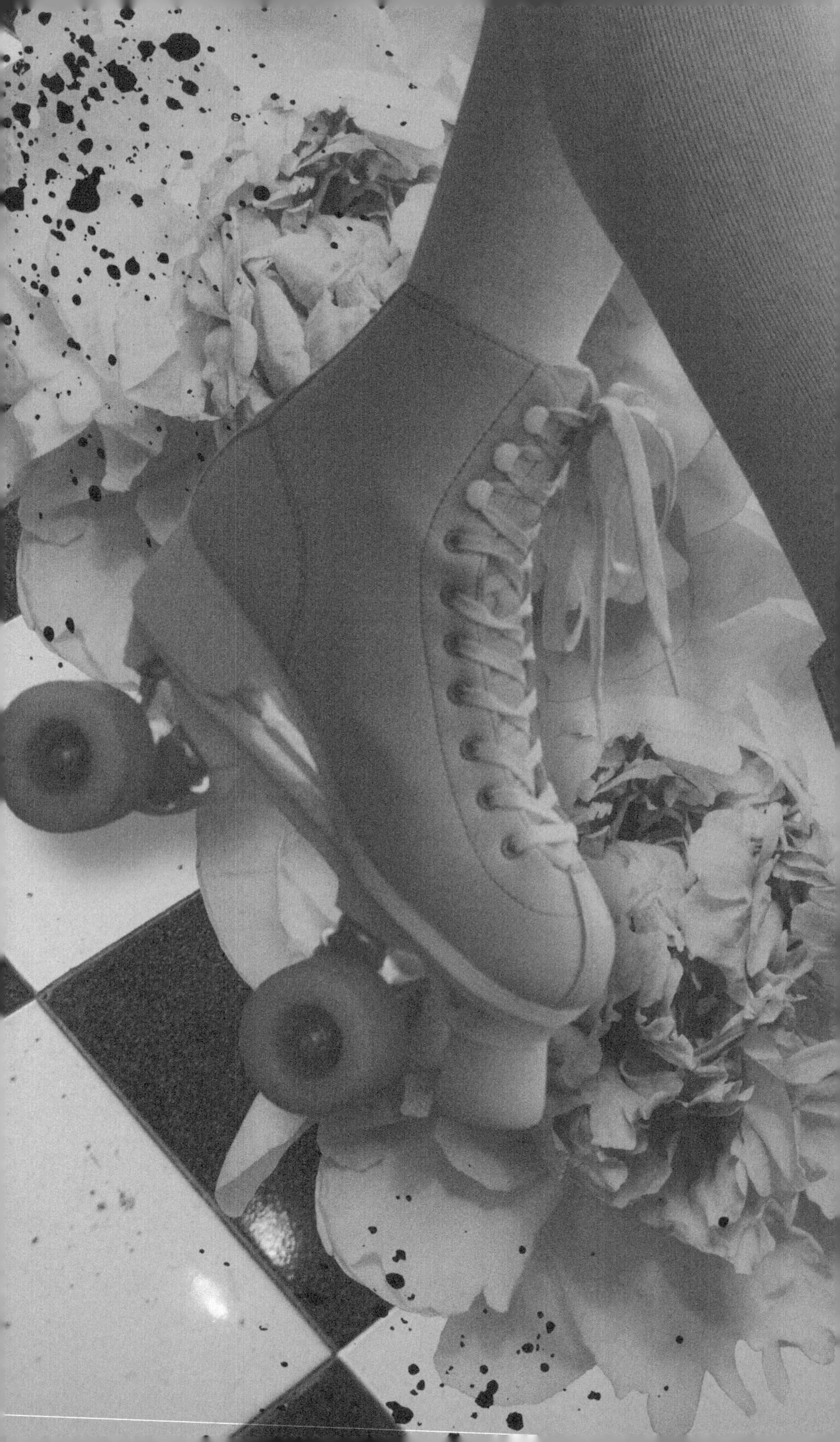

29

MILLIE

THE NEXT FEW weeks are a blur of chaotic lust that makes the days fly by, but I remember every single minute of it. Hayden keeps me up almost all night so I can match his schedule. He wakes me up multiple times during the night with his calculated mouth or his hypnotizing cock. He's the alarm I wake up to every night.

I've become his obsession. He recognizes how deeply my presence has him so demented that he doesn't want to seek retribution for it. Most of the night, he's gone doing whatever duties that are required of him since he's a Vampire Prince. Then he's back in his room, like right now; he just made me come so hard that my pussy is clenching down on his cock, and he roars my name when I orgasm.

"Look at me when you scream my name." He demands, husky and seductive. He sucks on my neck like a hungry beast that will never be satisfied. I can feel the warmth of my blood running down my neck and the moment it turns cold from the fall wind outside. His pace is slow, but his thrusts are deep, like he never wants to pull out of me. He fucked me on his balcony tonight, underneath a blood moon on a couch he had laid out. He fucked me like he always does. His hands in my hair, my breasts, his cock in my mouth, or my pussy, making me taste myself multiple times. Carnal, primal, and greedy.

He continues to claim me in ways that I crave and enjoy. Ways that I'm terrified to admit to him out loud that I love it when he mixes pain with our pleasure. My own blood stains my body, like I'm wearing his favorite jewelry. He claims me like he's afraid I'll die or run away from him. Hayden brings my dark kinks and fantasies into reality.

"I need to get on birth control, or I'm going to get pregnant," I warn him. I'm already past the three-month mark, and we still go at it every single night, sometimes even three times a night. He pulls out of me and pulls me onto his chest so that my face is resting on him. "My shot is up. I'm twenty years old, and I am not ready to be a mother yet."

"Ah...now there's my leverage. Do I have to get you pregnant? So that you will consent and let me turn you? *So that you'll stay?*"

I slap his chest gently, and his morbid humor turns into deep chuckles. "Don't say that," I scold him. I can feel his smile when he kisses the top of my head.

His skin is cold, as always. I run my fingers up and down his ab muscles while I rest my ear on his chest, wondering if this is all still a really weird dream. I long to hear his heartbeat, but it never comes.

"I'll have a nurse come in tomorrow morning to give you your shot..." He pauses, and we listen to the sounds of nature: the waterfall that runs down the mountains right by the Cathedral, crickets singing along with the occasional bat that decides to join the chorus.

He stirs beneath me, and a heavy yawn flows out of my sore mouth.

"I never wanted to be king, Millie. I never wanted to fall in love. I never wanted to be a father. I never wanted any of this, but then you made me fall in love with you by waking me up with your selfless sacrifice for me. No one has ever shown me that kind of mercy before. You're the only one who wants to help me...by rescuing me."

Where was his mother and father when King Davenport barged into my room like that? Where was Kallumt?

I can't imagine the loneliness he's gone through. Constantly being burned will eventually turn you into something you always promised not to be. Or maybe I do understand that type of isolation. Although, it's two very different paths.

"Do you want to be a mother?" he asks.

I sigh and think of my future. I picture myself cradling a third-trimester belly, holding life inside me, protecting it from a cruel, unforgiving world...a world where monsters exist—human and non-human. Then my illusion shifts, and I picture a tall Hayden behind me, with bright red eyes, holding the bottom of my belly from behind. Motioning his large, rough, cold hands in circles as he looks at me like I'm his favorite meal.

I shudder.

"I do want to be a mother, Hayden. But I also want to get my bachelor's degree. I have ambitions and goals to meet. I want to become a published author; I've wanted that since I learned how to read. I want to learn how to surf on hot summer days in Hawaii, and then, when I'm ready to settle down, I want to find someone who can grow old with me and raise our grandchildren together without having to run from the sunlight."

He stiffens like I've struck him physically. I instantly regret letting my candor get the best of me. I close my eyes and curse at myself internally.

Stupid. I should have kept that all to myself.

"If I were a better man, I'd let you go. But I'm not. I've never been a good man, and I've never led you to believe otherwise. I'm your monster and your future husband. I'm your future, and you are my forever. Stop denying us a life that is better than you think. You're going to come around, I promise. You can still do all of those things with me by your side, protecting you. I would rather get tortured at the Inferno than picture you grow old with some other human man. No one is good enough for you...not even me."

I furrow my brows. "The Inferno? What's that?" I think his mother told me about it, but I want to hear it from him.

He breathes heavily through his nostrils like he doesn't want to get into the subject matter.

"The Inferno is like our judicial system. The Kings of each region come together at the capital of Immortals Country, which is in New Orleans, Louisiana, and we torture the guilty before we execute them."

"When we were at the concert, that man, Cal. He mentioned your uncle. He mentioned that you hadn't attended that Halloween event in ages because you closed yourself off from your kingdom when he died. Did he mean a lot to you?"

"He was like my father." he prompts.

"How did—"

Loud knocks thunder from his bedroom door.

"Hayden!" A loud, crisp, southern voice echoes into our ears.

Hayden's father.

Hayden shakes his head, stressed. He kisses me quickly and softly before lifting me in his arms like a child. My legs dangle off his forearms, and he tucks me into bed. Bringing cold bed sheets to cover my naked body, and he starts to pull on his pants and shirt, dressing himself to look presentable to his father and not like he'd spent the past hour fucking me into oblivion after oblivion.

I grip the sheets, make sure it's up to my breasts, and stop at my collarbones.

"Go to sleep, baby. I'm sure whatever it is will be quick, and I'll return to bed to watch over you while you sleep," he promises me. I nod as he runs a hand through his black hair.

The sun will rise soon, and my eyes feel dry and slow. I rub them with my hand and try to get comfortable. He grabs his cigarettes from the dresser and tucks them into the back of his pants. He flashes to the balcony and closes and locks them with a key only he has. When he reaches the door to his bedroom, he gives me one last glance, turning slightly toward me, and stares for a couple of seconds like he's entranced. He stands there like a statue, watching me.

"I love you, Millie. I'll see you…" he clenches his jaw, waiting patiently for me to respond.

Weirdly, it gives me a warm feeling in my chest and veins. It's our little dark routine of words we do right before I fall asleep. He smiles, waiting for me to finish his sentence for him.

Dammit.

I'm falling for him. I'm craving him. I'm missing him already, and he hasn't left his room. He's caught me now…truly caught me like a mouse, and now I don't want to try and escape him.

He's won.

I return the smile, and his eyes brighten like I've never seen them do before. The blue in his eyes looks vast, sharpened, and full of hope. I think he knows he has me, too. I rest my head on the pillow and say, "I'll see you next moon." This time, the words feel and sound natural...like when the sun reveals itself after a treacherous rainstorm. I didn't force it out; it just came. The solace smile painted across my flushed face tells him everything.

His shoulders relax, giving me that dashing smile that could make any girl melt for him.

"We're getting married in just a few more weeks. Only your family and closest ones, like your parents and brother, can attend the wedding. They can attend the Cathedral. They will be unharmed by every single Northern Vampire, so you don't have to worry about that. They will have everything that they need. They will stay here in Montana for *only* the wedding... and then they must leave. *But you are not leaving me* or this town without me."

I TOSS AND TURN IN HAYDEN'S COLD, DARK ROOM, expecting another southern vampire to come to kill me. I'm expecting maybe even one of the Kingsguards to take me for himself, drain me, and unlock their powers, or whatever that means. On a positive, eerie thought, it's like no one would dare betray Hayden when he has a reputation for being merciless and unhinged when it comes to me or anyone who crosses him or his family. I mean, look what happened to Gerard.

I've become slightly paranoid, but after everything I've been through this year, it's hard not to fear my demise brought forth by monsters I always thought were fictional.

When an hour passes, I realize whatever Hayden's father wanted from him was more important than he thought.

Dawn is here, but there's no Hayden. Usually, I'm long

asleep, curled up against him, or he's holding me with my back to his chest. I'm in my velvet-textured, black nightgown, turning the pillow over for the colder side with sweat forming on my brows. I find myself drifting off to sleep, thinking about my father and *my mother*.

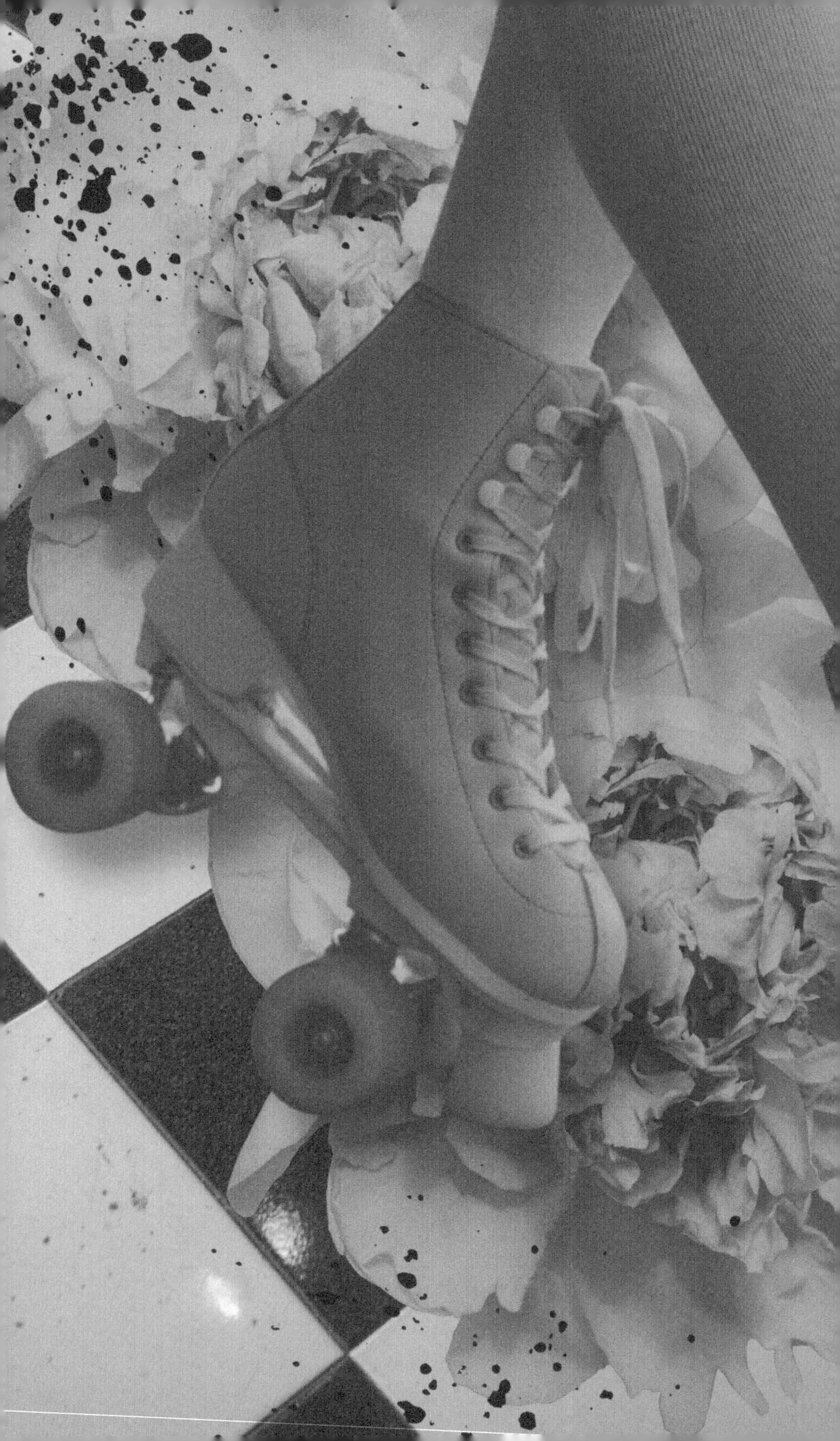

30

MILLIE

One Year Ago

I KNOCK on my mother's door. I hold potato salad and pieces of Turkey in a tray wrapped perfectly in aluminum foil. It's still relatively warm here in South Texas, so I'm in a light orange sweater and tight black leggings. It's Thanksgiving day, and I spent the day at my grandparent's place. After battling for the bread rolls, tamales, and cranberry sauce with my cousins, my grandmother tasked me with an assignment. She wants me to take food to my mother's house since she didn't show up, even though my grandmother extended an invitation to her and her boyfriend.

I stand there, knocking on an all-white door with a fall wreath. After three knocks, I wait for what seems like the longest minute of my life, but she doesn't open it. I turn over my shoulder and spot both of their cars parked in their driveway, so they must be here. I smell turkey stuffing through the door, and even though I ate about an hour ago, my mouth waters. Turkey stuffing is one of my mother's specialties; she passed down that recipe to me.

Suddenly, I hear the locks being played with and turn, and I wear the same welcoming smile I always do when I see my mother—the smile I refuse to give up on because one day, my mother will return one to me.

The door swings open fast, and I startle. I take one giant step back when I realize it's Santiago. My smile falls straight to the floor, and I turn away from his reddened, irritable, contorted expression and face the front window of their house. He doesn't say anything to me—not a respectable-mannered hello or even a happy Thanksgiving.

I never expected him to act like a civil human being or treat me like his girlfriend's daughter. He whips past me and almost brushes his shoulder against mine aggressively, but I dodge it in time. I watch him get into his car, turn it on, and reverse out of the driveway with harsh purpose, like he's trying to run away. He speeds down the road faster than what anyone should be driving down a neighborhood street.

Oh god. Did they really have a fight? On Thanksgiving day? A day that is supposed to be full of peace, forgiveness, gratitude, and family? I shake my head and suck in a breath until my lungs can't take anymore and prepare to walk into mayhem.

Sure enough, when I step in, my mother is a sobbing mess. On the floor, with red cheeks and swollen eyes. "Mom?" I ask with clammy hands. She doesn't greet me with a glance or respond.

I place the food on the kitchen counter, far from the edge, before I jog toward her again. I stand behind her and listen to her soft sobs while she wears her dark, auburn kitchen apron. Her brown hair is tucked behind her ears, and I watch tear after tear fall off her nose.

I hate seeing my mom cry.

"Mom, what happened?" But it's like she doesn't hear me. She's so utterly broken that it makes me wonder, where is she mentally? Where is her mind when I'm right in front of her, begging her to look at me? I start to circle her back with my palm as she continues to cry, and an intricate lump forms in my throat. I hate seeing my mother cry. The unconditional love I hold for her does that to me.

"Mom?" I ask again, but I'm returned with silence. She continues to weep on her knees. I act. I throw my arms around her and hug her, hoping it will wake her. I wrap my arms around her side gently. I haven't held her in what seems like a very long time. I hold her like that for a second, and she stiffens. She doesn't push me away, though. She lets me hug her while I place my cheek on her shoulder. She smells like flowers. She always smells like flowers.

I want her to hug me back, but it never comes.

Finally, she breaks the silence.

"He cheated on me. He cheated on me with someone who is barely old enough to drink, and now he wants me to forgive him for that." Her voice breaks and turns into a bellow of cries. She sags in my arms momentarily before she picks herself back up and stands.

"Mom. Don't you dare forgive him, please? You deserve better than this. It's not too late for you to get your happily ever after. You know, I read so many books. So many stories where there are men out there who would rather die than dream about hurting the woman they love?"

Her red, watery hazel eyes darken, and she scrunches her nose like I said something appalling.

"Millie, this isn't one of your silly romance novels! This is real life! It's time you accepted that."

"Mom! They do exist! I know they do...they have to."

"Millie! Look! I cheated on him, too! Happily ever afters aren't for everyone! Santiago loves me..." She shakes her head like she can't find the words. She brushes her red cheeks with frustration and pulls at her hair slightly. "I'm going to forgive him! Now, please, get out!"

"But mom? It's Thanksgiving, and I—"

"Get out! Now! Before Santiago comes back and sees you here."

"*Por favor, ma...*" I plead as I try to reach out to hug her.

She turns to me with a broken expression and pursed lips.

"Don't you understand?! I don't choose you, Millie." Her words poison me like venom. My heart shatters.

Can you die of a broken heart? Can you die after learning you'll never get to have your mother's love? Because my chest hurts. It burns, and I swear, the pain starts to intensify, causing my heart to palpate dangerously. I freeze from her revelation, and now I'm the silent one who can't find the words to speak. She's abandoning me all over again.

She continues unapologetically, "I choose him. I will always choose him."

Now, I'm full of tears. My mother is pushing me away *again*, chipping the light I try to maintain in my soul away and still choosing a man who has betrayed her in disgusting ways. Sleeping with other women when he has my mother, who gave up her children for what she deems is love.

I stand there, with wetness down my cheeks, and walk away. I exit her house, get into my car, and start to drive.

She will always choose to chase her happiness over Nash and me. All I want is for her to see herself the way I see her.

A few minutes later, it's like I don't have control. I seek comfort. I seek...*him*. I let my body take over on autopilot while my mind is full of dark thoughts. I head for the one person who makes me feel like good men are still out there.

I'm knocking on Cole's door.

He lives in a two-story house on his own, right next to a country club. I know Cole comes from money, but he never likes to talk about it. This house is just one of his family's properties. As always, he doesn't take long to answer.

He opens it. His brown eyes light up, and he smiles. But then it falters, his lips turn into slits, and his brows pinch together worriedly. He's clearly stunned, with widened eyes and pinkened cheeks.

"Millie?"

"Can I come in? I know it's Thanksgiving. Oh, shoot! Is your family here? Of course, they're here! I'm sorry..." I ramble and begin to stutter my words. "Crap. I'm sorry. I shouldn't have come. I apologize. It's a holiday, and I don't know what I was thinking. I'll get out of your hair."

"Wait!" Cole grabs my hand, and my heart jumps when his hand pulls me back towards his front step. "What's wrong? It looks like you've been crying?"

Shit. Did my mascara smear?

I brushed my knuckles near my eye, and sure enough, black traces of makeup formed on my skin when I swiped.

"Come in. Now." He demands. "My family lives more north, remember?"

I feel bad for not remembering that he's here only for medical school, and then he'll move away once he gets an internship.

He doesn't give me a choice. He pulls me into his chest, and his cologne wraps me up like a warm hug. Then his arms encase me into his strong body...and I let him hold me. I sniffle softly against his warmth, seeking comfort.

He closes his front door and leads me to his couch.

"Are you going to tell me what happened? Who do I have to hurt?"

I scoff out a short laugh and shake my head.

Another pause goes in between us as he cradles me on the couch.

"Is it your mom?"

My body goes rigid for a second, and then I concede with a nod. I've told him little bits and pieces about my troubled relationship with my parents. He knows I'm trying to make amends with my father, but I stopped mentioning my mother and Santiago months ago. Maybe I'm easy to read. I truly despise that about myself. Wearing my heart on my sleeve can be a good thing, but sometimes, it's a very vulnerable thing that people may take advantage of. I feel too much...which is something I'm working on.

"Parents suck sometimes. I know mine have their moments." He kisses the top of my head, and I retract from him. I analyze his drenched plaid shirt, and I palm it with my hand. I scoot my bottom until my back hits the back of his couch.

"I'm so sorry about crying all over you. Look at your shirt." I give him a half-hearted smile because the other half is crushed, feeling insecure about my entire being and my place in this world.

He shrugs and pulls at the ends of his shirt. He analyzes the damp mess I made and then looks at me with warm whiskey eyes.

"You're right. I should get another one." He smirks.

"You should," I tease back, crossing my arms after I swiped my palm over my reddened cheeks.

His smirk widens, and he looks at me with that same look he gives me...*desire*. It's no secret Cole wants me more than just friends. Every time we hang out or joke around at the coffee shop, there's a moment there between us. It's a moment full of tension, but it always depletes because it's like we're both afraid to make the first move. I'm surely not brave enough to, and maybe he hasn't wanted to pursue that yearning passion that's been building since we both started working at Nostalgia Coffee Shop because he's afraid it'll ruin our friendship.

His smile turns into something primal. His dimples disappear, and then he curls his long fingers underneath the end of his shirt and starts to pick it up, fast. He first exposes the hair under his belly button, and my cheeks light up, and my eyes widen.

What are you doing?

I try to form the words, but they're too stuck in my stunned throat.

He throws his shirt off, and it lands on the wooden floor. I'm staring at what was once an always cheeky, dorky guy who can take my funny jokes and throw them right back. But right now? He's transformed into a man who's done playing this push-and-pull game that's been going on for the past few years.

His chest moves up and down fast, and he rubs his face, starting from his nose down to his chiseled jaw, like he's trying to conjure up the courage to do something. He places one hand on either side of me, caging me on the couch, and I'm trying to sink into it to disappear from the emotions that are so volatile that they're burning into my core, making familiar lustful emotions swirl into an infinite circle. I'm intimidated and inexperienced when it comes to sex, never mind making out...

He licks his lips and cups and tilts my chin to meet his eyes. He senses my unease like he knows I want to say a funny joke to break the ice. But he's going to break it, and I know he's going to do it with his lips on mine.

"I'm going to kiss you now," Cole murmurs softly. His voice is rough and demanding.

I nod fast. "Yes, please." I blink fast, and he leans in slowly, and suddenly, I lose the ability to breathe. I close my eyes, and as soon as I do, his lips sink onto mine like an anchor in the ocean, finding its new home. They move and move until I feel his tongue lick me, begging for entrance.

My heart flips, and our kissing turns into a tornado of tongues. He pushes me down until I'm lying on my back, and he's nestled himself in between my legs.

What am I doing?! This is Cole! My close friend I can tell anything to, *my supervisor*, not someone I do things like this with. My hesitation is evident, and it gets the best of me when I break our overheated kisses, and look up to meet his darkened eyes.

Damn.

This is a side of Cole I've never seen before. I should be swooning. I should be in a puddle, ready to finally give up my virginity to someone who cares about me on levels only he and I connect with. But my heart doesn't reciprocate those emotions.

"Cole...we shouldn't do this." My eyes dart from his full, swollen lips to his front door.

He pulls back for a second and stares into my soul and then my mouth like he wants to dive back in and continue to move forward until he's inside me.

"This will taint our friendship, and I care about you too much to take risks or watch it change," I confess as my core heats and I open my legs.

"Millie, *you know me.* You know me, and I know you..." He kisses my lips once more, but it's a quick peck on the lips. Cole moves down to my jaw, and every single second that goes by feels like an eternity. He kisses my exposed chest right above my breast, and then he lifts my sweater until it reveals my lower belly. He plants a kiss on my raw skin, making goosebumps scatter all over, and I moan. He smiles, satisfied against me, and hovers right above my jeans' waistband.

He starts to unbutton my jeans quickly, and then he pulls them down until they're at my ankles.

"This will not ruin our friendship unless we let it, and I don't want to lose you. I don't ever want to hurt you. Right now, I want to show you how much I care...not with words but with my actions. We can overthink this tomorrow, but right now, I think I need to remind you that you are worthy of love—worthy of everything good in this world."

My chest tightens, and I feel the weight of all the terrible things that can go wrong, run away. My muscles turn into mush, and I let myself relax, ignoring all the negative intrusive thoughts as Cole begins to kiss and lick my clit.

"Overthink tomorrow," I grit out as I close my eyes tight and twitch with euphoric sparkles.

A ROAR AND A LOUD THUD WOKE ME FROM MY DREAM. The memories of Thanksgiving last year came back to me in my deep slumber, and now they're gone because something jolted me awake.

What awakened me?

I jump from Hayden's bed, palming the bed sheets for support. I look vehemently at his bookshelves, his turned-off TV, and his front door, which is still locked. I pant and place my hand on my chest to calm my thundering heart. I search for any vampires, red or blue glowing eyes, but nothing, and no one is here to harm me. I keep expecting to turn around, and the

Southern King will be here, rising from whatever realm he went to and finish the job he so desperately wanted to do.

Hayden had told me to stay here, but curiosity always gets the best of me. I swallow my nerves and fix my hair by placing it into a ponytail with a vibrant chrome scrunchy Hayden bought me. I climb out of bed, put on my slippers, and head for the door, hoping Charles or any other guard isn't there to stop my investigation.

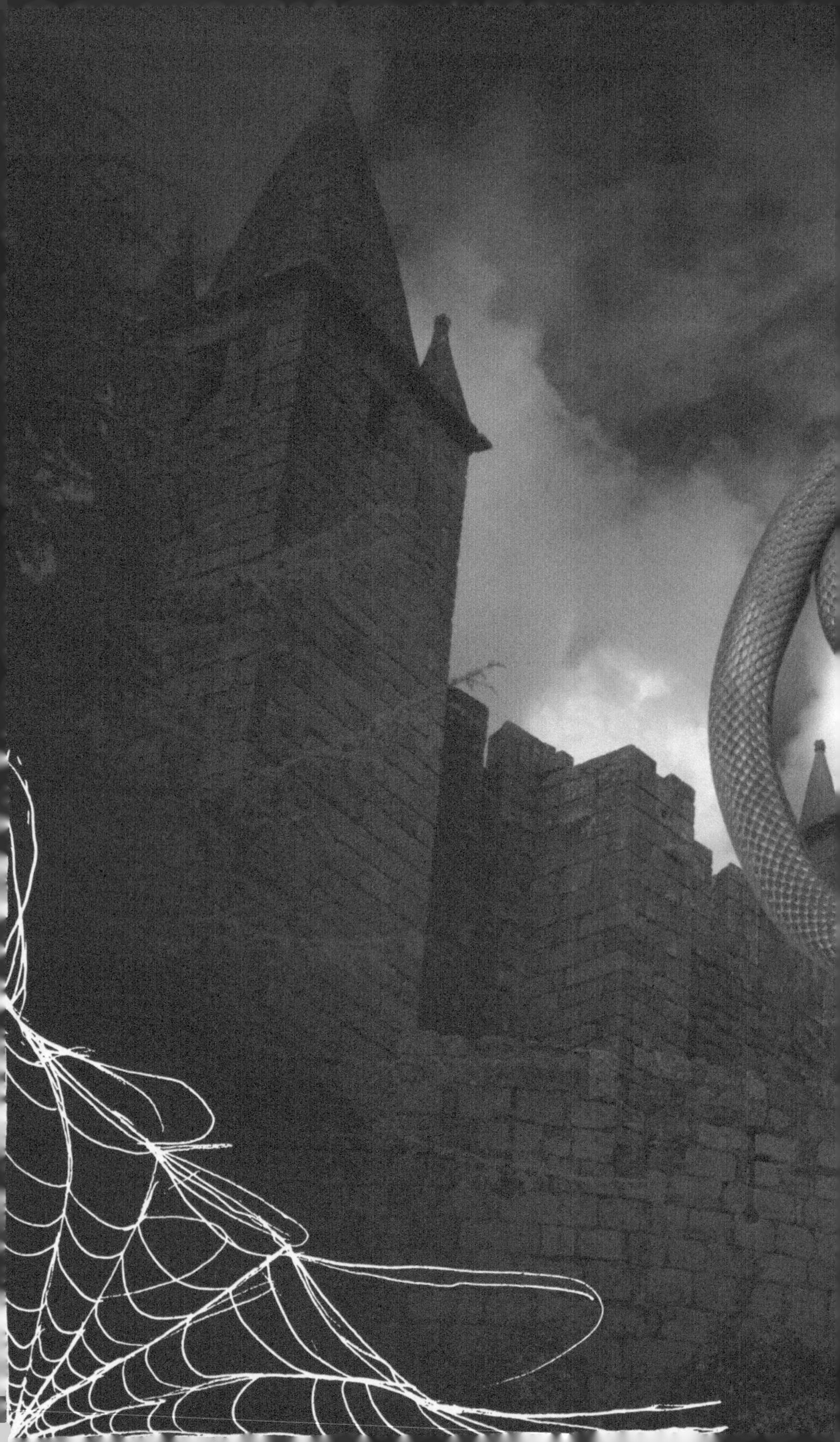

31

HAYDEN

"YOU'VE FOOLED around with her enough, Hayden! Initially, I approved of her marrying you because maybe I do like seeing my troubled son find some type of peace. A new leaf he's turned since meeting her and a break from his demented outbursts and immaturity. Now that I know she doesn't want to *truly* join our family, kill her and initiate your powers! Since she's a Valkyrie, her memory doesn't erase after you drink from her. She's a risk. A risk that is too golden to let go to waste!" My father roars, with eyes so heartless they look empty. As usual, he's disconnected from me and unable to understand that I've fallen in love with a person who is forbidden. He doesn't understand what that's like. His journey with my mother was always smooth sailing.

I plan to change that when I become King. When Immortals find themselves a Valkyrie, it's written in what we deem our version of the bible and commandments that we must leave them alone because the sin of Greed will lead to lust for power. Terrible, terrible sins that lead to carnage and bloodshed amongst each other.

I was keeping her alive for my selfish reasons, and it paid off because the Southern King jumped at the opportunity to steal her back, and now I have evidence that this was his evil plan from the beginning. Keeping her alive spared me from going to trial...and it worked. I got my revenge, but what I hadn't planned for was to fall in love with Millie. But now that I have, everyone and everything can go fuck themselves because there's no way I'm ever letting her go. I've always been selfish, and now that I have someone that makes me feel alive? I'm supposed to just let her go?

NO.

She is my prey, and I am her hunter. She is the ethereal of light in my vast, never-ending darkness. She is my undeserving forgiveness for all of my mistakes. I know she is. She has to be. Why else has God made us cross paths?

Before her, religion held no place in my blackened heart, but after meeting Millie. There is a God.

"Killing Valkyries is against the law!" I remind him of the laws put in place after the war between all Vampire Kings took place centuries ago in Europe. "Why would I tarnish the Drago name by putting our family line at risk by doing that? Millie and I love each other!"

"You forced her to!" he interjects. Spit flies out of his mouth as he snarls. "Don't think I don't know what's been going on between these halls of our Cathedral!" His eyes are beaming red, expecting me to recoil from his horrifying outbursts.

It won't work on me. Not this time. Not ever again.

I transform and let my emotions take over. I fix the cuff of my sweater, as I always do when trying to keep the monsters in my head at bay, especially when it comes to my own family.

"I will marry her, Arthur. She wears my mother's ring perfectly. I have my mother's blessing, and that's good enough for me. As soon as I take reign, I will propose a new law that says we can marry a Valkyrie. They're rare, and we haven't encountered one in hundreds of years. But if another immortal has the luck to find one and fall in love, then they should be allowed to marry them. When it comes to the powers, well...I'll leave that up to the council to decide. All I care about is marrying her. I don't give a fuck about the powers!"

His nostrils are flaring, and his long, thick fangs glint underneath the red stained glass illuminated by the sun outside.

"Don't you talk to the King like that!" Holland blares over our snarls. He walks with a cane and gets in between us as if he'll be able to de-escalate the situation when he only riles me up even more. Kallum stands in the corner, watching with fear, drinking blood from a red crystalized cup.

I smirk; it's sinister and conniving. Hollands hates it when I grin because he knows whatever comes next out of my mouth is never good. I've never given him a genuine smile. He grips his cane and takes a step back.

"His reign is over," I tell him, slow and unremorseful. "There's a new King in the North. I'm marrying Millie this week. We don't need a grand wedding. She doesn't care about money or such things like that." I grab my cigarettes and take one out. "I take it if you're such a rule follower, *father*, you know that once my marriage to Millie is finalized, you can retire with my mother and move to Europe like she's been wanting. You can't stop me. The only thing that can stop me from taking reign is my demise. But you wouldn't dare do that to your"—I tap my chin mischievously—"your villainous son? I think that's what I remember you and Mom telling me. That's what I'm good at, right? Playing a villain when I need to be?" I challenge him.

He stands there quietly and lets out a heavy breath.

"Big brother, why are you so invested in her? You know

how your relationship will end if she doesn't consent to turning." My body runs colder when he brings up the facts I've been pushing far back into my head, hoping I'd forget about the truths.

I turn to Kallum and light my cigarette. The bitterness kisses my tongue harder than usual. I look at Kallum as he swallows the blood in his cup, and he meets me with those brown eyes he got from our mother.

"If you turn her, her heart will stop beating, and you will unlock your powers whether you want it to happen or not. Everything about her is forbidden," Kallum continues nonchalantly.

"I'm hoping that marrying her will cancel out that fact. There's a law in place allowing us to marry humans. And at the end of the day, she is a human," I retort, throwing my cigarette to the floor.

"You're living on hopes and dreams that will send you to your damnation in the Inferno," Holland cuts in, his eyes sending daggers my way, but I send them right back with glares of my own.

My father has checked out. He sits on the couch and pours himself a drink of red like he's given up on me. Good. I don't need him to tell me that Millie isn't mine. She's mine and always will be, despite the truth.

"It doesn't have to be hopes and dreams, Holland. We're living on laws that were made centuries ago. It's time all Immortals change with the times," I spit back venomously.

"She's sick! She's going to die anyway. Drain her for your powers, big brother. Her pussy can't be that hypnotizing that she's changed you. You've had hundreds of women before!" Kallum tells me, slurring his sentence. He must have laced his drink with alcohol because his honesty is taking me by surprise. I know he doesn't mean to point out these facts, but he can't help it sometimes. He always has to be right. It's like he's driving a thick wooden stake through my chest.

"No, stop fucking talking!" I try to interrupt him, desperation getting the best of me. I want to fall onto my knees and put my hands to my ears, but I stay standing, burning holes through my little brother like I'm about to ruin him.

"Or have you forgotten that that's why their blood is rare?!" Kallum interjects me with an amused tone. "That that's why they're hard to find? Because they all die by the age of twenty-three! That's why they're called Valkyrie's!" Kallum blurts out, downing the rest of his drink.

I don't want to think about losing Millie. I can't... I won't.

"No...no...shut the fuck up! NO!"

I black out. I forget where I am and let the demons possess my body, and I can feel them grin sadistically inside my head as I let them take control. The thought of losing Millie drives me to the point of insanity and delirious rage. She is everything to me! I can't focus when she's not around. Millie Flores is the angel that's cursed me with her love. She forgives my sins and I teach her to welcome hers. I need her like the Earth needs the sun. I crave her like the ocean needs the moon. I will always burn infinitely for her.

I grab the closest thing I can find and destroy it. I break into it over and over again until it's in pieces. I stare at the broken chair as if that'll solve all my problems. It isn't enough, so I start to grab all of my dad's precious bottled-up blood and start smashing them.

"Millie is going to die anyway when she turns twenty-three! You might as well put her out of her misery! Do the humane thing and let her go home and return to her family. Let her spend the last moments of her life with her loved ones who miss her. Or kill her." My father growls and watches me. "Stop this madness! You've been trying to prolong her demise. Her death. You're going insane just to keep her heart beating. You're destroying yourself to find a way to keep her here with you! Enough!"

"If you dare look at Millie or talk about her in disgust, I won't hesitate to end you, *father*. You don't know her like I do. I know that she's found her family within me. I can protect her! I can save her!" I roar, and I'm blinded by my own rage that I have tunnel vision. I only see what I want to see. And that's my future with Millie Flores. My little Bambi. My angel.

"Stop it, son! Stop destroying my bottles!" He blares over the sound of glass.

"I am *The Depraved Prince*! That's what everyone calls me, right? I'm just living up to my name and the monster *you raised* because you wanted me to be a strong King, able to take on everything thrown my way in this cruel world we live in! I'm just"—I smash another bottle—"Living up to my name!" I throw another bottle, but this time, it hits the side of the door, and my eyes widen with shock, paralyzing my senses. The beat of Millie's heart replaces the sounds of glass shattering. I was so enraged and so lost in my outburst that I didn't feel Millie come near. I'm always able to sense where she is, but I blacked out so severely that I didn't listen.

Millie stands at the doorway, pale and shaken, with tears running down her cheeks. The room grows quiet, and the air feels tight. I'm frozen with every terrible, sick emotion overriding me.

"I'm going to die?" She looks at me with eyes full of hurt and betrayal. "I'm sick?" She questions me, her voice breaking, and it makes me want to die even more to see her look at me like this.

She's looked at me like this before. The night I saved her the first time when she had a broken wrist. When I took her back home the first night we met. And then again the night she stabbed me with her kitchen knife. But over time, she changed the way she feels about me and hasn't looked at me like that since I made love to her.

The TV my father keeps in the corner of his room joins the chaos. I must have accidentally turned it on when I started to smash things and pressed the remote. Millie turns to the TV, and we can all hear *his* voice, which makes Millie's blood heat up and mine boil into wrath.

"We believe and have evidence pointing to whoever took Millie is the same person that killed Pete Flores, her father." I watch Cole wipe away a tear, and a news reporter replaces him. A woman wearing a light purple suit holds the microphone tight in her manicured hands as she continues.

"Turn it off!" I snarl at Kallum, but he's as glued to the TV as everyone is. But no one moves...hell, nor can I. It's like watching an accident; all the secrets I've been keeping from Millie have finally unraveled. The truth of my father's plans for her...what it *truly* means to be a Valkyrie are all out in the open, and there's no coming back from this. I can only watch as the one soul I've connected with...watch her world get destroyed, and there's nothing I can do about it. I tried to protect her from this, even if it meant lies and deception. I wanted to protect her from our dark world and destiny that she didn't ask for.

I failed.

"Twenty-year-old Millie Flores went missing about four months ago. The house was found broken into, and her father was found brutally murdered around the same night she disappeared."

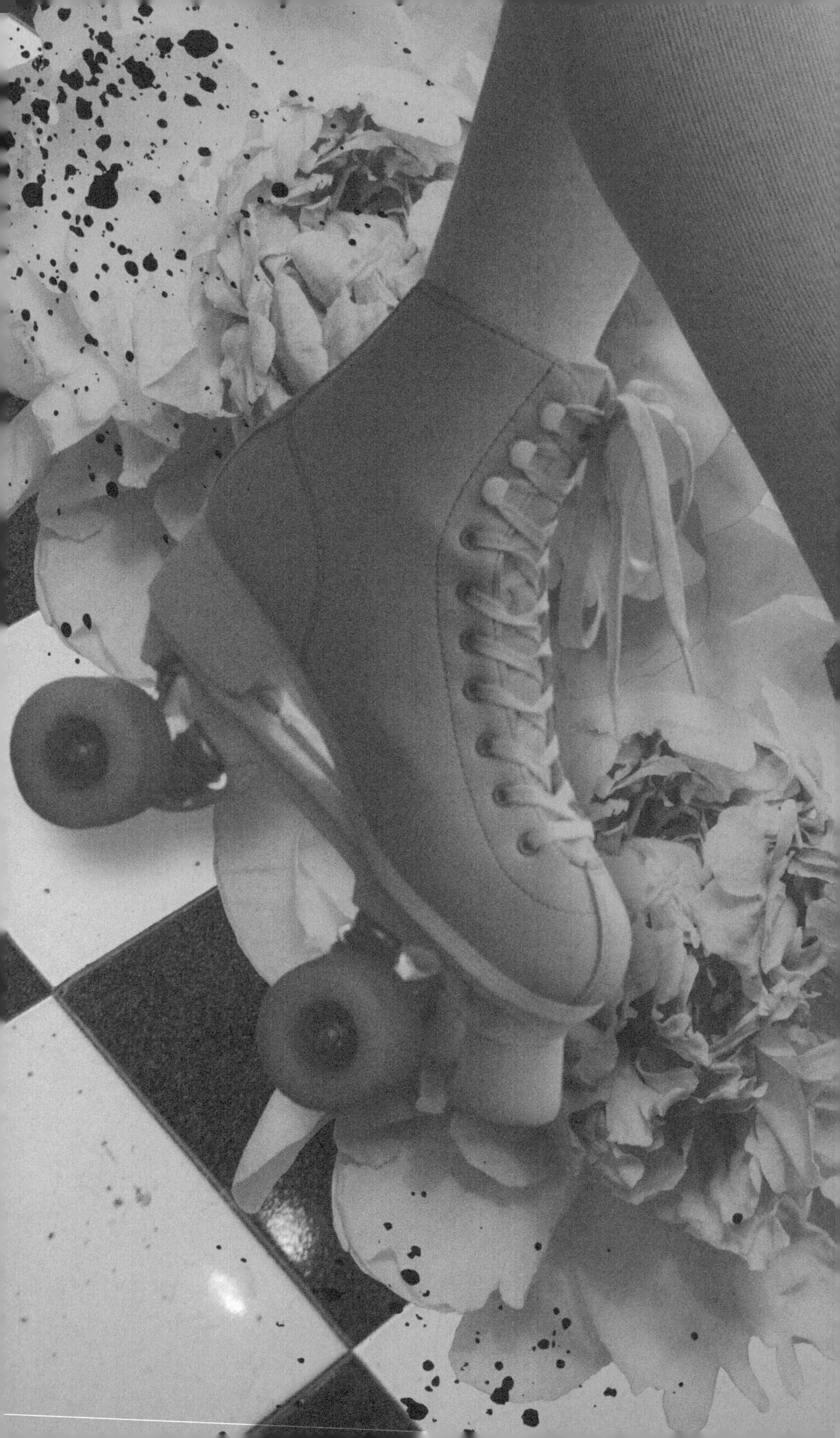

32

MILLIE

I THROW my diary on his desk, which slams against the wood. That's how he knew things about me. Things I've never told anyone! He took it from my room, invading my boundaries even further than I'd thought. He stares at it with guilt written all over his blue eyes. I charge him, and something wild comes over me. I slap him across the face hard.

"My dad is dead? I'm going to die? Is that why you want me to become immortal like you so badly?" I slap him again. His head whips to the side, and redness paints his cheekbones. His black hair hides the despair in his eyes and masks his scrunched nose with flared nostrils. "I'm sick, and you've known all this time!"

It doesn't do anything. He takes it and takes it with emotionless eyes, like whatever piece of sanity he had left in him isn't there anymore. I slap his chest and face again and again, and I'm sure it's hurting me more than him. The tender joints in my hand throb in pain, but it's not enough to stop me.

My father is dead? *I'm going to die?*

What the hell is going on?!

"How could you! You killed my father! You told me that he would be safe if I went with you all those months ago! You monster! You fucking killed him!"

When I realize it's not doing anything to him, I grab the scissors he used to cut open my bandage when he took care of my wounds for me. I raise it to stab him in the chest but freeze. My vision blurs with hot tears, and my chest heaves with pure devastation.

"Do it. It won't kill me, but if it'll make you feel better..." He shrugs with a broken tone. "Do it." He grabs my wrist and tries to make me stab him in the chest. His grip tightens, forcing me to inch closer to wounding him.

My nose scrunches, and my eyebrows pinch together painfully. I feel a type of poison inside my soul, making me feel like I'm demented. The thought of putting a blade into Hayden's unbeating heart kills me. Even though he's everything I fear, I don't want to hurt him.

"No!" I drop the scissors, and they fall between us with a loud clang. "I'm not like you, Hayden! I never want to be like you! I want answers from you!" He looks at them like he wants to retrieve them for me and put them inside his own chest.

"I'm tired of thinking there's good in everyone! Some people just bleed pure darkness. I'm sorry that I thought I saw something different in you. You are irredeemable. I hate you!" I shout as my vision blurs, my throat rasps and scratches my words with animosity.

"I'm sorry, Millie. I know there are no fucking words to express the magnitude of what I've done. I...*blacked out*. I can't remember anything from that night. Just that I took you away and...fuck! I'm sorry! I hate that I don't remember. My blackouts are uncontrollable. You know I suffer from this! You smashed the lamp against me and I raged. I became blinded by wrath and depravity and—" He grabs my hand and pulls me to him, but I fight him as much as I can.

How can he fuck me like this, knowing he's a monster? How can he tell me he loves me when he's killed my father? How does he think I would marry him and never find out? I push him away, and this time, he lets me have some distance from him.

"I don't care if you black out! If you are seeking forgiveness from me, you're crazy! You chose to murder my father! I need to leave! I hate you!" I shout, seeing red. My heart has shattered. This is all too much. I feel like I'm going to faint and enter the same dreadful headspace I've been in since I was a child. Getting taken from Hayden... I can't explain what this has done to me, but I've forgotten about my troubled past when I'm with him because he chases it away when we're together.

"Don't tell me you hate me. Don't say those three words again! I'll fucking break if you do. Don't rip me apart by telling me that!"

I purse my lips together as my vision blurs.

"I. Hate. You."

I'm seething. I'm breaking. I'm drowning in his messed-up world.

Black tears start to fall out of the corners of his eyes, but I can't stop. He kept these horrible secrets from me.

"You said that you fell in love with me the moment we met. Yet you killed my father. He and I...we were fixing things! He was trying to be a part of my life and you ruined that forever! You don't kill the father of the one you love! I did what you told me to do!" I grab at my chest, seeking relief from my living nightmare but nothing helps. I shut my eyes tight as all the memories of my father hit me.

My dad is dead...this is unbelievable. All this time, I've been falling for my captor's lies. His lies were so wrapped up perfectly in a bow of our desire for each other. He's my father's murderer?

"I'll kill anyone who tries to take you from me, Millie. I don't care who it is. I'll. Kill. *Anyone.*" He admits it with no remorse and the darkest of tones I've heard him mutter.

He doesn't regret killing my dad?

I shake my head at his brutally honest confession. I know he's obsessed and would go to limitless lengths to keep me with him...but this? This is unforgivable. My situation is insanity.

"God, Hayden!" My lips twist into repulsion. "I'm sick? What does that even mean?! Tell me the truth!"

He's quiet, and finally, he can't look at me anymore. The lies, the deceit, everything is coming together like a map, and I've just reached the ending to my destination—the ending of our unstable relationship.

"Tell me!" I'm begging for the answers I deserve.

He starts to tap his foot, shaking his knee up and down anxiously.

"All Valkyries...*are sick*. They all die at the age of twenty-three from rare or mysterious illnesses. The book says that it can be from heart failure, tumors...or cancer. Whatever it is... it's incurable nor treatable."

Cancer?

More tears fall down my cheek, and I grip my arms for comfort. I lick my dry lips, trying to process all of the information.

"That's why you want to turn me so badly?" I whisper, blinking slowly.

He nods, looking at me like he's being torn into a billion pieces by having to utter words he's been trying to avoid. Well, now I have what I needed to hear, and I don't know what to do but ache.

"Do I have cancer?" I ask him, but Hayden just flexes his

jaw hard and looks at me with tortured eyes and a tormented soul.

"I just wanted to protect you from death..." he tells me instead of answering my question, his tone turning deep and husky.

"By keeping all of this from me? You think I was going to marry my father's murderer?! You're a liar! You wanted me for revenge...you want me for your powers! You want me to be your prisoner until you take me for your selfish ambition!"

"I don't give a fuck about the powers! All I care about is saving you and keeping you with me until the end of time!"

"Your father has wanted to kill me this entire time, hasn't he?" I interject.

Silence. Shame is written all over his beautiful satanic face.

"That's why he looks at me like that? With hatred?" I taunt for an answer. "He wanted you to kidnap me, didn't he? To beat King Davenport at his own game?"

He shakes his head twice; his face is full of sorrow. He plays with his ring, twisting it around his finger over and over again.

"Let me go home. I'm done...Hayden. *I'm done.* I want normal. You are not my haven, and I am not yours. I need to get away from all of this derangement and brutality...I need to get away from *the Depraved Prince!*" I shoot back with toxins fueling every vowel.

"No! I can't fucking do that!"

Finally, he snaps and balls his fist like he's about to melt down and grab me. He stalks forward, each step loud and indignant. He reaches for my face, his fingertips barely able to graze my hot, fuming flesh. He cups my face, harshly forcing his lips on mine. He kisses me as he presses his body against mine by gripping my waist tight, bruising me surely. But I'm too angry... too broken to feel anything else.

I contort my face and pull away by pushing against his chest as hard as I can, but of course, he doesn't move an inch. Instead, he allows me to break the kiss, and he shatters even more when I don't return it or match his movements.

"You must let me go! I don't want you!" I scream until my throat bleeds with pain.

"I love you! I can't!" he yells back at me, this time accompanied by that same horrifying vampire snarl that they all do when they're angry or hunting. It's so distinct I shiver every time I hear it.

"Ahh!" I shout, frustrated. I've had enough. I'm boiling over and impatient. I try to grasp anything that will get me out of this situation and away from him. I grab the scissors again and hold them to my throat so he understands the level of depth I'm willing to go to to escape him. Hayden stares and goes rigid. His eyes widen with excruciating misery.

"If you don't let me go home, I will end my life right here and right now! I'd rather die than be with you!"

"Jesus fucking Christ, Millie! Drop it now, goddammit! I can't lose you!" He pleads and tries to grab the scissors, but before he can, I press it into my skin until I feel a sharp pinch, signaling I've cut through my flesh.

"Don't, baby, please don't! Don't hurt yourself!" he continues to plead. His shoulders relax when I pull back the sharp blade.

"Then let me go, or I'll finish the job for you and your father!"

He immediately steps away from me and creates space so I can walk towards the door. Black tears flood his broken blue eyes I've come to admire...and, finally, *despise*.

"I'm going to spend whatever time I have left, and I will do it without you. At..."

Home?

I want to say home, but it doesn't feel like it. Hayden started to feel like my home—this Cathedral. I...fell in love with him. I tried to make him feel good and give into his selfishness along with mine. But I got lost in his lies.

"Where? Tell me where?" he begs.

I don't speak. I look away from him and start walking toward the door. I can ask Kallum to put me on a plane.

"My mother's place. Or maybe my brother. They're the only ones I have left."

"She doesn't want you. Your brother left you! They don't love you. But I fucking do. I love you with all that I am. I love you all the time, from the moment I wake up until the second I fall asleep. And even in my dreams, I love you. No one cares about you the way I do. I'd sacrifice my entire world just to *look* at you."

For a moment there, I want to break and give in, forget that he's kept things from me, and forget that he was the one who killed my dad.

No. He's lying. *He just wants his powers.* He's the one that's sick.

"You made me think this entire time my father was alive! You deceived and betrayed me." Hot tears continue to leak, and I sniffle as I rub my nose.

I continue to make my way out of his room, but he keeps calling out for me. He hates that I'm giving him silence.

"Millie," he warns.

I grab the doorknob and turn it.

"Millie!" He shouts with a pained voice. "At least tell me where, baby. Please. Don't go. I...I can fix this. Give me time. I have all the time in the world, remember? Please. Don't leave me. Don't fucking leave me! You're not safe without me! My enemies will find you. I need to protect you. You're all that matters to me! You're all I want! The cruel demons that I endure are only worth it if I have you here to kiss them away. The duties I have to execute..." he stammers before continuing. "Tell me you'll see me next moon?"

I grab my hand, and my face twists into wrath.

"You are the cruel demon in my life."

I pinch the ruby engagement ring on my finger and throw it on the bed. Hayden watches the ring land on it and falls to his knees. He's shaking uncontrollably like he's lost, his jaw clenching with catastrophic failure. This time, he doesn't get what he wants. His eyes have turned crimson, and his fangs protrude over his bottom lip. His shoulders sink, but I refuse to spend another second with him. I grab my diary from his desk and tightly hold it to my side.

I open the door and walk out, slamming the door behind me. To my surprise, he lets me go and doesn't follow me.

With every step, I cry. I cry for my father. I'm crying because now I realize what happens to Valkyrie's. I'm crying because I've fallen in love with an evil, murderous vampire and hate myself for it.

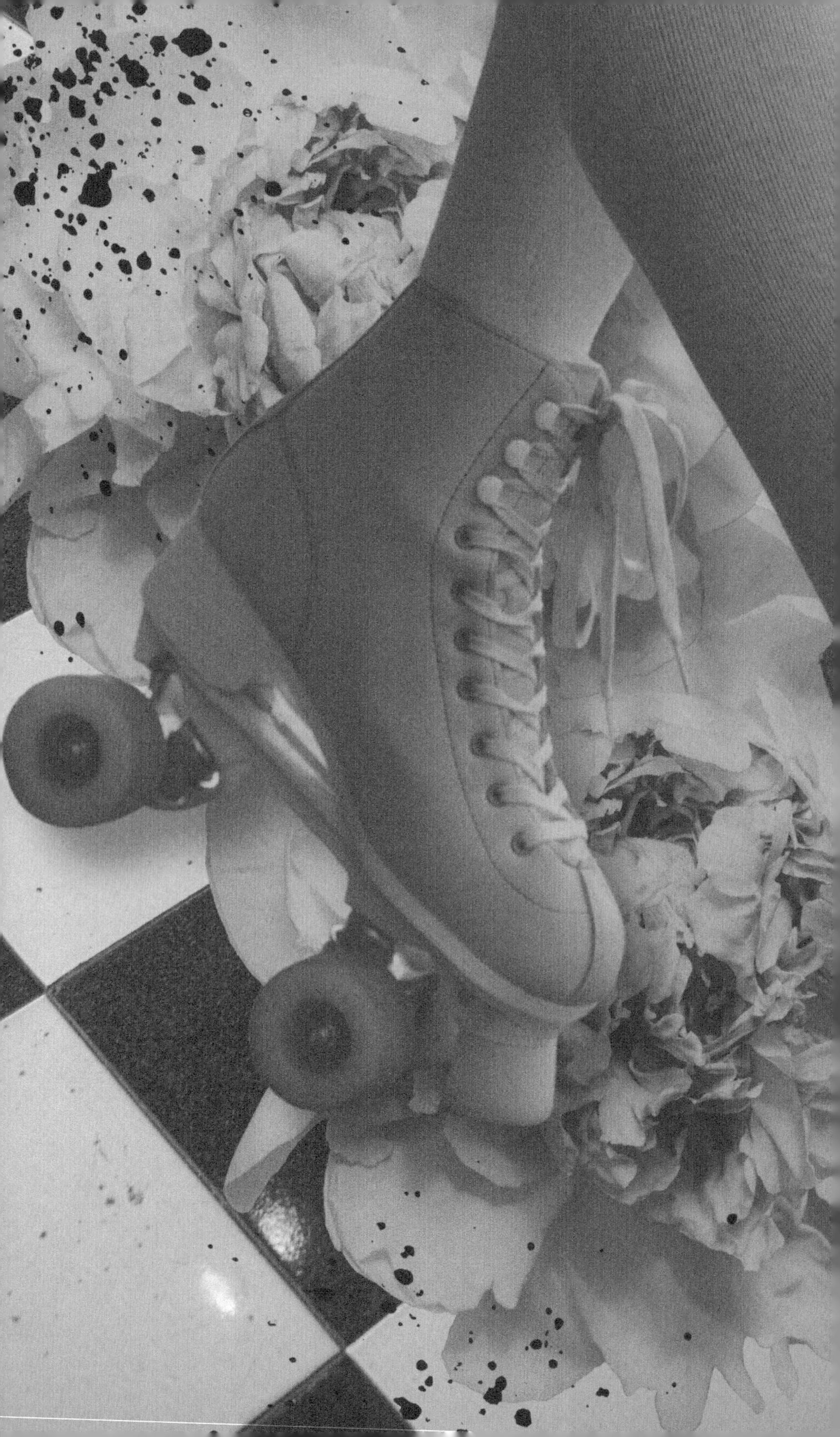

33

MILLIE

IT'S ALMOST midnight when I make it back home. I stare at my father's house like I can't recognize it. I grip the front porch railing tight until the white paint chips underneath my nails. I can't walk in knowing my father won't be there to greet me. Usually, he's there on that one side of the couch he always sits on. He's either watching a sports game or the National news. Or to have awkward conversations about how my day went at school or work because he was still trying to be the best version of a dad he could be since he missed out on years of my life. I can't walk in knowing that I won't see him gearing up his fishing gear because it's the weekend, and he loves to fish for bass on his days off alone. He would always invite me, and I would always say no because work and school had consumed my days. Now I regret it.

We were trying to repair our troubled relationship, and I could tell he regretted leaving my siblings and me. But he's gone now, and I haven't been able to accept it. I need closure, and I don't know how to get it. No one knows I'm here yet. I just wanted to see it without being bombarded with people intruding into my space. There's so much I have to do, but I wanted to start here.

Fifteen Years Ago

"Daddy...when are you coming home? Nash and I haven't seen you in a few days," I asked my father after my mom handed me the house phone. She walked away but never strayed too far so she could hear everything we spoke about.

They had another fight behind closed doors about a week ago. Even though they closed the door, I heard muffled, distressed shouts coming from their room. I sat beside Nash as he played Pac-Man on the Atari 2600 while my parents' behavior attracted my attention. I got up, pressed my ear against the door, and could hear how broken they were beyond repair.

I knew what was coming. Daddy is leaving again.

"Umm...soon. I promise. I'm going to stay at your grandmother's for a bit and visit when I can, okay?"

"No..." I shake my head, refusing to take that answer. "I want you home! I want you and Mommy together. Just like my friends at school."

My father sighs, and his tone breaks into a strangulated sob. He's doing everything he can to hide his sorrow. He doesn't want me to hear that he's hurting too. He shuffles around the phone for a few seconds as I wait patiently.

"Millie, how about this?" he offers. He's changing the subject like he always does, so he doesn't have to tell me the truth. I'm holding my breath as I sit on my mother's bed, staring at a family photo of us at my grandparent's house—a day with all my cousins on Easter, celebrating with a barbecue. I'm in my dad's arms as a one year old while my older brother holds onto my mother's dress, standing in a Lakers Jersey.

"I'm going to take you and your brother to Disneyland. Just

us three, and we're going to get ice cream, watch fireworks, and see all your favorite princesses." He's forcing enthusiasm as he speaks like he wants me to picture our future vacation. I cut him off before he could make his broken promise.

"I don't want to go to Disney, I don't want ice cream, I don't want to see my favorite princess. I want my daddy. I want mom and dad together. Come back home, please!" I sob into the phone.

Silence. Pure silence. He disagrees with me. He's not coming back home this time, is he?

"Millie..." my father murmurs.

I shake my head and cry silently. I run off the bed, clutching the phone tight as my father distantly bellows my name repeatedly for me to answer. I place the phone back into my mother's hands, leaving it without hanging up as my father waits for me to respond. I rush past my worried mother, retreat into my brother's room, and close the door.

Present

I showed up in nothing but the same clothes as the ones I had left Drago's Cathedral in. Kallum made sure to have me on a plane that flew directly to my hometown. He gave me a debit card, which I only used to pay the Taxi driver because I didn't want to give Hayden the satisfaction of needing him ever again.

He killed my father.

I glance at the window in the center of the front door and stare at my reflection. I don't recognize myself. I can see the bite marks that have scarred my neck, as Hayden promised. I palm it and shudder. I feel gross, like I need to scrub my skin until I'm raw and bleeding, but I know that it won't get rid of the imprint he left inside my soul, no matter how many showers or therapies I seek. He'll always be inside me. I feel disgusted with myself that I fell in love with my father's murderer and gave myself to him fully and willingly. I loved it.

No. He forced me to fall in love with him.

My eerie thoughts dissolve when the front door swings open. I gasp, and my muscles tremble. Is that a vampire behind my door?

Everything is starting to hit me all at once...everything that I went through these past few months is not normal, and I want to run away from this world and jet into another, far from these monsters that hide in the night. I turn, my feet craving to bolt into a nearby tree or bush.

I pivot my foot on the porch when I see Nash standing there with Cole and Leah. They're all side by side, somber expressions on their tired faces. All three of them were mid-conversation when their vision pins to mine, and I hold myself again for comfort with my hands. I don't know when I started to do this when I'm anxious, but it's become my routine.

They all stop in their tracks; Nash's sports shoes squeak with friction. They're all stunned, like they're watching something paranormal happen before them, and their faces pale as snow.

I can't talk. I can't move. Or breathe.

I push my long, overgrown bangs out of my face and wave awkwardly. I bite my lip and try to hold myself together until I find the right words.

What the hell do I say?

Hi? I was held captive by a vampire billionaire?

No, that doesn't sound right. They'll throw me into a mental institution if I say that out loud.

Leah is the first one to move. She lunges toward me and practically tackles me into a hug. She starts to bellow uncontrollably as she pushes her body against mine so tight it knocks the air out of me. I cough into her chest as I try to steal the air back that was thrown out of my constricted lungs.

I want to hug her back and join in her tears of relief, *but I can't*. I keep waiting for my vision to sting and my throat to ache, but nothing comes. I feel numb. I'm absolutely numb...*because of him*. I crave to be held by someone who has destroyed me beyond repair...instead.

"Millie! You're here. It's actually you! Oh my God!" Leah cries out.

Cole and Nash appear behind her. They both place their hands on my back, rubbing it in circles to ensure I'm real. I peek a glance through Leah's hair.

"Millie...you're alive. You're okay and in one piece." Cole tells me as his eyes brighten and his cheeks pinken.

Wow. I miss his voice. Was it always that deep and smooth? Have I been gone that long that I don't recognize Cole's voice?

"Where the hell have you been? I'm sorry! But please tell us everything. What happened to my baby sister?!" Nash whisks me away from Leah. He pulls on my arm, wrapping his hand around my elbow, and crushes me with his massive body. Nash smells like he always did before. Before he moved away for college, I see that he still wears Dior Men cologne with Old Spice deodorant.

He wraps his arms around me, suffocating me in his embrace, and I feel him cry. His chest and chin twitch against the top of my head with agony mixed with relief.

Shit.

I've never, ever, ever seen my big brother cry before, and it actually kills me. He pulls back and tightens his hands on my arms, gripping my skin firmly.

They all look at me with vehement, curious eyes, dreading the answers they so desperately seek. But...I'm not ready to give them any yet. I bite my lip and ask myself the one question I need answers to.

"Is it true?" I pause, looking at Cole, Leah, and finally, my big brother. "Is it true Dad's dead?" I stammer with a broken, soft voice.

He purses his lips, nods slowly, and his Adam's apple bobs tensely. "Yes, the night you disappeared, Cole, Hayes, and Leah went to check on you after you quit your job at the coffee shop. He was worried about you, everyone was, so he went to check on you a few days later and found father...he—" Nash pauses, unable to finish his sentence. "He..."

He looks away from me and stares at the floor like he's picturing my dad's dead body. I'm trying not to do that myself, but darkness clouds the corner of my vision before I know it. My once-taut muscles now loosen like I'm about to fall over. I blink briskly, trying my best to pull away from the weakness, but it's overpowering and swallows me whole until I'm in the shadows.

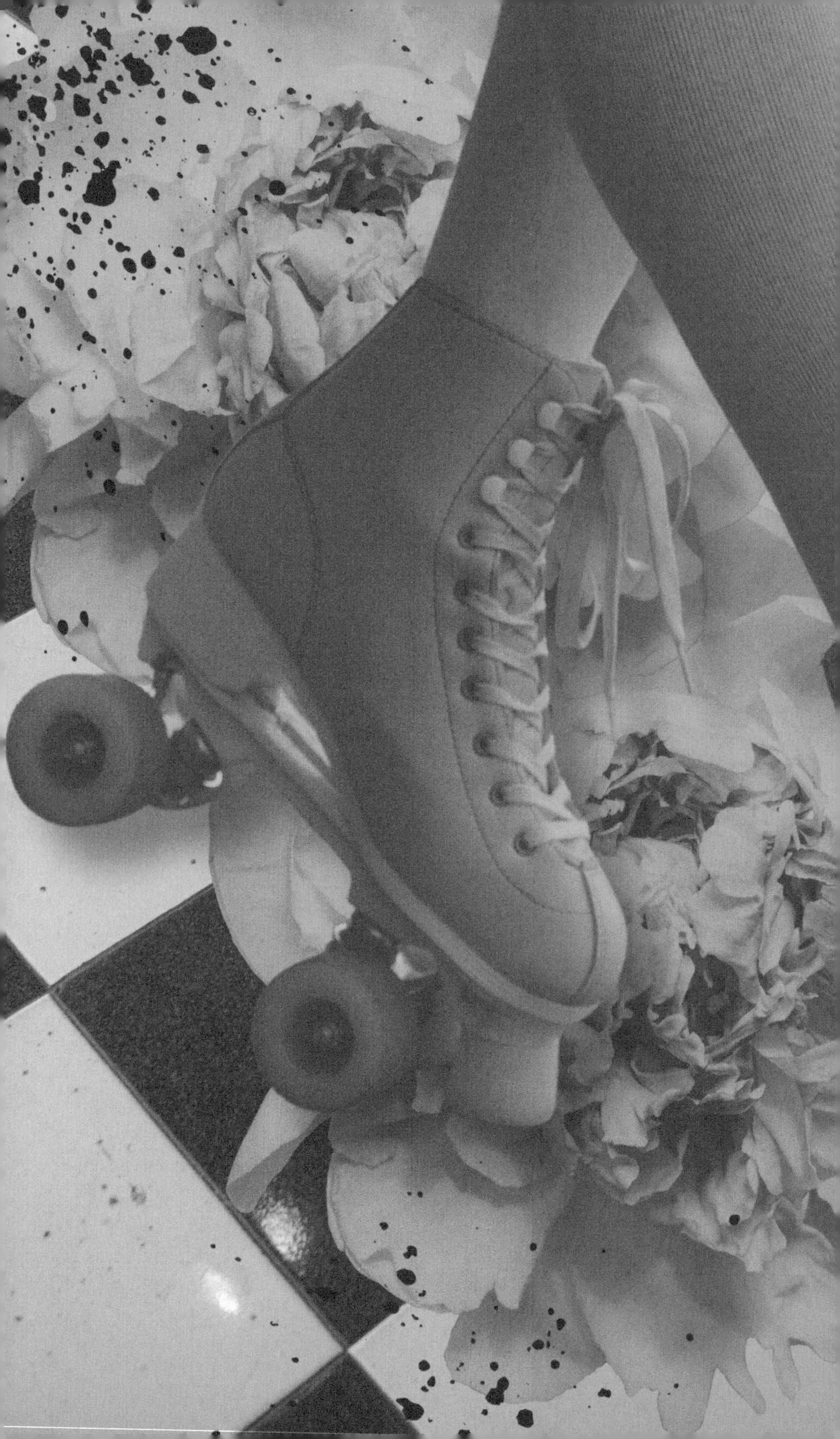

34

MILLIE

Three Weeks Later

I FAINTED after Nash tried to explain. I spent the next two weeks surrounded by doctors and police in the hospital. Nash took me in when I went unconscious, and because I had to know if Hayden and Kallum were telling the truth about 'Valkyries,' I asked them to run scans all over me and dive deep into my blood.

Doctors ran multiple tests on me but could not find any cancers, disease, or tumors. They said something small popped up, and they sent it in for tests, but I won't get those results for a while. So, I think my death will most likely be caused by heart failure. Or maybe the cancer won't show up until I turn twenty-three. Either way, I felt like I had escaped fear, only to be thrown back into it. I would wake up every day wondering if my heart would stop beating.

My face and return to my home have been on every single news network, and I hate it. I hate that I'm now known as a girl who mysteriously disappeared and has now returned safely, but I won't give any details about what I went through.

I'm just not fucking ready. I don't think I'll ever be prepared to share. The police are trying to push me for answers, as well as the therapist they hired to come to my house once a week, but I don't want to talk about it. So I talk about my parents instead.

Or maybe you're still trying to protect Hayden and the ones you love by not revealing his existence. You still love him.

Either way, I cannot form any sentences about Hayden without wanting to cry. So, if I think I'm going to get to a place where I feel like I'm going to scream or break, I push away and avoid the conversation. I explained to Nash that he needs to respect my boundaries by letting me open up to him when I find the perfect moment. He told the police and everyone who was invested or cared about me to back off for now, and everyone agreed.

Leah and even Cole offered me to stay at their place so I wouldn't be alone. I reassured them that I wanted to take on my healing journey *by being alone*. I haven't been alone. I want to grieve my father and what I went through...alone. I need to learn to find solace in solidarity, even if it's one of the lowest times in my life.

I want space and time to think about everything that I went through and losing my father. It doesn't feel real. It's like I refuse to accept my horrid reality where vampires exist and my father is gone.

My mom has called my father's house multiple times to check, and we've talked. The conversations are short, but at least she's checking on me. It's weird to see my mom care about me, but I'm still getting used to it.

Cole told me that our entire small town was on edge because nothing wrong ever happens here, so when I went missing and news of my father's death spread, rules were put in place, and now Santana was on curfew by seven.

The first night in my house was terrible—rough is an understatement. Every time the house creaked, I screamed. Whenever the trees hit my window from the wind blowing a little too hard, I would jump and look around for unusual, vibrant, glowing eyes and sharp teeth.

I tossed and turned, but Cooper would lick my hand, reassuring me that I was okay. It's incredible that dogs can sense when something is wrong internally. I know he can feel the emotional battles I'm fighting.

As Hayden promised, he follows me in my dreams. When I close my eyes, I see him. But I don't picture the depraved side; it's always the moments that made me feel something good when I lived with him.

Even though I managed to get away, I'm still *his prisoner*.

I dreamt of him holding me when I confessed to my suicidal attempt as a teenager. I dreamt of him caring for me while watching my favorite comedy show and cuddling in bed when I had a fever. I dreamt of us both looking at each other brokenly, searching for solace and love within each other because we never had something so pure and rare growing up. I even dreamt of the times we made love with that beautiful giant red ruby ring on my finger. His touch was euphoric, unique, and distinct and I don't think any man will ever be able to match the way he made me feel those months. I wake up flustered, but then I cry when I remember that he forced me to fall in love with him. Everything was built on lies.

He's a monster.

"Do you want to cry and let me hold you while you do that?" Cole breathes out, with sincerity laced in his deep tone. I tilt my head upward on his shoulder. Even through the dark night, the moon and lights from the street illuminate his handsome face. I look into his eyes and watch his blonde, shaggy hair move with the wind. He seems different...more masculine, and fit. It's probably just me, and he's always looked like this.

I asked my brother to get me out of the house. I wanted to start facing my fears one by one, which was the moon. How embarrassing is that? But it's because I know that our world is full of creatures that come out to play during the night and are out for blood, but knowing that Hayden is far away and the Southern Vampire King is dead, I feel a layer of immunity.

Unfortunately, Nash said he had much studying to catch up on, so he invited Cole to come over and take me out. It's the weekend before Thanksgiving, and I need a breather from being isolated in my house.

Being with Hayden was suffocating, yet the most alive I had ever felt. How could those two coexist?

Nash has been grocery shopping and doing house chores. He's been sleeping downstairs on the couch. We both can't step inside our father's bedroom without feeling a never ending sorrow that hits us like a wave that'll drown us in grief. It's like we're both afraid to admit he's gone and never coming back.

"Millie?" Cole's concerned tone brings me back to my cruel reality. I blink rapidly, forcing myself to concentrate on my present. Because I'm not in Montana. I'm not with Hayden.

I'm with Cole, eating popcorn and drinking soda at a drive-in movie theater, watching The Faculty next to other college students in groups and young couples making out.

My eyes fall to his pink lips, and I can feel his muscles tighten when he catches my gaze. I give him a slight curve of my lips as I turn back to the projector in front of us. "I'm done crying. I just want to smile."

He holds me tighter, and the memories of when he gave me oral sex a year ago come back. I always thought he would be my first; maybe I should have taken it further that day, but I knew our relationship would be based on unsure feelings if I had.

Because, yes, he's a good man. He's been there for me since we started working together at Nostalgia Coffee Shop, but I didn't crave him like he needs and deserves. I learned what that truly feels like earlier this year from a sinister monster with hypnotizing features.

Right after Cole went down on me that day and made me have my first orgasm with his tongue, I felt bliss, but then the pizza man rang his door, interrupting our moment, and then we spent the rest of the holiday together watching movies, and I even helped him study until he took me home. He's always respectable, always patient, and a gentleman.

We sit there watching a movie about aliens attacking a school, and I find myself finally forgetting a little about Hayden. Cole's finger circles the skin of my arm right by my tricep, and I stare at it.

"I missed you." Cole's blatant confession warms me.

I clench my jaw, fighting the flutter in my stomach. I don't want to talk about my absence.

A jump scare plays in the movie, causing everyone to gasp and scream. I look around and try to focus on my breathing.

"I knew something was wrong when you quit, and then you disappeared... I felt *guilty*. I felt like I should have tried to pry better and protect you because that's what friends do, right?" Cole explains with a stern tone. "I love you, Millie. I'm telling you this now because I regretted not saying it before you vanished. I love you in many ways. I love you like a coworker, a friend, a lover..."

I stay focused on the movie and purse my lips. "There's nothing you could have done. Please don't feel bad about what happened to me."

"What did happen to you? What happened to your father? Do you have any idea who did that? Is it the same person that took you? Do you know where this criminal asshole is?" He sits more up and leans forward until his cheek is centimeters from colliding with mine.

"Millie? You can talk to me—just like old times. I've never betrayed your trust, and I never will. You can tell me anything—"

I cut him off and snap.

"I can tell you anything, *huh*? How's this? The person who took me and killed my father is a monster. A monster that I fell in love with. How's that?" I fight the lump in my throat as I shift in the passenger seat.

His eyes widen, and he swallows nervously. His teeth grind, and I can only imagine he's thinking about what *falling in love with my captor* entails, but I will spare him the details of fucking a vampire. By the way his body slumps and his hands tremble with anger, he gets the idea, and it crushes him.

"I'm scared of everything right now. I'm scared that he's still here, watching me. I can still feel him inside me. I can still feel the way he moves and walks. I'm scared that if he sees you holding me right now or even looking at me the way you are, *he'll kill you*. And he'll take pleasure in hearing you scream just because you care about me the way he does."

There it is again, a sting pricks my eyes and threatens to

break me, but this time, I relax my shoulders and suck in a shaky breath. Cole tenses and his warm fuzzy aura about him diminishes into a cold stare. His forehead is clammy, and I can feel his outrage radiating like a magnet.

"He's the one that should be scared. If I ever get my hands on him, he'll regret ever touching you," he threatens as he balls his fists.

I scoff and tilt my head side to side because he has no idea that when I say monster, I mean an immortal vampire.

"Cole. He's bad. Very, very bad. I don't want to think about anything. I don't want to think about missing my father's closed-casket funeral because he was so badly mutilated that they could only identify him by his teeth. I don't want to think about anything, *please...*"

What am I pleading for exactly? For Hayden to come back and pretend that he's actually a good guy and hold me because it's his arms I want to melt into right now? Or for my heart to fail so I can be with my dad? Because I refuse to turn into a creature that craves blood and lives a malice outrageous lifestyle that will have me damned to hell.

I feel so lost.

Cole forces a smile through his tortured face, hearing me fall apart. He grabs my hand, pulls it to his lips, and kisses my knuckles.

"I'm going to get us some M&M's before they close the candy stand. I'll be right back." He tucks a strand of my bangs behind my ear, and I stare blankly at him. He's waiting for confirmation.

He knows those are my favorite chocolates.

"Come on. Show me that smile I've missed," he teases.

I squint my eyes at him like he asked me something ridiculous. He pokes my stomach with his two fingers right below my ribs, where he knows I'm the most sensitive from our past tickle fights at work on our lunch breaks.

"Cole," I seethe jokingly. "Don't you dare."

He does it again and again, causing me to flinch every time he pokes me, but then he starts to move his fingers using both hands.

"Stop!" I hiss, keeping my voice low, not wanting to disrupt the movie with my giggles. He wins.

"There's that smile that makes me so fucking happy," he tells me. He laughs and continues to tickle me. He pauses for a second and gets close to me as he closes the distance. His lips are right in front of mine. There's that moment again. The same look he gave me on Thanksgiving right before he kissed me...*everywhere*.

I grin and try to fight and slap his hands away until I'm full-blown laughing and chuckling with him. Both of us have broad smiles, and we're twisting for dominance. I love seeing Cole like this; it reminds me why he's one of my close friends.

He leans in closer like he's about to kiss me. I slowly blink, like I'm lost. What do I do?

Then lightning strikes in the distance, causing a flash of bright blue light to illuminate the drive-in theater momentarily. Thunders follows suit, rattling the car's windows and the metal on Cole's hood.

Suddenly, I see a familiar shade of crimson.

Vibrant. Glowing. And ominous eyes on me.

Hayden.

I scream. Lightning strikes again, causing the movie to jump and the screen to go black for a few seconds. It's enough to distract me from the eerie, tall figure behind Cole and hidden in the trees behind him a few feet away. I look back to the dancing trees, but he's not there anymore.

Am I seeing things? Or is he really here? Watching me?

Planning to kill the rest of my family because I escaped him? Either way, he's haunting me. Will I ever truly evade him?

I grab Cole's hands, pull them off me to protect him, and jump in the passenger seat. Fear invades my vessels, and I palm my scream with cold hands. Everyone in the drive-in theater turns to me as I try to catch my breath after finishing a loud, high-pitched, blood-curdling bellow.

Cole's in my face, inspecting me. "What's wrong, Millie? It's just lightning, darling." He cups my jaw, forcing me to look at him.

But I can't talk. I can't even look at him because I'm so concentrated on the trees behind him. Tears fall from the corner of my eyes, and I dig my fingers into Cole's jacket fiercely.

"Get me home, now! I want to go. We have to go, okay? Please?" I hold onto his arms like a lifejacket. He nods and kisses my forehead.

"Looks like the rain came early tonight, anyway. Let's get you into bed." He closes the windows and turns on the vehicle. He carefully reverses his truck, and we pull out of the field. Soon enough, rain patters the windshield, and Cole turns on the wipers. During the drive, Cole plays Oasis, and I try to focus on the trees. I keep waiting to see red eyes or dark brown hair again, but it never comes.

It couldn't be him. I'm being paranoid. I know it wasn't him because if it were, Cole would be dead right now, and I'd be getting dragged back to Montana against my will. It couldn't be him...

As Cole walks me to my house, Nash waits for me at the door, arms crossed and worried.

"Do you want me to stay the night? I can stay downstairs. Or in your bedroom? Whatever you want. I don't feel good about leaving you alone," Cole offers sweetly when we get to my porch. He walked me to my door like the perfect gentleman that he's always been. I smile, and I'm on my tip-toes to reach his cheek. I brush my lips softly on his winter-kissed skin.

"I'll be fine..." I lie. He knows it, Nash knows it, and I know it. I'm sure Nash has told him about the nights I wake up screaming...

I'm back in their Southern Vampire territory, and I know I may still be in trouble deep down. Even though Hayden was unhinged and unstable, he would never *actually hurt me.*

I rush into the house before Cole can complete his farewell. Nash tries to stop me.

"Millie...wait! How was the movie?"

But I'm in the house half a second later. I dart inside the living room, passing the television that plays a Christmas movie. I barge into my room and start packing my things. I need to leave. I need to become a ghost if I want to live the last two years of my life in peace, knowing that my family will be safe from all the vampires that know where I live. The longer I'm around them, the more I put them at risk, and I can't have that hanging over my head.

I'll spend one more day here and catch a flight to Alaska. I have some money saved up from the coffee shop, and I'll use it to fly. It should be enough to keep me afloat for a month until I find a job.

Still, before I go to bed that night, I stare at my work roller skates as I wonder about Hayden and his mother, with whom I formed a strange, unusual bond. I keep pondering whether he ended up marrying another vampire. His father wanted his marriage to be finalized this month, and since I am no longer with him, it makes sense that his title and position would move forward, and he would be the new vampire king in his region, with or without me.

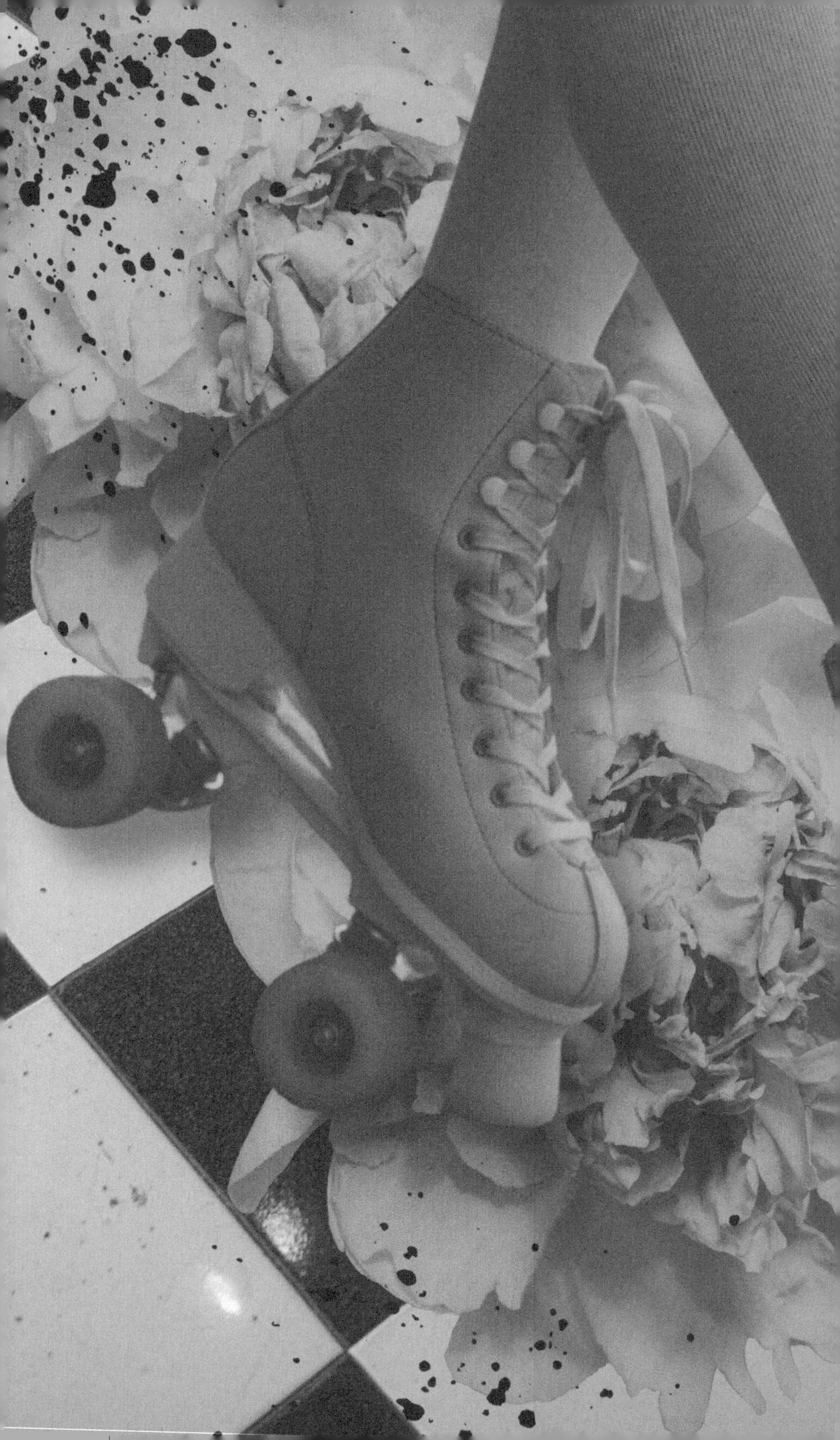

35

MILLIE

THE NEXT DAY, Nash and my mother ambushed me. My flight doesn't leave until tomorrow morning, but I wanted to spend the day hanging out with Leah. I haven't really been able to hang out with her since I've been home, and I wouldn't feel complete leaving her behind without a decent farewell.

"Millie, you need to tell the police about the man who kidnapped you." My mom breaks the silence. I still hadn't turned in Hayden, although I know if the police were to try and go after him, they would never find him.

I play with the ends of my sleeve anxiously in the living room. The fireplace is going, and it helps ease my nerves. No one knows I'm going to disappear again tomorrow. I have it all planned out already. I'm going to leave a note ensuring my safety and call them every other month to check in so they're not worried sick.

"Mom...why do you care? You've never cared about me before. It only took for me to disappear and for my father to die for you to realize you have a daughter who needs you," I quip as my frustration paints my tone.

My mother purses her lips and clicks her tongue.

"I love you. I know I don't say it often enough, but I love you both. You are my children," she responds while darting her hazel eyes at the both of us. Nash fidgets uncomfortably as he holds a book in his hand.

"Actions," I murmur as I watch the flames crackle behind her. My tone is bland but concrete.

"What?" she questions me, confused with narrowed brows.

"Actions speak louder than words, Mom. You say you love your daughter, but who still lives in the home you raised us in?" I ask, biting my lip.

Santiago.

"You say you love us, but when's the last time you asked us how our day went or showed up for anything, like picking me up from work when I didn't have a ride? Or show up to my high school graduation when I made valedictorian? Where were you?"

With Santiago.

"You say you love us, but growing up, who is the one that always came first before us?"

Santiago.

"That's enough!" My mother stands.

"All I ever wanted was to protect you from him, make you open your eyes, and be the person to make you realize that you deserve to be loved faithfully and kind. To show you that I'll always be your daughter. Why do you shut me out when I try and help you? Be there for you like you should be for us?"

"I will not be here to listen to this!" she pouts, grabbing her purse and starts for the door, but I keep going.

"Do you know that I'm scared all the fucking time? I'm scared because if I ever find someone who genuinely wants to be with me, and when they tell me they love me, I can't believe them."

Hayden and Cole pop into my head.

"I'm afraid to commit to a man because I'm afraid he'll cheat on me or leave me." My voice cracks as I remember all the memories of growing up and seeing my mom failing to find the one to show her that true love exists over and over again after continued failed relationships and that it doesn't have to always come from a man. It can come from various things. It can come from family...or friends.

Nash wraps his hands around my arms and tries to hold me from behind, but I gently remove his hands from me. She opens the door to my father's house, and I sniffle. With a tear rolling down her cheek, she stands and places one foot onto the porch.

"I pray every night. Every night since I was a child, you would finally leave Santiago, choose us, or choose yourself and chase a true happily ever after because I believe in them. *No matter what anyone tells me, I believe in them.*"

Again, Hayden pops into my head, and I hate myself for it. Hayden wanted me to have children with him. He told me one night that he would always ensure his children and wife were first. He was faithful to me the entire time we were together and promised to stay devoted to me, and I believe him. I consumed him from the moment he went to sleep until we saw each other on the next moon. Despite his flaws, he never beat me; he cared for me. He's afraid of the same thing I'm scared of.

Abandonment.

And I left him.

It hits me at this moment, and it strikes me hard. That Hayden still has me under his spell. I palm the scarred bite mark on my neck, pressing my hand on it, wishing I could hear his voice echo in my head whenever I strayed too far, like the concert or whenever I would take care of his mother's garden.

"You know...the man that took me is the only person that

made me feel seen, heard, and—" I trail off, thinking about the way Hayden would touch me, hold me, kiss me, and look at me like I was the only person in our world.

Desired. Loved.

I can't say it. The way my mother and brother are looking at me right now, I don't like it. Nash furrows his brows, confused and disappointed, while my mom looks disgusted as her face turns slack.

I don't want to feel ashamed for falling in love with Hayden. He's a broken soul like I am. I can relate to him in so many ways...our trauma, but I cannot save him, and I cannot fix him. That conclusion of inevitable reality hit me when I found out he killed my father and lied about what exactly I am.

I look away from them and stare at the pictures of my dad and me on my first day of college above the fireplace. He holds me with his arm around my shoulder in front of the university mascot. He never smiles in photos, but he did in this one. I like to think he was proud of me. The familiar dull pain pulls at my throat and chest, and I let out a heavy exhale.

"How could you say that?" She shakes her head. "Goodbye, Millie." Mom closes the door, and I sink onto the couch where my dad used to sit.

"Goodbye, Mom," I whisper and silently hold myself.

"A SERIES OF ANIMAL ATTACKS HAVE RESURFACED AND left five people dead. Curfew was lifted when Millie Flores returned home safely, but now the Mayor is taking more precautions. We may have a serial killer in town, the same one police are after, and since Pete Flores' case remains unsolved, the entire town is on edge again."

I hear the news reporter as I walk to the kitchen. I cross the living room behind Nash as he sits where my dad used to be.

"Turn it up, please? I want to listen to this," I ask him, and he quickly turns, catching my worried gaze. He scatters for the TV remote and turns it off. Like I just caught him watching something vulnerable and wrong.

"Why'd you do that?" I try to reach for the remote, but he stands up and tucks the remote in his jeans. He stares at me, forcing his big brother smile like he's trying to comfort me.

"I'm still your big brother. I still need to protect you. I'm the man of the house now, and I say, TV rots your brain." He pulls me in and tucks his arm over my shoulder. He hooks my neck with his bicep, squeezing, and starts to nudge his knuckles into my head playfully.

"Stop, get off, jerk," I joke as I push him away.

We both stand there in an awkward yet warm exchange between us. It feels like old times before he moved away for college. He's trying hard to take care of me and distract me from falling into depression again. He knows I struggle with battles against myself. But I don't need anyone to do that for me. I can do it alone. He's trying to rekindle our sibling relationship but doesn't know how to. He breaks the silence.

"I'm going out tonight to study with some friends over a video call. I'm still able to do group projects from home. The professors and the university have understood our entire situation."

Nash starts to pack his things from the dining room table. He places his books in there and grabs his car keys. He heads for the door.

"I just paid off all of Dad's debt that shifted over to us, by the way. Like his house, the funeral..."

Cooper licks my hand, and I smile down at him and pet him repeatedly. "Wow, our community is awesome." I get on my knees just as Cooper rolls over to his back, his tongue hanging out happily, and I give him tummy rubs.

"Yeah. No kidding. One person made a one hundred million dollar donation. I put the rest away in a savings account."

Something pulls at me, and a lightbulb goes off. I immediately think of one person I know capable of having that much money and wouldn't blink an eye to drop that amount. I clear my throat and stand. I ball my fists.

"Who was it?" I ask in an accusatory manner.

"We don't know, it was anonymous." Nash shrugs and takes a bite of a Gala apple.

I stare at him pensively.

"When did they make this donation?" I pry further. I tighten my eyes and rub my lips together. I lean against the wall and cross my arms against my chest.

He starts to chew slowly like he's weirded out. He shifts on his feet. His dark black hair moves to the side when he blows his shoulder-length hair out of his brown eyes that try to figure me out.

"The night you came back home..." he sing-songs like he has no idea why I could be upset by this. I'm questioning him like it's a horrible thing because I know who gave us that money.

Hayden. It had to be him.

"Return it!" I stalk off toward my bedroom. My footsteps thud against the tile, and I'm seconds away from pushing open my bedroom door and looking for my own car keys so I can go to Leah's house.

"Umm, no? Millie, what's wrong with you?" he roars after me, but I can't face him because if I do, I may word vomit out of emotion, and I need to control myself. I tense up as Nash grabs my hand and pulls me back a little into the hallway before I can escape into my bedroom. Cooper stands on his two back legs and whines. He barks at the both of us like he's trying to tell us to stop arguing.

"Talk to me, dammit! It's been weeks since you've been home. You know something. You know who did this to Dad, and it's like you're protecting them! Is that why you don't want to say anything?" He accuses me. His forehead vein bulges, and my protective, authoritative big brother is back. The one that isn't scared to hurt my feelings or crush my boundaries.

"Back off, Nash!" I pull my hand away, and he lets me go.

"No! He's my father! We need justice!"

I want to scream at him. I want to tell him everything, but I must protect Nash from what I've seen and know. If that makes me a villain in his eyes...*to save his life*, then I'll be that.

"Please...leave it alone," I beg with tears clinging to my eyes.

He grinds his jaw and breathes heavily through his nose. His white shirt moves up and down as he tries to calm himself down. We stare at each other in the hallway. I have no words but beleaguered emotions that speak a thousand words when I don't have to.

He takes a deep breath, nods apologetically, and leaves the house. Great. This will be the last time I see Nash, and it had to be an argument. I get lost in my thoughts once again. I've come to terms with my father's death. It hurts. Our plans are dead alongside him. I feel partially responsible, but I try to push that out of my head. I know it was out of my control, but I can't help but feel like everything is my fault. I didn't ask for any of this to happen. I'm focusing on readjusting my future one day at a time.

I shake my head, passing by my dad's redwood wallpaper; I grab my keys and head to my car with one destination in mind.

I haven't told Leah anything. I didn't tell her I was showing up tonight, either. I've been so lost in my head that I forget where I am sometimes. Thankfully, I remember how to get to her house by memory and our countless hangouts before Hayden took me.

She still lives about ten minutes away from my house, in a neighborhood that's right by the mall. I park my car two houses down because it seems that Leah's neighbor is having a party and leaving nowhere to park in front. As I walk down the street, I can smell good old Texas BBQ and brisket being cooked in the distance, and it makes my mouth water. Country music plays, and I know it's George Strait.

I get closer to Leah's front door, walking across the front lawn to get there. I pass her bedroom window, and I get the same temptation to scare her by tapping on her window like I always do when I come over.

Grinning mischievously, I feel like my old self again—at least for a split second—because when I walk up to her window, her curtains are open, like she always loves to keep them. My playful demeanor vanishes when I'm holding up my hand to knock against the glass. I freeze like I've been caught in the middle of something I don't want to be in. I see my close friends together in a way that makes me go sick to my stomach, and I'm tempted to retch up my dinner.

I wish I could erase this from my memory. I wish I never came here. Because then I could pretend that my two best friends were still in my corner. But this is real life, and shit happens.

Cole is getting sucked off by Leah. His shirt is off, his triceps flexing hard as he tugs on her hair. He's fucking her face slow and gently. His eyes are on her mouth, and she looks like she's choking on him from how rough he's being with her throat. But she smiles like she's enjoying it through her gags. She's bare naked while Cole has his pants hanging down by his thighs.

They're looking at each other the way Hayden and I used to. Are they in love?

I tear my eyes away from her window, and my blood runs cold. I take off running back to my car, pressing the unlock button over and over again when I'm still a few feet away. I can't hear George Strait anymore, just my pulse thundering. I get in my car, slam the door shut, and peel out of her neighborhood. The entire time I drive home, I'm sobbing and gripping the steering wheel until the rubber pinches my skin from the friction.

I don't know why I'm crying. I think it's just from shock.

Every single minute I get closer to my dad's house, I hope Cole didn't catch me. There's no way Leah did because I could only see the back of her head. I don't need them to know that I saw that. They're free to do whatever they want.

What did I expect? I was gone for months. They probably turned to each other for comfort and did the cliche thing and started to fuck their grief out. But why am I hurting? Why do I care?

I never saw Cole in that way, anyway, but I guess it's the principle of feeling like they kept it from me that shocks me. Either way, how could they explain their relationship to me? I've been trying to heal. I'm an emotional person overall, and I guess I just wanted to say goodbye to Leah by watching our favorite Rom-Com movies and playing board games in her room until we got full on popcorn and snacks.

But things are different. I'm not the same person I was since I got taken the first time by the blonde vampire who broke my wrist. I'm not. But I'm determined to live the rest of my remaining life to the fullest.

When I get to my house, I run inside and lock the doors behind me. However, when I get to my room to try and finish packing up the rest of my things, the house phone rings.

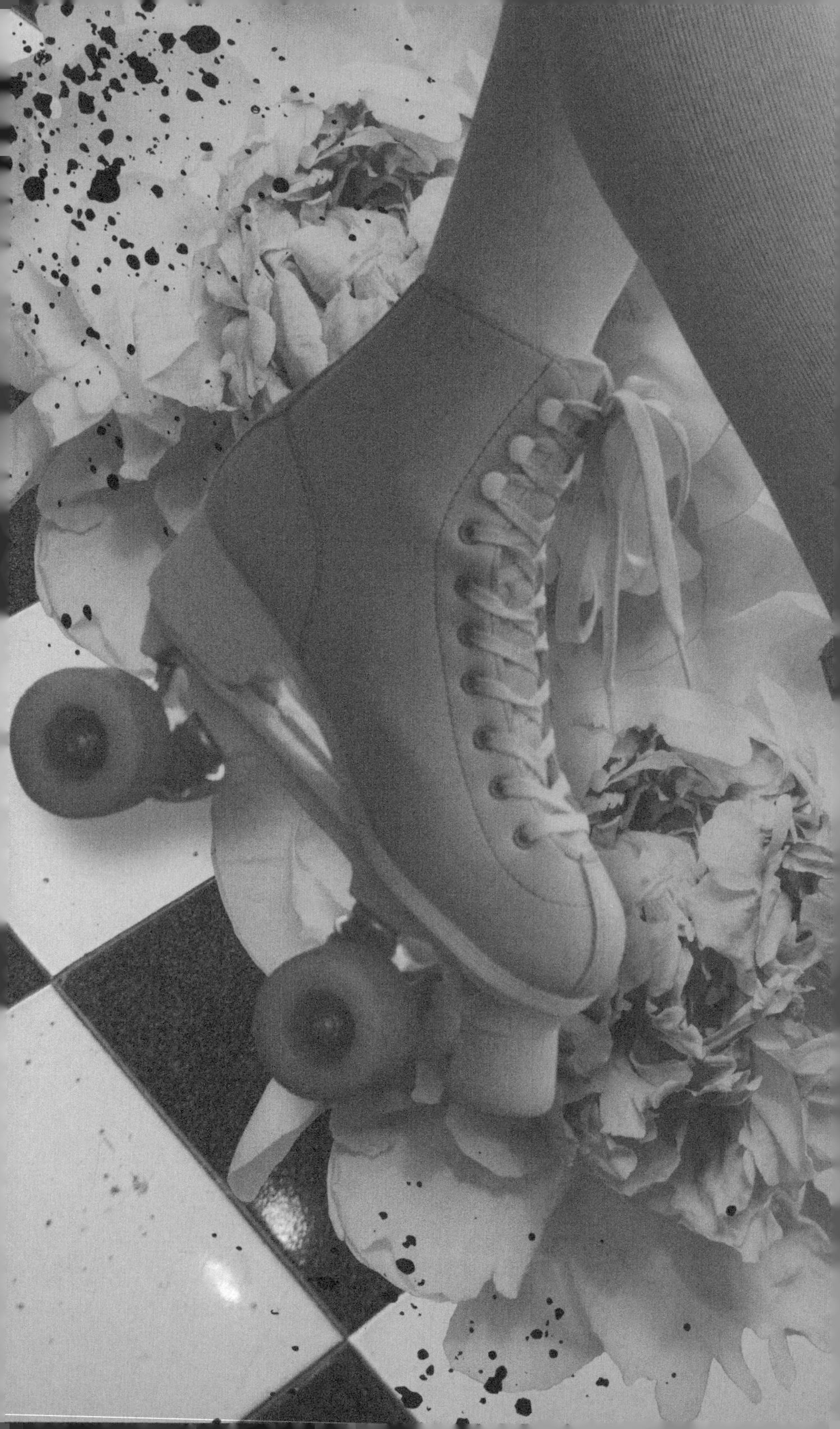

36

MILLIE

I DON'T WANT to answer it. I've been avoiding the constant ringing of my house phone like the plague because, most of the time, it's the detective from the local police station on my case or family members who have never checked on me before, wanting to invade my space. I stare at it as it hits the fourth ring. I curse under my breath, and my anxiety slowly withers away.

"Hello?"

"Hey! My older sister Penelope told me you drove by?" Leah tells me sleepily.

I start coughing and choking on my spit.

I'm caught.

"Are you okay?" she asks with a giggle.

I suck in a breath and try to clear my tangled nerves. Shit.

She knows I was there...

"Yeah. I did, but I..."

"Sorry, I was so tired from work today that I napped hard. I just woke up. Why'd you leave? Come back. We haven't hung out, and I miss you!" she chirps happily.

Why is she lying?

"You know Leah...you don't have to lie to me. Even if the truth hurts, I can take it. But lying to me about being with Cole tonight is just weird. If you guys are together, that's fine. I want you to be happy, and if it's with him—"

"Millie? What are you talking about? I've been alone since I got home from work. I mean...yes, Cole and I talk, but we've never done anything romantic or past friendship. I would tell you if we were dating. I just got you back. I don't want to ruin our friendship."

"Leah," I call her out, appalled. Why is she lying and doing it so confidently? "I saw you with him tonight through your window." I pause, shuffling the phone to my other ear. The front door to my father's house slams shut, and I don't think twice about it. I know Nash is back home from studying.

"I saw you...with Cole. I went up to your window and was going to try and tap on your window like I always used to do. But then I saw that you were quite occupied, and you were..." I shake my head, blinking rapidly, trying to keep my voice as casual as possible. I don't want those images in my head right now. "I left right away, and it's okay. I—"

Leah interrupts me. "I swear on my mother, Cole wasn't here. I've been napping!"

I try to respond, but then I hear a dead tone. All the electricity flickers momentarily before it goes out, and the phone dies. Did she hang up on me? She wouldn't do that to me. She's not like that. She's the type of friend who addresses harsh topics until we find a solution. Never angry or close-minded.

"Leah?" I ask, ensuring we lost connection. She doesn't respond, and I get a horrible feeling. Trepidation crawls into my skin, and I grip the phone tighter than I should. Darkness floods the entire house, and rain starts to tap harshly on the roof and windows, joining my shallow, fast breaths. Thunder explodes and rattles the windows.

No.

No.

We're not doing this. Everything is fine. I'm okay. I'm safe. No vampires are here, and I am leaving tomorrow.

Optimism.

"What the hell?" I place the phone back on the wall. "Nash! What's going on? The electricity is out?"

I'm returned with silence, which fuels my negative thoughts more.

Why isn't he responding?

"Nash? Are you home?" I walk into the living room and expect to see him on the couch, but he's not there. I furrow my brows, confused, and continue to call out to him.

"Nash!" I bypass the dining room and the kitchen, opening the door to my father's room, and pause. I don't know why I hesitate, as if I'm about to see my father walk out of his bathroom to tell me to stop my shouting. Flashes of him in his work uniform, fatigued red eyes, and darkened under circle holding my dinner plate for me. But it's just that. A flash of a memory with nothing to support it. He's gone.

I will not cry...

Swallowing the lump in my throat, I close the door and turn around to face the dark hallway. I check the parking lot through the front window by the living room, but I don't see Nash's Jeep.

Huh?

I must have left the front door open when I came back home. I must have forgotten to close it because I was so jumpy from seeing Cole with Leah that I wasn't careful.

I need to find a flashlight. I rummage through the kitchen

drawers, pulling them out individually, but I don't find any. I only see utensils, random batteries, and postcards.

Cooper follows me everywhere I go, his nails clacking against the tile with each step. I give him a small smile as I push through my dad's things in the drawer. I lean forward a little to get a better look and bend my knees slightly for a better angle to reach things through the cupboard.

"Do you know where Dad kept the flashlight, baby boy? I swear it's always by the—" I always talk to Cooper like he'll be able to talk back to me magically. My question gets cut off and replaced by another one.

"The pantry?" A man asks me in a tone I don't recognize.

I stop moving, paralyzed by the sudden intrusion. I slowly turn around, dazed and suspicious, because I didn't hear my close friend come into the house, never mind walk up to me. I whip around to find Cole in the kitchen with us, pointing my father's flashlight at me, waving it in circles like a game.

"Cole? What are you doing here?" I ask, stepping back until my behind collides with the kitchen counter.

Wasn't he just with Leah? Why is he inside my house? I mean, I don't mind.

It's Cole.

Cooper starts to growl beside me like he's warning Cole to stay away from me. He turns off the flashlight, and the lights in my father's house come back on. The light from the hallway gives the kitchen dim lighting, barely enough to see that Cole's dressed in a white jacket, black pants, and Converse. He's not wearing his glasses. He's looking at me like never before with devious, cruel intentions.

Is he mad I saw Leah and him together?

"I'm here because..." He looks me up and down like he's trying to undress me with his eyes, and I cross my arms over my chest. "Because it's time you tell me the truth, and I want to hear it from your Northern Vampire fucker mouth."

I gasp, and my mouth drops wide open. He takes a step closer to me, and I grip the counter tightly, looking for something to protect myself. Cooper starts to bark at him furiously.

Is Cole here to hurt me? How does he know about vampires?

"I don't know what you're talking about, Cole. Why are you here?" I ask, keeping my gaze on him. The hair on the back of my neck stands up.

He never takes his eyes off of me. His silence is deafening, and the only thing I can hear is the blood rushing to my ears, thunder shaking the walls of my house, and my heart thumping in my chest.

"I loved you, Millie. I fell in love with you slowly over time. I could relate to you with having shitty parents that didn't want you—being the second-born son with hard-to-impress parents. Well, I have my fair share of trauma. But don't we all? They always overlooked me because I wasn't born first. But now, I've been called for a deeper purpose, and I had to give you up once The Depraved Prince murdered my older brother!" Cole crushes my father's flashlight in his hand when he squeezes it, and I watch all the bits and pieces fall to the floor. Cooper barks louder and starts to walk in front of me like he wants to pounce on Cole.

"What are you talking about?!" I ask, dumbfounded.

"So you want to act clueless?" Cole grins wickedly. He laughs slowly, and then his teeth become large fangs, slowly popping over his lips. Teeth I've come to know too well, and his eyes transform into a glimmering vibrant blue contrast to his original brown ones.

Is Cole a Southern vampire? Since when?!

"Oh my god. You...you're a vampire?" I breathe out while my shoulders sink, and I rub my eyes with my palms.

I swallow my nerves, almost choking on brewed anxiety. I start looking for a knife, desperately seeking protection. Even though I know it's not enough to protect myself, maybe it'll help.

"I didn't want to turn, but your boyfriend changed everything for me and my family. Or maybe he's an ex-boyfriend because you're back home now, and I don't see Prince Drago anywhere near you."

"Get out!" I yell, grabbing my father's pocket knife from the drawer, and holding it in front of me. Cooper senses the tension and the danger we're both in and lunges for Cole's throat. He flies forward, barking, snarling, and biting, and my heart sinks into my stomach.

"Cooper! NO!" I try to pull him back, but it's too late. Cooper bites his forearm and tries to dig his teeth in, but Cole is inhumanely fast. He grabs Cooper aggressively, forcing him to cry out and yelp, and Cooper goes limp with low whimpers on the floor.

"You evil monster!" I shout, gripping the knife harder, desperate to put it inside him. "Did you just kill Cooper?!" I'm seeing red.

"Come here, get on your knees, and find out." He dares me with an evil smile, pointing to Cooper. I dart my eyes to the floor, and thankfully, I can see he's still breathing but too weak to move.

Asshole. And there's nothing I can do to kill him but wait until the sun rises, and even then, it's still hours away.

"Does Leah know about you?" I bite out while my eyes well with tears.

"Didn't your boyfriend tell you? When we drink from humans, it erases their memory. They can't remember anything after. Leah doesn't remember the reason why her throat is so bruised from my dick tonight because I bit her right after. Unfortunately, it doesn't work on you because of how *special* you are." He throws air quotes around the word 'special.' He scoffs and glares. "Leah was so eager to get a taste of me...an easy whore for me to use, and she doesn't even remember it the next day. Pathetic." He chuckles as he throws his head back, satisfied as the memories play back into both of our heads of their sexual encounter.

"Aww, are you jealous of Leah? Want me to fuck you too?" he continues.

"Screw you. I would never let you touch me!"

"*Let me*? Poor little Millie. You naive bitch. I'm going to rape you over and over again, suck you dry, and dismember your body, then send it to your boyfriend."

"Cole... I cared about you! Why? What have I done to you?" I narrow my eyes and grip the knife handle harder, ready to use it.

"Well, one. You should have given me your cherry when I had the chance. But you gave it up to my enemy. Two, you're back here, and I know you're planning to leave for Alaska. Once you cross territories, I can't touch you. I wanted to kill you in front of him, but it looks like I'm going to get to have torturous fun with you for a bit longer. Let me take you home to my mother and show her I got the New Northern King's little pet under my leash. A Valkyrie."

I try to run for it, but then he's in front of me, blocking me, and I halt before I bump into him. I raise my knife, ready to fight for my life, but he grabs my wrist, the same one I broke earlier this year, and twists it until I feel pain.

"Ah!" I scream. "No!" I don't think it's broken, but it hurts enough for me to let go of it.

I struggle in his hold, but he doesn't let up. He pulls my

hair to the side while I punch him everywhere I can. His gaze locks onto my neck with a wide smirk, but then it falls when he sees Hayden's mark.

"He marked you?" he murmurs, his tone full of shock. He loosens his grip, just like he's trying to process the information. "The Depraved Prince actually fell in love with you?" he scoffs, disgusted. His face turns red like he's about to rip me apart from envy.

Is that what it means when the teeth marks don't disappear? Is that a vampire thing?

Still, he holds me tight, and I swear if he could kill me with his murderous gaze, I would be dead. Still, if I can't kill him with my mortal body, I can wound him with my words.

"Wow, Cole. You're going to use me to get points with your mother? *I think you're the pathetic one*," I spit out venomously with a forced smile. But my words cut too deep, and my eyes bulge from my skull when I realize how far those words struck his evil spirit. He picks me up faster than I can register or defend myself and throws me to the wall in my living room. I'm mid-air for a second or two before my back hits the fireplace, and I shut my eyelids tight, trying to catch the breath that was forced out of me with his heavy blow. I palm my ribs as I try to regain my strength. Everything burns. I hear his footsteps thud closer to me over the ominous ringing, and with each second, I dread it.

He picks me up by my hair, pulling it so hard I think he's going to scalp me. He drags me on the floor as I kick, hit Cole's body, and scream for help, hoping the neighbors can hear me, but the sounds of nature swallow my pleas for survival. He throws me to the couch, climbs on top of me, and pushes his entire body weight on me, crushing me.

He pulls my neck to the side, exposing my unscarred skin, and does what he promised. He sinks his teeth into my flesh and immediately starts to suck my blood out. He tightens his grip on the back of my head like he's punishing me.

"No!" I try to push against him, but it only makes my situation worse. Cole growls and slaps my face until I see stars. It gives me a whiplash to the point where I swear I can feel my brain convulse and collide within my skull.

"Millie, before you go unconscious, I need you to know something," he snarls hungrily.

Blackness starts to cloud my vision from how hard he pummeled the side of my head with his hand. I try to breathe, but my lungs have betrayed me and won't work. All I can do is try to keep fighting when my mind can't signal my body to move. There's a disconnect, and I'm going to suffer for it.

His lips brush against my ear, and I feel my blood drip out of my neck.

"I was the one who killed your father," Cole tells me proudly, and a sinister smile paints his darkened face.

My body runs cold at his confession. My eyes open weakly, and my chin starts to shake as the sobs are caught in my throat.

Cole killed my father.

Cole is my father's murderer.

Not Hayden.

He reaches for my skirt and pulls on it with his fingers hooked into my panties until the fabric tears.

"I bet I can fuck you better than he can," he murmurs into my ear chillingly.

"Get your fucking hands off of her!" A deep voice snarls, full of pure lividity and vengeance. That voice. It drowns me in a chemistry I'm addicted to like a drug. But I can't move, can't speak or breathe. I can't run to Hayden or fight Cole off me as he continues to drain me, and I pass out.

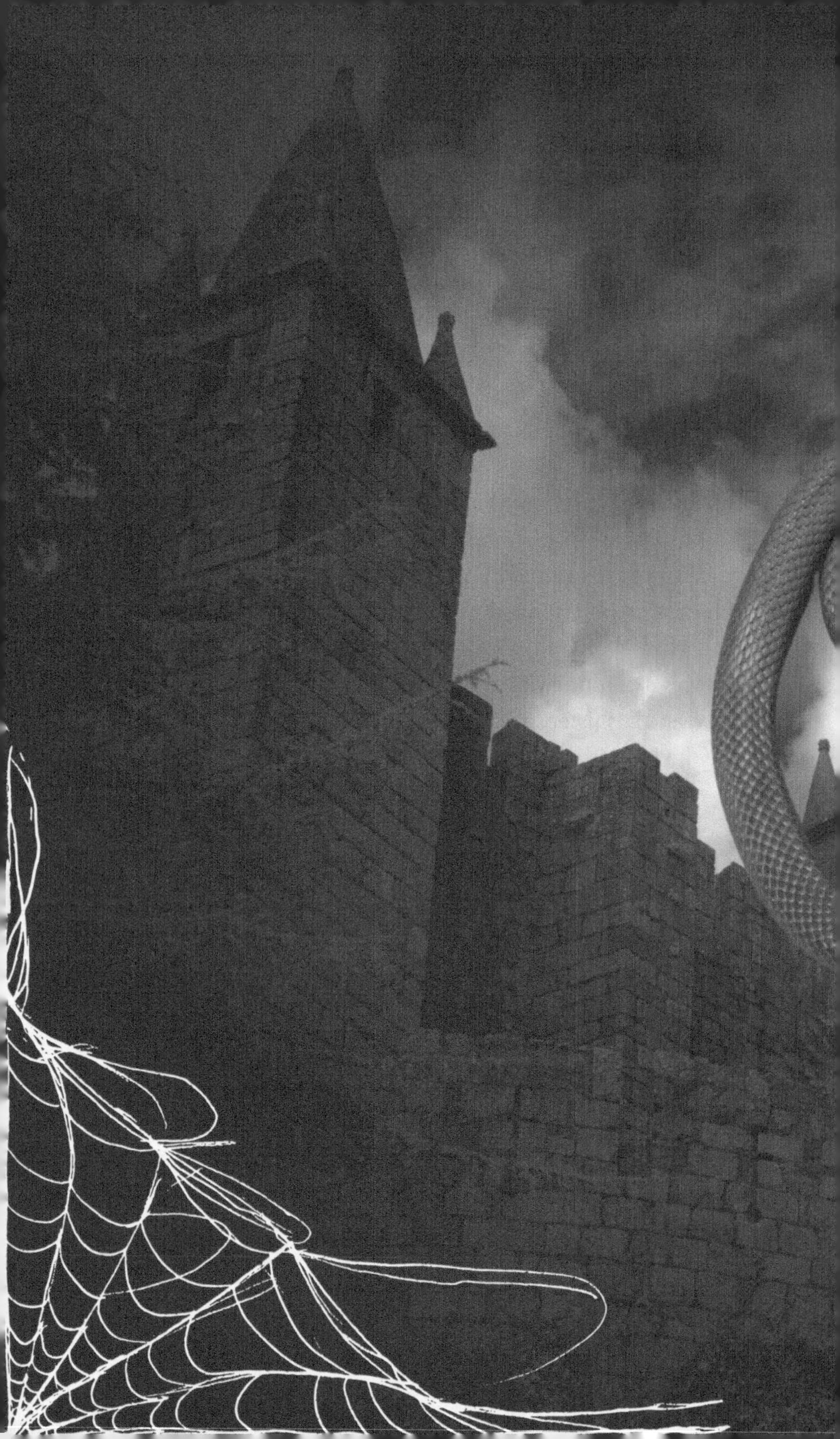

37

HAYDEN

One Day Ago

"WHERE IS MILLIE? My peonies will die soon. I haven't felt her presence in the house these past few days. *Son?*" I'm staring at the white peonies my little Bambi cared for when she was still here. I'm in the garden, the moon shining over me and my mother, and we admire the imprint she left on both of us.

Even my mother misses her. She wants her back, too.

She and my father leave for Europe this week, leaving me in charge of our region. I can begin my reign...wifeless. With tensions rising between the North and the South, the council agreed to let me start my reign without a wife for now. They bent the rules for me out of fear. I've been on edge, and everyone knows it leaves me unpredictable.

Everyone is scared of me.

"I did something...very bad," I admit, still trying to remember the events of that night I captured Millie from her home. It's all fuzzy, and no matter what I do, nothing changes, and it's driving me crazy. I tuck my hands into my suit, pacing back and forth. I stare at the balcony I used to fuck her on, under the moonlight, and then we would stargaze together right after. I would listen to her heartbeat like it's my national anthem, as she would listen to the bats fly by and the waterfall crash against the Earth. She's everywhere, even when she's not.

"What did you do?" Her voice softens like she's afraid of the answer...*afraid of me*. "Is that why you've been so irritable? Drinking all night and snapping at everyone who talks to you? Why did you let her go?"

It's true. Alcohol is a funny thing. Lately, I've been craving it more than blood. It twists my pain until all I can feel is numbness. The old me wants to make a comeback. Where meaningly fucks and drinks were my favorite way to spend my nights.

"I've been asking myself that same damn question since she left!" I snarl and let my demons that I've been holding in arise from hell, and the depravity takes over.

"I blacked out and killed her father," I murmur as I take out a cigarette. I light it up, waiting for it to burn. I take a hit and watch the smoke swirl into the cold, crisp air, and my heart sinks when I see those pretty brown eyes with golden sparks deep inside my soul. She's in my head, she won't fucking leave my head, and if it's the only place I can see her, I'll gladly live in my mind like it's my new prison.

"Ahh. Yes, that'll do it. Humans can be sensitive to their boyfriends murdering their parents. It's not a good look, son," Mother snickers like it's a joke.

I scoff. I just wish I could remember it. I don't remember killing multiple Kingsguard men in our own Cathedral; why would it be any different when it came to her father? I hate that I black out sometimes from rage. It's a factor that's a part of my DNA. Only Millie makes it go away.

"I sent them a donation for my mistake. I know it's nothing. I know I'm vile and cruel, and I can't bring her father back, but if I can take that financial burden off her shoulders and her brother, then so be it."

"How much?"

"One hundred."

"Billion?"

"Million, they wouldn't let me add a zero."

I take another hit, trying to block out flashes of us tangled up together. I can still smell her. I can still taste her. I can still hear her moans, her voice, and her laugh, even though she's thousands of miles away. She's haunting me.

I meant it when I said I'm her prisoner.

I can still feel the way she used to run her hands through my hair when we would watch movies together after I made love to her fiercely. I can still feel the way her pussy tightened around my cock when I hit that one spot inside of her over and over again. I can still feel how she looks at me...like I'm not a monster, but a man capable of giving her the world.

She's inside me. She's torturing me by denying me, and she expects me just to let her go? The only reason why I'm not there, hauling her ass back to my bed, is because of the way she looked at me.

She sees the monster everyone else sees, and it taints my strength to run after her. If this were any other day, I would be in Texas, grabbing her by the neck and forcing her back with me. But something chipped inside me, and I still don't fucking understand it.

Yes, I threatened everyone she loves if she were to leave me so that I could have her all to myself. And I would do it again even though it backfired. I know who the hell I am, and I've come to terms with it long before I met Millie. I crave her all the time, morning, day, and night; I breathe Millie in like my oxygen. She's more than my obsession. She's more than my queen. She's the entire kingdom.

She's out there, left unprotected, and I can't do it anymore.

She's stubborn. She's fighting me because she's scared of her feelings for me. I may have killed her father, but I know she still wants me.

"How does it feel to be King?" My mother asks me as she strides to the door to the Cathedral. She holds the knob waiting for me to answer.

"Pointless," I rasp and run a hand through the beard I've been growing out these past few days. It's astonishing how our bodies are selective with human traits. I drink in the air as if that'll deflate the emptiness Millie left in my heart.

"Everything is pointless without her," I repeat. "Like I'm walking a road with no end and nothing to look at but never-ending, vast, black-and-white walls because the color in my life has dulled further down than ever before."

I've never known how to keep something good in my life because I don't know how to hold onto it without destroying it.

"You remind me a lot of your uncle. The way he loved Adriyana was admirable, violent, and, most of all, frowned upon and unaccepted by the council. He never gave up on her, even when they executed him." She opens the door to the cathedral. "I'm leaving for Europe with your father. All I ask is that you take care of Kallum." She pauses before she vanishes. "What you did to that poor girl is wrong, but I will no longer interfere in your life, son. I've had enough. Maybe I feel responsible for how your father and I raised you, but you're still my son. No matter what you have done in the past and what you will do in your future...you are still my son."

THE DEPRAVED PRINCE

"To King Hayden Drago! The Depraved Prince is now the Depraved King...drink up, boys!" Landon shouts, and everyone holds cups of alcohol in the air, cheering with vibrant ruby eyes. Their glasses chime together, and I sit numbly on the chair by the bonfire. I tap my feet anxiously as I watch the trees sway before me.

I finally gave in to Landon's request to celebrate. I stopped showing my face around the North after my uncle was executed, but now I have a duty to the people and obligations to meet. So I can slowly ease myself into it by letting one of my loyal friends hold this party for me.

Everyone is drinking, dancing, and even fucking at Landon's home. Everyone brought their little human pets to the bonfire, and I don't carry the temptation to snatch one away like I always did before. It's nonexistent.

Landon, Kolton, and the rest walk away, leaving me to sulk in the imprisonment of my own mind.

I don't enjoy anything anymore.

I. Loved. Life.

It was the only thing I could say that I loved.

Now? I love Millie.

The world and my ambition sound like static. Boring, and hellish.

I hate waking up, knowing that my Bambi isn't breathing next to me in my bed. I miss waking up to the scent of strawberries. The feel of her warm, soft, naked skin touching my cold, dead one. I'm in fucking pain, and she's back home in Texas, unprotected and going back to her old life, pretending that I don't exist?!

I haven't been able to stay fucking sane since she threatened to put a blade in her throat to get away from me.

Well, have I ever been sane?

I killed her father. I get it. She needs time. But she doesn't have time. She only has about three years left before the Reaper comes to collect her soul and I need her to spend them with me. I'll convince her to consent. I won't hesitate to go to extreme measures...if I fucking have to force them out of her stubborn fucking beautiful lips, I will.

I bring the bitter beer bottle to my lips and swallow. I get lost in the flames of the bonfire. Watching and listening to the fire crackle while getting lost in Millie. Where is she right now? Is she working back at the Nostalgia Coffee Shop on those cute roller skates of hers? Is she with...Cole?

Fuck!

I can't stand these thoughts. These demonic voices in my head are telling me that she doesn't love me. She doesn't crave me anymore. I'm a piece of shit who deserves everything bad that gets thrown my way.

You don't deserve anyone good.

She's going to die and you're going to live alone for eternity like the depraved blood lust evil vampire that you are.

Is she spending time with him? Touching him? Letting him kiss her the way I love to?

I can see it now. I can picture her with him and wrath builds inside me as I have these mental pictures of them together.

Him holding her, consoling her, being there for her when all he's thinking about is fucking her.

Fuck him.

If she tries to get another boyfriend, I'll find out and I'll kill anyone she tries to go on a date with. They'll all die and she'll realize that I'm the only one for her. I smile and lick my lips at the thought of killing any man that tries to take my Bambi on a date.

A woman walks in front of me, cutting into my thoughts of

Millie away. She has curly red hair and long legs and stops like she's trying to get me to notice her.

"Is there anything I can do for you, King Drago?" she pouts seductively. Her voice twirls with heat, and she's practically drenched underneath her underwear. I can sense it. She grabs a piece of her hair and plays with it by wrapping it around her finger over and over again. She's another vampire.

I ignore her and take another swig of my beer. I refuse to look at another woman, never mind talk to one. She sighs and forcefully sits on my lap. She plops her ass on my groin, and I tighten my muscles. She won't take my silence as her answer, but a challenge.

"You don't have to talk to me. I'll do all the talking for you, babe. I bet I can turn that frown upside down without you saying one word to me..." she says as she starts to tug off my belt.

Now, I'm ticked off. "What's your name?" My eyes flash to red, my voice vibrating with unease. I clench my jaw, forcing my fangs to stay tucked in.

"Debby." She giggles and bites her lip. The familiar motion sends an image of Millie doing the same thing when she's stressed. Millie always bit her lip when she was frustrated or angry. Libby or Debby—whatever her name is—winks at me and starts to palm my cock over my jeans, up and down, trying to get me hard.

I tuck a strand of hair behind her ear and grin with disdain. "If you're name is not Millie Flores, then you and everyone else can leave me the fuck alone." I point to her friends, who are lined up for me behind her, ready to join us on the couch.

Before meeting Millie, I've been known to fuck...*and fuck a lot*. One night, I had five girls licking my cock and balls at once. Before, it was a good time. But now? It's rather dull and distasteful now that Millie owns me, even if she isn't *here*.

I stand up, forcing her to her feet, and walk away. She groans, pissed off by my rejection, and returns to her group of friends. I smash my beer bottle on the ground with pure fucking wrath as I stalk toward Landon. The glass shatters, quieting everyone in the party except for the music. "Simple Man" by Lynyrd Skynyrd continues to play.

I haven't given up on Millie and me. And I never will.

"Hey man, where are you going? The party just started. Stay with us. If you don't want to get your dick wet, that's fine, but hang out with us," Landon quips.

"No. I'm good. I'm going to call it a fucking night." I say casually, forcing the resentment I have for my Bambi to stay inside.

Landon tries to stop me again. He places his hand on my shoulder, and I quirk a brow at him.

"Come on, we just got news today that King Davenport's other son will take over. We just want to let loose before—"

Another son? Who the hell is Davenport's other son?!

"What?" I'm seething.

"King Davenport's youngest son?" Landon replies dubiously.

"I thought Eleanor was going to take reign?" I quirk a brow.

"No...her mother and everyone else in that region voted against a woman taking power." Landon rolls his eyes. "Lame. I would have loved to see Eleanor be queen. Despite who her father is, she's a good person, and—"

Thoughts are screaming at me. Bad ideas are at the forefront of my mind, and missing pieces are coming together. I have this strange feeling that Millie is in danger. To be honest, I'm always paranoid that she's in danger.

"We have to go. Why wasn't I notified of this before? Holland always filled my father in with important updates like this. Why am I the last to know?!" I snarl, grabbing him by the collar with both of my hands and teeth, ready to bite his head off. I'm about to break him into pieces if he says the wrong thing.

"Hayden!" He tries to untangle my hands off of him, but he's unsuccessful. "We've been trying to tell you, man, but you haven't been listening!"

Landon looks at me with sincerity. His words strike me hard like a knife, and I want to rip him apart just because I can. It's what I'm known for anyway. So why not?

"You haven't been listening, man. *And it's okay,*" he reassures me. He knows the damage my little Bambi left in me. A few beats of tense silence pass between us as my sanity continues to crack. "Let's go," Landon tells me, keeping calm even when I'm shaking with murderous intentions. Nostrils flaring, muscles constricting, I let my head and hands fall. I let him go and walk away with all the guys following me.

"I'm going alone!" I shout as I race to my private plane with the Kingsguard by my side.

"The hell you are!" Kolton, my other close friend, blares behind me.

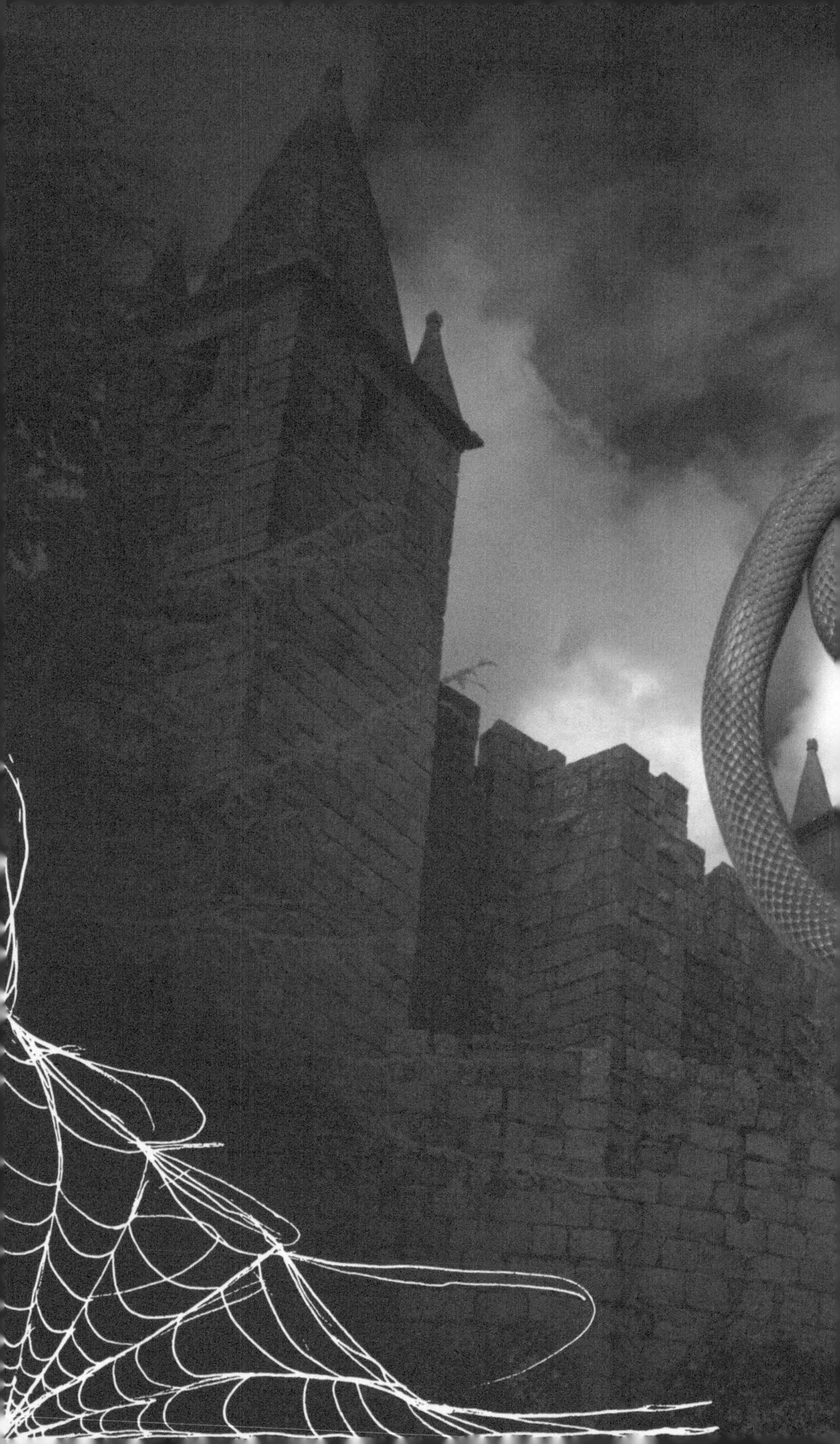

38

HAYDEN

THE SITE before me makes me sick. His waist is pressed into Millie's like he's about to enter her. Her underwear is torn, and his fangs are inside her neck. He's feeding on her; I can almost taste her blood from where I'm standing.

I'm going to add his eyes to my crown and throne by the time this is all over.

"Get your fucking hands off Millie!" I growl loudly; my entire body shakes, and I want to rip him apart piece by piece slowly, but what is the fun in that?

No, no, no. I want him to rot in his mistake of trying to take what's mine. He needs to get a taste of why I earned the name of depravity amongst our world of immortals.

He stiffens, and Millie goes limp on the couch. Her black waves of hair fall off the cushion, and her sleeping, pained face breaks my spirit. She's whimpering in her sleep.

I'm flexing my jaw so hard it burns.

Finally, he gets off her with a victorious smirk to taunt me. And it's working.

"When you are known as The Depraved Prince and when

Millie found out her father was dead, it was so fucking easy planting it in everyone's heads that you were the one responsible. No one blinked an eye. No one suspected it could be a lie when all you're known for is being a selfish, evil vampire." Cole confesses as he licks Millie's blood off his lips with a sinister smile. I can feel myself wanting to implode from the madness. No one gets to taste what heaven is like, and he has. I'm going to fucking turn his power of immortality into a joke. He has his hand on her chest like he's ready to rip her heart out. He stares at me, antagonizing me like I've fallen into a trap.

"There are rumors about your blackouts in the community, King Drago."

How the fuck does he know?

I stalk forward, about to flash to him and kill him, but his threat shatters me.

"You come closer, and I'll rip it out of her chest." He points to her heart, and it makes me stop.

Motherfucker. He knows I'm nothing without her. Everyone in our world knows the Depraved Prince has fallen in love.

"I had to turn earlier than scheduled. I was forced to avenge my father's death...just like you avenged your uncle. Revenge just tastes better when you get to do it in front of them. Isn't that right, Drago? How did it feel when you killed my father in front of Millie?"

"Not as good as it'll feel when I rip your head off," I snarl.

He scoffs before laughing, and I return the demented smile at him. My teeth almost slice into my lips as I try to keep my demons inside.

"Here's what's going to happen, Cole. You're going to leave this house, and I'll grant you a head fucking start to run away from me. Give me my girl, and I'll spare you tonight. But only tonight." I offer him mercy. I never propose weak deals, but I'll do anything to save Millie.

His vision darts to me and then to her sleeping figure on the couch. He grabs her wrist, the one that was broken, and squeezes it. Millie is so out of it she doesn't feel him hurting her.

"What the fuck do you want?!" I hiss so loud the entire house shakes.

He lets her hand go and looks dead in my eyes with his vibrant blue eyes. "I want you to suffer."

He knows killing Millie would end me.

"This is a war, Hayden. And the war isn't over. It's just begun." He grabs Millie, lifts her into his arms, and uses her as a shield to walk out of the house. His palm is on her throat, making sure I see that he's a second away from ripping her throat out if I come too close.

A shotgun racks loudly, and a gunshot goes off midair. Cole and I growl towards the source.

Who the hell has a gun?

Nash stands in the doorway, holding a giant cross with Jesus Christ tight in his palm. Cole starts to laugh at Nash like he's a joke.

"Drop my sister, you bloodsucker!" Nash demands while the grip on his weapon trembles. His long black hair sways in the wind from the rainstorm outside. He holds it still, pointing straight at Cole's face. Lightning strikes and thunder erupts right after.

I take advantage of Nash being a decoy. His finger is on the trigger, and I lunge for Cole. The blow from tackling him into the wall forces him to drop Millie. I can't look at her, or I'll die if I see that she's bleeding or hurt.

I have to focus on ending the man who tasted my little Bambi. Cole and I wrestle. He clocks me in the jaw which only makes my grin more potent. I laugh as blood spurts out of my crooked smile. It's another battle of princes, and I know I'll win. Anyone who looks at Millie, let alone cause her pain will know what it's like to fear me. Our brawl doesn't last long. My age grants me the upper hand.

"I'm going to end you!" Cole growls. He lunges for my throat while I take joy in making him squirm for his life.

"Yeah, yeah, whatever." I twist his neck until it breaks. It won't kill him. He'll heal, which is precisely what I want right now. He falls to the ground, unconscious. Landon, Kolton, and others swarm inside fast to chain him in silver. Chains that will have him under control until I get him back to the Cathedral. I love to fight my battles solo. Even if it ends in my demise, I love the journey.

It takes every dead patient bone in my body to refrain from ripping him to shreds. I have beautiful plans for him.

I fall back to my knees with shaking muscles and bittersweet nerves. I've been dreaming of our reunion every single day, waking up in a cold sweat, turning in my bed, pretending she's right by me. Then the disappointment follows right after, and I want to destroy Drago's Cathedral because her absence demolishes me. Now I have her again.

I turn Millie around so I can see her. I need to touch, feel, and smell her. I need to awaken the fire inside me by ensuring she's real.

When I scoop her into my arms, she groans sleepily. She makes that same sweet tune when she's peacefully resting. I've grown fond of it over the past months of having her in my arms when we sleep every day. My lovely, sweet, angelic Millie that has a fire in her heart and hope that lasts mountains high. She's alive. She's okay. And she's all mine again.

My wife. My little bride. My haven.

I hold her tight, my rough palms securing into my body. I

smile as I descend from her father's house and prepare for the rain outside. I don't make it three steps before Nash points his shotgun at me from behind and racks it.

"Where the fuck do you think you're going with my little sister, you evil vampire! You're the one who killed my father, aren't you?!" Nash threatens with panic laced in his voice. I tilt my head to the side, my red eyes brightening and daring him to challenge me. I will kill anyone who tries to get in the way of the life I have planned for Millie and me, including her brother. I don't give a flying fuck who it is.

I smile. He's scared of me. I can feel it.

"The blonde-haired man with the bad haircut?" I point out Cole.

Nash narrows his brows at me, confused, with a slanted, bewildered mouth like he doesn't know who I'm talking about. He still doesn't lower his weapon, and my patience is growing thin.

"The man whose neck I snapped? Cole. He's the one responsible for the death of your father. Not me, believe it or not." I shrug nonchalantly, not caring if he believes me or not. Either way, I'm walking out of here with the love of my life. She belongs in Drago's Cathedral, not here in Texas unprotected.

"Let her go," he insists.

I scoff out a chuckle, raise my brows, and darken my eyes.

"No," I state simply.

He puts his finger on the trigger, daring me, and I'm about to snap this boy's gun in half.

I sigh heavily. "She will be safe. I love your sister more than life. More than me. More than anything. I won't hurt her. But she's mine to take. Not yours. I'll have her call you when she wakes if that makes you feel better."

"I just got her back," he murmurs sadly.

He regrets leaving her behind when she was a child. But I don't give a fuck.

She's mine.

"I know..." My throat rolls. "But so did I," I reply with no remorse. A tear falls out of Nash's eye. I've had enough of all these emotions. I've met my limit of chaos for the night.

"Nash," I growl.

"Yes?"

"Do not tell a fucking soul about our kind. If you do, and *I will fucking know if you do,* I will kill you myself, and you will never see your sister again," I promise him as I hold his sleeping little sister in my arms tighter. I bring her sleeping body closer to my chest and walk out with my little bride.

"Where are you taking her? Are you going to hurt her? Kill her? Turn her into a vampire?!" He racks his gun again and points it at me. I stop walking and turn to him. He places his finger on the trigger, and I reach out and lower his gun.

"I don't care that you're pointing the gun at me, but don't you dare point it while I have your sister in my arms!" I snarl protectively. He complies, but his stern gaze never wavers. He drops the weapon to the floor after putting it on safety. Cooper stirs and limps toward Nash, licking his hand. Millie's dog looks at me with a softened glance.

He's finally warmed up to me.

"If those were my plans, and if weapons could kill me, I'd grab that gun of yours and shoot myself. I'd rather die than have one thought of harming her cross my mind. I love Millie with all that I am. I'm keeping her, and you're going to let me. No one can keep me from her anymore. Not even herself."

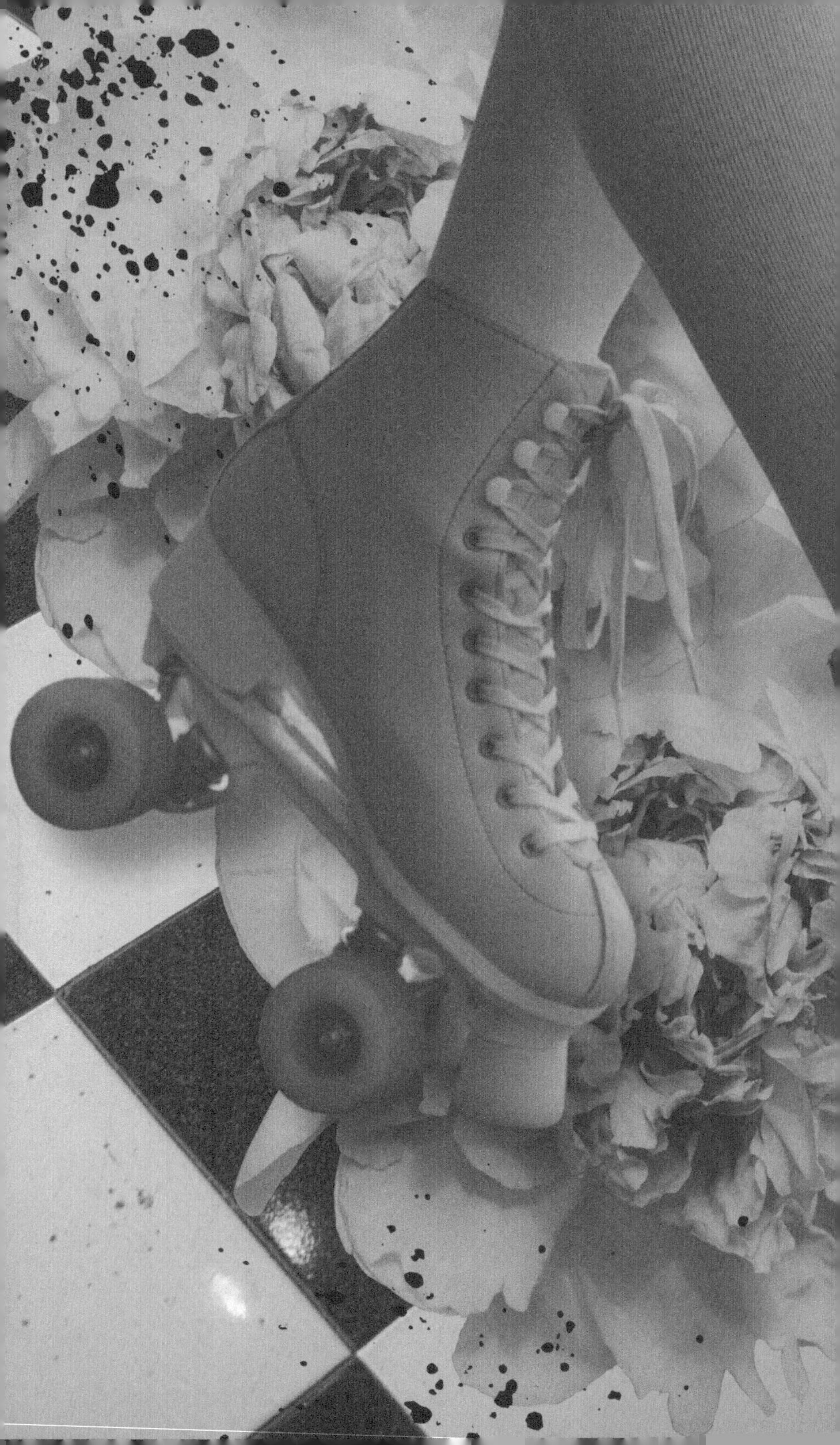

39

MILLIE

I SWEAR if I get knocked out by a vampire one more time, I'm going to lose my shit.

Thankfully, this time, I know exactly where I am. I recognize that stained glass color anywhere. Even in dim lighting where the candles stay infinitely burning, I know I'm back in Drago's Cathedral. The smell of wood, mint, and the man I love to fight surrounds me like a warm fall blanket.

I'm alive. Protected. Safe.

"Hayden. Is it you? Is it really you?" I grumble through the darkness.

"It's me, my little Bambi. Wake up now. I need you to wake up, baby. Can you do that for me?"

His voice slips into my ears, reminding me I crave him as much as he craves me. I've tried to block him out since I came back to Texas, but he's there imprinted in my blood and soul like a virus. I want to be sick with his obsession. Because now, I fear I'm obsessed with him, too.

Although my twisted heart desires Hayden, there's uncertainty.

I groan when the inflammation and soreness in my neck remind me of Cole's mouthful. My best friend is my dad's killer, and he tried to kill me. The betrayal is sickening. The trust issues I already have heightened. But Hayden. Hayden...is my nightmare-turned-lover. Dark passion intertwined with thrill. The man who loves me dangerously yet gently.

I sit up on his bed and lick my lips. I rub my eyes and realize I'm in a black satin dress. He likes to dress me in his favorite color. Black.

Those familiar cold, callous hands tilt my chin up.

"There's my Bambi girl. I missed those honey eyes on me," he tells me with a clenched jaw. His dashing smile, which masks the pain he holds within his spirit, isn't there. The morbid humor he likes to throw at me is nowhere to be found. His tone is agonized. His pulled-in dark brows and eyes are crimson like a fire, pushing me into a storm of regret.

"I fucking missed you. Don't ever make me experience what that word feels like again, Millie. I won't be able to live another fucking second if I do," he growls. His fingers drop from my chin. He sits next to me instead and glues his eyes to me.

"Some things are a bit fuzzy," I truthfully say as I rub my neck.

"You're back in Montana...with me." He takes my hand in his. He grabs something from his pocket. It's the same massive ruby engagement ring I threw at him. He grabs my ring finger and places it back on.

"You're never taking this off," he murmurs.

I stare at it, and it shines back at me. This must be worth a fortune.

"How long have I been out?" I raise a brow and tilt my head to face my handsome vampire captor.

"Too long." He kisses my forehead.

"How long?"

"Twelve hours."

I shift uncomfortably.

"Hayden. Is my father really dead?" I croak out, doing my best to avoid choking up. Fuck. Grief hits me like a stab to the heart.

He leans over me and kisses my lips this time. He clenches his jaw and nods. He stops pressing his lips against mine and instead rubs my cheekbones with his thumb. "Yes."

"Is Cole really the one responsible for killing him?"

He nods again. "Yes."

"I need to get out of here, Hayden. I can't forgive you for everything that's happened to me. I..." I place my feet on the floor, ready to stand, but Hayden grabs my hips and forces me back down on the bed beside him.

"Stop it! No more running. No more fighting me. Let me fucking love you!" he shouts. "I'm not letting you go. I will do everything in my power to help you grieve your father but don't make me live one more moment without you. I love you. And you love me. I can feel it." He cups my face, and I look into his darkened, wide eyes.

I shiver.

He's been showing me unconditional love and devotion this entire time, and I run from it because I'm scared he'll eventually leave. *Everyone leaves.* But not Hayden.

"I love...you," I whisper with a heavy breath. My tone almost breaks, but I swallow the shakiness back down. "I'm sorry. I love you, Hayden."

"I know you do. You run from me, but then you want me to follow. You fight me, but then you want me to hold you tighter. You're my little Bambi girl. I know your soul calls to mine even when you think it doesn't. And I'll gladly burn the whole world for you to understand that I love you, and you're only mine to look at. I'll burn it all with a smile on my face just so you'll know you can never outrun me."

A tear escapes my eye.

"I don't want to run anymore," I concede.

"We'll see about that..." he jokes and kisses my lips. I move against him and enjoy every second he devours me with his mouth. He tastes like he always does. Sexy. Rough. With a hint of cigarettes. His tongue spins with mine in a passionate dance before he lets me go. I grip his thick thighs tightly once more, practically digging into his skin over his jeans.

"I want to show you what I do to those who hurt the only person I fucking care about." He breaks the kiss, and his words hold a cruel, vindictive tone.

"What do you mean?" I ask breathlessly. "I don't want to go anywhere. I want to stay in bed kissing you until I forget my own name. Help me forget."

He smirks as a lock of hair falls over his face. His eyes turn from blue to bright red. He stands, intertwines his hand with mine, and pulls me up.

"Let's go. I have a surprise for you."

I'VE NEVER BEEN TO THIS PART OF THE CATHEDRAL before. Hayden holds me like I'm his property as four of his guards walk us to wherever he's taking me. He stops when we reach two massive, tall and wide double black doors with the family crest in the middle. A terrifying, detailed bat with a snake wrapped around it.

"Where are we?" I ask Hayden as I hold his arm tighter. He looks over his shoulder and smiles at me with those drop-dead stunning aqua eyes. He returns me with silence, then his teeth sharpen, and he's in full-on Drago vampire mode.

The doors split in half once Hayden pushes them open—the wood creaks and echoes amongst the tall Victorian walls. I gasp as I take in the mesmerizing scenery. It looks like a throne room. He holds my two hands with one of his behind his waist. I take in the painted murals on the ceiling. Beautiful and elegant.

Hayden lets me go, leaving me with his guards. Finally, after his massive, tall frame sways to the side, I see what he wants to show me. My body goes rigid, and a wave of anger hits my chest. I ball my fists, and a rock in my constricted throat is born.

Cole is helpless, with his hands tied behind his back. Black tears roll down his cheeks as he struggles to stand but the guards keep him restrained on his knees. He kneels in front of what looks like a chair made of crystals—red, blue, green, and magenta diamonds sparkle.

Hayden smiles like he's having the time of his life, and Cole's suffering is his favorite form of entertainment.

"The council is in favor of the Drago family. Your father and brother really fucked up this time, didn't they?" Hayden taunts like it's a game to make Cole miserable. Hayden rolls up his sleeves and circles Cole three times.

Cole screams. "Let me go, Hayden! I don't want revenge anymore. I'm...I'm sorry! *Please!*" he bellows out his apology as he tries to escape his chained wrists. Cole glares at Hayden with pure hatred.

"You're sorry? Please?" Hayden mocks. "I fucking hate that word."

Hayden shakes his head. He walks away from Cole as another vampire with beaming red eyes, and a cane hands him a sword.

"Thank you, Holland." Hayden admires the weapon like a true King and thanks the man. Its blade is thick, and the handle looks like it weighs about twenty pounds. The diamonds from the throne glimmer against it, casting rays everywhere like a disco ball.

"One thing about me, Cole, is that I love problems. I get excited when I get to solve them, and you know what my favorite thing to do is with people who piss me off?" Hayden roars with depravity. He looks at me and locks his vision with my blurred eyes. His jaw flexes as he shows me the side of him I fear.

I can't look at this. I can't watch the man I love be possessed by revenge. I hug myself as I stare at the black floors but keep my ears open.

"Millie..." Cole calls me.

My old friend is trying to seek mercy through me. He pleads for me through his whiskey eyes, and I almost feel bad for him. Hayden flips the sword in circles, keeping a sinister grin who's taking pleasure in Cole's dread.

"I like to make them scream and regret the day they ever met me." Hayden raises the sword high in the air and slices Cole's head off before Cole can say his last words. His blood splatters all over the floor. I jump up at the sound of his head being severed. The sound of his head falling onto the floor and rolling will forever haunt me. Hayden roars with laughter as his friends rally behind him with cups of red, chanting and cheering his new name.

The Depraved King! The Depraved King! The Depraved King!

Cole's body slowly melts and turns into ash. Goosebumps prick at my skin as I watch my old life and Cole disappear forever. I belong to the Depraved King now.

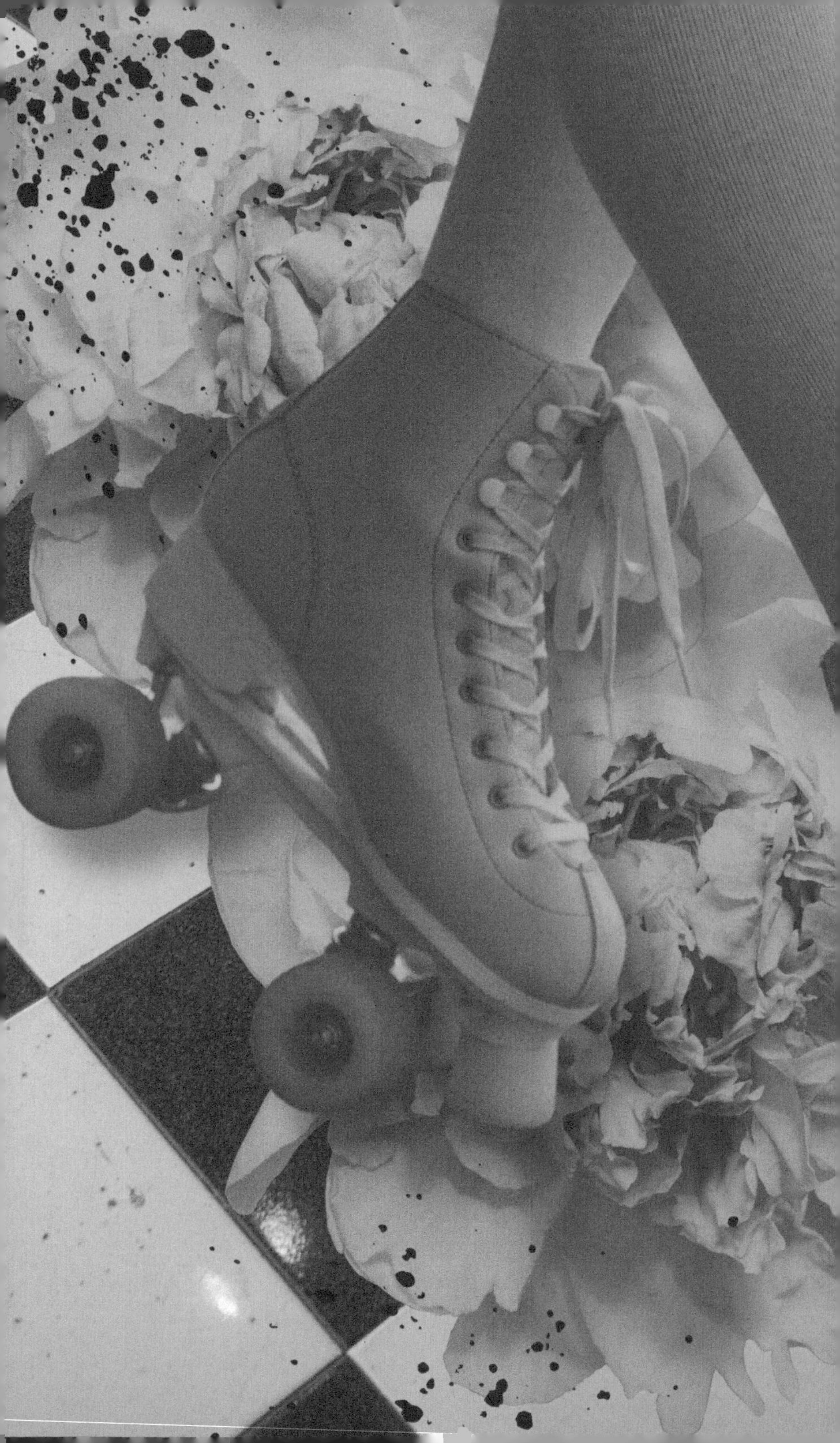

40

MILLIE

AFTER HAYDEN CELEBRATED KILLING his enemy, he ordered everyone out of the throne room. He and I are staring at each other, and the unknown is killing me. He's watching me like a deer in headlights, afraid I'll gallop away.

What happens now?

At the end of the day, he's still forcefully taking me. But this time, I don't want him to let me go.

I pull on my lip with my teeth and walk toward him as he stands in silence. Blue eyes, dark hair, and facial hair around his jaw. He's always clean-shaven, and it's a new look for him. I like him in every single way. He's enchanting, and he doesn't even have to try.

"Is this the part where you redeem yourself? The part where if you set me free, and if I come back to you, then we were meant to be?"

"No." He rips off my dress. My body jolts from his needy aggression to get me naked. He throws it on the floor, leaving me vulnerable. He walks behind me, and I feel his icy breath on my shoulder. "This is the part where I remind you the way I like to fuck. This is the part where I remind you of the man you fell in love with. Because, *no*... I don't care about doing the noble, good guy thing. This is the part where you let me drown in you because the only time the darkness is away is when I'm inside you. This is the part where I remind you that *this time*, you're not going anywhere and that you're mine. You've always been mine since the night we met. The only way I can go on peacefully with my life sentence in this cruel world is knowing you're safe, *and that's only with me*. So accept it now because there are only so many games of chase I can do before I just chain you up to my bed." He growls into the shell of my ear, and I shudder. My nipples point and harden when he stands in front of me like a hungry, angry beast.

He gets down on his knees and smiles sinfully.

"Woof," he says as he smirks, and my lips tilt with a smile. His tongue dives into my wet slit, and he begins to suck, lick and bite.

Oh, God. I inhale sharply, and my eyes roll back from the dark desire.

"I have a kingdom to run, and I need my queen." He circles my clit faster and more brutally with that illegal tongue of his and breathes my scent in like I'm his only oxygen to survive.

"I love to lick this perfect, tight pussy." He stands before me and sits on the throne of vibrant crystals. He grabs my hair and pulls me closer. Still standing, he grabs my hand and kisses the engagement ring.

"Tell me you won't leave again." He bites the inside of my thighs, and I moan.

"I won't leave you again."

"Tell me that you're my queen." He bites me under my ribs. His fangs puncture me ruthlessly, and he sucks my blood out for a few seconds until it drips and spills over the sides of his mouth. I claw at his hair, begging for the *real* thing.

"I'm your queen," I breathe out. The overwhelming lust is too much. I need him, and I need his beautiful thick massive cock inside me now.

"It's not fucking good enough. All the trouble you've caused like a bad fucking girl." He grabs my hips and throws me over his lap. A high-pitched gasp escapes my lungs, and I squirm. He takes off my panties and rubs his palm over my ass. Then he raises his hand and smacks it hard. I can feel my skin ripple, and his hardened bulge pokes into my ribs like he's satisfied from watching it bounce.

"My little Bambi deserves a fucking spanking for thinking she could ever leave me. You know what happens when you try to play a game of cat and mouse with me." He slaps my ass again, and I yelp, but I take it. I rub my thighs together to stop the aching. He knows how to work my body every single time. He's more experienced and has hundreds of years under his belt. He knows all the right buttons to push and has me under his spell.

"You haven't been my good girl, and because of that, I'm going to punish you." he slaps my ass again and again. The sound of the spanking and my whimpers echo everywhere. Three of his fingers enter me, bringing me to the edge. He pumps them as he hums with dark satisfaction. He rails me with them deep and brutal as my clit throbs and nears an explosion. I'm dripping all over his hand as my orgasm builds. Fuck, how does he manage to get me to my end in just a few seconds? I'm about to come, and he knows it but doesn't let me cross the finish line. He stops rubbing my clit, and I cry out. My eyes widen, and I hiss at him, but I turn to face his signature sexy smirk.

"Let me come, please, Hayden!" I'm begging for it with no shame.

He thrusts his fingers faster, and I try to finish what he started. I need a release from my built-up orgasm that wants to wreck every single particle that makes me, me, but as soon as I try to touch my clit, he smacks my hand away.

"My baby girl wants to come, does she?"

I nod, biting my lip.

"Beg for it, baby. Beg me to let you come."

"Let me come, I'm begging you."

He removes his fingers from my pussy, picks me up so quickly, and makes me straddle him. I thrust my hips over his waist, so needy for him.

"Take off my belt." He demands, rough and sensual. We're making out, devouring each other like we can't get enough of one another.

I'm twitching with excitement. Fuck I love him. I fumble with the metal, take it off every loop, and throw it on the floor, panting and ready to beg for forgiveness from the devil in front of me, who smirks so beautifully because he knows he has me captured for eternity.

"You want me to let you come?" he asks as he grips my thighs and grasps tight.

I nod, breathless. "Yes."

"You want me to believe you when you say you'll never leave me?"

I nod again and kiss his lips. I push against his cold lips, needing him to feel how desperate I am to show me how feral he is for me. I want him to consume me like he always does, and he's holding back to make me suffer. I love it when he fucks brutally. I'm admitting it to him. Surrendering whatever I have left in my life to him.

"Yes, Hayden. I promise. Let me taste you. Let me suck on

you this time. I want you to feel my devotion when your cock is inside my mouth."

I pull down his pants, and his cock springs free with glistening pre-cum. I put the head of his dick in my mouth and suck.

"Baby..." he throws his head back onto the throne, grabs a fistful of my hair, and closes his eyes as I bob up and down on his thick, veiny length. "Fuck..." he moans, and it's the sexiest 'fuck' I've ever heard a man groan out sensually. He hits the back of my throat, making me gag, but I don't quit. He tastes too good.

He pulls out of my swollen, throbbing lips after thrusting into my throat a couple more times. Saliva drips off my chin, and he hums, deeply aroused at the sight of my spit all over his cock.

"Prove it to me *more*. Prove it to me right here and right now and forever by taking all of me inside you." He lifts me until I feel the head of his massive thick cock at my entrance. I'm dripping all over him, and he slicks himself with my wetness. I sink onto him willingly, and I gasp at the fullness. I knew it was going to hurt, but my pussy welcomes him like always. I'm so full, his thickness stretching me as he yanks me further down. I scratch his abs, leaving trails of blood until I stop at his groin.

He roars with pleasure and grabs my jaw, forcing me to look him into those red eyes that are blazing with devotion. "You're going to prove it to me by sitting on my cock, riding me until you shatter with my name falling from those pretty little lips," he growls into the shell of my ear, with my blood dripping down the corner of his full lips. I don't let him finish. I begin to roll my hips, fast and hard, bouncing on him like he's my haven. I've missed him. I've missed him so much, and I hate myself for it. Despite the hatred, he makes me feel good, and all my doubts dwindle.

He takes my tits in his mouth, practically biting on my nipple, and I moan as I pull on his hair. Up and down my waist goes as I fuck the Depraved King on his throne.

"Fuck. Yes, baby girl. *Prove it to me. Prove it,* just like that. Jesus Christ, Millie. Just. Like. That!" He slaps my ass and grabs a fistful of my hair, yanks my head to the side, and licks my neck. "Milk my cock with your tight pussy." He sinks his teeth into me, and the lust overflows, simmers into my veins, and poisons me.

"Use me, take me, fuck me," I whimper, which intensifies Hayden's hold. He sucks my blood faster and harder like I'm his favorite last meal. He snakes his hand into my waves of hair. His thick black ring with his family crest is at the base of my scalp as he tugs.

"You're going to let me fill you up with my cum, aren't you?" Hayden tells me; his deep voice vibrates against my sore throat, and my hot blood rains down my neck and onto my collarbones.

"Yes," I moan, and he sucks my blood out faster, greedy and impatiently.

"You're going to carry all of my babies?" he demands an answer, but I keep quiet. His dick is that good. It stuns my ability to speak; I'm too busy trying not to shatter all over his dick. I want to make this last a bit longer.

"Aren't you?!" He growls voraciously and starts to take over the pace, making me weak, and he begins to pound away brutal and carnal. Like he's trying to tattoo my pussy with his cock.

Oh. My. God.

"Yes! Give it to me. Give me all of you," I concede.

"Baby, you already have all of me," he exclaims softly and gently. "Look at you bouncing on my cock like the fucking liar that you are. You can't deny that you love me. Look at your sweet tight cunt taking it all."

Hayden spills inside me with a growl, his teeth lodged into my flesh. I look up at the ceiling as he gets his fill, staring at the painted murals.

I don't know when it happened, but I'm dozing off while Hayden clutches me tight and takes us into his bedroom. He carries my drained body through the black halls. He closes the door, locks it, and the next thing I know, we're both naked in his bedsheets.

"You're going to die of heart failure when you turn twenty-three." His voice trembles as he rubs his hand over my naked back in soft circles. I can't move. I let the words of my future demise sink in, and I try to process the information.

"Have you given it more thought? Will you let me turn you?"

I suck in a breath, hoping it'll relieve the tension all over. And it does, but only for a split second, but everything feels heavy again.

"I don't know, Hayden. This life you guys live in is painful, brutal, and full of unpredictable horror. I wouldn't be tied to you forever but to all the downfalls of being a vampire. A war has started between you and Cole's family, and I think it's far from over. Or what if you make more enemies? What if they try and kill me? What if we have children and they try to take them? What if—"

He puts his hand on my mouth, hushing me. His brows pinch together ruthlessly like he's in pain.

"I will always protect you. No would dare take you from me. And if they do, they'll wish they hadn't. Falling in love with you has made me see the world differently. *This life, differently.* Becoming a vampire was something I welcomed easily. I love life. I love waking up, knowing it'll never be my last. But now?

I'm terrified." His voice is deep and full of stone. "I'm terrified of waking up and finding out your heart has stopped beating and your soul is no longer trapped inside me. *My purpose is you.* You are the reason why I want to *continue* to fall in love with life, but if you leave me for Death, pretty girl..." A black tear falls out of his eye as he tilts my chin up to meet his cold red eyes. He's surrendering himself to me, letting me see his dark soul behind the shield he hides behind. "I will fight any God who tries to stop me from entering those gates of Heaven where I know you'll be. And I will find a way to you, like I always did before and like I always pledge to do." His declaration sends me into a mess. I want to open my mouth, but if I do, I'll give in to him despite everything we've gone through.

"Spare me that misery and stay with me. Here. In this cruel world." He climbs on top of me, pushing my hair out of my face. He looks at my lips with divine admiration and crashes his lips against mine. He enters me, slow and careful.

"Stay with me forever. Tell me you'll see me next moon, *please.*"

"Hayden..." I close my eyes and feel them roll back from how magnetic and hypnotizing this man is. He thrusts in and out while he makes his promises. He kisses my neck, trailing kisses down to my collarbone.

"You're perfect. God-like. You're an addiction I've tried to break, but you won't let me detox from your toxic possession. I will always see you next moon because fate is in your favor, and I no longer have any fight in me to pull away from you. I'm in love with you. I love you so much it scares me." I cup his face with my hands and kiss him hard. Fire burns through the both of us. We're two hurt souls coming together to make each other feel something good. It's more than euphoric. Our tethered connection is powerfully blinding. I break the kiss, and it kills me not to keep our lips an entangled mess. I love him with all the broken parts of me. He broke me, like he's been wanting to do, but not in the ways I thought he would. He broke my trauma and healed me in demented, everlasting ways.

"Don't ever leave me, Hayden. Promise me that I can trust you. Promise me you won't ever hurt me. Promise me that our love will last forever...and surpass your infinite lively sentence... just please don't abandon me. Don't leave me. Everyone in my life has left. Everyone in my life hurts me. But you haven't. Will it always stay like this?" I whisper, searching for his answer vigorously with watered eyes. He grins that billion-dollar one that always makes me turn into his prisoner willingly.

"Millie..." He smirks. "Until the moon and sun collide and the oceans dry. I will love you infinitely."

Hayden

SHE SMILES AFTER I MADE LOVE TO HER FOR THE THIRD time tonight. We interlock our limbs, and I hold her naked, warm body close to mine. Her hand trails my upper back right behind my neck. It's the first and only tattoo I'll ever have.

"When did you get this? It's my handwriting...from my diary, isn't it?"

Millie

"I got it a few days after you left."

She kisses the tattoo and smiles against my tricep.

"*Volo unum esse cum morte.*"

My eyes circle, and if my heart could sink, it would.

She's consenting.

She smiles harder and repeats the words.

"*Volo unum esse cum morte.*"

I palm her mouth with my hand before she can finish.

"Don't," I order her, forcing her to stop. Her eyes widen with hurt. Her brown eyes flicker with sadness and confusion. But I just smile and slowly let my hand fall from her mouth. Instead, I kiss her hard. I swear I've never felt so fuckin happy to hear those words fall from her mouth.

"But I thought? Why not?"

I trail my vision to her eyes, her lips, her perfectly swollen breasts, and finally, her lower belly. I place my hand on it and kiss her lips again. I wanted to wait to tell her this, but there's no other perfect moment like this one.

"Because you will carry another heartbeat inside you, and the only way for that to happen is if you stay human. If I turn you, you won't be able to become a mother, and I know that's something you want to do in your human lifetime."

She nods as I palm her stomach.

"Yes. I do," she admits and holds my hand.

"Tell me..." I stand from the bed and grab her journal that I packed before we left her father's house. "Why did you write so much?" She grabs her journal from me and opens it. She flips through the pages and then closes it again.

"Because reading and writing saved my life. I haven't finished writing *everything*. There's more. There's more you don't know about." She sighs and places her diary on the nightstand. She crawls on my body and pulls the blankets over us.

There's more?

"Who do I need to make scream and beg for their life? Whose car do I need to blow up next? Who do I need to torture?" I hiss.

"Hayden!" she scolds. "I'm not a victim. I refuse to be. I can handle my own battles." She giggles.

She knows I'll do it, and I always follow through with my threats. If anyone tries to hurt her, they'll be dead faster than they can blink. She stiffens and stops rubbing her hand over my chest.

"Wait, whose car did you blow up?!" She sits straight in the bed with pulled-in brows.

I smile mischievously. "Santiago's."

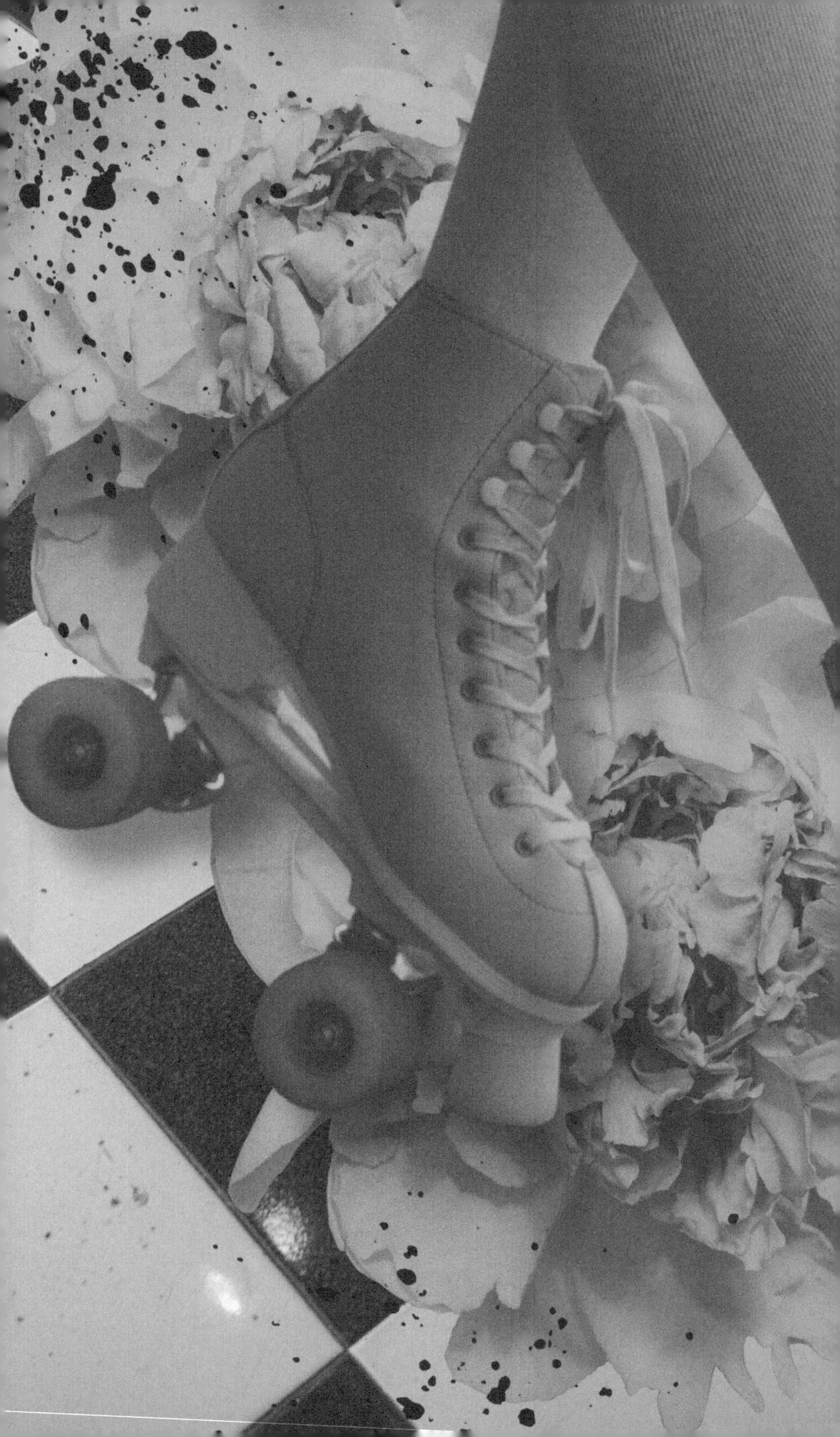

41

MILLIE
ONE MONTH LATER

HAYDEN HAS BEEN adamant and consistent about convincing me we can still do all the normal things I can do with a human boyfriend. It's been a week at the university near the Cathedral, and so far, I'm living my life like it's normal to have a vampire fiancé who doesn't give me any other choice but to choose him.

I emailed Hayden from the library computer on campus and wanted to stay longer tonight. I don't need one of his human bodyguards driving me home tonight as they have been doing since I started my junior year of college. He hasn't responded, and I don't expect him to.

I'm keen on perfecting my studying skills. I want to ace my first English literature exam, so I stayed longer on campus. Hayden is asleep during the day, anyway.

There are faint noises of people typing on their computers, light chatter, and books closing. The library is quiet and smells of wood and old books. It's my favorite scent, and I feel a sense of complacency in my new life. When I registered for college,

Hayden insisted he pay for all my classes in full. I fought him on that as best I could, but there's no winning that battle.

It's been a breath of fresh air to be able to do things I've set out to do before my Valkyrie demise at twenty-three. Hayden will turn me when I consent on my twenty-second birthday. Out of fear of how powerful, ruthless, unremorseful, and unpredictable Hayden has become, the Council doesn't want to challenge him to turn me. Everyone fears him—every single King and person who breathes fears Hayden.

He killed King Davenport & his sons, leaving only a woman named Eleanor to take reign. No one has been able to do the things he's done, making Hayden the most powerful, heartless Vampire to walk this Earth. Because of his actions to keep me alive and protected, no one wants to challenge him, granting him peace to alter the laws like he wants.

Everyone fears him.

As I close the doors to the library, I look at the ticking clock above it.

9:37 p.m.

Shit!

I lost track of time. Hayden will be worried. I told him I would take a Taxi home. I hold onto my backpack tighter as I jog out of the library. Darkness and crickets greet me with a gust of fresh wind that runs through my wavy hair. I turn the corner of the building toward the parking lot and bump into something hard.

"Oh, ouch!" I yelp as I drop my college textbooks simultaneously. Blinking rough and fast, I search for my three books that I was holding. They landed by my feet...and someone else's.

A pair of black converse shifts awkwardly. I reach for my books, and their hand brushes with mine accidentally.

"I'm sorry. That's my bad. I should've watched where I was

going." A man apologizes. He takes one book while I grab the rest. I stand back up, and straighten my back. I reposition my backpack on my shoulders and realize I'm face to face with my English classmate.

"Jared Whitlock. Hi." I stutter as he hands me back my textbook. I take it and decide the best place to put my textbooks is back in my backpack. I unzip and throw them in quickly as he watches me.

He tucks his long sandy blonde hair behind his ears and readjusts his sports bag over his shoulders. Jared Whitlock is the captain of the baseball team. I don't know him too well, but I know enough. He's charming and intelligent, with a dashing smile and the brightest green eyes I've ever seen. All the girls in our class giggle and blush if he glances at them for one second.

"Hi, Millie Flores." His pink lips curve but fall back down when he spots the engagement ring on my finger. "Or should I say future Mrs..."

I dart my eyes to my ring and back to his friendly smile.

"Oh, yeah...this." I wave my ring finger, and it glistens under the moonlight. "Future, Mrs. Drago, I guess you could say." I roll the r and huff out an awkward laugh. I walk towards the parking lot in front of the administration building, and Jared follows.

"Drago...why does that name sound familiar?" He shrugs his shoulders as he walks. "You're so young to be getting married. How old are you? Nineteen?" He inquires.

"I'm twenty, actually." I laugh light-heartedly.

"Nineteen—twenty. Same thing." He chuckles. "Were you in the library studying?" He points to the building behind us. The sound of crickets and owls sing as we walk.

"Yes. I don't like failing. I'll study all night if I have to."

"You could never. I think you're the smartest one in class. I've seen the grades you get." His voice lowers shyly as he throws his head back with another chuckle. "And you're definitely the prettiest girl, too, if I might add." I almost stop walking when his admission sinks in. His stare blazes the side of my face, but I'm too focused on returning home to respond or meet his eyes.

"Well...thank you. I—"

Jared interrupts me before I can tell him I'll see him tomorrow and bid my farewell.

"Come see me play one of these days," he interrupts me. "I know I'm pushing my luck, but I would love to see the prettiest girl on campus cheer me on."

The sound of multiple engines breaks through the crisp air and rattles my bones. I whip my head toward the direction. They get louder as multiple lights flash over Jared and me. I look to my left, holding my hand by my eyes, and squint to see what the hell is going on.

Motorcycles.

Millie...

Hayden growls into my head as he talks to me. I still don't understand how he can whisper into my mind, but it works every time we're close to each other. And right now, he's fuming by the way he just said my name.

The engines roar, and the volume almost makes me want to cover my ears. They all stop driving and plant their feet on the ground.

Finally, through the thick fog of the night, I see that it's my fiance and his friends—Landon, Kolton, Kade, and a few others I don't recognize.

Hayden and his friends are together on their bikes, surrounding Jared and me like sharks ready to pounce. Hayden has a cigarette between his teeth, black sunglasses on, and a black leather jacket hugging his massive muscles. A silver chain with the bat wrapped in a snake hangs around his neck and rubs against his tattoo of my name.

He takes a drag of his cigarette, hollowing his cheeks as his friends stare at me while grinning wildly and mysteriously. It's like they're excited about what's about to happen. I can't read Hayden like he can read me, but I know he's not happy about seeing Jared right next to me. I'm sure he heard everything.

This isn't good.

Hayden throws his cigarette on the ground and stands tall. He steps on it with his black boot, drops his head back, and faces the sky. He blows the smoke out, and I watch it in slow motion.

"Is this Mr. Drago?" Jared asks hesitantly. Fear is evident in his shaky gulp, and his Adam's apple bobs up and down slowly as he quivers.

"Yes, I'm going to get going now. I'll see you in class," I say fast as I shake. I've got to get out of here; Hayden is unpredictable.

"Whoa, whoa, whoa. What's the rush, baby? Aren't you going to introduce me to your new friend?" Hayden rushes over and stops when he's right in front of Jared and me. He wears a giant devious smirk across his handsome face and I just know he's staring daggers at Jared behind those dark sunglasses. His intentions are anything but welcoming. I know that sinful smirk all too well. It's seared into my soul.

He grabs my hand, pulling me to his chest as he throws his arms over my shoulder possessively.

He reaches for Jared's hand.

"I'm Hayden. Millie's fiancé." Jared stares at Hayden's hand like it's going to bite him. He studies the family crest ring he wears on his middle finger. Jared slowly holds his hand out, and Hayden takes it with confidence.

"Jared."

"Ahh, Jared...let me guess. Captain of the baseball team, straight A's, lots of friends." Hayden scoffs. "Looking for your next baseball bunny to fuck after games?"

My mouth drops open, and I tug on Hayden's arms.

"Hayden. Don't." I pull on his leather jacket harder, urging him to leave Jared alone. He's being ridiculous.

"Look, man, I think Millie can make her own choices whether she wants to go to one of the games. She did tell me that she's new here, after all. I'm just being friendly." Jared straightens his back, puffing out his chest defensively. Still, Hayden is taller and easily towers over Jared's build.

Hayden glances at me over his shoulder and clenches his jaw tight. It flexes over his sharpened and pointed chin with dark enthusiasm.

"Friendly...huh?" Hayden takes a step toward Jared, closing the distance more, and I swear I feel like the Earth is spinning. Hayden takes off his sunglasses and grins ominously.

"Let me show you how friendly I can be when someone tries to take what's mine."

"Hayden!" I shout at him over the sound of engines being revved and all of his friend's dark laughter behind us like it's entertainment. They're egging him on. "Let's go home," I plead.

"Yes, my angel. Anything you want...but right after I finish saying goodbye to Jared." He stares at Jared's shoes, and I hold my hand over my chest. My heart pounds ruthlessly, skipping beats, but I can't unglue my eyes to what's about to unfold in front of me.

"Tell me something, Jared..." he murmurs, still looking at the floor, but then Hayden lifts his head slightly, and his ocean-blue eyes change to crimson red. He smiles with long, dangerous fangs and taunts Jared. "Do you believe in Vampires?"

THE DEPRAVED PRINCE

JARED PISSED HIS PANTS FROM FEAR AND ALMOST PASSED out when Hayden transformed into vampire mode. Kolton pounced on Jared, sucked his blood until he got his fill, and then left him. Hayden reassured me he wouldn't remember anything from tonight because of the venom that gets injected into Jared's system.

Still, *I'll remember every little detail about tonight.*

I thought after I came back and set a wedding date, he'd be less possessive and depraved, but he's only gotten worse. I cling to his waist as he drives us toward a lake near the Cathedral alone. I'm swearing in my head about twenty times. I'm so mad at him. After twenty minutes, he parks his bike right next to the lake. There's a full moon that reflects against black waves. It's the prettiest view I've seen.

As soon as he puts the brake down, I jet off the bike and let go of him. It earns me a low creature-like growl from Hayden, but I don't care.

"Don't you fucking dare think about trying to run from me!" Hayden blares as he still sits on the bike and holds the handles so tight I'm surprised he hasn't torn his bike apart.

"He's innocent! You promised you wouldn't do this! You promised you wouldn't do stuff like this! You can't kill or almost kill guys that talk to me or just...*look at me!*" I palm my waist.

"Yes, I fucking can. He talks to you again, and I'll fucking kill him!" He drawls as he holds out his hand and calls me over to him by curling his fingers. "Come here, Millie."

"No," I grit out.

"Come here, Millie, and sit on my cock. I know you want to," he demands, rough yet silky simultaneously.

I hate that he senses the sensation that sparkles in between my thighs. Even when he fucks up, and we fight, he senses when my body burns and ignites, waiting for him.

"No!" I yell, bewildered by his relaxed nature. "You almost killed him just because he asked me to go to his game! You keep acting recklessly, and one day, people will start to notice that vampires exist and come after you! You're being irresponsible and jealous!" Instead, I no longer face him and pace around, anxiously looking at the water as I run up and down the shore. I continue to vent with no filter. "You're an asshole sometimes! I hate—!"

"Millie," he seethes, warning me to stop. "Watch your words before I do something that you'll *really hate*."

I stop pacing and glare at him.

"I hate that you keep doing stuff like this. You can't kill everyone who hurts me, Hayden. I just...I'm..." I drift off, trying to find the right words to form. Finally, the realization hits me, and my throat tightens. I close my eyes as I walk closer to him, still fuming with heat in my cheeks, flared nostrils, and crossed arms over my chest. I stop before him as his curiosity builds in those entrapping light blue eyes. He frowns as he watches me intently.

"I'm scared of losing you," I murmur. "Stop putting yourself and your kind at risk. I can't lose you." I cry softly as I close my eyes. "You're being reckless. Exposing yourself and your vampirism is not safe. Don't make more enemies, you have enough already." The thought of people finding out about vampires and coming after Hayden makes me physically and mentally unstable. I crumble at the thought of someone finding out about vampires and killing Hayden. What if people find out and try to kill every vampire that walks? Although I know it's nearly impossible with how powerful and unremorseful he is, it's still there. An unknown gnawing situation I don't ever want to encounter.

Hayden picks me up quickly as my tears fall, forcing me to straddle him. I try to lift myself off. I'm still upset with him about the Jared situation. But he keeps me restrained down by my waist. I'm forced to sit on his very hard, thick cock that's restrained by his jeans. It's begging for release.

"That's not possible, Bambi. You will always have me. I promise. I'm not going anywhere. Wherever your soul goes, mine will follow. It doesn't matter where or how far." His cold fingers trail up my thigh and snake underneath my plaid skirt. I hitch a nervous breath as he trails circles over my damp throbbing pussy. "I'm obsessed, addicted, and tethered to you for eternity. I love you."

I meet his now red eyes as I run my hand through his dark, disheveled hair. He's clean-shaven, like he likes to be. His throat rolls up and down as he meets my watery eyes, locking with them as his fangs flash. He tugs the back of my hair and pulls me into him. He trails his nose at the middle of my breasts. His cold tongue drags amongst my skin and kisses each breast as I moan. My entire body explodes with goosebumps, and I shiver when he rips my shirt open—making my bra no longer usable and my breasts fall out.

He groans, satisfied, and places his mouth on my pointed nipple. He sucks hard as his fangs beg to puncture me, but he holds himself back.

"I'm still very mad at you." I declare over my thundering heartbeat and hot cheeks as his cold three fingers enter me. My front teeth dig into my bottom lip, rough as he glides in through perfectly as always. My wetness coats his rough skin as he pumps them in and out. Every time we touch, it's like an electrocution of fire, bliss, and erratic wild lust that turns into a tornado of emotions. Loving Hayden and all the darkness that comes with his tortured soul is a thrill with storms and rainbows. Each day, each kiss, and each breath I take with him by my side is a gift.

"If this is you mad, I'm going to piss you off some more." He pulls my neck into his mouth, and sinks his fangs inside my pulsating sensitive flesh just as he pulls my underwear aside. He unzips his jeans and enters me roughly. The head of his cock bulldozes its way inside me as he sucks my blood from where he marked my neck. The scar he forever tattooed on my body from when he first bit me. Pure madness rages on as he controls the speed.

"Fuck, Millie. You have a body that can make demons worship angels," he deeply grunts into my neck. The noises he makes turn me on so high.

I roll my hips fast and needy, making a mess of myself as I whimper from the pain of his bloodlust. His teeth always cut into me like butter. As I move, warmth leaks down my neck. It's my blood. We make love to each other on his bike, with teeth, blood, and craze. Our bodies become one as we fuck underneath the moon and right by the water as he gets his sweet tooth satisfied by my blood.

"How do I feel?" I moan and scrape my black polished nails into his back.

"*You feel like mine,*" he drawls deeply without missing a beat.

Hayden

Fuck. Every time I sink all the way home into her tight pussy, her walls welcome me perfectly because she was made for me. No other man will ever get to experience the way her soul lights up a room or the way she comes with *my name* on her lips. I don't know how I'm going to survive knowing she attracts other men just by breathing at the university. Her presence is a glowing gift and everyone notices her when she walks into a room, it's inevitable. I'll be watching closely, even when my back is turned. I'll always be watching. I may be paranoid, but I'm doing everything I can to keep her alive before she consents. I'm watching her all the time when she thinks I'm not. The evil shadow inside of me grows by the day.

I am the most powerful vampire King in Immortal's Country.

"You're so beautiful, Millie. You're every single dream I've ever had come true. I don't regret scaring that little asshole away tonight. I'll remove any man's eyeballs from their skull if they look at you like that," I groan as her honey-brown eyes sparkle in the moonlight.

"Creep" by Radiohead plays as I continue to rail her deeper and deeper on my bike until the head of my cock destroys her pussy. I pull on her skirt, fisting it to keep her in place. Because every time I thrust, she jolts from how much power I drill upon her body. As always, I have to restrain my strength because I'll end up killing her if I don't. My girth is too thick and long that every time I pump, it hits her cervix *and* sweet g spot. She moans, and I know those sounds all too well. Those sweet melodies she makes me when she's close to meeting her climax.

"Always keep these legs open for me...*and only me*," I growl. I continue to feed from where I engraved my teeth marks like a tattoo. Her hands thread into my hair, pulling me closer to the base of her neck as if it'll help ease the pain. The taste of her warm, Valkyrie blood is another blessing I don't deserve but one I will cherish for eternity.

"Hayden, my love, it hurts. You can stop now." A whimper follows suit out of her pink lips that match her flustered cheeks.

She tries to push me off her neck with her palms, but my demons want me to keep going.

"No!" I growl, defying her and continue to drain her from her neck. I thrust harder, faster, a deep creature like snarl vibrates against her hot flesh as I hold her tighter. I can't help it. It's too fucking good. "You can take it," I command through a full mouth of her metallic addictive blood. How does she expect me to stop? It's like trying to defy gravity. She's too delicious, too beautiful to refrain myself.

She snaps me out of the darkness.

Her dainty and slender fingers connect with the side of my face and temples. I growl and my vampirism slowly retreats. I stop drinking. I lick my ice lips as her hot blood drips all over the both of us.

"I'm sorry," I apologize weakly as I pull back.

But she doesn't stop riding me. She yanks my hair and throws her head back as we fuck. She's covered in red just the way I love. Her pussy clenches down on my dick as she moans my name over and over again. She's coming all over my cock.

"I hate you sometimes. Oh...*fuck Hayden*," she moans harder as her orgasm rips through her, and her cheeks pinken.

I grin proudly, watching her come undone. Her walls are closing in tighter around my nerves and I implode. I spill my cum inside her with a feral growl, bliss clouding my thoughts and the demons fade away to the point I don't know my own name.

I love her. I love her so fucking much. When she's not with me, *I'm lost*. I would turn her now if I could but she wants to experience being a mother and I'm going to honor that before Death comes knocking on her door.

"We're going to have our little family one day. You will carry my children. And we'll never let them feel what we did, right?" I groan into her neck, kissing and licking at her wound.

She's heaving, her chest coated in sweat despite the freezing temperature. Millie looks as if she doesn't want to come back down from the oblivion I just fucked her in. She nods as her blissful climax still lingers between the both of us. She presses her lips to my cheeks.

"Our own little family," she concedes. "You always get what you want...even if you have to take it."

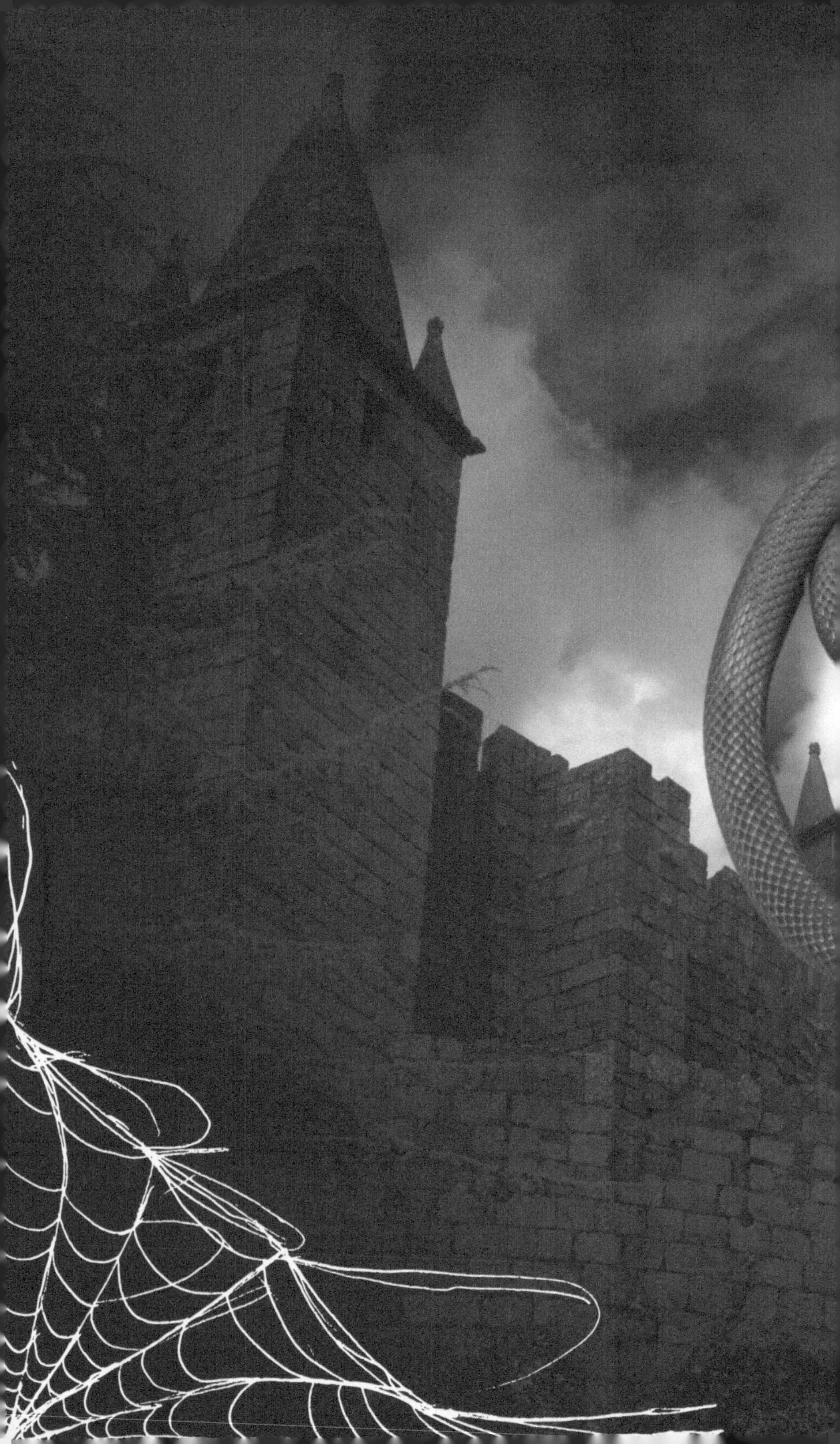

42

HAYDEN

I WAKE up the next night to Millie's sobs in the bathroom. Throwing the bed sheets off my body, I run towards the sound of her fast heartbeat. Every step I take, I can't help but wonder who I'm going to hurt for it. Walking behind her in nothing but my boxers and silver chain with the Drago emblem down my neck, her warmth calls to me like it always does.

"Baby, what's wrong?" I urgently ask, gripping her shoulders comfortingly. She stands in front of the mirror, and I watch her skin dip in where my fingers are in the reflection. She's in her silk black-laced gown that flows just below her knees, and she's already drying her tears with her knuckles. She has something in her hand, gripping it tight like she's frustrated.

"It's nothing, my love. I'm sorry for waking you up." she apologizes softly. I reach over her shoulders slowly and take her hand. She looks away while I pry her trembling fingers open.

It's a pregnancy test.

I swear my whole world stops, and I have the biggest smile on my face.

"It's...negative. I'm so sorry, Hayden." Millie sits down on the closed toilet with her face in her palms, hiding her disappointment while using her black waves of hair to mask her emotions further.

I place the test back on the sink and tense up. Scratching my temple, I close the distance.

She really wants this. I really want this. I wish I could take that disappointment away from her. It breaks me to see her sad after every negative test. She wants to become a mother so badly before she has to consent. It breaks my heart, but I know it will happen. It took my mother around six months of trying with my father to conceive me and two months with Kallum. We talk about having our first child almost every night. We spend our nights making love, teaching her about the underworld of Immortal's Country, picking out boys' and girls' names and nursery themes while I work and she studies.

I pick her up bridal style and take her in my arms, and she holds me tight. The entire time, I kiss her everywhere, and I can *feel* her body relax as the seconds go by.

Once I make it to the balcony, I sit her on the rail and open her legs until I settle in the middle of her inner thighs. I tilt her chin up to meet my gaze as the moonlight and crisp air dance against our skin.

"You are a blessing. You are perfect. I promise we will have our little Drago running around soon. I love you, and you are enough for me." I press my lips against hers, and she lets out a heavy sigh as she kisses me back harder.

"How do you manage to always say the right things to make me feel better? To make everything just...*better*?"

"Just comes naturally," I sigh with a careless shrug, move her hair out of her face, and tuck it behind the shell of her ear before continuing. "I have this effect on everyone." I sneer with a wink, hoping it makes her smile. Her mouth drops open, and she pushes my shoulder away playfully with a scrunched cute nose and a smile that will always have me on my knees in a split second.

I place my hands on either side of her waist, caging her in.

"Your nightmares have stopped." I point out, changing the subject. For nights since after I brought her back to the Cathedral, she would dream about losing her father to Cole. Just thinking about the man who got to taste and see Millie's pussy makes me want to revive him just to kill him all over again.

"Yeah, they have ever since you chased them away every night with how hard you love me." she swings her feet side to side.

It's true.

I spend every minute making sure she has everything she needs, and when I'm not with her, she lives in my head.

"I miss my dad," she admits through pursed lips.

"I know."

"I won't be able to see him again once I turn into a vampire, right?"

I grind my teeth at the thought of her dying to reunite with her father. I don't know how to answer that.

Cooper comes strolling through and nestles his head underneath Millie's hand. He's licking her fingers until she pets him back on the top of his head. He's a part of my guardsmen. He guards the Cathedral and always protects Millie. She asked Nash to give Cooper to her, and he obliged.

"When can he start sleeping in his own bed?" I groan, frustrated that I have to share Millie with Cooper. I cross my arms over my chest, teasing her.

"Never," she turns over her shoulder with a pout as she scruffs his neck. She knows I can never say no to her. A knock on the door causes Millie's smile to curve into a frown.

"Meeting on the phone, Hayden. King Bane wants to talk."

Holland announces on the other side of the door. My shoulders fall, and I cringe.

"Duty calls." I sigh as I turn to the closet, ready to clothe myself.

"Can I come?" Millie's hand stops me before I can walk away.

"Millie, I don't want to bore you with my work, and you have to study. You have an exam next week."

"I want to go." she hops off the railing and walks past me like she's not asking anymore. *She's telling me.*

"A CONGRATS ARE IN ORDER." KING BANE'S ANCIENT VOICE booms over the speaker with a cold tone. King Bane is the Immortal King of the East. I sent him an invitation to the wedding, and I'm guessing that is the reason for the phone call.

"Thank you." I quip, taking a drag of my cigarette as Millie wanders around the room, studying every corner like she's intrigued by the history.

"I'll do my best to attend the wedding. I would love to take my wife and sons to meet the new future queen of the North. I haven't been to Montana since..." I tune out King Bane's voice when Millie gets on her knees between my legs with a mischievous smirk. She always manages to distract me just by breathing. She pushes my knees apart and unzips my pants. Every single nerve inside me explodes with liquid fire at the anticipation. Before I can move, she shakes her finger, side to side, like she's ordering me to freeze as her cheeks pinken. I sense her slick pussy already dripping beneath her underwear, making my mouth water.

I can't believe she's doing this. I can't get off the phone, and she knows it.

"Millie," I warn her to stop with gritted teeth as she takes hold of my cock and pulls it out. Pre-cum already glistens at the tip, but before I can say another word, her tongue flicks it like she's eager to taste me.

This woman.

"I'm sorry?" King Bane's voice pulls my attention away, and I stare at the phone in a hypnotizing daze.

"N-nothing. I thought I—"

Millie's hot mouth closes in on my cock, and she starts to suck. I close my eyes and grind my teeth when her tongue flicks me up and down. I tilt my head to the side.

Oh, she's going to pay for this.

"Okay," King Bane clears his throat. "Listen up, King Drago, not everyone agrees with you marrying a Valkyrie, but because—" I tune him out again as Millie takes me to the back of her throat over and over again until tears leak out of her eyes and down her cheeks. My dick twitches and grows harder, and she just smiles like it's a challenge to get me off the phone. Saliva drips down her chin as she gives my tip another world-shattering suck before she inhales another deep breath.

I grip the chair handle until the wood chips. I'm about to destroy this whole fucking room if I don't get inside her right now. I am pretty lustful for her blood, and I could drink her in as I punish her.

She stops sucking, and I groan out, frustrated.

Why did you stop?

I growl into her head so King Bane can't hear.

"It seems to me you're on a very important call," she whispers.

She's fucking teasing me.

She walks away from me, making my balls draw up tight,

and I'm begging for her to finish what she started. But King Bane's voice forces the nirvana she encases me in to drift away the more he goes on about how the council favors me due to fear.

If you don't finish what you started, expect to be punished.

She ignores me, and that drives me even more crazy. She shrugs as she snakes her hand into her panties and starts to finger herself. She sits her tight perfect ass on the edge of the table so I can get a good view. She closes her eyes as she pleases herself on her palm. Rubbing her swollen throbbing clit in treacherous circles, making me fucking feral.

She's close to climaxing. Her heart rate speeds up, and her toes start to curl. Is she about to finish without me? I don't fucking think so.

Her mouth pops open, and she brings her other finger inside her mouth, sucking it like she's begging me to fill it with my cock.

Goddammit, Millie.

I bite down on my knuckles, my fangs slicing into my hand until dark blood flows everywhere and drips on the phone.

"King Bane. An emergency popped up, and I have to let you go. I'll call you back soon." My tone is murderous. Millie recognizes the change in my demeanor; her eyes shoot open, and she drops to her feet. She's going to run?

She springs away, darting towards the door. She didn't think I would end the call, and now she's going to regret it.

"But King Drago, I'm not finished." King Bane protests with a stunned tone.

Click.

I grab her, slam her ass back down on the table and wrap my hand around her throat as my tongue dives inside her mouth. My pants slide down to my ankles, and I drive my cock all the way home into her tight pussy, not letting her catch her breath.

"You thought you were being cute? You thought you were going to tease me and let another man hear you come? You thought you would just distract my work and important phone calls and get away with it?" I snarl into her ear as I rail her hard and unremorseful.

"Take it. Take every inch and every drop of my cum, Millie."

Her eyes roll to the back of her head as every single thrust hits that one spot inside of her that drives her crazy. She wraps her legs around me as she moans.

"I'm sorry, I—" I cut her apology off with the palm of her hand as I continue to fuck her.

"No. Too late for that." I pull her hair back, grab a fistful, and expose her neck. She screams as I bite her, and everything feels out of this world as I drink. The only time I'm happy is when I'm inside her, hearing her heartbeat.

"Taste yourself." I swipe her blood with the tip of my finger and drive it into her mouth so she can taste what I do. She sucks like a good fucking girl, and I grin as my cock grows harder.

"Hayden, oh my, *fuck*. Don't stop!" She chants and bites her lip. With blood dripping down her neck and chest, she cries out my name as I mix pain with pleasure. Her breasts bounce, and her nipples harden against my chest as I continue to fuck her ruthlessly against the table until she's begging me to stop for the entire night, and cum is dripping down her trembling thighs.

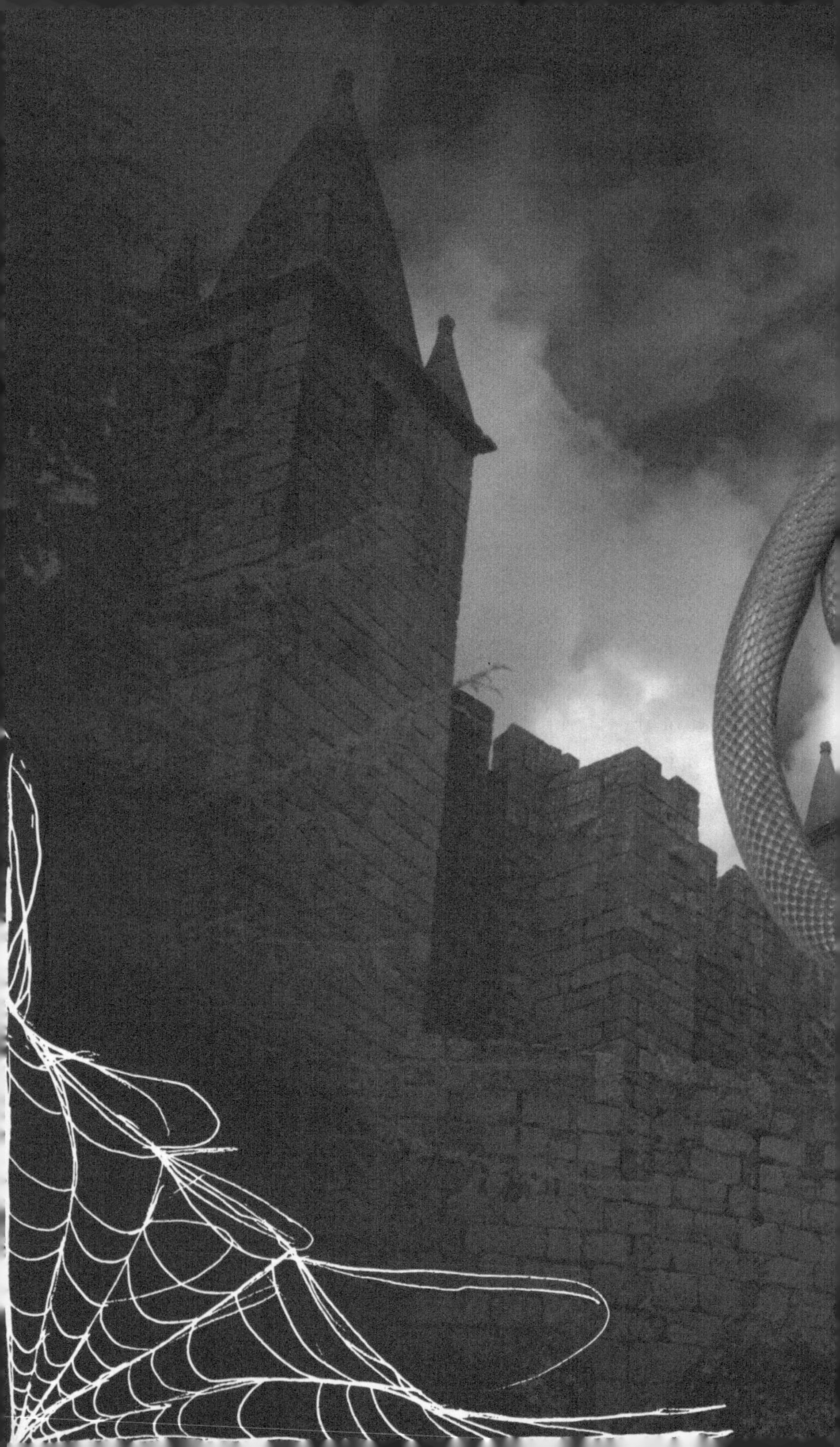

43

HAYDEN

SHE LOOKS as beautiful as the day I met her. But in a white dress that she wears for me?

Perfection. Flawless. A goddess.

It's really happening. Millie is happy. Millie Flores will be Millie Drago, and we get to start the life I never thought I could have. My first and only love is looking at me like no one ever has before in my three hundred years of life.

She wants me.

She looks like an angel who found peace after fighting the battles in her mind. She looks like she's finally taken a solace breath after drowning in the depths of the darkness she's endured. She looks like she's learning how to love herself after being taught to hate herself.

But most of all, she looks like mine.

"Put Your Head On My Shoulders" by Paul Anka starts to play. It's the same song that played in the car the first night we met as I drove her home.

She walks down the aisle like the most precious, delicate, rare jewel I've ever seen. She's nervous. She tries to bite away her smile with her front teeth like she's ashamed to be so happy. I think it's cute when she does that. She deserves all the happiness in the world, and if I can't give it to her with my blackened dead heart, I'll spend all the money in the world to give it to her.

She stops in front of me. Kallum presents her hand, and I give him a farewell nod. Cooper sits beside me like my best man, with a wagging tail.

No one showed up for her but her brother, Nash. There's no doubt her father would be here. I have nothing against the men in her life, but I need to be the only one she can count on because it's true. I will never fail. I failed my parents and the people of this kingdom by being known as The Depraved Prince, but that will change, now that I have *her*.

Her black hair is curled, framing her cute heart-shaped face and full cheeks. Her blood rushes to her cheeks whenever I'm near. The way her heart thunders like a song, it will always be the anthem of my eternal condemnation to hell. Her eyes sparkle joyfully, looking at me like I'm her haven.

The white dress flows down her elegant curves, and she holds a bouquet of white peonies in her soft, glowing hand. Her skin is so smooth, velvet, and perfect.

"You are and will always be the most beautiful bride. Your beauty is out of this world, Millie. I'm just the lucky bastard to live in it."

She smiles, and I kiss her.

"I haven't even started yet, King Drago," Our officiant complains, clearing his throat.

I keep kissing her, and she kisses me back. Everything, absolutely everything, gets tuned out as we get lost in each other's lips like we always do. The only thing that plays is our song in the orchestral version.

We were fucking made for each other. And if we weren't, I

would do anything to mold myself to meet her pieces like a puzzle.

"Are you okay, my Bambi?" I ask her while taking her hands in mine. She looks ill, and my heart races at the thought of her Valkyrie destiny coming true earlier, even though the book says not until she turns twenty-three. We still have two more years before I turn her.

"Yes, I think." She forces a laugh.

"Not getting cold feet on me, right?"

"No, it's not that at all. I have a headache...not feeling too well, but I must marry you. Nothing is stopping me from becoming your wife today." She forces a weak smile, and I brush my finger against her cheek worriedly.

"After this, I'll have the medical staff come look at you. We'll postpone our honeymoon plans to Alaska if that's alright with you?"

She nods. "As long as I'm with you, I don't care where we go. I just need you, Hayden." Her cheeks flush a hot pink, and I'm tempted to bite them.

The grumpy officiant clears his throat, and everyone who was standing sits down, taking their seats. Nash sits at the far left corner, wearing garlic underneath his clothing as a protective chest plate and neck armor. I smelt it when he came in. I couldn't help but laugh at the cliche rumor that garlic keeps vampires away from biting him. He'll be disappointed to find out it doesn't.

The officiant continues, placing a crown full of ruby red diamonds on Millie's head. I've all about tuned everyone and him out, staring at Millie like I'm the luckiest damned man in this world. *Fuck.*

I love her. I love her so fucking much. It hurts, burns, and breaks me, but I will always gladly succumb to those feelings... *for her.*

"King Drago?" The officiant clears my headspace and interrupts my longing gaze at my wife.

Right.

I grab her, pull Millie in by the waist, and push her against me until her dress rubs me. I know it's not the part of 'you may kiss the bride' yet, but I don't care. I press my lips against her hard, and she returns the kiss as we dive into our secluded bubble. I let go, and she flushes while grabbing my arm. She looks into my eyes, and all I can hear is Paul Anka playing in the background as her eyes sparkle and her heart skip beats.

I break away and stand up straight, trying hard not to fucking tear up. But I will always fall apart and unveil my emotions like a man desperate and violently in love.

"My entire existence, I've earned a justified reputation for never showing up and always being selfish. While the self-serving aspect of my life is still true, I'll never give you up, Millie, and if that makes me a bad guy, then I will wear that title with honor. Because I have you and our future family, a heavenly vessel of pure innocence and true love that I vow to protect for the rest of your lives. The day we met was the day I was reborn into my new forever."

WE'RE MINUTES AWAY FROM THE RECEPTION ENDING. WE stand outside by the waterfall, watching the fireworks erupt for by the mountains. Our nearby town of Bozeman does this every year.

Millie rests the back of her head on my chest as I hold her waist from behind. She turns around, with my jacket on her shoulders to keep her warm from the unforgiving winter on her human body. She tilts her head, and meets my gaze with simplicity and peace shimmering in her brown iris'. Her breathing has changed, and her heart starts to slow, but I'm too distracted by the tears in her eyes to think about it more.

Pop. Pop. Pop.

Another firework screeches above us, diving into the stars and thunders like lightning when it pops. Red sparkles litter the clouds, and I sway with my wife by her hips as music continues to play softly in the background.

"You know, I always thought...that my mother and father didn't want me. I blamed them for the way I can't trust people and the way I can't believe it when someone tells me they love me. And then I realized that *we all suffer from shattered scars and pieces.* We're all just trying to survive in a world of unavoidable mistakes and demons that infiltrate our boundaries. They're just hurt people who hurt people. I don't resent them anymore. I understand now. I get it." She shivers against me, and I don't like to see her like this.

Pop.

Screech.

Pop.

"Baby..." I brush my knuckles on her face, trying to take her pain away by wiping the tears off. "You're still so young. It took me centuries to come to terms with who I am and the shit I've gone through. It's okay and normal to break down. Just never stay there in the darkness. And if you feel stuck, and can't be strong for yourself, I'll be your voice, I'll be your shield and I will love you enough to help you heal. We fight our demons, together, okay my Bambi girl?" I tilt her chin up with my ring finger and place a kiss on those perfect lips of hers.

She kisses me back for a few seconds. She pulls away and arches a brow. Her face is pale, and she gives me a tortured smile.

"My dad wasn't here to walk me down the aisle. And she isn't either, and that fucking sucks." She scoffs out a laugh as she sniffles. "My mother...she's—" she swallows nervously, clearing her throat. "She's a broken soul. She's a victim. And I forgive her. I forgive my dad. Forgiveness is something hard to give and receive. But I'm able to do it because of you. You've taught me this, Hayden. Love can be a million different things in the eye of the beholder. No matter how you see yourself as a monster, my love. You're not." She lifts her hand to my face, and her flesh is cold. "You've sacrificed everything for me. You breathe for me even though your body can't. You've given me your naked soul, even though you think it's damned to hell. You're like breathing in an ocean. I never thought it was possible, but you make drowning in the darkness *beautiful*."

I reach down and cup her face, kissing her like I always do. She presses her lips back against me harder, and we move perfectly together like we always do, but then she stops.

"Hayden? I don't feel so good." She freezes, and my eyes pop open worriedly when she goes lifeless in my hands. She drops her bouquet of peonies that she helped my mother grow, and then I see my worst fears come to life. She's bleeding from everywhere. Red drops from her mouth, nose, eyes, and ears. Red is everywhere on her dress and the flowers.

What the hell is happening?!

"Millie! Talk to me. Tell me what's going on!" I hold her and lay her down gently just as the fireworks come to an end, and every single northern vampire cheers happily. They're happy, and I'm fucking dying.

"Millie! Oh my God! Millie! Wake up, baby. Wake up!" I hold her shoulders tight, and I feel her heart come to a stop forever. It's stopped beating. Her rhythm, which I've come to know as my national anthem, has stopped. The music of her breathing has come to an end.

Everyone from the wedding surrounds me. My friends, guards, parents, and Nash are just as confused and petrified. My mother falls to her knees and tries to help.

"What happened to her? Isn't she twenty? It's not her time yet!" My mother frantically shouts as she brushes Millie's hair out of her face. She's assessing her wounds, as am I. We're both erratic and helpless as she tears off pieces of her black dress and cardigan to plug her bleeding ears.

How do I wake her? How do I make the blood fucking stop?! Did I misread something in the book? Kallum, indeed, would've told me by now if I missed something!

"I don't know! Help me, mother! Help me save her! Her heart doesn't beat any longer! Help me!" I plead with manic desperation. I punch the grass with my fist. My eyes beam red, and my fangs flash with havoc. Black tears drip onto her peonies.

"Oh, Hayden...she's gone. I—there's nothing we can do. She didn't consent, did she?" my mother trembles.

I shake my head, refusing to believe this is my reality. I hold her tight to my chest, trying to comprehend what could have led her to die like this. I've been careful and gentle with her, worshiping her every need. *We had plans.* We had fucking plans to start our family. We were already trying...*she wanted to go to Alaska.* My Bambi girl still wanted to do so much.

"No! I refuse to accept this!" I bite her. I bite her all over, trying to see if my venom will miraculously turn her into a vampire without consenting. Everyone watches me with black, confused tears running down their distraught, pale faces.

After minutes pass by like years, and I perform chest compressions to try to get her heart beating, nothing is working, and I'm forced to live in my worst nightmare.

"No...no...*Millie!*" I wail with an inhumane roar. The

guards start to push everyone away from us as I hold and grieve my person. "Don't go with Death." I cry into her neck.

"I'll find a way to you, baby. I'll see you next moon, right?" I mumble our signature farewell to her. "Say it back. Say it back right now! *Please.*" The word I fucking hate falls off my lips so effortlessly.

Please.

I keep holding her as her blood makes a puddle. I sit and let my knees drench in it as I kiss her soulless forehead and lips. She's cold. Where's her warmth? Where's her honey-brown eyes that sparkle? *Where is she?*

"I'll see you next moon." I groan into her neck, where my mark still lies.

I'll see you next moon.

"She had more time! This doesn't make sense!" I shout into the sky. I hope God can hear me. I hope he can listen to my pleas to give her back to me.

Please give her to me. Give me back my little Bambi.

"What the fuck is happening to my sister?!" Nash's livid shout slices through the thin air. He loses control but my guards restrain him within the crowd, forcing him to watch.

"King Drago!" One of the maidens holds up a cup. She was the one that helped get my Millie dressed in her wedding gown. "She was poisoned!" Everyone gasps in horror while I do everything I can to not destroy and kill every single guest.

Who would poison my girl? Millie shouldn't have any enemies with evil intentions to end her life and if she did, I'd make sure they never got a fucking chance. She's adored by everyone in this Cathedral.

My mother flashes to her, pulls the cup from her hand, and smells it. She's careful not to touch it with her mouth. Not one more second passes before she pushes the bronze cup away from her lips, revolting. Immediately, my mother's eyes bulge, and she goes still.

"Who gave her this drink?" I snarl, but I don't move. I can't leave my wife. I can't let her go...

She points to Holland.

He drops his cane and snickers demonically. He stands there clapping with an evil grin, his eyes beaming red with glee.

"Checkmate," he spits with hatred. I knew he hated me, but I didn't realize his hatred for me cut this deep. He's willing to kill and take the only person I love away.

"You...you?" I'm shaking, aching, breaking. Tragic is an understatement. Has our love blinded me so much that I hadn't been focused? I hadn't seen the chest moves were being moved from inside of my own kingdom? I still don't have it in me to let go of Millie. My blackened eyes dart to Holland and my bloodied bride. My father takes initiative for me when I can't. I'm frozen with a destroyed soul. Even the demons that live inside me are absent, granting me this moment to endure it in silence. I don't have the energy to feed them. I'm drained from the inside out.

Millie...wake up. Baby. Please...

I plead with her through her mind like I used to do but only silence greets me.

My father rushes to him and restrains him. Holland doesn't fight him as thirty more vampire guards help assist my father.

Holland played us all. He's been the true enemy all along. Pulling the strings behind enemy lines.

"You don't deserve anything good in your life. You always get what you want, and I'm sick and tired of it. But guess what? In this cruel world, we don't always get what we want, Hayden, and it brings me joy to see you suffer and learn one of life's hardest lessons. You're a monster trying to change the times for a human? For love?" he scoffs with amusement. "Don't forget who you are...which is The Depraved Prince."

44

SCARLETT
YEAR 2024

"IN THE END, The Depraved Prince became The Lost King. The Lost King who fell out of love with life and in love with the idea of death. It's a tragic story of revenge and love that hurts. His father warned him time and time again that this would be her ending. She was always supposed to die. He was always supposed to lose her." My aunt closes the book.

"And what happened to Holland?"

"Hayden tortured him until he killed him. It turns out he was the one who leaked Hayden's uncle's relationship with King Davenport. He was the one who turned on the TV so Millie could find out about her father dying, and he was the one who let King Davenport into the Cathedral so he could get to Millie to unlock his powers. It's all written in this journal."

"How?" I quirk a brow, biting my fingernail with a broken heart.

"How? What?" she repeats.

"How did Hayden torture Holland?"

"Those details aren't important, sweetie." She groans out.

She removes her reading glasses and stiffens, probably thinking about the answer to my question. I'm sure it's in that journal.

"Milie's death destroyed him, and there are other stories about him. Stories that he turned into something far worse. Some stories are so horrifying I refuse to believe they're true." She widens her eyes and shakes her head. "Or maybe he's gone from this world and into another, haunting Millie until he finds her again...nobody knows."

My *tia* closes a pink, outdated journal with the title Millie and peonies decorated on it. She places it on her bookshelf, tucked far into the corner. My tia is a vampire enthusiast. She hoards everything she finds like a collection when she travels around the world. She seeks out urban legends and mythical creatures. Millie's journal has been sitting on that shelf for a year or so.

Tia believes vampires exist, but no one believes her. Everyone in our family thinks she's crazy for it. But me? I believe her. I plan to investigate and hunt for the truth of their existence. I want to find an immortal vampire myself.

"I don't want to believe that she's dead."

"Well, she is. Her tombstone rests in that Cathedral." My aunt sighs heavily. "Revenge is an ugly emotion. You can't fight fire with fire and expect to win. You must never act on it, Scarlett."

I shift in my chair and drink my cup of tea.

"What happened to her mother?"

My tia tears up and holds her cross necklace like she's dreading to answer my question. She pulls out her journal again and finds a letter. She gives it to me and wipes away a tear from her cheek.

She hands me the letter, and I take it slowly. I open it.

"The letter was in the journal. Millie's mother...well, she ended up leaving Santiago. She left him the day before Millie and Hayden's wedding. She tried to reach her but instead wrote this letter."

> *To my daughter,*
>
> *It turns out I believe in happily ever afters after all. You made me believe in them, Millie. Not the kind that deals with a man but the kind that gives my soul peace. The kind that makes me believe in second chances at life and the kind that gives me hope. The kind that makes me feel like it's never too late to try and be better. The happily ever after I choose is my children and the little girl in me who believed in myself and loved myself when no one else did.*
>
> *I love you, Millie. I see a lot of myself in you. If you can take anything from my mistakes, it's this: I want you always to love yourself and never depend on anyone else to make you feel worthy—because you are. You always are worthy and deserving of an all-consuming life story. I'm sorry. I'm so sorry for the pain I've caused you. Your pain is valid. You are valid. If you allow me the privilege to be a part of your life again, Mom is here, and she is here to stay.*
>
> *Love, Mom.*

Wow...

What a cruel way to end The Depraved Prince. All Millie wanted was to see her parents get their happy ending, and she died before finding out her mother chose hers.

"That gothic-looking Cathedral up in the mountains...the one with the closed-off trail to get there. Is that where King

Drago lived with his family?" I ask, tapping my nails on the desk before me. It takes about five miles to get to that place. I've never tried because it's a strenuous hike, and people have died mysteriously trying to get to it.

Walking past me, her face hardens as she grabs her teacup, and I watch the steam flow over the white and baby blue glass swirling right by her mouth. She pushes her gray hair behind her ear, and her light brown eyes turn into slits. She places the teacup down and sits at her coffee table. She looks out the window into the night sky. I already know what she's looking at. You can barely see the beautiful architecture above the tall trees. You can only tell it's there if someone points it out.

"Don't ever try it, Scarlett. No one believes me, and that's fine. I'm known as the crazy lady who believes in vampires, werewolves, ghosts, and demons, but I know deep down, you believe it, too. Promise me you'll never go there?" She turns away from the window and looks at me with scolding eyes of protection.

I swallow nervously.

"Yes, *tia*."

THIS WEEK HAS BEEN ONE CRAZY, WILD RIDE OF storytelling. It was raw, tragic, but honest. She skipped over the explicit romantic parts, but I get the point as an eighteen year old.

Before I went to bed that night, I put my newly bought telescope to use. The next day, I went to the store downtown in Bozeman and bought it. My *tia* told me *I couldn't go there*, but she said nothing about a telescope or spying. I can't get Millie's and Hayden's story out of my head. I think it'll live with me forever.

It's midnight, the day before Halloween. Instead of trick-or-treating or binge-watching classic horror movies, I'm looking through the scope. Finally, after finding a good angle to set it up, I spot the Gothic black cathedral through the mountains and trees.

There's greenery all around it, and it looks abandoned. Red stained glass is on every single window except one.

It's broken.

I adjust the scope until the blurriness goes away. My retro vintage radio that I left playing shifts to a radio station I've never listened to before. A 1950s song starts to play. I stare at the song title just as "Put Your Head On My Shoulder" by Paul Anka plays statically.

Huh? That's never happened before...

I bite my lip and return to my scope. An electrocuted sensation of horror runs through me when I see something mysterious. There, where the broken stained glass is, is a tall, massive shadow figure in a black suit staring straight at me with glowing red crimson eyes.

A blood-curdling scream slips into the eerie night, and I drop the telescope.

THE END

AUTHORS NOTE

I really wanted Millie and Hayden to have a happy ending, but this was their story *for now*. And I hope I told it with care. Millie didn't know how to feel or accept the love and protection Hayden offered her time and time again, which resulted in her running from it. Every single time Hayden showed her this in his own way, she wouldn't let herself accept it after everything she'd been through in her life because she never knew how it felt to be loved unconditionally. She finally gave in to him at the end.

If someone can relate to their struggles, my heart is with you.

Thank you.
-Lexie

ACKNOWLEDGMENTS

To my husband and my little family, thank you for your patience and support during my journey as an author. To my parents, I love you both with all my heart. Thank you for supporting my ideas and continuous words of encouragement. To my grandparents, thank you for being here, always.

I'm eternally grateful to my street team, ARC Team, my cover designer, book besties, Dani, Destiny, Nicole, and every single soul who supports my stories and gives them a chance.

ABOUT THE AUTHOR

Lexie Axelson is a Hispanic author from South Texas. She is a military spouse and mother. She's a foodie, who loves traveling, spending time with her family, and binge-watching horror movies. If she's not in a bookstore browsing, she's reading a book. Her passion for reading and writing started a young age. And she hopes to bring more book boyfriends to your bookshelves!

Made in United States
Cleveland, OH
22 December 2024